BOUND FOR THE HILLS

RAIN TRUEAX

The elusive Will Tremaine
and the 'Last Taggert' in the
wilds of the Arizona Rim country

Bound For The Hills
Arizona Historicals
Book 7
The Taggerts

is an original work of Rain Trueax.
All rights reserved.
Copyright © 2016 Rain Trueax

ISBN: 978-1-943537-07-5
Paper Back

Prepared and presented by:

Seven Oaks
Monmouth, Or.

Sign up for new release notifications at http://raintrueax.blogspot.com

Personal Contact and Rights Agreements write to: raintrueax@gmail.com

❀ Created with Vellum

CHAPTER 1

September 5, 1905—Mazatzals, Central Arizona

Wilhelmina Agatha Tremaine Butler listened with pretend concern, to the driver of the wagon carrying her to the cabin she had rented for three months. Since he repeatedly said the same things, it was difficult to be polite, but she was trying. She knew Amos Contrell meant well even if fear seemed his main stock in trade.

"Ya ever lived in wilderness, Miss Butler?" he asked sneaking a glance over at her. Since she'd heard that exact question at least five times since they had left Payson, she knew her answer would not satisfy him.

"No, but I am very excited to be doing it soon."

"Them Mazatzals is rough country. There's a reason nobody but bears and cougar live there. Ya ever seen a black bear, Miss Butler?"

"Not other than in a photograph."

He shook his head. "Wal, the ones up here, they'll walk right up to ya if ya let 'em. Ain't scared of folks, cuz they ain't seen many. If ya try to run away, they'll chase ya." He turned again from his mules to see if she had properly grasped the seriousness of the situation.

"I remember what you said, Mr. Contrell, and also that I should always look around before leaving the cabin. Also not to put out garbage to attract them—bury it deep or burn it."

"That's right. Then there's them renegade 'paches. Now the 'tals are a long way from the Rez, but some come sneakin' around anyways. Some jest won't stay put. They come by that thar cabin and see ya are by yore-self..." He shook his head as though the possibilities were too dire to pursue further.

She suppressed the smile. "I do have a rifle. A repeating rifle and know how to use it," she told him for perhaps the tenth time since they had left Payson at least an hour and a half earlier. She saw he had little faith in it being true. He meant well. She understood that but at almost twenty-nine, she was hardly a girl. She may not be wise to the ways of the woods, other than what she'd read, but she understood, perhaps more than he, that the world had risks.

"That dress of yores is plumb pretty."

"Thank you." She guessed the plain cotton of her black dress had nothing to do with what was coming next.

"Not much to protect you from brush, rattlers, skunks..." He hesitated, obviously searching for more words to indicate why her lightweight fabric was not adequate for wilderness garb. "You got anything tougher? Warmer? Ya know cold weather comes sooner in the high country."

"I didn't come up here with a ball gown," she said teasingly but saw he didn't think it was funny. "But I do have a heavy coat, boots, several shirts made for boys, heavy socks, and a pair of jeans." She didn't mention her cotton skirts. They would do nothing to reassure him.

"Jeans?" He looked scandalized.

"My friend, the one who told me about this area, she wrote of the clothing she had needed. I bought some before I left home and more in Payson. I think I will be warm enough."

"Stocking cap?"

She grinned. "Yes, and a cotton hat for sun protection."

He sighed and then started in again with the warnings of the dangers she would be facing. She listened, then didn't listen as she thought of her own concerns which had nothing to do with wild beasts or not being properly garbed for wilderness living. Because of other items she had to bring, her clothing items had been minimal, but they were in several weights for varying weather. She was not naïve about mountain living. Even what she had packed hadn't made it easy shifting from the train to the stage and finally hiring Mr. Contrell to take her to the cabin. Living at the cabin for three months, she did need to be properly outfitted for even the possibility of snow.

Half an hour later, topping a rise, Mr. Contrell halted the wagon. "Thar it be," he said sweeping his arm in an arc. Below was a small valley. Part of a beautiful blue lake was visible. It did not appear to be a large one-- even if the tall trees blocked most of it. Above the lake set a perfectly proportioned log cabin. She hadn't expected it to have flowers in front of the porch. Although she had only read descriptions of the setting, it lived up to all the land agent, Chester Gibbons had promised.

Mr. Gibbons also had worried at a woman going off by herself to live in a lonely cabin. He had tried to convince her that Payson had lovely cottages. "Why not one of those? If not those, there were places that would give you privacy heading east along the Tonto Rim. At least then, there'd be those passing by if you ran into trouble," he'd said.

She had smiled and insisted she needed a more remote location and finally he had told her of this one. "Jared Smith had it built but his wife hated it."

"It was poorly built?"

"Beautifully built, as pretty a cabin as I've seen, but it was so far from everyone else. Oh, an occasional miner might come through but otherwise, she felt she'd go insane being so alone. She tried. You can tell that by the shrubs she planted but it just wasn't home to her."

It had sounded perfect to Willy and she'd smiled and asked for lease papers.

"I will draw them up with an option to buy. That will ensure that you don't have someone buying it out from under you."

"Thank you. I didn't know it was for sale."

"It has been for someone with cash." He had handed her the papers. "I hope you are notifying your family where you will be," he'd said as she perused them before signing.

"My family is all gone on now, Mr. Gibbons."

"Then friends."

"I told those who I felt would care. I trust you won't tell anyone where I am should someone come asking."

He'd huffed a little as he'd assured her of course he'd never do that.

"If a problem should arise," she'd said at the door, "send a missive with Mr. Contrell. He will be coming out with fresh supplies every two weeks."

Mr. Gibbons had nodded approvingly. "He's a good man. I am relieved you arranged for that."

"I am not a fool, Mr. Gibbons. There are reasons I need this level of privacy. I am glad you will respect that."

Nodding, he had again looked affronted.

As she had headed toward the freighting office, she had realized she didn't trust Mr. Gibbons but she'd had no choice. She needed the cabin.

Before she'd left San Francisco, she'd written Holly Jacobs of her plans and of her father's death. At the freighting office, waiting for Mr. Contrell to finish readying the wagon, she had asked for pen and paper and written a quick note to give Holly further details as to where the cabin was, which she'd hurried to the post office to mail.

She had not worried about her decision, but something told her to let Holly know she was fine and that this was to be a grand adventure. That part of her plan, she knew Holly would approve, as her friend was the reason she had even known about Payson and these mountains. At Yale, Holly had spoken of her desire to do an archaeological dig in the mountains of Central Arizona. The research Holly had done then had excited Willy about the country and had made her a bit envious. But she'd had her own path to follow, and the two had lost touch.

As Mr. Contrell drove the wagon down the narrow lane, she found her mind wandering from where she was to wondering where Holly was. She hoped her letters would reach her, and they could reconnect as friends. In neither of the notes had she attempted to explain all of why she had come so far and why she had needed this respite. Perhaps if they met someday, she would explain the rest. Half of what she was feeling she couldn't even explain to herself.

Pushing the concerns from her, she smiled as Mr. Contrell stopped in front of the cabin. She jumped to the ground, heading immediately for the porch. The key worked perfectly in the padlock, and she entered the cabin into a large room, with a stone fireplace at one end. There were more furnishings than she had expected with a leather sofa, two small chairs, and a braid rug in front of the fireplace. On the mantle were two brass candlesticks and candles. A long table and simple wooden chairs stood not far from the door she assumed led to the kitchen. The other door had to be to what had been promised to be a downstairs bedroom. Open stairs led to the loft over the great room and the second bedroom.

She sniffed the air. Although a little stale from having been closed up, she smelled no mouse dung, which meant the cabin must be tight enough to keep them out. She walked into the kitchen. The wood cook stove appeared large enough to prepare meals for a crew. She opened the oven and approved its size and cleanliness. Long counters were on both sides of it and a brass box for kindling alongside. There were two large cupboards, and a pierced metal pie cabinet. Someone had wanted to make this a full-time home. It felt a little sad that it had been abandoned.

She turned to Mr. Contrell. "What was Mr. Smith hoping to do up here?"

He put down the box he'd carried into the kitchen. "Why ya askin' that?"

"It just looks it was meant for more than an occasional visit."

"Can't say for sure. You heard his missus didn't like it."

"I did."

"Seems I heard talk it might've been mining what brung him."

"Might?"

"Or prospecting. Lots of silver in these hills. Them White Hills to the north, been more than a few figure maybe it's where them gold nuggets was found."

"I hadn't heard gold was up here."

"Jest rumors." He took off his hat and rubbed his baldhead. "But the Tonto 'paches, they had gold nuggets. Nobody ever found out where they come from. I kinda figured Smith thought it was around here, which is why he bought it. Only he found nothin'. Mostly how it works with them looking for a pot of gold." He chuckled.

"I have been told that, Mr. Contrell, most often by my father."

"Ma'am, you s'pose you could call me Amos? Mr. Contrell sounds like *my* pappy, and he's been dead now twenty years."

She grinned. "If you call me Willy."

"Willy? Yah got a boy's name?"

"It's the one I prefer. Wilhelmina never felt like me." She laughed.

"At least, it'd sound like a female."

She grinned. That was a bit ironic. "From the time I was old enough to say what I wanted to be called, it was Willy. In school, if a boy didn't like it, he got punched in the nose."

"Lady like you punch someone in the nose?" Again, he looked scandalized.

"I had to learn the lady part, Amos."

He nodded. "Maybe you'll do better out here than I been expecting then. Although I still worry."

"I am a city girl, Amos. I don't know this world, but the city can be brutal also."

"Spect it can. All right, I better get back to unloading as I need to be back in Payson afore dark. Don't want the night beasties to get me." He chuckled again as he headed back outside.

When Amos returned with a square box, she directed him to set it on the long table. "Would you mind helping me slide the table in front of that big window?" When they had it properly centered, she opened the box and lifted out her Underwood typewriter.

"What kind of contraption is that," Amos asked, looking at it skeptically.

"A writing machine, far better than handwriting something as with the carbons, I can make several copies as I go."

"What fer?"

She ignored that. "I was afraid the rough roads might've jammed its keys." She lifted the top and saw the levers were all perfectly aligned, the ribbon and carrier undamaged. She put the boxes beside it. She would be able to watch the lake, maybe see deer or the bear he warned about, while she worked.

She should have been exhausted after the train ride from San Francisco, the twelve-hour stage ride to Payson, two uncomfortable nights there in a hotel, where the lumpy bed and noise on the street made sleep hard to find, then finally this last leg of her journey, but instead she felt invigorated. She had done it. She had changed everything, and she was ready to move on to the next step—make that steps.

Carrying in the last of the food boxes to the kitchen, Amos turned to look at her without moving toward the door. "Jest don't like leavin' a pretty little thing like you here."

She had to exercise restraint not to push him out the door. "I'll be fine." She managed a smile despite her impatience with her work.

"Ya even know how to light that stove or the fireplace?" He narrowed his gaze as he studied her from the doorway. "Nights can still get cold here in September."

She'd laughed. "I know how to strike a match, Amos. I was told there was plenty of kindling split, as well as dried moss to get fires started easily. Mr. Gibbons assured me the owner had left enough wood to last even a hard winter, but I will only be here three months,"

"Ya won't be lasting that long," he grumbled.

"You did say you'd come back with more flour, bacon and such in two weeks."

"I will or I'll send my nephew James. We won't leave ya out here without even a hoss."

"I would not be better off with a horse since I don't ride. Besides, I'd just have to feed and care for an animal, which I know nothing about."

"Wal, that's so." He stepped back up into the wagon and gave her one last concerned look. "Wish ya wouldn't stay though."

She smiled. "I will be fine."

Shaking his head, he cracked the reins over his two mules' backs. When he was finally out of sight, the forest and feeling of wilderness closed around her. The silence was the first thing she noticed and then a bird calling. She felt a sense of relief. She had done it. She stood on the porch, stretching her arms wide as she could. She wanted to take this world into herself, to hold onto this moment forever.

Tall pines loomed to the right, down a slope from the cabin the lake came up to a small beach, huge boulders were along one edge. It would be a good place to swim as long as the good weather held. She took a deep breath of the pine-scented air and smiled with satisfaction. Other than those deer, bear and cougar, her nearest neighbor was supposed to be over a mile away. Perfect.

Her first morning in the cabin, when she woke, she lay watching the light slowly increase, relishing the sound of birds, and the whisper of a breeze through the pines. She had opted to sleep in the loft. Through its shakes, she could see the sky. The mattress was on the floor, but it was soft and very comfortable. The bedding had been clean, and there had even been pillows. She decided the loft was to be her bedroom.

The outhouse was close enough to the kitchen that it didn't take long to take care of that and assure herself the owner had been right--plenty of firewood stacked in a protected back porch. In the kitchen, she found one cupboard had dishes and pans including a coffee pot. She brought in enough kindling to get the cook stove going, pumped water, and soon had coffee brewing.

Her morning was spent unpacking boxes of clothing and foodstuff. Rye and white flour, powdered milk, sugar, baking powder and soda went with the salt into what looked to be a rodent and bug secure cupboard. Although she'd still seen no sign of mice, she'd read enough books about log homes to believe they might be lurking under something to appear at the first scent of food.

On the off chance she had an accident while in the mountains, she had filled a kit with a small flask of whiskey, a roll of gauze, scissors, needle, thread, surgical tape, carbolic acid, and aspirin, which she had read was good for reducing fevers and pain.

Partly from her own interest, and partly as research, she had taken a class in first aid when at Yale. It had given her the rudimentary facts of treating various wounds, as well as let her meet Clara Barton, who although old, was a legend. What Barton had learned, with her work nursing the wounded during the Civil War, had led to improved medical procedures.

Willy had no expectations that a few days in that class would have given her expertise in medicine, but it had been good for her writing, as well as given her confidence that she could take care of any scrapes or cuts she got. Research before she left San Francisco let her know how to handle a snakebite. Despite the fears of Amos and Mr. Gibbons, she felt prepared for any emergency beyond perhaps a fatal accident. And that could happen anywhere.

For her noon meal, she sliced bread and smoked ham to make a sandwich, then sipped some black tea. Although she had looked longingly at the Underwood as well as the lake, she had important things to tend to first. The bread she'd brought would not last long and her plan was to make sourdough loaves. It sounded simple in the books. Add rye flour and water into a crock and wait. It would start bubbling within twenty-four hours. The only real problem they warned was too much starter. What was too much?

Putting the rest of the cooking supplies in places she'd be able to easily access, she brought her *Boston Cooking-School Cook Book* into the main room to study recipes. She'd heard of it while in the university as a new approach to cooking using measuring cups and spoons, which she had been sure to also purchase before she left San Francisco, unsure whether such would be available in Payson.

With the book, she was sure she could master cooking. Improving her cooking, would give Willy a needed break from serious writing. She'd prepared the basics, of course, but had little experience beyond that as after her mother had died, her grandmother, her father's mother, had taken over the home until she died while Willy was away at college.

As she skimmed through the book, she felt some amazement at some of the recipes. Calf's head? Who ate that? She'd never eaten tripe or even heard of it. Other recipes looked more promising like chicken cutlets, or apple fritters—if she'd thought to bring apples.

To resist the temptation to dally away her time, she had brought no other books, none of her treasured classics, certainly none of her many books—not that she read her own work after she sent them off to the publisher. Trash.

The book she intended to write next would have meaning, be important, be part of her new life, and offer something to the world. Its creation had been one of her two purposes in coming to this wilderness. The second involved her father's papers and journals. She supposed she'd not have had to come so far to understand why he had hidden them and what they meant. For that matter, she could have stayed in San Francisco to write the great American novel that she was sure lay buried under her lesson plans and many dime novels. So, why come so far to do what was possible in the city? For a woman, who believed she used logic to make her decisions, she'd used little of that with her quick and abrupt decision. It could only be explained by instincts.

She unpacked her father's journals, the box of receipts and invoices. Besides stacks of paper, carbons, and erasers, she put five lined tablets along with pencils and pens with ink. She had not known the journals existed until months after her father had hung himself. Her desire to find a reason for his suicide, the strange certainty that someone had been in their home the day of the funeral, all had led to her searching the house, but only when her summer school classes had ended did she have time to put more into it. A place by the pantry that didn't look like the wall around it had led to finding a panel. A fingernail into what only appeared to be a groove in a doorframe popped it open.

Inside had been four journals and boxes of billings and business papers. Looking at the journals had been a disappointment. Although her father had written with a fine hand, the words had made no sense. It was no recognizable foreign language. Why had he gone to the trouble of creating a secret cupboard, fill journals with gibberish, and gather boxes of receipts, invoices and letters? Her desire to figure that out as well as a need to get out of San Francisco, to try something different, had led to the abrupt decision to leave town. Instinct had led to her not telling anyone.

Did any of it relate to why her father had hung himself? He had worked for the Hemstreets for many years and seemed happy with his accounting responsibilities. The last few years though she'd been wrapped up in the responsibilities of teaching at Golden Gate University. She'd paid less attention to what must have been a growing depression. Did the boxes of material that he amassed relate to his decision to take his life? She felt tears in her eyes but brushed them away. She'd cried enough over his death. It was time to do something about it, do something with what he'd apparently left in secret knowing only she would find it.

As the sun began to sink in the west, she lit a kerosene lamp, ate a slice of bread with butter and then poured herself a sherry to sit on the porch. A roughly hewn bench was along one side, and from it, she could enjoy the colors reflected into the lake and how they transformed the water from blue to purple and then a fiery red. Sipping the sherry, she thought about her life and how many changes she had known in her twenty-nine years.

With her mother born to wealth, which she'd turned from to marry her father, a lowly accountant, Willy had been taught about the fine things. She snickered as she thought how difficult that had been for her mother to impress on her. Oh, she knew of good china, fine silks, homes with all the conveniences, but they'd never mattered to her.

Even as a child, what Willy had valued was what her father had— education, knowing things, learning about fine literature, and lasting philosophies. What made the ideas of men like Plato and Aristotle such that many generations later, people still discussed them. She had hungered for a higher education, but it had been out of the question, even with her excellent marks.

Ironically, it had been her last year in high school when two events changed her life. A friend loaned her one of the popular dime novels. She had snickered through it at the same time she was writing a thesis on Nathaniel Hawthorne's *Twice Told Tales*. The praise for the book had come from the greats of Hawthorne's own time, not the least of which had been Longfellow, who stated the short stories and Hawthorne's writing was "characterized by a large proportion of feminine elements, depth and tenderness of feeling, exceeding purity of mind." Her mind had begun to spin with the possibility of merging the action of that dime novel with the elements of classic plots and her own writing style. She had to learn about guns and such, but she found them rather interesting anyway.

A month later, she had sent off her first manuscript to one of the dime novel publishing houses. A contract returned quickly, with an option for more. She would be publishing them as Will Tremaine. Was this her making or her downfall? In some ways, she thought, as she took another sip of her sherry it had been both. She had sold out the classics as she mined them for plots on which she created a western tale.

When requests came for the mysterious author to appear at book signings or to give lectures on the West, her editor, Matthew Jefferson, the only one who knew there was no Will Tremaine, brushed them off with various excuses. Having these lusty, sometimes brutal westerns written by a woman would never do was his reason. She had her own.

The royalties paid her way through first Wellesley and then to study for a doctorate at Yale. Better than any of that was meeting the truest female friend she would ever have. Holly came from wealth. She never questioned from where Willy got her money. It was not difficult to keep it that way, which she did feeling some shame at what she was writing. Hers were far from books that would become classics.

Her last hero, her ultimate hero, the man with no first name, the last Taggert, had been a combination of every classical hero she'd ever read— most especially those who were sacrificial. She went with him through battles that nearly cost him his life but always he succeeded and went onto a greater adventure. She understood that if she ever wrote his last book, it would have be his death. She could not bear to do that, to turn him into the ultimate martyr. With her teaching career established, she had a steady, if not large income, and told her editor, there would be no more books—Taggerts or otherwise. He was clearly horrified.

"Is it money?" he had asked when he made a trip to San Francisco, at least in part to change her mind. "I can get you a larger percentage."

"It's not the money."

"But what about the last Taggert? Doesn't he deserve an ending?"

Knowing there could be only one end for him, an end she was

unwilling to write, she had shook her head and only smiled. "He didn't exist, Matthew. Remember that. Yes, he came out of a factual outlaw family in Kansas, who are likely long dead, at least having nothing more written about them and no one seeming to know what happened to them. That's why it worked—part real and part fantasy."

"He seemed real to me and thousands of readers. I still get letters asking when book eighteen will be out."

"Find another hack. It's not difficult. There are dozens out there."

"But not like Will. He got not only into the heart of the outlaw heroes but also the women who loved them."

"It's not happening."

"Think about it, Willy. You know I regard you as a friend, not just another writer."

"I know. I am by the way going on a little vacation."

"Where?"

"It's a secret." She had smiled at his frustration.

He had shaken his head. "I thought you regarded me as a friend as well as your editor." He was at least twenty years older than she, happily married, and so she didn't suspect him of ulterior purposes. Still, the less who knew where she was going, the better. She wanted no visitors.

"I do, and we will talk again… but I won't change my mind on the westerns."

She had understood how Matthew felt. She also would miss the last Taggert. While she had written him as an outlaw, he had the heart of all heroes. He had stayed away from the woman he loved, Lucy, for her own good.

She felt tears in her eyes as she considered the raw emotions she'd felt as she'd written him being put on the train to Yuma, his wrists handcuffed behind his back, with Lucy sobbing on the train station platform. Maybe she'd also fallen a little in love with the outlaw, the man she'd never given a first name despite giving him stories full of daring deeds.

She would miss the imaginary image she had created. She knew exactly what he looked like with a tall lean build, an angular face, dark hair, and a kind of crooked smile that warmed any woman's heart but was, as often used right before he pulled his six-shooter to right a wrong. He was no whiner. He did what he needed to do but never asked for a reward. He was her dream man. How could he not be when he had come from the best of all classic heroes.

Still, she'd never respected her writing of him anymore than the earlier gunmen and outlaws. They became heroes to so many, and they should not have been. They broke laws—even if for good purposes. They used guns to solve problems. And in the end, they were only creations—if not hers, someone else's. They weren't real. She was taking money for fooling people.

Her father, Holly, her best male friend, Nathan Hemstreet, none of them knew her secret, which was just how she wanted it kept. When no more books appeared, people would quit wondering where Will Tremaine was. They would forget the last Taggert.

She wondered then about Holly. Has she married? She felt an urge to see her and decided she would go to Tucson before returning to San Francisco. Holly had intended to rent a cottage in Tucson from a friend called Rose. One way or the other, she'd find her. That would be a fitting end to her adventure. She was in no hurry to return to her lonely home, but eventually she would have to do it. Not only had she grown up in San Francisco, it was where she could support herself with her professor's salary.

Overhead, the sky turned indigo and then black, as stars and planets twinkled. The waxing moon was still a week from full as it tried to rise above the ridge. In the distance, she heard an owl, the swoop of wings, then a rustle in the brush. She supposed she should have been afraid but instead she felt enlivened—more than at any time in her life. She may have been born to the city, but her soul belonged in the wilderness.

Tucson, Arizona, September 7, 1905

"Cole, who told you that you could get out of bed?" Holly shrieked as he limped into the kitchen.

"Don't recall needing permission since I was a child," he said with a grin as he eased himself into a chair stretching his sore leg out in front of him. "Got any coffee left or did my brother get it all?"

His sister-in-law frowned at him but went to the stove and poured him a cup. "You are lucky to be alive, you know."

He sipped the coffee. "That's been true a time or two."

Holly sat across from him and rubbed her swollen belly. Pregnancy, of course, was not discussed between a man and woman. From his brother, he knew the expected date was less than a month away.

"Where is Josh?"

"He's pretending to take a nap." She smiled. "For a two year old, he does still need them—even if he doesn't believe it. Maybe I should correct that to the typical male."

"If I needed one, I'd take one."

"You were shot. Your body needs to heal."

"It wasn't a bad wound."

She grimaced. "Marshal Trask should have never asked you to go with him to arrest Mitt Jackson."

"It's what I do."

"Arrest people?" she asked,

"I reckon that was rhetorical since you know the answer."

"You could find something safer to do."

"I could... sometime."

"Do you have another contract now, and it's why you're in a hurry to get back in the saddle."

He grinned. I wouldn't put it that way. But..."

"We want you to stay here with us this time, not go heading off after more bad guys."

"Or to help good guys," he reminded her. He liked to think of himself as a paladin, a man who worked for the good but without a regular payroll limiting him as to what jobs he could take. As his reputation had grown, as not only a man who could use a gun, but also a man who knew how to avoid using it, jobs had been plentiful. All he had to do was sort through to those he could offer a benefit. Travel had taken him around the West, and only a week before he had been shot, back to Tucson.

"You've drifted long enough. It's time you settle down, get a wife, have some children."

"Like my brothers?" he asked with amusement as he sipped the coffee.

"Vince and Jesse are happy."

"And so it's what I need?"

"You could try it."

He laughed again. "You can't try it. It's for keeps, and when it's miserable, that's for keeps too."

"It does not have to be that way."

"So I hear."

"When we get our adobe out at the ranch, it will be good for families there. You could build one too. There is more land available."

"It's not my thing. Give it up, my beautiful sister-in-law. I won't be changing."

"You have before." He got a kick out of her stubbornness. Vince had been a lucky man. Well, so had Jesse. He knew his brothers were happy or more than happy. It didn't mean he would be.

"I'm getting too old to change," he said rubbing the large muscle in his thigh. The bullet had gone in a little above his knee, luckily or he'd have been walking with a gimp the rest of his life, but the muscle spasmed now and then from the shock of it. He was forcing himself to walk normally, not to cater to the injury. It was the only way to get back to where he'd been. He'd had enough wounds to know that.

"You used to not like guns," she said narrowing her eyes.

"Still don't."

"But now you use them."

"Only when it's the last resort—which is how I got this."

"Vince never told me how it happened, and I didn't ask," she said as she got up to pour tea into her cup.

"No big story. Mitt acted as though he was going to go with us. He had a gun in his pocket and shot through his coat. I dodged to the side but not fast enough. Bill and I both shot him. No telling which bullet killed him. Maybe he preferred to go out that way."

"Would you have?"

"Then go to prison? You bet." He worked to manage a smile to reassure Holly. A woman in the family way should not be upset. "I don't break laws though; so…"

"Good. But if you moved out to the ranch, you'd be with us, and family is support for each other."

"You do not give up."

She smiled again. "Jeremiah would like his sons all here. He's worked to improve himself, even took a class to learn some history of Tucson."

He snorted, as he wondered what his father's motive had been for that. "Maybe. Anyway let's talk about something nicer."

"Like what?"

"Jesse. Every time I see him, he seems more the man he was born to be. I won't say he doesn't have his times where he gets stumped but overall, nobody would know what he was like before he met Lily."

Holly smiled as she sipped her tea, a softened expression in her beautiful blue eyes. "It can work wonders. Love that is."

"So I hear and back we go."

"You should lie down."

"You should quit being a mama."

"Not possible, at least not for twenty some years. Deal with it." She grinned.

"You might have Vince twisted around that little finger of yours, but you don't have me… quite yet." He knew it was close to that though as she had become every bit a sister to him after marrying his brother.

Boots on the porch had both them looking toward the door when Vince came through. "You don't obey orders worth a damn," he said as he kicked off his boots and walked to the table.

"When they make sense maybe… sometimes." Cole smiled and shook his brother's hand. "You quit work early."

"Had some mail." He set a pile of letters on the counter. "Saw this in town too." He handed Cole a paperback book. "Thought while you were laid up, you might like to read the new one."

Cole looked down at the cover of the book where a man stood, legs spread wide with a gun pointed at the reader. "What the hell is this?"

"The latest edition of the Taggert family outlaws." Vince laughed.

"Taggerts?" He stared at the title—*The Last Taggert Faces His Fate with Guns Blazing*.

"Haven't you seen them before?"

"You are joking? You have this made up to be funny?" Disgusted, he threw it down on the table.

Vince poured himself some coffee as Holly rose to get the now protesting Josh. "Not at all. There are more of them out there. I figured you had to have seen them."

"Who is this Will Tremaine?"

"No idea."

"You don't think Pa would be writing these?" It would be just like the old man.

"He claims not when I showed him the last one. I think this is the seventeenth."

"My God, why?"

"They sell. That's the reason things ends up in stores."

"How come our name? Just a coincidence?" This would not be good for his working for law officers or had it been better than he imagined. He wondered if Trask had seen it.

"You tell me. Family came out of Kansas with guns blazing." Obviously, Vince found it amusing. Cole didn't see it likewise. He'd worked to live down that name, and here was this jasper making it infamous. He'd like to find Will Tremaine and poke him in the nose.

"It'd just make it into a book," Vince said sitting across from him with his coffee. He chuckled.

Cole skimmed through the book. It started off with gunplay and looked as though it didn't let up. This Taggert could take down seven men in a shootout and not even consider it an unusual day. He'd have laughed if it hadn't been carrying his name. He wondered if someone like that could be sued to get them to stop. "How long have these been out?"

"I didn't see the first ones. They come out and disappear as fast as they are on the shelves. I'd guess some years since there are seventeen of them."

"This Tremaine fellow write about more than us? That is not us but using our name?"

"A lot more. He's pretty famous. People wait for the next one. From what Del said at the store, these go the fastest, but I saw one about a marshal, someone called the Dancing Outlaw, not sure of the name, then the Frisco Kid. That fellow came from San Francisco and…"

Cole interrupted him. "You read them?"

"Just the Taggert ones. They're kind of fun. I like the invincible part especially." He grinned as he saw Cole's irritation. "You're taking this too seriously, brother. Relax. They can't arrest us for what happens in a dime novel."

"You sure?"

CHAPTER 2

San Francisco September 10, 1905

Nate watched as his mother's irritation grew when ringing the bell wasn't enough to get her the service she desired. He could have said something, but he was studying her. She seemed to have forgotten he was sitting at the other end of the library.

Terrence Cooke came through the door looking only at Eleanor Hemstreet. Nate had become the invisible man. Fine, he liked that idea.

"You rang, madam?" Terrence asked with his usual polished manners.

"Where is Mr. Hamilton?" His mother smoothed down the rich purple brocade of her dress.

"I have not seen him since early this morning, madam."

Nate saw her purse her lips together and suppress whatever she wanted to say. "Thank you."

When he had left, she rang the bell again. When he returned, she said, "Pour me a brandy." Terrence looked at her for a moment, perhaps thinking ten in the morning was too early for liquor, or wondering why she would not have gotten it herself from the sideboard only ten feet from her, but he was too well trained. His face was expressionless as he handed it to her. Again, he didn't look at Nate. Terrence probably did know he was there. Not much got by him. Nate wondered how much he had observed of the goings on in the Hemstreet mansion.

"May I do anything else for you, madam?"

"No, nothing." She sighed. "Just leave me alone." She waited until he closed the door, took a sip of the brandy, and then walked to the window to look out at the city. Although his mother was not quite sixty, her face looked older. He felt it was her dissatisfaction with anything or anyone. She had one of the finest homes on Nob Hill. Ten bedrooms, modern bathrooms with the finest fixtures, a parlor large enough to hold a ball, a table that seated fifty in the dining room, a staff that... but it never was enough. She wanted more. He saw the fury on her face and debated what would ever take that away. Perhaps only death. Sad.

For the first time, she looked over at him. So, she had known he was there all along. "Ah Nathan, and what have you been doing today?" she asked sipping the brandy again.

He knew his riding outfit and the boot he had crossed over his knee would have told her where he'd been, but she liked to control. She wanted to force responses.

"Golden Gate Park," he said.

"Was it nice there?" she asked, boredom in her voice.

"Very."

As she stared at him, he wondered what she saw. Her dissatisfaction with everything extended to him. As her only son, he never was all she wanted him to be. He had quit minding years earlier.

"Did you ride with Miranda?"

"No, by myself." Miranda Compton was his mother's idea of the ideal mate. Her family's wealth doubtless figured into that as much as her comely figure. The problem was Miranda was an incredibly shallow young woman, whose greatest interest involved finding a new ball gown. Nate would sooner mate with a trained monkey.

He had not realized before but his mother clearly was dying her hair to keep it the same gold it had been when she'd been girl. It didn't somehow work. Doubtlessly, her aging was bothering her, but it was one thing she could not control even if she could attempt to hide it.

"She's a lovely girl," she said narrowing her eyes as she moved to sit on the chair across from him "You and she would make beautiful blonde babies. They'd probably be tall like you and your father, rest his soul."

"I am not interested in her or in marriage, Mother."

She gave him a disbelieving look. "Not marriage to anyone?"

"I didn't say that—just not now."

"Are you interested then in the businesses? You know I had hoped you would be, that you would be my right hand man, and then someday take it over."

"I know what you hoped."

"You aren't still moping over that girl are you?"

He knew whom she meant and smiled. She didn't like to use her name. "What girl?" he asked feeling a little mean himself.

"You know who I mean? That worthless accountant's daughter."

"You didn't see him so worthless when he worked for you."

"I didn't know... didn't realize until he killed himself that he had been cheating us."

"There is no proof of that."

She looked away. "I wish..."

The tap at the door interrupted what she might have said. When it opened before she could say enter, he knew who it would be. Only Thomas Hamilton, his mother's majordomo had that kind of arrogant confidence. He wondered what the man held over his mother. While he was in the room with them, he'd never learn. Hamilton went to the sideboard and poured himself a whiskey before he turned back to her. "I heard you had asked for me, madam," he said with a rather snide smile. He was portly but muscular, not nearly as tall as Nate, but with his broad shoulders, he had a demeanor that caused men to back off, his mother also.

"Nathan," she said, turning to him, "would you mind giving Thomas and me a moment of privacy?"

"No problem." He rose and left the room, shutting the door firmly behind him. He walked down the hall letting his boots make enough noise to make them confident he had left, then he quietly returned to the door. Whatever as going on, he wanted to know.

"If she left by train," Hamilton was saying, "she didn't use her name. Would she have reason to use a phony name?"

"I don't know." Her voice sounded concerned.

"She could have hired a driver? Did she have money for that?" Hamilton had moved to take one of the chairs by the fireplace—another proof of his power over his mother.

"Aren't you supposed to be the expert in this sort of thing?" Annoyance was in her voice.

"Not about women running scared." He obviously had no worry at displeasing her.

"You think she is?"

"I don't know, but why go without telling anyone? We have never found Butler's papers, none of the stolen material that we know he amassed."

"You think she'd have taken it with her?"

"Again, I don't know. The day of the funeral, I sent men to look. They found nothing. I thought there was nothing but then she takes off in the dead of night—and after six months. What if she found what he stole?"

"Perhaps it was just a vacation." Her voice didn't sound confident of that.

"There are ways to be certain of the papers not being in the house."

"What did you have in mind?"

Before Nate could hear the answer, he heard footsteps coming down the stairs. He couldn't be found listening at the door. At this point, he had no idea who in the staff he could trust. He moved away and then turned back to the door and opened it, interrupting the conversation but also protecting his spying. "Sorry to interrupt," he said as he looked at Hamilton, seeing the annoyance on his face.

"Thomas and I have finished our business," she said glancing at Thomas and then back at Nathan. "I am glad you came back as I did have something more to talk to you about."

Hamilton rose. "I will take care of that detail, madam," he said and was gone.

"Please sit with me a moment," his mother said as she patted the spot on the sofa beside her. He took the chair Hamilton had vacated.

"Why do you need that guy, Mother?"

"He's our majordomo. You know that."

"Is that all?"

"He keeps our home running smoothly. We need a chief steward and Thomas is an excellent one."

"If you say so."

"I had meant to ask you to come with me to the opera tonight. It will be *Falstaff*. I know how you like Verdi and bought an extra ticket with the hope you would join me."

"No."

"It's a comedy. It would do you good to laugh."

"Perhaps, but the answer is still no." With that, he left the room wishing he had heard the end of the conversation. What papers were they looking for? He thought about going to the Butler home and looking for some kind of secret room. Was it why Willy had left town so abruptly without telling him? He had thought they were good friends and yet she'd given him no clue where or why she'd left. What stolen papers? He needed to go to the Butler home and look around. The answers might be there. Was whatever they had been talking about connected to Samuel Butler's suicide? He had liked the man, spent time with him as well as with Willy. He didn't believe him to be a dishonest man, certainly not cheating the family. No, but what else could it have been?

Tucson, Arizona September 11

Cole came in from helping Vince shoe his mare only to see Holly sitting at the kitchen table, a letter held loosely in her hand and staring into space. "Bad news?" he asked as he washed up at the kitchen pump.

"I am trying to decide. Perhaps being in a family way has me more emotional than need be."

"Want me to get Vince? He was moving the horses into the lower pasture."

She shook her head. "Not necessary. I just... The letter is from a good friend from Yale. She and I were close back then, but we drifted apart once I got to Tucson, and she began to teach. I think about her regularly but hadn't realized how long it had been since I had written or gotten a letter."

"Is she sick?"

"No, or at least I don't think so."

"If you don't want to tell me, I'll go and leave to your thoughts."

"No, I'd like to tell you. I'd let you read her letter except that would seem an abuse of her privacy although she didn't ask me to keep what she said a secret exactly but..."

He felt his instincts kick in, the ones that had repeatedly let him see into what someone was feeling, beyond the words. "She's in trouble?"

"I think so."

"Tell me something about her." He sat at the table.

"She's brilliant, funny, curious, beautiful, brown hair that glows red in the sunlight. She had earned a scholarship to go to Yale where I met her. Her mother had died years earlier and that is probably something we had in common. Her major was English. She wanted to write and teach. When we graduated, we did correspond for a time, but then my father, died and I got caught up in the business in Chicago, then coming to Arizona to do my exploration. I think she wrote last and embarrassingly, I didn't answer. I hadn't even told her I was married or about Vince."

"So how'd the letter find you?"

"You know how Tucson is. Over ten thousand people but still has a small town feel. My first and maiden name, of course, were on it, and the postmaster knew Vince, had seen other business come to us. He forwarded it."

"You aren't smiling, so this was not good news."

"I'm trying to decide. Want some tea?"

He didn't, but he nodded. "Where's Josh?" he asked as she got up to put tealeaves and then hot water into a rose-colored china teapot. He hoped she'd not use the fine china teacups, but she set two on the table. They never seemed to fit his hands right. One day he'd break one and then feel guilty.

"He's with Lily. He and Tyler wanted to play."

"They're lucky to be so close in age."

"Very fortunate."

"Back to your friend," he suggested as he stared at the tea she poured, took a sip, and tried not to grimace. How did anyone drink this stuff?

"Her letter told me on what she's been doing since our last contact in evidently 1901, right after I got to Tucson. She has been teaching at a small private college—Golden Gate University. It was a perfect fit for her as it had been born from several literary reading groups." Tears came to her eyes. "I am so ridiculously teary these days."

"To this point, it doesn't sound like you have a reason to feel upset for her. Sounds like she's done well. She'd not married?"

"The return address was her maiden name; so I would guess not."

That would make her almost thirty. Sounded like the kind of educated woman, who did not intend to marry. Nothing wrong with that. At thirty-eight he had no intention of getting himself hitched either. "There is more," he said as he made himself take another sip of the tea. Holding the cup felt awkward, but it pleased Holly.

"I am blaming myself. I've been to San Francisco twice since then. Vince I went on buying trips. I didn't even think to look her up. Some friend I was."

"Life can be that way."

"Friendships take nurturing. I failed my end. I would have expected her to be angry with me for not writing, but she wasn't. She wrote as though we'd just talked to each other."

"Was there a reason for the letter now, the one you can't get a handle on—like maybe she needed a reference or was fired?"

She shook her head. "She asked for nothing. I am sorry to be so confusing. I am confused. She lost her father last year. She seemed to manage that all right but then something happened that led her to take a trip. She remembered my talking of my desire to go to Central Arizona. She said she was traveling there to spend a few months."

"I still don't see the problem."

"She'll be alone. You know Central Arizona, don't you?"

"Pretty well." He'd been on manhunts twice up in the region west of where he'd been with Holly and his family on one of her digs. It was rugged country, but some of the small towns were pleasant. "Where exactly did she head?"

"She didn't give me an address. I think she was going with the intention of figuring out the exact place once she got there."

"She reckless or irresponsible?"

"Certainly, she wasn't but… She headed for Payson."

"Payson? Why in hell's name would she go there?" That made no sense for a university educated, city gal.

Vince came in. "Want me to go get Josh?" he asked and then looked at the two tensely staring at each other. "What's wrong?"

Holly repeated what she had told Cole. "That doesn't sound like a problem to me," Vince said. "I've been in Payson a lot of times. Small town but nice enough, no problems like say Holbrook. What's got your tail in a twist?"

"How crude," she said with a grin.

Vince winked. "Let's have it."

"I am in a family way," she reminded him.

"I did have reason to know that." He laughed and poured himself a shot of whiskey, handing another to Cole.

"Well, being pregnant might make me more emotional."

He raised his eyebrows. "Might?" He laughed again.

"All right, does. But you are right. It is silly I am being. She's probably nicely settled in a Payson cottage and… I can write her there."

"You can."

"In the meantime, want me to go pick up your son and you two can wrestle through this," Cole suggested.

"You sure your leg is up to it?" Holly asked. He gave her that look and she smiled. "Fine, it would be very nice of you. Or both of you go."

"Not leaving you alone here," Vince said, "not with the due date so close."

"All right, then Cole." She looked up at him, those beautiful blue eyes wide. "Bring us back our son. He'll love riding home with you more anyway."

"The big bad outlaw?" Cole asked as he rose and pulled on his hat at the door.

"Those books still bothering you?" Vince asked with a sly grin.

"And they don't you?"

"Hell no. They give me some prestige in the bars, having an outlaw brother." He laughed as Cole snorted and headed out the door.

Mazatzals-- September 13

After three failures with the sourdough starter, and her conviction that she was never going to get the recipe to work, Willy had second thoughts about making bread. For the evening, she ate the stew she had prepared from onions, dried beef, potatoes and carrots. Again sipping her sherry on the porch, she stared across the lake to see an elk coming to the edge and drinking, then three more. She had yet to see a bear or cougar but she did take her rifle with her when she swam in the lake, which the weather had enabled her doing every afternoon. At first, she had felt the need to wear her undergarments, but the last time she'd swum nude. Nobody but a deer might see, and it was remarkably freeing.

What she had yet to do was get a start on her masterpiece. She almost laughed as she thought the words. Of equal concern, she had been no more successful in understanding her father's journals. The piles of receipts had proven beyond her. Nothing made sense or even felt connected. Why hide it all and then make it impossible to decipher? Or had he not been sure she'd be the one finding it?

She hadn't gone to Nathan for his help in putting all this together. It wasn't a lack of trust but more the feeling it involved his family business, one that his mother had run since his father died. Perhaps she should have gone to him, but...

Mrs. Hemstreet had never liked her and made little secret of that. She supposed the woman had worried more than friendship might develop between her son and the girl who had come from the lower economic class, who had a father who worked in an office, where little money was ever available. Better things were planned for Nathan. She could have reassured the woman that Nathan, handsome as he was, held no appeal for her. If he had felt otherwise, he'd never given her a hint. She did care for him but as a brother, certainly nothing more.

With the information he'd put together, was her father trying to hide his own wrongdoing or someone else's? If he had been involved in sundry dishonesties, he had never appeared to profit from it.

Back in the cabin, Willy lit the kerosene lamp and sat in front of her typewriter. She wanted words for her new book. Nothing came. Writing about the dangerous Taggerts had been so easy. In the beginning, her male protagonists had been mostly outlaws and met their comeuppance at the end of a rope or a bullet.

Then she got interested in a family and one particular man as a heroic character, even a tragic figure who sacrificed himself for the sake of others. His love for Lucy had softened him and led to his downfall. If she wrote of him again, she would want to take him out of Yuma and give him a happily ever after with Lucy. She could not do that nor could she let him meet his demise. Instead, she was releasing him, this nameless man who strode through life by himself, doing good for others and never for himself. He was a fantasy that she'd half fallen in love with despite his nefarious background.

She went into the kitchen, restless and realizing that much as she loved the idea of the wilderness, she'd never experienced so much quiet, so much solitude. She had supposed that to be good for writing her book, for solving the puzzle of her father's enigmatic notes, but it appeared it wasn't doing that. Living in cities, with the noise of commerce right outside her window might have proven easier for her to work.

For the first time she regretted not bringing some of her books with her. It had made sense at the time, but she'd had one she much looked forward to reading by Edith Wharton, *The House of Mirth*. It had been highly praised. She'd bought it and then put off reading it because she knew it to be a tragedy, the downfall of a woman in society. Having only months before buried her father after his suicide, she couldn't bear reading of heartbreak. Now it might have been just the thing to assure herself her life was better, at least than the ill-fated heroine in Wharton's book.

She wandered back into the main room and stared out the window to the dark lake. To the east, the sky was lightening enough to let her know the moon was rising. As it came over the ridge, it was almost full. With almost a magical quality, it was perfectly reflected in the still lake. She wished she painted, as that moment should be captured. Holly had talked of using photography in her archaeology. A camera might be the thing to capture what she saw. Well, she could use words. It would not fit into her future book, but she should write what she saw. Outlined now against that reflected orb, a deer walked along the lake bank.

Typing as fast as her thoughts could go, Willy described the scene. More than the physical reality, there were feelings the moon inspired. It went to a larger truth of life. The timelessness of the moon and the way it went through its cycles, the constancy it offered to a world that was always changing. This same moon had looked down on this land before any white man saw it. Most likely, before any man saw it. Yet it wasn't the same moon.

Smiling, she only stopped when the moon had risen high in the sky, no longer connected to the lake. She had recorded what she had seen and felt. Maybe she could submit the piece to *McClure's Magazine,* which she enjoyed reading when she had time. They ran stories about nature.

She laughed at herself. Did her writing only have value when she could sell it? That was something to ponder. When had she reached the point where teaching writing or selling it were all that made it of significance?

Upstairs in her bed, she pondered it all. For the first time she understood the value solitude offered her. When she had kept busy, preparing her lectures, going to the theater, walking along the bay, shopping, meeting Nathan for lunch, she didn't have to question herself in regards her own life path. Out here, with only the basics to accomplish, she not only could write a book, but she could look at herself in a deeper way than she ever had. Always she'd had a plan, something to do, tasks to perform. Thinking always was focused on a thing or an action. Here at this small lake, in the Mazatzals, she was free to look at life and herself in a new way. She smiled as she fell asleep.

Tucson, September 14th

"Cole, do you know where Vince is?" Holly asked as she came out onto the porch and saw Cole repairing a harness.

"Why?" he asked looking up with concern that maybe the baby was coming.

"I need to talk to him. No emergency." She smiled, and he knew she had realized his concern.

"Last I saw, he was on the other side of the barn. I can get him."

"Maybe you are who I need to talk to." She sat on the porch bench.

He put down the strap, needle and thread. "All right."

"I finally had a chance to look at yesterday's mail. I got another letter from my friend."

"Not good news?"

"No, she wanted someone to know where she had gone, but I was not to worry."

"Payson you said."

"She didn't stop there but went beyond it into the Mazatzals. From her description, into wilderness."

"Your friend is beginning to sound a little unstable to me," he said rising to join her on the bench.

"She said she had a reason."

He shook his head. "Holly, that country is rugged, unforgiving of mistakes, not to mention the hermits and fugitives who use it as a hide-out." She frowned and he saw the tears at the edge of her eyes. "Sorry I said that," he said. "I can see you're worried enough as it is."

"If I wasn't so close to, well, you know, I'd ask Vince to go find her and bring her down here to us."

"No idea why she'd want to hide out up there? You sure she's not running from the law?"

She gave him a look. "Of course not. Willy would never do anything against the law."

"Willy?"

"Wilhelmina but she's always hated that name."

Watching a rider approaching, Cole realized it was his father. This was definitely not going to be his day. He knew what Holly had to want and that was for him to head north and check on her crazy friend. He supposed he'd have to do it. He only hoped she didn't ask his father to tag along.

The old man dismounted slowly and tied his mount to the rail before he stepped onto the porch. Cole rose and shook his hand, then went into the kitchen to bring out an extra chair, letting his father sit beside Holly.

"What brings you up here?" Holly asked with a smile. "Of course, we are always glad to see you."

Jeremiah smiled. "Gotta see my grandson once in awhile," he said.

He was taking a nap or I had hoped he was," Holly said. "I'll see if he's really just playing in there."

"Be nice of you," Jeremiah said, and then looked at Cole, who had straddled his chair.

"Your leg good?"

"It was not much of a wound."

"Not how I heard it."

"Well, it's what it was."

"What did you want me to do?" he asked, used to how his father operated.

"Had news for you."

Cole had an urge for a cigarette. He hadn't smoked for six months. Too often, he took it up and then got the habit. At the moment, it would be worth later having to break the habit. "Good news?" he asked with a smirk. Clearly, his father wasn't coming with good news.

"Remember Albert Johnson?"

Cole had not killed so many men that he had forgotten any of them. He nodded.

"He has a brother."

"And this matters why?"

"His brother has been riding with the Black Handkerchief gang."

Cole resisted laughing. Every gang had to have a title. "I am supposed to know them?"

"If you worked much in New Mexico."

"I don't."

"Clement Johnson has put out the word that his brother was shot in the back, and he wants revenge."

"He was not shot in the back."

"Knowing you. I knew that. But others don't. You have quite a rep these days."

"I don't. It's that damned book."

Jeremiah chuckled. "In this case, you're the one who's been out there.

Jesse and Vince have kept a low profile since they got married. And you are the one who shot Al, aren't you?"

"I was with Sheriff Evans. Johnson had rustled thirty head of cattle. It wasn't the first. Steve asked me to go along. I did it as a favor." A sheriff, in a small town like Springerville, didn't have the money to hire him. He had liked Steve. He hadn't expected it'd lead to shooting. Who kills someone over a few head of beef? It turned out Al did or would have.

"You shot Al." It wasn't a question as his father lit a cigarette.

"He acted as though he was surrendering. Steve, thinking it was over, reached for his reins. Al took advantage of that. Yeah, I pulled out my gun, ordered him to drop his. He didn't and turned it on me. He missed. I didn't." It was what Cole hated about guns. At one time, he had avoided carrying one. Now it seemed it was what kept him alive but maybe also would end his life. He should have stuck to his original belief—leave guns alone.

"I understand, but Clem has been working up a grievance. He managed to talk Sam Collins into joining him. Maybe another."

"Where are they?"

"Rance said in Holbrook but heading this way. Might be smart if you laid low for a while."

"Run?" He snorted his disgust at that idea.

"Just give him time to get over the urge he's got to get himself killed."

"The shooting was a little over a year ago. Why now?"

Jeremiah looked over at him with a sly grin. "You likely know the reason."

"Tell me anyway."

"The books. The last one was a real ripsnorter and talk is nobody could take you in a fight."

"Me? I still don't see what makes it me. What about a cousin?"

"The description."

"That bastard described me?"

"Right down to the dark hair, tall, slim but muscular build, that crooked grin you get sometimes like now."

Damn. Who could know him well enough to do that? He knew no Will Tremaine. So the writer had to be using a phony name. Who the hell would do this to him? "Is it you who wrote them?" he asked grinding his teeth together.

"I ain't a writer. No, hell no. Besides, it's not like I want one of my sons made into a target. Had to be somebody who knew you though."

"I don't know any Tremaines. I don't know any writers."

"Wal, the books are plumb popular."

"Don't tell me you read them too?"

This time his father's smile was uncomfortable. "Tremaine's a danged good writer. He really does write a story that makes you keep reading. Makes you want the next one."

Cole rose and stood watching as Vince rode up to the house. He was beginning to think coming to Tucson had been a mistake. When Holly came out with Josh in her arms, the look she gave him let him know he'd not have a choice for going north. It had nothing to do with Johnson coming after him. It would be to relieve his sister-in-law's worries. He hoped it would do that. From the sounds of her irresponsible and naïve friend, it might already be too late for her. The Mazatzals were not kind to fools.

"You don't have to do it," Holly said after they'd eaten the evening meal and Josh had been put to bed.

"I know."

She handed him the map she'd drawn, following Willy's directions. "I'll fix you food for the trail."

"Pack enough for two. I'm going along," Jeremiah said offering the one thing Cole most did not want to have happen.

"No need," Cole said trying to smile.

"It's not about need. When are you leaving?"

"I told you that it's not necessary. I'll be riding fast. You won't be able to keep up."

Jeremiah chuckled. "Then leave me behind. I'm going. What time in the morning?"

Vince laughed and handed them each a whiskey. "Give it up, Cole. He's going, and you'll be glad he did."

"Want to put money on that?" Cole asked sipping the whiskey. He glanced over at his father. "I'll leave right after breakfast."

"Which way ya going?" his pa asked.

"If you're going with me, you don't need to know, do you?"

"You are a surly cuss," his pa growled.

"Learned from the best."

"I need to talk to you," Vince said to Cole.

"Fine."

"Alone."

"All right." The two went out onto the porch.

"You be careful," Vince said.

"Of course."

His brother chuckled then handed him something. Cole looked down at what had been placed in his hand—packaged condoms. "And I need these why?"

"Don't know that you will, but there are all kinds of ways to get in trouble."

"This kind of trouble is easy to avoid. Just say no."

Vince laughed. "You haven't run into much temptation to which you cannot say no, I take it?" He chuckled again.

"Why would you think I would this time? I am going up to help someone, make sure she's all right." He remembered Holly's description but felt it likely had been exaggerated. "She's an old maid schoolteacher, right?"

Vince laughed more loudly. "Yeah right. Like you wouldn't find an educated woman a temptation."

"Just because you did, doesn't mean I would."

"Better safe than sorry as they say."

"They say that do they?" This time Cole chuckled.

"Take them and if you don't need them, you can give them back."

Cole shook his head but shoved them in his pocket. He'd bought them before, when he intended to visit a brothel, but this was not going to be this kind of trip. Vince pulled him into one of his bear hugs. "Remember what I said. Be careful and not just of the woman."

"Sure. Pa will keep me out of trouble."

Vince snorted. "You think you fooled me? I know you don't intend to take him."

"Well, don't tell him." With that, he left and headed for his room. He could pick up supplies in Apache Junction. Opening his saddlebags, he stuffed in a spare shirt, coat, scarf, long johns and socks. In a small bag, he put the condoms, toothbrush, bar of soap, razor and brush.

Where many men of his time preferred beards and mustaches, Cole liked his face clean-shaven, although changing his appearance was beginning to sound appealing. Maybe later he'd put up with the annoyance of an itchy beard. His bedroll was leaned against the wall and he put it with the saddlebags. Three nights sleeping out should get him there.

He didn't want his father knowing his route, but he had already worked it out. He'd head north from Oracle toward Apache Junction, cross the Salt and pick up the ridge trail east of the Verde River to Jake's Corner and into Payson. His gelding, Boomer, was good on steep places and a sturdy enough built horse to handle the rough ground, not to mention put on the speed when required. His last night out should be in the Mazatzals. From there, head up the valley to Payson. If he got lucky, she'd have had the sense to go back to Payson and be settled in a cottage there. Otherwise, he'd have to follow Holly's map to the cabin and hope she wasn't dead already.

With a nearly full moon, he would not need sunlight to ride. As soon as the moon was high enough, he'd head out, leaving a note explaining what he'd done and telling his pa to go back to bed. He wanted to ease Holly's mind about her friend. God, he'd do pretty much anything for that woman, but he didn't need to be slowed down or stuck with his pa for days on end. It was bad enough to be trying to help some woman who wasn't using the sense God gave her.

CHAPTER 3

San Francisco September 13

H is mother sat at the head of the table. Nate took the other end and waited while he was served, before pouring himself a snifter of whiskey from the cut glass decanter. After the day he'd had, he needed it. They ate in silence. He didn't voice the questions on his mind, as she'd only lie. He poured himself another shot when he'd eaten all he could stomach.

"What is wrong, Nathan?" she asked as she studied him with that expression she had mastered that indicated disapproval and concern in equal proportions.

"What makes you think something is?"

"You don't generally drink so much." Her voice sounded nervous. Her eyes darted to him and then away.

What he was thinking, he was in no mood to address with her, and yet he had to know. "Did you hear about the Butler home burning to the ground?" he asked, deciding to confront it directly.

"It was in this morning's paper. Tragic. A blessing that no one was home at the time."

"Was it?"

"That was a cryptic comment."

Not half what was possible. He smiled knowing it held no humor. He could still smell the smoke though he knew it was his imagination as he'd scrubbed too well to believe any was still tainting his hair or skin.

"You've never said where Miss Butler went."

He didn't answer but moved up the table and took a chair next to hers. "You care?" he asked with what he knew was some bitterness that he couldn't or wasn't willing to hide.

"Just idle curiosity. She teaches at Golden Gate University, does she not?"

'You know the answer to that."

She looked away and then back. "If she left, she should have sold the family home. Then she'd not be out its value."

"You know she didn't?"

"You are very much in a mood, aren't you?" She rose and moved away from the table to stare out the window at the dark street.

He was in a mood, all right but he'd not be telling her that he had been in the Butler home, looking for what no one else had found, when he heard a window breaking and others entering. He'd slid out into the yard and watched as those inside set fires in enough places that no fire department could save the structure. The arsonists had then gone outside and watched as the firefighters arrived, unable to do more than stop the fire from spreading.

From a distance, he'd been unable to recognize the arsonists, although one had a build like Thomas Hamilton. The other three looked like paid toughs. When they left, he'd have followed them, but he had been on foot and they lashed the horses pulling their buggy and quickly left him behind. Had Hamilton been one of them?

"You aren't really listening to me, are you, Nathan?"

"I was distracted. What did you say?"

"Just that I was surprised Miss Butler would leave such a good job. I thought she enjoyed teaching."

"Why would you think that?" he asked sipping his whiskey. "You hardly ever talked to her."

"She is not a friend of mine if that was what you mean. Barely an acquaintance through you. I would be polite to her, of course."

He smiled at that as he sipped the whiskey. He had thought he knew his mother. Now he wondered if he ever had. Since his father had died when he was away at university, he'd spent little time with her. It had been avoidance but perhaps a mistake. Exactly how ruthless was she? Had his mother wanted the Butler home burned to cover up something? If so, what? Would Hamilton, do something like that on his own?

"Nathan, did you hear what I said?"

"Guess not."

"What has got you in a tizzy?"

He smiled at that but didn't answer.

"Will you let her know about the fire, or does she have perhaps a friend here who would?"

"I'm not sure."

"You don't know if they will or you don't know where she is?"

"Both."

"I would love to help her with her losses. Should I ask Thomas to try and track her down?" Her countenance told him all he needed to know.

"No," he said as he finished off the whiskey.

She pulled the cord for Terrence. When he arrived, she said, "Do you know where Thomas is?"

"No."

"Find out."

"What do you want him for, Mother?" Nate's instincts said that he knew the answer but didn't want to believe it.

She went to the sideboard and poured herself a brandy, obviously too nervous and upset to want a servant doing it for her. What was the desperate need she had for Hamilton? He wasn't just a steward. For the first time, he wondered if the two were lovers. His mother was much older, but Hamilton wouldn't let that stop him when money and power were at stake. He waited, certain when Hamilton arrived, that he'd be asked to leave. That was fine with him. He now had his own plans, and they didn't involve telling his mother.

"You wanted me, ma'am?" Thomas said as he entered again without knocking. He looked over at Nate. "Good evening, Mr. Hemstreet."

"It is, isn't it?" Nate said. He couldn't read the man's eyes as he looked at him with a bit of a squint. It looked as though Hamilton was unsure of him. Had he caught a glimpse of him at the fire?

"Nathan, would you mind leaving us. We have some business to discuss," his mother said.

"No problem. See you in the morning," he said as he strolled from the room.

In his room, he shoved clothing into a valise. In the small drawer, he checked under some papers and was pleased to see the $500 he had stashed was still there. With morning, he'd be on the train heading for Tucson. He had checked the schedule and gotten his ticket after observing the fire. He didn't know if Willy would be there, but her university friend had lived there. They had at one time corresponded. Maybe they still did. He would find her and from her, he would find Willy.

He didn't know why Willy had left San Francisco, but as soon as he had seen the men burn her family home, he'd been sure that she was in danger. If they would burn down a house for whatever it was that they wanted, Willy would be no consideration. He had to get to her and warn her. He only hoped he'd find her in Tucson with Holly Jacobs.

He thought then of his mother. Despite knowing of her selfishness, her values that seemed only about amassing wealth, she was still his mother. He didn't want to believe she was behind what had happened. It could all have been unrelated to her. He knew it wasn't, but why? It made no sense to risk arson. What was important enough for that?

Mazatzals, September 16th

Coming up from the lake after her swim, Willy dried in the sun by laying her towel on the biggest boulder and lying back to enjoy the warmth. Her frustration in getting nowhere with the investigation of her father's work was not going to ruin the day or her time in the mountains. In a few days, Amos would return with more supplies. She had expected by then to have a good start on her new novel. She had nothing. She began to think she should have remained in San Francisco.

When the brush rustled, she pulled on her shirt and jeans. Holding her rifle, she watched for a wild animal to appear. What came out of the sage appeared at first to be a wolf and then she realized it was a dog, a small brown dog. She saw its ribs and a potbelly indicating starvation. Its coat was rough and tangled with briars. Poor little thing. Wherever it had come from, it had not had an easy time.

"Hello," she said hoping the dog was friendly. It sat back on its haunches and watched her, apparently as wary of her as she was of it. She walked back to the cabin and tried to think what she had that might be good for a starving dog. She was uncertain of its age, but it was small. She took some of her dried beef, mixed it up with the powdered milk and water and put it into a small bowl.

Back outside, at first she thought the animal had run off, but then there it was at the edge of the pines. Putting the bowl on the ground, she sat on the edge of the porch. Time passed, perhaps as much as an hour before the dog moved slowly toward her. It walked a few steps, then went down on its front legs with its back legs in the air as it crawled toward her and the food. It stopped and watched again.

"What's your name?" she asked modulating her tone to be as soothing as she knew. "If I guess it, will you come to me?" She began to try the few dog names she knew. It watched with what looked to be curiosity. She supposed she was taking a risk. Maybe it meant her harm. Dogs could kill humans if the human was foolish. Something though in this one's eyes gave her confidence that it didn't mean her harm. It was skinny but no frothing at the mouth. Its eyes appeared clear. Its only concern was her intentions toward it.

"Chester?" she asked with a smile. "How about Dennis? Micky? Are you a girl or boy dog?" She couldn't see enough of the dog to be sure. Actually, she wasn't sure she'd know the difference anyway. What she knew about biology had come from books and schooling. She'd had no pets growing up and very little experience with them as an adult. Her father had talked sometimes of them getting a dog, but there was often barely enough money to feed the two of them from what he made. When she began to make money from her books, she had forgotten about her onetime desire for a puppy.

Finally, the dog came to the food and sniffed it, looking at her a little nervously before it grabbed one of the chunks of beef and ran a few feet to woof it down.

"Don't choke on it," she said trying to be reassuring.

The dog returned twice to get the rest of the meat and then just stood and watched her from a safe distance. She thought about reaching out her hand, but maybe it would see it as an aggressive move. "How'd you get out here so far?" she asked. "Don't you worry about being eaten?"

The dog just looked at her. It started to turn and walk away, but then when she did nothing to stop it, it came back and this time a little closer to lap the milk.

Willy walked into the cabin but left the door open. She headed to the kitchen to check her last failed attempt at making a sourdough starter. Still no bubbles, nothing that looked remotely alive. When she looked into the great room, the dog was sitting on the braided rug and again watching her. She pumped some water into a bowl and set it a few feet from the dog. She went to the door and slowly closed it, giving the little dog every opportunity to run outside. It only watched with those big eyes.

She wasn't much of an expert on dog types but the size and coat made her think of terrier mixed with something else. "What are you doing out here?" she asked as she sat at the table next to her typewriter. "You need a name," Willy said. "How about Zeus? Do you like that?" She had begun to think of the little creature as a male but had no firm reason for it.

Zeus had perked up his ears when he heard the name. Maybe he liked it. She knew she liked the idea of having someone to talk to. When Amos arrived with her supplies, she could ask if he recognized it as a lost animal. She hoped he wouldn't. Except how would he fit into her life in San Francisco when she finally had to return? This was no time to worry about something so far in the future. Besides maybe, the dog would leave her long before she left the mountains.

She turned toward the table, opening her cookbook again trying to get a handle on how her sourdough starter had failed now four times. It only required three things, if she didn't count some warmth—water, flour, and the crock to put it in. The crock had to be clean and she had washed it between each failed batch. The flour couldn't be a problem. It had no bitterness. It had to be the water she was pumping from the well. Maybe it had something in it that was working against the process.

She walked into the kitchen and picked up a pan, went out the door, leaving it open for the dog to leave or stay and headed down to the lake. The large rock made a convenient place to lean forward and dip out a pan of clean water. When she stood, she saw Zeus had followed her. Maybe now he would leave.

When he followed her back to the house, she felt pleased and again closed the door. She took the water into the kitchen, started a fire in the cook stove and put some of it into a pan to boil. Looking back at Zeus, who was now standing in the doorway to the kitchen, she opened the cupboard, took out the remains of her bread, broke off a chunk and held it out to Zeus. "Want this?" she asked as she knelt. The dog edged closer and then took the bread from her hand in an almost delicate bite. She smiled as Zeus then woofed it down. It was the beginning of a promising relationship, she hoped anyway.

An hour later, with the lake water having cooled sufficiently, she tried again with the clean crock and her rye flour. For her supper, she heated back up the stew she'd made the day before. Leery of Zeus being so close to starvation, she gave him a little dried beef that she had softened. Assuming he might have a need to void, she opened the backdoor. She headed for the outhouse while he went toward the bushes. She wasn't sure if he would return, but when she returned, he did also.

With evening, she lit a kerosene lamp, enjoying the now waning moon as it again rose over the lake before she decided to head for bed. She'd accomplished nothing of what she'd come to do, but she felt good about the day anyway. Walking up the stairs, she wasn't sure how Zeus would handle that or if he'd be content to stay on the braid rug. He surprised her by following and then settling at the bottom of her bed.

"So you did know a loving human at some time, didn't you?" she said as she reached out her hand to let the little dog sniff her fingers. "You don't have to be afraid of me. May I pet you?" She reached slowly for Zeus' head. He didn't move and let her stroke down his neck. His coat was rough but she felt if he'd let her work with it, she could work out the barbs and snarls. She felt what appeared to be an old scar, but he didn't flinch. It must have been long ago. That could have happened in the wilderness or had he had a mean owner? As trusting as he had become, and so quickly, she wondered if he'd gotten lost. It would be risky to put too much love into him until she asked if Amos had seen him.

She blew out the lamp and lay again staring at the ceiling. Between the cracks in the shingles, a few stars were visible. It was so beautiful. The quiet still amazed her. Then she heard a wolf. She'd heard them a few times before, but this one sounded closer. She was glad Zeus had opted to come in. The howl went on for a few minutes and then she heard a response from farther away. Zeus had gone alert at the bottom of the bed. The howling sounded like a song, perhaps mates calling out to each other. Had they been apart, due to hunting, and now needed to reconnect, to assure each other that they were still alive and cared? Was it the alpha and his mate? Was she being silly?

She smiled, as she knew she was turning animal behavior into human emotions, the mated sort. She actually knew little of human love of the mated sort. Friendship, as with those like Nathan or Holly, that she understood but not the kind of love that she'd written between Lucy and the last Taggert. She'd imagined what that would be. She had almost seen him walk toward her and then turn away to keep her safe, felt her own doubts as to how much he loved her, or had he made excuses?

When writing the last of those books, she had been both herself and Lucy with her doubts and love. She hadn't tried to answer the question of love in the last book, but she knew what she believed. He was noble, sacrificial and he'd loved Lucy more than his own life. Since she'd created him, it was her prerogative to make him into what she wanted. He was what she would have wanted for herself, had she ever desired such a love—which she hadn't and didn't.

She snuggled down in the quilts and felt Zeus move up the bed a little to be closer to her legs. It felt good.

Payson September 17

Riding into Payson, Cole reined Boomer to a stop in front of the general store. He'd bought food in Apache Junction, but he'd get more here, if he must head into the Mazatzals to find her. If she had settled into Payson, he'd stable Boomer at the livery and let her know how much she had worried her friend. Inconsiderate, shallow woman that she doubtless was.

Inside the store, an older man looked up. "Can I help ya, stranger?"

"Cigarettes, whiskey, flour, bacon, beans, biscuits, some jerky." He would get oats at the livery. Boomer deserved them. He'd proven to be the best horse he'd ever owned, and that was going some. "Another box of shells for my Colt, I guess." He had taken to wearing it on his hips and it wasn't all due to the possibility of Clem Johnson catching up with him. He had worked enough with the law to know the unexpected happened more than any would like. While the revolver might deal with an emergency, it also might make the emergency more likely to happen. Ironies abounded in his life.

"Coffee's hot if ya want some," the clerk said as he gathered the supplies into a flour sack. His wife came out from the back and helped him with the order.

Cole poured himself a cup. "I am looking for someone, new to the community."

"Someone got a name?"

"Miss Butler." He sipped the bitter coffee.

"And who are you to be asking?" the woman asked.

Cole never liked giving his name but not much choice for it. He wasn't going by any phony name as though ashamed of who he was. "Cole Taggert."

The man looked up from the tally he was adding. "The Cole Taggert?" he asked.

"There are more than one?"

The clerk chuckled. "Wal, guess he never had first name in the books. The last Taggert. You ain't him air ya?" He studied Cole more carefully. "Look like him some."

"He's fiction, mister."

"Shore seemed real. Loved that last book. *The Last Taggert Faces his Fate, Guns Blazing*." He grinned widely. "The man is a real hero. Sure it ain't you?"

"It's not me. How much do I owe you?"

The man ignored his request. "Why ya want the gal?"

"A friend was worried about her."

"Good reason. She rented a cabin. Amos knows more about it."

"Amos?"

"Contrell ran her out there. He runs the freighting business other side of the livery."

"Thanks." He finally was able to pay, picked up the sack and tipped his hat to the sullen looking lady, before leaving the store. He felt irked with himself at buying the cigarettes. Most of his life, he'd stayed away from the devil weed. He should throw them out. But he didn't.

At Contrells, he saw an older man in the side yard repairing a wheel. He looked up as Cole approached.

"Howdy. I hear you took Miss Butler out to a cabin in the Mazatzals."

The man took off his hat and wiped his baldhead as he studied Cole. "Reason you be askin', young fella?"

"A mutual friend has concern for her."

He considered that a moment. "You wantin' me to take ya out there?"

"No need for that. I just wanted to know if she was still there."

"I go there on Tuesday with supplies. Don't suppose, you'd take out some jest in case she's runnin' low ahead of time."

"No problem at all." He felt relieved the old timer hadn't asked his name.

"What's yore name?" He had felt relieved too soon.

"Taggert."

"All right then, let me get what I was thinkin' she might be needin' if I can't get out there when I promised."

"Long trip out there for a wagon," Cole said as they walked back to the general store.

"Over two hours." That told Cole he'd do it in a little over an hour.

"How'd ya be knowin' where she was?" the old timer asked.

"She wrote a friend, and her friend was concerned, asked me to check on her."

Contrell chuckled. "Her friend's a smart one."

"She is."

"Willy was too to be tellin' her, more than I was fearin'."

"Maybe." Cole had his doubts.

An hour later, he was on the road west with confidence as he came to various splits in the road that Holly had done a good job in the map. He would be there before late afternoon. What happened then, he had no idea. It wasn't like he could drag her out of her cabin and take her back to Holly. What would Holly expect from him?

He gave Boomer a break to drink water and eat some fresh grass before moving a little faster on the last section of the road. When he came to a rise, he saw a small lake and cabin. He edged Boomer down the road, looking toward the cabin for movement when he realized the movement was in the lake.

He looked out and saw a shapely female bottom as the woman swam out into the lake with easy, powerful strokes and kicks. What the hell. The sunlight hit her wet hair and he saw it was long down her back, brown with a reddish glow in the sunlight, and... Damn. He watched even as he should have turned away. She was like a water nymph or something out of one of the Greek mythologies Holly had given him one Christmas. He edged Boomer down toward the lake and saw the pile of clothing and a rifle propped against a huge boulder. When he looked up again, the swimmer had turned, was heading back to shore.

Instead of looking away, he leaned forward on his pommel and watched until she was close enough to stand up. She did it when she wasn't showing more than her shoulders above the water. "Stranger, get out of here," she yelled, her beautiful face showing her anger.

"Can't do that, ma'am," he said "but I can turn the other way." He didn't want to, but he did it and heard her splashing to shore and then the sound of clothing being hastily pulled on. The next sound he heard was of a shell being levered into a chamber. He grinned and turned back to her, dismounting from his horse but not moving toward her.

"Get out of here," she repeated. The barrel of the rifle didn't waver. "What did you do with my dog?"

"Never saw a dog, ma'am, and I came too far to quit now." He stood his ground and watched as she stalked toward him, the rifle barrel still pointed right at his chest.

"What do you want then?" She had a deep voice for a woman, strong, determined. He guessed it fit with a woman who would rent a cabin out in the middle of nowhere. Didn't seem much like he imagined an English professor would sound though. Of course, he hadn't known many of them. Actually no educated woman before Holly.

"You wrote Holly. She was concerned and asked me to assure her you were all right."

"Holly? Why would she do that?" She hadn't lowered that rifle. So long as she wasn't shaking holding it, he was fine with that.

"Didn't you figure it would worry her? Woman heading alone into land men don't even travel, without they have a good reason and even then, not without some worry."

"A long way from people often is the safest place to be," she said and finally lowered the rifle. She stared at him for a longer time than was comfortable. He couldn't read the expression in her green eyes before she turned and looked toward the brush. "Zeus," she called until a small brown dog emerged, still looking uncertainly at Cole.

"Your guard dog?" he asked with a crooked smile.

"He is afraid of strangers, I guess. All right, if Holly sent you, I guess you are safe enough. Do you want to put your horse in the corral out back and then we can talk?"

"Sounds fine." He watched then as she headed up the slope to the cabin. Damn, this was nothing like he'd figured. She cut a fine figure in a cotton skirt that had a way of showing its outlines, when the breeze blew. What he'd seen of her buttocks, when she was swimming, was an image he'd not soon get out of his head.

He unsaddled Boomer and let him loose in the split rail corral. He threw his saddlebags over the top rail. He grabbed the flour sack of supplies, pulled his Winchester from the scabbard, and walked to the cabin. Nice setup with a sturdy looking, two-story log structure, shed, corral, and that lake. Having seen how Miss Butler handled her rifle, he figured she was as safe here as probably anywhere-- that is if she didn't hesitate to use it when required.

When he stepped up onto the porch, he saw she'd left the door open for him. He let out a breath thinking he was not going to be comfortable in there, not with a woman like her, but he couldn't come this far and then leave without talking to her. Inside he smelled coffee with something else cooking. He realized he hadn't eaten since a trail breakfast early that morning. He stacked his rifle by the door, unbuckled his cartridge belt, put it on the small bench, and walked inside.

Pulling off his hat, he saw she was in the doorway to what appeared to be the kitchen. "Please come in and tell me about Holly. I wasn't very polite to you and am sorry for that."

"You did what Holly would've with a stranger approaching that way. Sorry I startled you, Miss Butler."

"You have come a long way. Would you like a cup of coffee, something to eat?"

He handed her the flour sack. "I did bring you some supplies from Payson."

She looked in the sack and smiled. "I don't smoke." She handed him the Luckys.

"I don't always either, but there are times." He put the pack into his shirt pocket.

She smiled. "Like when you are sent after a crazy woman?"

"That would qualify." Reluctantly, he grinned.

"I'd love to hear how Holly is, but why don't we eat first. I started a pot of beans this morning, flavored with ham. I think they're ready."

"Sounds real good, ma'am."

"Willy."

He smiled then as he followed her into the kitchen where there was a small table with two chairs. She set down a small bowl for the little dog and then dished up their food.

After eating, he sat back in the chair and studied the beautiful woman across from him. She was nothing like he had expected.

"You haven't told me your name," she said as she poured them each another cup of coffee.

"Cole Taggert."

CHAPTER 4

W illy was unsure how she managed to avoid spilling her coffee, as a shudder went through her body. She remembered a term she'd read only a year or so earlier—déjà vu. She felt the blood leave her head and wondered if she might faint for the first time in her life.

"Are you all right?" he asked, his dark eyes showing his concern.

"I... Yes, I'm fine. I... Just your being here and Holly and... Please, can we go into the parlor where you tell me how she is?" She needed a moment to collect her thoughts. What was going on here? How had her fictional character seemingly appeared from out of nowhere? How was he connected to Holly?

She sat in the chair by the fireplace and he took the one across from her. She hadn't studied his face when he'd ridden up or even when they'd eaten. She'd seen him as tall, dark-haired, handsome. Almost afraid to do so, she looked up. My Lord, the same strong jaw, angular face, thoughtful gaze. She looked down at her hands now clasping each other on her lap and tried to understand how this could be happening.

He was the man she'd been writing about, the last Taggert, the man without a first name. The man she'd sworn she'd not write about again, not just because she regarded the books as rubbish, but equally as much because she'd become infatuated with her fictional hero.

She was only grateful she had written her books under a pseudonym. Even if he had heard of them, he'd not know they were hers. She certainly couldn't bring herself to tell him. He didn't look like the sort of man who would be reading such books or was she being foolish about that too?

She'd created a fictional character-- look like him or not, it wasn't this man.

"Can I get you something?" he asked and again she looked up and met his level gaze.

"I do have a bottle of sherry in that cupboard." She pointed to it. "Would you also like a glass?"

"Not really my drink, but in that sack, if you'll recall, there was a whiskey bottle. I'll get you your sherry and myself a snort, if you don't mind."

"No, not at all. Thank you."

A few minutes later, he handed her a small glass and sipped the first of his whiskey. "Are you all right?" he repeated.

"I will be. I just need to wrap my head around... Tell me about Holly. Is she all right? I wrote, but left before I could have gotten a response from her. The last time I heard from her was... I guess 1901 when she was heading for Tucson and her investigation of her dreams and that ruin."

"She told you about that then."

"Yes, and then I guess she got busy, and I was too. I was teaching English and wrapped up in trying to get my lesson plans right. This spring, my father... killed himself."

"Holly didn't show me your letter. Did you tell her of the suicide?"

"No, I thought it would be better told, when I saw her." She wondered what he was thinking as his face gave away nothing. She'd called that a poker face in her books. She now understood what that meant. "How is she? Did she find her answers in her ruins?"

"I guess you could say she did. She's fine. Married. Guess you didn't know that either." She shook her head. "They have a boy, well, soon there'll be another which is why she didn't come up here herself."

"She's got a family. How wonderful. Is it wonderful? Is it a good man?" They weren't always.

"I might be biased. It's my brother, Vince."

Dear God, this couldn't be worse. Holly was married to a Taggert. She'd never forgive her. Why hadn't she taken a different name for her outlaw series? Too late to lament that now. She usually was good at putting from her what she couldn't change. She hoped that would be the case this time. She tried to smile but was unsure she had succeeded.

"Drink some of that sherry, ma'am," he said as he took another sip of his whiskey. "You're pale."

"Sorry. I..." She took a sip of the sherry and let out a breath. She had to get herself under control. "I'm fine, just surprised and happy for Holly. She had never spoken of wanting children, but I guess that changed." This time she managed the smile.

"Falling in love does that, they tell me."

She managed to even her breathing. "You never have been in love?" she asked knowing it was a rude question to ask a stranger, but she wanted to know. Was Lucy real too?

He smiled and met her gaze. "No ma'am and not wanting to either."

"Most people do want to. I guess Holly fell madly in love enough to forget her other goals?" She couldn't imagine that strong of an emotion to send a person on a new track, but she'd read about it. Never mind that, she'd written about it.

"She still did digs until the little ones. I think it's in the future for them. Vince is a trader. Holly said she felt guilty that they had even been to San Francisco, and she hadn't tried to find you."

"They were there?" she repeated feeling dumb for the inane question. Why not be there?

"It was to establish a trading business for the tribes in Arizona. They brought crafts from here and then took back money and sometimes sophisticated items for Tucsonans who wanted a taste of the big city but not enough to go there."

"Are you then also a trader?" She was being nosy and normally would have never thought of such an invasive question for a man she barely knew, but she was curious about this stranger who didn't seem a stranger.

"No, ma'am."

"Please stop with the ma'am. My friends call me Willy. I hope we can be friends since you are related to my best friend in the whole world."

"She said the same thing about you, Willy." He obviously made himself use her name.

"I guess it sounds like a boy's name."

"It does."

"I am not a boy."

He smiled. "No, you definitely are not."

She looked back at him uncertain what to say. This was a dream or maybe a nightmare to have her creation show up as a reality. Could she be dreaming? She looked down and saw that Zeus was sizing up the stranger. "He's not sure what to think of you," she said.

"Kind of like you," he said in a teasing tone. He reached out his hand to the little dog and let him sniff of it. "You trust me?" he asked as he ran his hand down the dog's back. With that, he reached down and put the dog on his lap. Willy knew one thing for sure, he had no fear, not of her rifle or a dog he had just met. Zeus though didn't seem uneasy with the action. He let Cole pet him and then rub his tummy.

"You might want to consider a new name for the dog," he said with a teasing smile as he looked up at her.

"Well, he is small, but I thought Zeus might be an encouragement."

"Because he's a she. And my guess is, pregnant."

"You don't mean that." She looked at her dog and finally assessed the belly, which she had equated to being nearly starved.

"Might be why she got tossed out." He felt of the dog's belly again as she didn't protest at all. "I feel bodies in there. How about Zoe?" he said with a smile.

"I don't know anything about birthing. How soon, do you think?"

He felt again. "Can't say for sure but they have puppy shapes." He grinned, and she knew it was at her obvious dismay. She had come to love Zeus… or make that Zoe but puppies. What did she know about that?

"She couldn't die with them could she?"

"Dogs don't usually, but I have to admit I haven't whelped any either."

"My God." She took another sip of her sherry. "Should I be preparing anything?"

"Don't think so. Now I have a question."

She hoped it wasn't the one she feared but nodded.

"What brought you out here? It's not exactly the place I'd pick for an English professor or someone from the Bay area."

"You've been there?" She was delaying an answer but also curious.

"A time or two."

"With Holly and her husband?"

"No."

He sure wasn't one to give much information. She debated as she watched him stroking her pet. How much could she trust him of her own story?

"I found some information which I felt would need time to interpret," she said.

"Have you done that?"

"No. I wonder… Could we talk about that in the morning? I feel exhausted right now."

He nodded and put her dog down. Zoe didn't move far from his legs as he rose. "You have a shed out there, I'll bunk there tonight and we can talk in the morning."

"You don't need to sleep outside. There is a bedroom here on the main floor." She pointed toward its door. "Why not sleep there?"

He seemed to consider that for a moment and then smiled. "And you sleep up there?" He gestured toward the loft.

"Yes."

"I'll do better outside. It's a warm night."

"Suit yourself."

"I will."

"The outhouse is out back but maybe you already know that."

"I didn't, but thanks."

She lit a lamp. "I will fix breakfast and then try to explain what has gone on."

He nodded and was out the door.

Cole didn't sleep in the shed but instead threw his bedroll by the corral where he had stacked his rifle. In the distance, he heard the wolves. For the first time in over half a year, he lit a cigarette and lay smoking as he contemplated the sky.

The moon was just rising above the ridge to the east, and the sky was already full of twinkling stars. He should have learned their names. He knew just enough to use them to mark a trail. Some were the names of Greek gods.

He thought then about Willy and naming her dog Zeus. She had been nothing like he had expected. That was bad. He could not remember the last time that he'd been attracted to a woman. Maybe it was seeing her swimming, but he knew it was more than that. She attracted him physically, of course, but even more mentally. He had no idea why she had ended up out in the Mazatzals, but he now sensed there had to be a logical reason.

He doubted he could help her with her problem, whatever it was. He let out the smoke. He would want to. That made him mad at himself, but it was what it was. He had always had a sort of sixth sense and it had served him well when growing up with the family he had. Now that sense told him that Willy was in trouble, maybe more than she knew.

In the cabin, he had noted the typewriter, stacks of paper, piles of receipts, and who knew what else. He was no accountant but he'd worked with numbers enough to see someone had amassed all of that for a reason. Several possibilities came to mind, none of them leading to good news. Willy had been a teacher; so no obvious need for that kind of documents. Although he had worked with law enforcement, he'd also taken private clients, some of those had been in trouble economically and needing someone to look through their business. Having run his father's hard-scrabble ranch for as many years as he had, he'd learned to get around figures pretty well. Maybe Willy was working through debts of her father's, but if so, why leave San Francisco and come to the wilderness? Nothing tallied up.

Then there was such a beautiful woman being unmarried. Education could do that to a woman, he supposed. Holly had said she thought she'd remain single even after falling in love with Vince. Independent women saw life differently or so it seemed from his sisters-in-law. They though were wealthy women. He had no sense that Willy came from wealth. Holly had said she'd gotten scholarships to go to college. Marriage was good for women who couldn't earn their own way. But then, Willy did with teaching at a small university. Maybe she'd seen what he had with his parents' marriage, the bickering, the dissatisfaction on both sides. That had certainly soured him on the idea of getting hitched.

His brothers were both happy with their marriages, with a family life, but Cole had no sense that it would make him happy to find a woman. He'd had most of his lifetime taking care of others. When he'd finally felt free of the obligations of family, he'd done what he pleased for the first time. He didn't need a wife, certainly not to have sex now and again.

He couldn't deny being attracted to Willy. In some ways, the very craziness of her taking off and getting this cabin had an appeal to him. He guessed if he ever wanted to tie himself to some woman, it'd be the independent sort. Not her though. The two of them came from a very different world. No, he would find out what had led her to this wilderness and see if he could help her. Then, he'd try to forget he'd ever seen her swimming, her beautiful backside lit by the sunlight and that hair... Damn, he had to quit thinking about that moment or he'd drive himself crazy.

When he woke at first light, he pulled on his boots, took his rifle, shaving gear, and walked down to the edge of the lake. Taking off his shirt, he bent to scoop up water, wash, and then work up lather enough to shave. Cold water made the shave a little rough, but he wasn't going to build a fire just to shave and he didn't like bristle on his face. When finished, he stood and waited until his skin dried to pull on his shirt.

Staring out at the lake, as the light changed its colors from dark to brighter. Soon, there was a rosy-hued sunrise, in all its glory reflected into the still water. It was easy to see how a person could get used to a view like that. He'd lived his life not wanting to like anything too much and that included a view. He picked up his rifle and slung his gun belt over his shoulder.

When he turned to look back at the house, he saw she was on the porch with her dog. They were both watching as he walked up. He wondered for how long.

"Good morning," she said smiling. "What would you like for breakfast?" She was wearing a turquoise, cotton skirt with a plain white blouse. She had brushed out her hair, and it hung down her back. Her feet were bare. It was hard to believe this woman also taught a college English class. His, sometimes hard-earned, stereotypes were flying out the window.

"What do you have?" he asked stowing his weapons against the log wall. He was thinking her lips looked very kissable, full, kind of warm looking as though she'd been kissed first thing in the morning and liked it. He knew it was all his imagination, but the feeling wouldn't go away nor the temptation. He turned to look back at the fading sunrise to get his head back where it

belonged.

"Hotcakes," she said. "I'm afraid I ate all but one egg two days ago, but I have maple syrup and some bacon, which I saw you also brought; so you must like it."

"I do like it. Coffee is the main must."

"I made a big pot." She and her dog went in and he followed her, again noting the table with papers spread out across it. She'd been typing something. He resisted the temptation to see what and followed her into the kitchen where she was stoking up the fire. "Cups are on the shelf," she said pointing toward them.

"Can I help?" he asked.

"May I," she corrected and then gave a little laugh. "I am sorry. I can't seem to leave the teacher behind when I go on vacation, and no, I don't need any help for this. I had put the ingredients together earlier so it's just getting the pan hot." The bacon was quickly sizzling in a second fry pan. "This house was very well equipped in terms of pans, utensils, knives, all that one could want for living here, which I guess the owner hoped to do."

He poured his coffee and then sat at the table watching her. She set a small crock of butter on the table and a jar of what he guessed must be syrup. "I have had some trouble figuring out the right amounts of everything to bring and then when Ze... Zoe came along, it cut into some of what I had to feed her up. She was all bone, still is skinny but I guess some is being... in the family way."

He smiled, not surprised that she was uncomfortable saying pregnant —even being a sophisticated, college-educated woman. Funny thing about how people were nervous when discussing what was so natural to life. "You going to call her Zoe?"

"I can't think of a better name yet. I had tried different names on her, but she didn't respond to any until the Z word."

"How about Zinnia?"

"I like that. Zinnia, what do you think of it?" The little dog looked up at her, but probably it was the soft tone in her voice—one he'd noticed she shifted into whenever she talked to the dog.

The batter hit the sizzling pan and soon the fragrance of pancakes filled the kitchen along with that of bacon frying and coffee. She kept cooking them until he held up a hand. "No more. What about you?"

49

"I will have bacon and coffee."

"You'll stay skinny that way," he said as he fed Zinnia a piece of bacon and half of his last hotcake. She woofed down both.

"Mr. Contrell will be here later today or tomorrow and restock me."

"I met him in town. Seems like a dependable guy."

"You stopped then to ask questions." She sat across from him and nibbled at the bacon.

"I thought it possible you'd be back in Payson and not enjoy living this far away from others."

"I guess that was possible. Instead, I fell in love with this place. I wish I had the money to buy it."

"It's for sale?"

"Mr. Gibbons said it would be with a cash offer. I didn't ask how much because I have no spare cash."

"How many acres come with it?"

"I didn't ask, but Mr. Contrell may know."

He wouldn't ask because he wasn't about to buy it. Settling down anywhere wasn't in the cards. His life demanded he not care too much about anything.

"Shall we take our coffee into the parlor and I will try to explain my situation." He smiled and rose, taking a refilled cup and again sitting in the chair in front of the fireplace. She took the one across from him. "I guess it starts with my father's death. In March, he killed himself."

He didn't know what to say to that and so just nodded. Sorry was such a pathetic word.

"I was teaching and living with him but not there a lot."

"You found his body?"

"Yes. He'd... hung himself in our basement, from a rafter, kicked out a chair and..." She stopped. He saw her work to control her emotions.

"Had he left a note?"

She shook her head. "No last word. That morning when I'd gone to classes, I didn't notice anything about his demeanor to indicate he was unhappy. It was... a complete shock."

"If you need to cry, I would understand," he said.

"I cried out all the tears, I guess." She sighed. "I had to get things together, arrange for his funeral, burial. I was in somewhat of a daze for weeks. I managed to teach but just couldn't concentrate on anything else. The day of the funeral though... I knew someone had gone into our home. A door that had been locked was ajar, things moved, but nothing taken. Since people do that, steal from those they know will be gone, I thought perhaps they'd been interrupted and left before finding anything of value, not that we had much."

"Did you come to believe they were looking for that?" He pointed to the papers on the table.

She nodded. When I came out of my daze, I began to wonder. I put together things. The day I found my father's body, I also realized his desk had been cleared of all papers, none of his notebooks nor the billings that so often cluttered it. That was unusual. Then, he... he had a way of enjoying the secretive." She smiled sadly. "He doubtless wished he had been a spy; so I thought perhaps he'd created a hiding place. Eventually, I found it and with it the journals and boxes of what you see on the table."

"No note?"

"No."

"You realize there are several reasons for hiding what he did."

"I accepted that, but for him to do anything dishonest, would have been totally out of his character and yet, well, I can't be sure."

"But you have to know." He understood that.

"Yes, if he had been cheating those he worked for, I'd have wanted to find a way to pay back what he had gotten. But once I got it all here and had time to look through it, the receipts, invoices, bills, statement of building supplies, orders, letters, none of it made sense to me and even more confusing were his journals." She walked to the table and opened one of the black notebooks. "They are gibberish. Not a foreign language but just words making no sense at all."

He followed. The penmanship was fine, great care taken to make uniform paragraphs. There were numbers but mostly words but not words he recognized either. "It's a cipher," he said as he looked for what might be vowels. Find the other letter for them and often finding the word became easy.

"You've seen them before?"

"It's not uncommon when someone has information that they fear falling into the wrong hands. It can though be difficult to decipher without a key." He saw tears in her eyes. "Maybe you'd rather not know."

She stiffened her spine. "I have to know. He left it hidden with the rest. I think he knew I was the one who could find it and then..."

"And it's why you wanted to get away?"

"One of the reasons."

"Are you a writer?" He pointed to the typewriter.

She whitened. "I teach English. We all write some."

He nodded and turned back to the receipts and billings. "I don't know if I can help you. This name appears regularly—Hemstreet Enterprises."

"He was their accountant."

"Do you have reason to trust or distrust them?"

"Nathan Hemstreet has been my best friend for many years, like Holly in that. His father died six years ago."

"From what?"

She had to think. "I was back East and… I just heard he passed on."

"And Nathan runs it now?"

"No, his mother Eleanor. Nathan has had little interest in business, but his mother has tried to bring him into it. He has said it's what she wants. He hasn't been sure it was his own desire."

"All right. Let's start with the journals and see if we can read them, and they may tell us why he collected what he did. This one is dated 1901. Are any of them older?"

"No, it's the first."

"Anything significant happen that year?"

"Nothing that I know of. It was the year I returned to San Francisco, and Holly and I lost touch. I had the offer from Golden Gate University, which was just starting up. It was exciting, demanding, and I became lost in the developing of lesson plans, my students, being back in San Francisco. I paid little attention to what was going on in my father's life. We often didn't even meet for dinner. I feel incredibly guilty now as I wonder if he ever tried to tell me, and I didn't listen."

"What if you find out that your father was cheating the Hemstreets and guilt led to suicide?"

"I'd be heartbroken but honor bound to reveal it."

"Because you love this Nathan guy?" He didn't know why he asked that. He didn't want to know the answer.

She shook her head. "I'd do it for my father because he hid all this for a reason. Maybe it was intended to be a confession to ease his soul."

"If someone believes in such." He didn't. Maybe she needed to believe in a purpose behind everything. He would rather think there was not.

"Yes, if someone believes in such. I have some pens, and you can take one of the tablets. May I help with it?"

"Sure, a brain like yours should make this kid stuff. First, we look for vowels as they are repeated the most in English. Or did your father speak another language?"

"No, a bit of German but I don't believe enough to write it."

"All right. To start, we look for repeated letters. Look also for words the right length for words your father used frequently in conversation."

"Sounds like I should start another pot of coffee." She smiled.

"Good idea." He pulled up a chair and began copying the first paragraph onto a pad. He resisted looking at the words on her typewriter. Maybe a letter to the man she thought of as a friend but was it that simple? Nothing usually ever was.

CHAPTER 5

Tucson, Arizona – September 18

Nate stepped from the train and onto the platform, waiting while the porter brought his bags. He had traveled a bit but never into the Southwestern United States. Approaching Tucson, the country had been rugged and tough looking. As the train pulled into the old depot, he saw a new one being constructed. With bags in hand, he headed for his hotel. The streets were wide, unpaved, but flanked by businesses looking much as they might in any other town. Not the Cowtown he'd been expecting. There also appeared to be a larger population than he'd anticipated. Finding Holly Jacobs might not be so easy.

After checking into his hotel, which was adequate if not exceptional, he stepped back out onto the street, debating how one found a missing person who wasn't actually missing. Maybe the sheriff's office, but it would be his last resort. He could use a drink. The bar closest to his hotel, the Pedrales, looked as though it would work.

Inside smoke choked the air. Although it was not yet dark, the room was busy with tables filled and men standing at the bar. He headed for that. "What can I get ya?" the bartender asked with a friendly smile.

"Cold beer?" He wasn't sure what was possible.

"Coming right up." He walked to the other end of the bar, opened a large refrigerator, returning with a bottle of beer and a glass. "This all right with ya?" When Nate nodded, he opened the bottle and poured the beer into a glass.

"Busy night for a Monday?" Nate asked trying to find some friendly conversation after he took a sip and smiled.

"About like average. You new to town?"

"Just came in on the train."

"Enjoy your stay." He grinned again before heading down the bar to another customer. Rarely having been in a bar like the Pedrales, Nate debated what would sound nosey and what might get him information when the barkeep returned. The more he thought about it, asking questions in a bar about a lady wouldn't seem smart anyway. He'd enjoy his beer, listen to the conversation, and try somewhere more likely the next morning.

"You looking for a game?" a man asked who sidled up to him.

"Not tonight."

"Not a gambling man?" The man was older than the barkeep. His smile came easy and made Nate wonder what he really wanted.

"Not good at cards or lucky at dice," he said taking another sip of his beer. "This is good," he said, not that he was any connoisseur.

"Can get pretty much anything in Tucson these days," his new friend said. "Town's growing up."

"I can see that."

"You coming here to live?"

"For now, just a visit." He didn't know this man well enough to ask about Holly Jacobs or Wilhelmina Butler. The slight slur to the man's words gave him a concern that he was going to end up with a problem.

"My name's Rance Evans. What's yours?"

"Nate Hemstreet." He took another sip of the beer. He hadn't wanted to give his name, not that the Hemstreet name was likely to be known in this Southwestern town.

"You from Frisco?"

He studied the man a little more closely. "Is that important?" he asked as he let out a breath.

The man put his hand on what Nate now recognized as the butt of a gun. What the hell kind of place was this?

The bartender came back. "Rance, you're drunk. Go home and sleep it off."

"Just trying to be friendly, asked a friendly question and..."

The bartender stopped him with a raised hand. "Where's Jeremiah?"

"He ain't my keeper."

"Somebody needs to be. You're drunk and have had all the drinks you are getting."

The man glared at him but finished his whiskey with a swallow. "No problem. I'm gone." And without a further word, he was.

"Thank you," Nate said when the bartender looked back at him. "I was uncertain if that was about to be a problem."

"Rance and his friend had a falling out last week, and he had to move into a hotel. He's not happy."

"So he's looking for a new friend?"

The bartender chuckled. "I don't think he knows what he's looking for. Maybe a meal ticket. My name is Ridge."

"Thanks for your help. You think he'll be looking for trouble later?"

"Likely won't even remember your name tomorrow."

Nate ordered another beer. "I don't fit very well here."

"Get yourself some western clothes and you will."

"You mean my suit is a giveaway?" Nate chuckled.

"Fit right in back East but out here, yeah. Not to say there aren't places in Tucson where men wear good suits, but this ain't one of them." He disappeared for a few moments to replenish some other drinks and then returned.

"What gives it away?"

"Tailored, fine fabric, that tie. That the latest thing in Boston?"

"San Francisco." He smiled. "Where is a good place to get the proper garments for Tucson?"

"Emporium is good. My pick though is Sicillas. They carry some of everything and western gear that'll hold up is definitely part of that. That is if you plan to stick around."

"Not sure, but I will get outfitted. I don't want being taken for a dude who is an easy mark."

"Throw in a few ain'ts, and you'll have it made." Ridge chuckled again.

Nate thanked him and headed for his hotel. It'd been a long day, and he had a lot to do in the morning. Tucson might look like any other small town in the country, but it was different. As he lay in bed, he heard a gunshot and then another. What kind of place was this southwestern town? And where the hell had Willy gotten to?

Mazatzals September 19

Willy hurried down the stairs, let Zinnia out and took care of her own needs before washing up and starting breakfast. She glanced toward the lake several times hoping to get another view of Cole shaving. She could hardly believe how wonderful that sight had been the morning before. She had only imagined what a man might look like with the sun just hitting the muscles in his shoulders and back, as they flexed, while he took care of morning ablutions. That morning, she had hurriedly settled at her typewriter and written all she saw with the mix of nature in the raw as well as the man half in the raw. She had no idea how she'd use the description, any more than she had when she'd written the moon rising. It didn't fit into her idea for a classic or a dime novel—not that she'd be writing more of the latter.

She'd been so into describing what she saw that she almost missed his heading up the slope toward the cabin. Leaving the writing in the typewriter had been a mistake, but she didn't think he'd looked at it. He truly was a gentleman. When he'd left for the night, she made sure to put that page with the others and stashed them with her clothes in the loft. She wouldn't want him coming across them and wondering what else she wrote. She supposed if she wanted to be honest with him, she'd tell him about the dime novels, but did they really relate to his life at all? That Taggert wasn't him.

Smiling, she heard boots on her porch. "Come on in," she yelled before he could knock. He had a little bristle on his jaw. Maybe he'd shave later. She liked that idea. More light and she'd see more of the definition of muscle as he moved. Why she needed to do that, she wasn't prepared to consider. "Coffee's ready," she said as he entered the kitchen. Again, she saw that he'd removed his cartridge belt and left his weapons outside. She appreciated the consideration. She'd never thought to have the last Taggert do that. Of course, since he had so many dastardly enemies, probably he could not have afforded to do it—fictionally speaking that is.

"I've been thinking about the cypher," he said. "Did your pa have a nickname for you, besides Willy, that is?"

"Not that I can recall."

"Not even way back?"

"You think it would be a key to the letters?"

"Could be." He sipped his coffee watching her over its rim. She wished she could read his mind. There was something in his eyes that mystified her. She looked down and realized she'd not buttoned her shirt all the way up. A bit of cleavage was showing. Living alone here, it hadn't mattered whether she buttoned all the way up. Would he think she was trying to seduce him? Not that she'd have the faintest idea how to go about doing that.

"I'm afraid all I can offer you are more pancakes and bacon. The sourdough didn't come out again."

"Cakes sound fine. Had a lot of failures with that starter, have you?" he asked.

"So far, total failures. At first, I couldn't get it to bubble, then when I did and added it to the flour, it went flat and way too sour to eat. Even my dog turned her nose up at it." She liked the sound of that, her dog.

"I might be able to help you with that later, if you want that is."

"Very much. It was my idea that I could make my own bread here between Mr. Contrell's deliveries."

"Good idea. When you expect him?"

"Today, I think." She pointed to the kitchen wall where she had placed a calendar, crossing off dates. So far from people, it was the only way to keep track of time. "He said though he might send his nephew if he got busy in town."

After they had finished eating, they moved back into the great room with their coffee. "You thinking of sending letters off when he comes?" he asked studying her with a look that again had her wishing she could read his mind.

"No, I hope Holly isn't worried, but I hadn't planned to write her. You can tell her I am fine when you go back, can't you?"

"Sure."

"I might even visit her in Tucson although I suppose she'll be really busy with a new baby."

"She'd still be glad to see you."

"I'd like to see her children, meet her husband. I am sorry we let so much time go. Being busy is no excuse."

"It is a reason though."

Outside, she heard the sounds of a wagon approaching. "This is much earlier than I expected Mr. Contrell." A few minutes later, she saw a tall, dark-haired man driving the wagon, as he brought it to a stop in front of the cabin.

"Howdy, Miss Butler," the driver said as he jumped off and walked to the porch. "My uncle couldn't make it today and asked me to bring out your supplies. I'm James Wilson, call me Jim."

"Thank you so much, Jim." She realized that Cole had come out of the cabin behind her but had stopped long enough to buckle on his cartridge belt. What was that about? Surely, he didn't see this man as a danger.

Cole helped carry in the sacks of goods.

"Uncle Amos didn't mention you had a dog."

"She showed up last week. Do you recognize her as belonging to anyone you know?" She hoped the answer would be no.

He studied the little dog who had darted behind Cole's legs. "Nope, can't say I do. Maybe some folks north of us or someone traveling through."

"I'd like to keep her."

"Seems there'd be no reason you couldn't." His gaze shifted from her to Cole. "Uncle said you were here. Glad to meet you, Mr. Taggert."

Cole took the offered hand but didn't look pleased. She felt Jim was just trying to be polite but had no idea why Cole saw it otherwise.

"You must have left at first light," Cole said stepping back and looking up the road and then back at the young man.

"I kind of hoped to spend some time out here. Always liked this place."

"You knew Mr. Smith?" Willy asked.

"Sure did. I helped build the cabin. One of the prettiest settings in the Mazatzals."

"It certainly is that. Would you like some coffee?"

"Sure would."

In the kitchen, Cole didn't sit at the table but leaned against the counter watching them as they drank their coffee. Jim Wilson looked up at Cole. "I had a question."

"Yeah?" It wasn't a friendly response.

"Do you know the author wrote all those books about you? I wondered if he based them on interviews or what?"

Willy nearly choked on her coffee, looking from Jim to Cole.

"Those books are fiction, Mr. Wilson," Cole said in a level tone, but his eyes had narrowed. "They are not about me. So far as I know, there is no Taggert like the books suggest."

"You read them?"

"Skimmed a little, that my brother handed me, but no, didn't read it. Just pure bunk, Mr. Wilson. I doubt the author knew any real gunmen."

"I don't see how you'd say that. The stories seemed real to me."

"You know any gunfighters?"

"Maybe."

"In Payson?" Cole's disbelief showed in his tone.

"Well, I ain't always lived there."

Cole smiled at that. "I guess I was being edgy," he admitted surprising both Willy and Jim.

"Didn't mean you wrong."

"I know but that book… It's been following me around for a while now. I'd like to get my hands on the author of it. People think it's me."

Jim sipped his coffee. "Does look like you."

"So I hear."

"A man come to town yesterday asking for you… or maybe it was the book one."

Cole's lips tightened. "Give a name?"

"Johnson, I think."

He drew in a breath. "He go on his way?"

"Not sure. I didn't see him again, but he was asking others. Might've stayed in the hotel. I don't frequent the bars."

"Wise." Cole walked out of the kitchen, onto the porch and stared out at the lake. Willy felt like following him. He hadn't encouraged her to do so, nor did she have any reason to think she could reassure him. She had seen by his response to the books that whenever she told him who she was, he wouldn't take it well. She wished she'd never written them and yet without them, she'd not have the college education, which led to her job teaching. She had though betrayed a man in using that name, a man she hadn't known actually existed. What damage had she done to his life with her reckless use of words?

Tucson September 19 afternoon

Having outfitted himself properly with jeans, cotton shirt, belt with a silver buckle bearing the head of a horned creature, a lightweight jacket, and cowboy boots, he debated an appropriate hat. The bowler he'd worn to Tucson didn't seem quite the thing. The Emporium hadn't carried hats that appealed to him or when they did, they were too small for his head. Tall as he was, his head was even bigger than the average man's. He'd gotten that from his father or so his mother had constantly reminded him.

Nate headed for the other possible store for hats. Inside Sicillas, the large room appeared divided in half, with womanly garments on one side and masculine on the other. A red-haired woman came from the distaff side. "May I help you?" she asked with the kind of smile that warmed a man to see.

"I hope so. I need a hat."

She led him toward the display in the front of the store. "Any particular style?"

He looked at the Stetsons. They would not be true to whom he was though he did admire them on men who lived the western life. "What do you think would be best, Mrs. Sicilla?" He took the chance she was married and there was a mister.

"Call me Connie. Well, what about this?" she asked handing him a gray hat with a slouch brim. "You can shape it as you want. They've been popular in Australia but also here as they don't make a specific statement. Just protect you from the sun which can be brutal in Arizona."

He tried it on-- pleased it fit. Looking in the mirror, he saw that it suited him, and as she said, didn't try to make him look like a dude pretending to be something he was not. "I like it," he said. "Sold."

"Good." She led him back to the cash register. "Can I get you anything else?"

He handed her the necessary cash. "Maybe some information. I am looking for someone." He'd also asked at the Emporium, but his lack of Spanish and the clerk's lack of English had gotten him nowhere.

"For good or ill purposes?" Her smile was teasing as she handed him back his change.

He set the hat on his head. "She would be able to help me find a friend. Her name is Holly Jacobs."

She studied him for a long moment. "Who is the friend? And then, I must ask, who are you?"

"My friend is Wilhelmina Butler. She and Holly were best friends."

"I might be able to help you, but I will have to send word to someone as it's not up to me to make a decision regarding a friend, who might not want to be found."

"That's fine. Should I come back this evening? How long will it take to notify this friend?"

"Where are you having dinner tonight?"

He shrugged. "I hadn't decided."

"Why don't you come back and have dinner with us."

He smiled at that. "You wouldn't trust me enough to tell me where Miss Jacobs is, but you would invite me into your home for dinner."

"That's about the size of it." She smiled.

"All right. What time?"

"Six. My husband, Del and I eat in our quarters behind here. Come in as the store closes, and then I will know what I can tell you… or whether I can help you."

He left the store, sure that the woman knew where Holly was and maybe Willy. He had confidence she would tell him. Walking toward his hotel, he ducked back into an alley when he saw Thomas Hamilton with two men. Damn, what was he doing here? The men headed for the Pedrales. What business could Hamilton have in Tucson? Did it relate to Willy or were his crooked operations more widespread than Nate imagined?

He went back to his hotel room, buckled his shoulder holster in place and made sure his 44-40 Remington was loaded before he slid the revolver into its holster. He put on the jacket to hide the weapon. He wasn't looking for trouble but on the other hand, he'd had enough experience through his father's business dealings to know it didn't always come when one was looking for it. Gritting his teeth, he thought of his mother, returning to the question of how involved she was in what Hamilton was doing. He believed the man had burned the Butler home. Now he wondered about the suicide of Samuel Butler, as good a man as he had ever known. Exactly what had his mother asked be done?

He walked to the hotel window and looked down on the street. It would be hard to wait for six. He wouldn't go directly to Sicillas. With no way to determine why Hamilton was in Tucson, he'd take no chances on being followed. His main hope now was that Willy had not in Tucson. He also hoped Connie Sicilla would get him the information as to where she was. Something told him that she was in trouble. More than she knew.

Mazatzals, September 19

After Jim had left, Cole had been quiet, saying little. They had worked again on trying to find the key to the cipher but neither were in the mood for it. When a rider came toward the cabin, she would have gone out, but Cole stopped her. "Stay in," he said. "Keep Zinnia in too."

"But…"

"Don't argue with me, Willy. Let me find out who this is."

She picked up her rifle, angry with him, but she stayed put, behind the window where she could watch. She did not recognize the rider until he dismounted by the porch.

"Looking for something?" Cole asked.

"My name is Chester Gibbons. Is Miss Butler here?"

Walking out onto the porch, she said, "How are you, Mr. Gibbons? Is there a problem?"

He looked askance at Cole. "Is there?"

"He is a friend of my family. Now what do you want?" she asked.

"Someone is talking of wanting to make an offer on the cabin and this land."

"I thought you said I'd be fine with it after having an option to buy."

"You have a month to exercise that option. I am sorry. I didn't expect this."

"It seems strange since you said that it had set empty for months."

"I thought so too. The family only recently came to Payson. They were told about this property and had a desire for a lake. I am sorry, but you will have a month unless you decide to exercise your option to purchase it."

"I can't do that."

"Perhaps it's a bluff, and they don't have the cash either. I run into that now and again with my business. Anyway, I just wanted to let you know." He looked then at Cole who had leaned against the post that held up the porch roof. "Who are you?"

"She just told you. Friend of the family," Cole said coldly.

"Well, I am sorry to be the bearer of bad tidings. I just felt I should let you know. Do I know you, Mister...?"

"You couldn't have sent a letter with James Wilson?" Cole asked ignoring the question.

Mr. Gibbons managed a small smile. "It just came up after lunch. You do have a month." He looked back then at Willy. "I hope that they are bluffing. I rode a long way though to assure myself that you had been fairly warned. I am so sorry." He turned back to Cole. "You look like someone I know."

"But I am not."

Gibbons' smile was toothy. "I can see that."

"You are aware that you need to give Miss Butler written notice of this offer and her need to vacate," Cole said coldly.

"I... Yes, I can do that. I am sorry about this, Miss Butler. If this turns out to be a serious offer, I will look for another suitable location."

"I appreciate that," she said still surprised at how unfriendly Cole was to now another stranger to him. What was that about? Despite his bad news, she would have invited Mr. Gibbons to supper, but she knew Cole wouldn't like it.

When the land agent had ridden off, she turned to him. "You don't like strangers much, do you?"

"Never found one brought me good news," he said.

"Surely at least one has."

He just looked at her. There had been no time to talk about the books, but she knew now that eventually she would have to do it. She wanted to find the right words to explain how she wrote about a man, whom she didn't know existed, only to find he did. Crazy is what it was.

"Chicken came with the supplies," she said putting the concerns from her. "How about fried chicken and mashed potatoes?"

He let out a breath. "I'd like to have a cigarette out here first, and then I'll help if I can."

"You don't need to help me."

He drew a cigarette from his pocket and lit it.

"It's a nasty habit and not healthy for you," she said, knowing she was again sounding like a teacher.

"A lot of things aren't." His smile was crooked. She had rarely seen him smile when he looked genuinely happy. She wondered if that ever happened. What had gone on in his life to make him such distrustful, toughened, even bitter man? She guessed she'd never know and headed into the cabin to start dinner.

Cutting up the chicken, she felt disappointment that her time at the cabin would be shortened. She had a month to get the money together. Holly and even Nathan would loan her the funds needed to buy this cabin, but she would hate to ask either. Besides, did she really want to own it? What would she do with it if she did? Her teaching responsibilities were such that vacations weren't easy to wrangle. She smiled as she used the word. If she hadn't written all those dime novels, she'd not have thought of such a word.

She had taught a summer class with the original intent of earning some extra money, as well as not wanting to think about her father's death. The decision to ask for the fall trimester off had come only after she found his papers and thought of turning her writing around. Having only taught at Golden Gate for four years, she knew she could have put her future there at risk with requesting the favor. With a yearly contract, she served at the pleasure of the board.

She still believed it had been worth the risk. Perhaps she could have done it without getting totally away from her home, from her responsibilities. Except, she had already learned things about herself that she'd never have learned in the city. She'd never have met the last Taggert. She smiled. He'd be angry if she called him that. She had constantly to remind herself that he was not that man. She still could not explain how she had described him never having met him.

Zinnia was not at her feet but had chosen to stay in the main room with Cole, who bent over the papers and journals was shuffling papers. He was dogged. She could certainly say that for him. Then she giggled at her choice of words. Putting the potatoes into the oven, which felt the right temperature, she dredged the chicken in flour with pepper and salt. She'd wait half an hour before setting the pieces into the cast iron skillet. She poured herself a glass of sherry.

"Would you like some?" she asked as she approached him. She looked down then and saw he had poured himself a shot of whiskey. "Finding anything?" she asked looking out across the lake and seeing four elk coming down to drink.

"I decided to stick to the billings. I'm ordering them in piles according to date and type."

"You know much about business?"

"No degree, if that's what you mean, but enough. I kept the ranch going up in Utah, then sold it for a good price, invested since. I get by."

"I tried to make heads or tails from it, but numbers aren't my thing."

"Well, let me give it a try."

She went back into the kitchen and soon had the chicken frying. In the supplies, three wonderful looking bunches of carrots had been included. She washed, then scraped them before slicing them for finger food. In the morning, she'd look for possible recipes to use them with the onions and potatoes. She rather liked cooking... despite the sourdough failures. She wondered what kinds of food Cole liked. Would it be what the last Taggert enjoyed? She shook her head at her silliness.

CHAPTER 6

Tucson September 19

Nate had chosen an evasive path to go back to Sicillas, arriving as close to six as he could manage. The store was quiet, the lights out, but the door was unlocked. He walked in and tapped lightly on the door to the kitchen.

"Come on back," Connie said. When he opened the door, a tall man rose from the table. He was dark haired, rugged looking, wore a gun on his hip and didn't look to be in a good mood. On the other side of him was an older man, receding hairline and a pleasant smile. "I'm Del Sicilla," the second man said putting out his hand. "The other half of Connie."

Connie had stayed by the stove watching but saying nothing. In some ways, Nate found her the most intimidating. There was something almost otherworldly about her. He resisted the smile as he thought of a fairy.

He turned back to the men. "I am Nate Hemstreet."

"I hear you have some questions," the dark-haired man said, without offering his name as he sipped a whiskey.

"Are you the one with answers?"

"Might be."

"I am looking for Holly Jacobs."

"And the reason being?"

"I need to find Wilhelmina Butler. Holly was her best friend at Yale."

The stranger looked at him with an intense gaze, which could have been intimidating but strangely Nate found it humorous. "If you don't know where she is, I should go," he said.

"Don't be so quick to take offense."

"I don't have time to waste."

Another man entered the kitchen, this one tall, gray haired, a thick mustache, but looking very like the man at the table. "Learn anything?" the older man asked. He was familiar enough with the kitchen and Sicillas to pour himself a whiskey.

"Actually, I could use one of those," Nate said.

The older man gave him a look but then poured a second shot and handed it to him. "You're the one with questions."

"I am." Nate took the whiskey and slugged it, holding it out for another.

"You hold your liquor well?" the older man asked. "If not, we won't be finding out much before tomorrow." He poured the liquor and smiled.

"If you people do not know where Holly Jacobs is, I am wasting your time and mine." He sipped this shot more slowly.

"We need to know why you want her or Wilhelmina?" the younger man said as he studied Nate.

"Holly would help me find Willy, who I believe is in danger. I can't waste time getting to her and warning her."

"And your reason being?"

"She is my best friend in the world."

"Nothing more?" the older man asked.

"That is her choice. I won't say it is mine."

Connie moved from the stove and put a large bowl onto the table. It smelled fragrant and obviously loaded with chili peppers. "Gentlemen, eat and then talk. Liquor on an empty stomach doesn't usually fare well."

The men smiled with a mix of chagrin and agreement, but nodded. An hour later, they took to the back porch, while Connie cleaned up the kitchen. Del poured them each another shot.

"You brought out the good stuff," the older man said as he lit a cigar.

"Figured this was an occasion for it."

"My name is Vince," the hard looking one said. "This is my father, Jeremiah."

"There a reason for no last names?" This was feeling strange or maybe the liquor was going to his head.

"We're Taggerts." He lit a cigarette.

Nate considered that. "Should your names mean something to me?" They didn't.

"Tell us more about this danger to Miss Butler, and we'll tell you."

"Willy's home was destroyed by arsonists. I believe their leader was my mother's majordomo."

The men didn't look as shocked as Nate would have expected. What kind of men were these? "There is more, isn't there." Vince said. It wasn't a question.

"The man who burned the home is now in Tucson."

"What the hell is a majordomo anyway?" Jeremiah asked.

"A hired thug, in his case," Nate answered.

Vince lit a cigarette. "Any chance he's in Tucson because he followed you?"

Nate shrugged. "That is the question."

"Could he have followed you here?"

"I was careful not to be followed, but I am in a hotel. He could easily find out where if he had been following me."

"Let's hear the rest," Vince said.

"While you tell me nothing?" He considered that.

"Holly Jacobs is my wife," Vince Taggert said. "You sure you don't know the last name?"

"Why would I?" He felt mystified at the question.

Vince smiled. "No reason, I guess. Holly did get a letter from her friend, and she was very concerned for her."

"Willy expressed fear?"

"Not her. My wife because of where Willy was headed."

"So you know where she is and it's not here," Nate said.

"Why didn't she tell you where she was going?" Jeremiah asked, letting out smoke in a circle.

"I would have hoped she trusted me, but I guess she didn't fully."

"And yet we should?" Vince asked.

"Maybe not. Sorry I bothered you." He rose to go, but Del put out a hand. "Let's go in and talk to Connie about this."

"Your wife? What would she know about it?"

"More than you could imagine," Jeremiah said. "I agree. Let's ask Connie."

The three men walked back into the kitchen where Connie was now sitting at the table and looked to be waiting. "Are you familiar with Tarot cards, Nate?" she asked as she shuffled what looked like a deck of playing cards.

"I've seen them used a few times by fortunetellers," he said as he sat across from her, the other men also taking their seats at the table.

"Do you respect the secrets they can reveal?"

"Not sure."

"Be sure," Jeremiah said. "With this woman, they tell truth."

"It is not required that you believe," Connie said. "Do you want to ask a question?"

"Would they tell you where Willy is?"

"Not that probably."

"Then I have no question."

"Do you give me permission to ask a question for you, one I believe may help you with your need? You don't have to believe it's anything. You are not bound by them."

"Fine."

"How many times should I shuffle?"

"Four."

She smiled. "And cut?"

"Six."

Finishing, she dealt out three cards face down. "Do these three feel right to you? Please put your hand over them without touching them."

"They're fine."

She turned them over. "They represent you as I thought they might. They reveal someone who is about to learn a new skill, develop a part of themselves that they had yet to know was there. The one learning the new skill is a wealthy man, who is also courageous. He is good, kind to others, a dispenser of largesse. Possibly the head of a business. The determiner card, as to what the skill will be, is the moon." She looked up from the cards and studied Nate's face until he felt uncomfortable. He didn't look away. "You have undeveloped psychic abilities. Did you know that?"

"Maybe." They had not been welcome.

She smiled again. "When you take control of the business you will inherit and need to run with better judgment than your parents, your psychic abilities, which could go in many directions, will grow until you are much like a wizard." At his expression of disbelief, she laughed. "Disbelieve me if you wish but it is what it is. There are those who will need your help, and you will be strong enough to give it to them. Especially Willy, you and the other. Even before your powers grow, you will give to the *other* what is needed."

The *other*? That made no sense. "None of this appears to help me get to her," he said feeling disappointed.

"Does enough for me," Jeremiah said as he leaned back in his chair. "I'll take you."

"Is she here in Tucson?"

Jeremiah chuckled. "Nope, four days, maybe five, you being a tenderfoot. It's a hard ride north of here. You up to it?"

"You sure it's safe to take him?" Vince asked, his face showing his lingering doubts.

"Willy needs to know what she's up against. I ain't met her, but I like her spunk going like she did, not asking help from anyone. Besides, the *other* with her, that one matters to me." He grinned. "I'll take him."

"All right, get your gear from the hotel," Vince said rising. "I'll meet you out front with a horse and take you to my place for tonight."

"All this from a card reading?" he asked still feeling a little mystified.

"Not just a card reading but Connie's," Jeremiah said. "Let's get, before them hooligans think to track you."

That sounded good to Nate. An hour later, he was riding a new horse, using a western saddle, alongside two men he had only just met and heading out of Tucson toward Vince Taggert's ranch. He felt confident that he was doing the right thing. Something about Connie Sicilla had inspired confidence. Except who was the *other*?

Mazatzals September 20

With morning and a fresh supply of eggs, Willy decided to fix Cole a large breakfast, ham instead of bacon, and even fried potatoes. She'd fed Zinnia chicken pieces and some potatoes from the previous night. She wasn't sure if ham was good for a pregnant dog. She wished she had some books on the subject.

"We've been getting nowhere on the cipher. I am thinking going for a ride might help clear our heads," he said after they'd eaten.

"I uh have never been on a horse." She sipped her coffee, trying to think of reasons to keep it that way.

"I figured you to ride in the saddle and I'll ride behind. Nothing to it."

"Unless I fall, and then it's a long way down."

He smiled, maybe the first genuine smile she'd seen on his craggy face. "You, the woman brave enough to come into the wilderness by herself, and now afraid to get on a horse?"

She nodded. "Besides what about Zinnia?"

"She'll stick close to the cabin. We won't be gone that long."

"Where will we ride? That is if I did decide to do it." The idea did have some appeal, but she felt a mix of that and still fear of being thrown. She'd certainly put enough people on a horse in her books, but had had no interest in trying it herself. She and Holly had once been going to go for a ride in Boston, but at the last minute something had come up, and she'd never gone.

"There is a ruin about maybe five miles from here. I thought you might like to see it."

"I'd have to ride astride."

"Didn't you bring some pants? Holly and Lily both wear them when need be."

"Well…"

He smiled again, and she knew that smile was having a devastating impact on her heart. "All right," she said finally knowing the main appeal would be to have him so close to her. They'd avoided that since he'd arrived. She wondered what it would feel like to lean back against what she knew to be a hard chest after having seen him washing up, now twice. She'd not had her own bath in the lake since he'd come, settling for spit baths, which were not nearly as satisfying. Still, she couldn't really go into the lake with him there, even if he promised not to look. If he'd gone in all the way, he'd done it after dark, as she'd yet to see him swim. Another sight she wouldn't mind collecting for the time he was gone from her.

She knew, from the few days with him, that she'd never known a man like Cole Taggert. He wasn't a man of many words, but the ones he used counted. It wasn't just that he looked like her imaginary Taggert, but his demeanor also surprisingly, again and again, what could only be called déjà vu. She was not a woman who believed in the mystical. Yet what else could explain this bizarre connection—one, which apparently only she knew existed. She was unsure what his response would be when she finally told him about her other name. She had a feeling it wouldn't be good. She would have to do it, but not today, not ruining what she felt would be an experience she would long remember.

Upstairs in her loft, she quickly changed from her dress to the boy's jeans, boots and a plain shirt. She carried a hat downstairs and onto the porch where he had tied his horse and was leaning against a post smoking a cigarette. Zinnia was at his feet. "Will I need a hat?" she asked noting he was wearing his black Stetson. It was some battered and suited his face in a way that a new hat would not have. He also had the cartridge belt around his narrow hips. She wished for paper to describe what she saw, then thought how foolish that was. No more dime novels.

"If you want one," he said, but it's mostly forested; so your choice."

She'd be riding in front of him. The brim might bump him. She threw it back on the table. Kneeling by Zinnia, she said, "You have to stay here." She looked up at Cole. "I don't suppose we could take her?"

"It'd be hard on her and for no gain. She seems like a pretty clean dog. Why don't you close her in the cabin to be sure she doesn't follow."

She liked that idea. Even if there were to be a mess to clean up, it'd be worth it to keep the little dog safe.

"I will help you mount," he said after she'd closed the reluctant dog into the house. "Put your left foot into the stirrup and step up, swinging your leg over, toes into the stirrup."

She did and then adjusted her seat until she felt comfortable. The ground did seem a long way down. He handed her the reins before leaping up behind her. He put his arms around her and took the reins. "For now I'll use them but later you can get a feel for how that works."

One thing that worked well, was feeling him against her back. She didn't lean into him, as she wished, but felt his warmth and those muscular arms around her, holding her securely in the saddle. She'd never experienced anything quite like it. She liked knowing her safety was in his strong grip, his easy balance on the horse. She began to enjoy the movement of the horse as they headed up the trail.

"How do you know of this ruin?" she asked as she tried to forget her nervousness.

"I was up this way two years ago."

"A vacation or do you hunt?"

She heard the smile in his voice. "Sort of a hunt, yeah."

"You have never mentioned what you do."

"Does it matter?"

"I suppose not, but you know what I do. You know why I am here." She felt guilty at saying that since he didn't really know all about her. Still, he wasn't telling her much about himself.

"Let's just enjoy the ride," he suggested as he turned his horse up a trail that led north. She'd had no idea there were so many trails in these mountains. "This led to a mine also," he told her as he pointed through the trees to a dark ridge that rose to the east. He stopped the horse long enough for her to see the hole he pointed to. "Silver most likely although sometimes they found gold."

"Mr. Contrell said that was what Mr. Smith had hoped to find when he built his cabin."

"Looking for gold seems the shortcut many want."

"Funny isn't it," she agreed as he gigged his mount in the side and got them started again.

"In a way but it also is tragic. Leads to a lot of mistakes, and in the end, what can they take with them?"

"Treasures in heaven," she suggested, trying to put a prim sound to her voice.

"You believe in that?" he asked.

She was so aware of the hard muscle in his bicep as it brushed her arm that it was hard to remember his question. "I don't have a lot of beliefs except maybe in education, learning, trying to do right for however long someone is here."

He didn't respond, and she thought he wouldn't, and then he said, "You asked about my background. Did you really have interest?"

"Of course. Do you have brothers, family?"

"Two living brothers and my father." He let out a breath. "One brother is dead."

"I'm sorry."

"Don't be. He was a murdering bastard and got what he deserved. Vince, my oldest brother killed him in self-defense."

She swallowed hard. What could one say to something like that? Her own story was sad, and yet she hadn't experienced that kind of brutality where one brother had to kill another.

"I shouldn't have told you," he said. "You have enough of your own troubles."

"That doesn't mean I am not interested in your life. What are your brothers' names?"

"Vince, Jesse, and Asa is the one who is dead. He's buried along the Salt River in an unmarked grave, which is actually more than he deserved. He... enjoyed tormenting others, scaring them, trying to break them. The world is better off with him out of it."

She thought of a million questions she would like to ask about how his death came about. Had Asa abused Cole? She asked none of it because she had heard in Cole's voice that he'd been reluctant to tell her what he had. She decided to change the subject. "And Vince is married to Holly."

"And Jesse to her sister, Lily."

"They all live in Tucson?"

"Outside of it. Vince and Holly are moving to be closer to Jesse and Lily. Their children are close in age. Jesse and Lily have a boy and girl. By the time I get back to Tucson probably Vince and Holly will also have two children."

"They are all happy in their marriages with their families."

"For now."

She smiled at that. "My mother did love my father, but she wanted material things. She married him knowing who he was but still, she missed much of what she had had. It made her unhappy that an accountant couldn't provide her with luxuries. I think it made him unhappy he felt he had failed her."

"How old were you when she died?"

"Twelve. She'd been sick though some years before that. It was as though she wasn't there."

"Any grandparents?"

"After they disowned her for marrying my father, I never met her parents. My father's mother came to live with us and she did what she could."

"It was good."

"She tried but she was older and impatient. She died when I was on the East Coast going to college. On my mother's side, I know I have cousins and an uncle and aunt even but they had no interest in us. I don't in them now."

"Bitter?" He stopped the horse at a small stream for him to drink.

She had to think about that for a moment. "I don't think so. Just nothing I'd care to know about them. You know that saying that blood is thicker than water?"

"I do know it."

"I don't think it's true."

"Let's us take a little break here too." She heard the smile in his voice. He slid off the horse and then lifted her from the saddle. She moved to a large rock to watch the stream. "They talk about places being God's country, but this certainly is all of that," she said.

"Do you mind if I smoke?"

"You are an adult; so it's certainly your choice about smoking." She put a note of disapproval in her voice. He might not care if it shortened his life, as some believed it would, but she cared.

"How did you get so smart?" he asked as he sat on a rock across from hers.

"I do have a doctorate," she reminded him with a teasing smile.

"You don't get that kind of smarts from books."

"How would you know? Are you a reader?"

"When I have time and a place, yes. I have one in my saddlebags back at your cabin."

She only wished it were her cabin. "What is it called?" She didn't believe it would be one of hers. She hoped anyway, as she watched the riffles in the stream. A leaf was caught in one and then got free and went on downstream until it would be caught again.

"*Moby Dick.*"

"I didn't imagine you reading a book like that." She looked up in surprise as she thought of her own books and their ultimate inspirations. The Melville epic had been at the heart of many of her western stories.

"Why not?"

"Well, it's not one that many find easy to read."

He laughed at that and again she heard real amusement in his voice. "And a cowpoke couldn't read something complex?"

"Well, I guess I was operating with a stereotype, wasn't I? What was the appeal though of Herman Melville's classic? It's considered tedious by many."

"How can it be tedious when a man is fighting against himself as he tries to kill what he doesn't like inside himself?"

She nearly gasped. He had gotten to the heart of the story. How much education did he have?

"The answer is only to eighth grade." He apparently had read her question without her voicing it. "But doesn't mean someone has to stop learning, does it?"

"No, of course not." She considered how this man was like her created hero and yet she'd never imagined the last Taggert as reading anything more than wanted posters. "What led you to *Moby Dick*?" she asked.

"In the beginning, the sea."

"You wanted to go to sea, and yet are landlocked?"

"No, I have no interest in being a sailor. I have seen the ocean though. The Pacific that is, seen a whale breaching. I suppose I was curious about a whaler's life—the life I don't have. Actually, the life I don't want."

"That is a good reason for choosing a book."

"In the case of this one though, you doubtless know more about it than me, but it also asks questions of evil, sanity, passion or would that be obsession and the likely end of that kind of fixation."

She thought then of her need to find an answer to her father's life, his death, the reason for all he had hidden away from her. "Have you had a quest like Ahab?" she asked unable to take her eyes off his handsome, angular face and those dark eyes.

"I could have at one time, but now, I don't think so."

"Can you tell me what it was?"

He considered that. "To find meaning to life, my life."

"That is weighty."

He laughed. "Tell me about it."

"You amaze me. I… what other books have you read?"

"Anything by Mark Twain, as you probably would expect."

She smiled. "I wouldn't even try to expect where it comes to you. You got sent on a quest up here by your sister-in-law, disrupting your own life and work."

"I would say this is not so much a quest as a task. It wasn't much sacrifice at the time. My work is somewhat flexible. You asked earlier. I take on jobs as they come. Sometimes it's for a lawman, helping to bring in someone wanted. It also has been for a person or business when they feel they are being defrauded by someone. I've helped solve murder cases. I get letters asking for my assistance. We work out a fee if I decide something sounds interesting or that I can make a difference."

"Do some involve guns?"

There was that smile again, the one that showed no humor. "Sometimes."

"And the Mazatzals? How did you know of this ruin and this country?"

"The first time I was up in the Mogollon, it was with Vince for Holly's dig. This was before she married Vince. I had tagged along out of curiosity."

"You appear to have a lot of that." She laughed.

"More than my share. It hasn't always worked for me either."

"Were you taken with archaeology, and it's why you came back up here?"

He shook his head. "I did like the kind of deductive process. I like solving mysteries but no, the second time I was up here on a job when I came across this ruin."

When he didn't offer what kind of job, she guessed he didn't want to talk about it. Not wanting to ruin the rapport they had found, she didn't ask further. She'd never seen him so open and willing to tell her about himself. Getting away from the cabin had been good for them, as he had suggested. It would have been a good time to admit to her own writing, but she couldn't bear to break the mood. Would he leave as soon as he learned she had created a fictional but shallow personification of himself without even knowing it?

He handed her his canteen to drink from but drank himself from the stream. "Why don't you drink from the canteen?" she asked when he levered himself back up to look at her.

"I'm used to this water. You're not."

She screwed back on the lid. "I could get used to it maybe."

He smiled. "Not today though."

Tucson September 20

Nate ate breakfast with the Taggerts, finding Holly to be the great beauty he'd been told by Willy to expect, as well as a gracious hostess to a man she didn't know. When he admitted it surprised him, she said, "You are a friend of Willy's. That's good enough for me."

He was anxious to get out of Tucson, but Jeremiah had things to do first, and so he was forced to wait. Since he had repeated all he knew about either his mother or Hamilton's words and the burning of the Butler home, there seemed little to talk about.

Josh had all the curiosity of a two-year old. He'd had zero experience with children; so they shared some educating each other. The little boy had a set of blocks that he delighted in building into tall towers before they fell. Nate remembered those years and so joined in with the activity. It helped to lessen his anxiety-- some.

It was shortly after lunch when Vince rode in, ate a lunch that Holly had prepared, watched as she put their son to bed, and then finally got to what Nate cared about. "I got you supplies enough for the trip. You can buy anything else you need in Payson," he told him.

"What do I owe you?"

"Nothing. You are doing this for Holly's friend. When Pa gets here, you two will leave."

"Good. I am anxious to get there, but how do we assure that we won't be followed?"

"Trust an old outlaw to know how to avoid that," Vince said with a grin.

"If we are, we'll have to turn around. We can't take the risk of leading them to Willy."

"Don't worry about it. I'll be your backup to be sure nobody follows you. I also talked to Sheriff Trask, who owes my brother a favor or two," Vince said as he poured himself a cup of coffee. "He's right now having a visit with Hamilton to see what he wants in Tucson. He does that with new arrivals, especially if some of them look like toughs. He'll ask enough questions about their purposes to keep them busy while encouraging them to head back from where they came."

"Your brother?" He had to believe that this was the *other*.

"Cole. A few weeks ago, he helped Trask with one of his apprehensions. Cole got winged in the doing of it, but he kept Trask alive, or at least that's how the sheriff saw it," Vince said.

Holly entered the kitchen and sat across from the table, rubbing her hands absently over her swollen belly.

"You okay, beautiful?" Vince asked with concern.

"Just be glad when this little one is here," she answered with a smile that probably was intended to comfort her husband, but Nate saw that it'd take the baby being born for that to happen. He could see how having babies would be a worrisome thing for a man. Women did die in childbirth. He thought then about Willy having a baby, maybe his baby. He stopped himself. That wasn't happening until she changed how she felt about him. Maybe his arriving at her cabin would help bring that about.

"Vince said that Connie saw you as having mystical powers," she said now looking at Nate.

"She did indicate that. I guess from the cards."

"You don't put much stock in them?" she asked.

"Not disbelief or belief."

"Connie has a pretty good record of nailing what has been or will be," Holly said.

"What sex is your baby?"

She laughed. "I didn't ask her. Should I have?"

"No need. I can tell you."

Vince gave him a look. "And you say it's…"

"Healthy baby girl." Nate grinned.

"Based on what?"

"50-50 odds." He chuckled.

Jeremiah came through the door. "Ready?" he asked.

Nate rose. As ready as he'd ever be.

CHAPTER 7

Mazatzals September 20

W hen Cole stopped his horse at the edge of a clearing, he pointed. "There they are," he said. What she saw were stone walls, built into an overhanging cliff. Overhead ravens soared. From photographs and Holly's descriptions, it was exactly as Willy had expected. Cole slid off the horse and then helped her down. He dropped the horse's reins.

"He'll stay here with the grass," he said, pulling his rifle from its scabbard before leading Willy forward.

"It's…" She sought for words, wishing she had brought a tablet to describe what she was seeing. She could almost feel the energy of the ones who had lived there, a simpler life or was it?

"This one is in pretty good shape," he said as they walked closer. "Last time I was here, there were even pots inside the rooms."

"Is it safe to go in?"

"After I check for snakes or something unfriendly."

"Like what?"

"Cougar or bear sometimes hole up in places like this. The spring over there is a draw to bring them a meal or two." She waited while he climbed up the slope to the doorways, looking in each. After a few moments, he waved her up. The slope was gentle enough that she found climbing it easy even with her leather soled boots. She entered the first room. The beams across the top were still in place, giving it a cozy feeling. With half the roof gone, light allowed her to look around. A large pot was in one corner, broken pieces in front of it.

"Holly said sometimes they broke their pots when they left if they didn't plan to return. Looks like they couldn't make up their mind on this one." She glanced up at him to see his smile.

"I'd love to take it, but it'd be sacrilegious."

"Could lead to bad luck," he agreed. "Bad as breaking a mirror."

She laughed. "Seven years then or would my soul be trapped in the pot?"

"Is that what causes the bad luck with breaking a mirror?"

She looked into his eyes, saw the glint of humor, and smiled. "It's what the Romans believed."

"They'd know a little about bad luck," he agreed.

"I think living in a place like this must have seemed like paradise." She walked out of the room and looked at the small clearing, the stream that seemed to emerge directly from the earth, and the scrub pines beyond.

"Be close to family."

"Right now I'd love that. I didn't have much family and now with my father gone, there's none. I would have loved to know what that kind of life felt like."

"Maybe a lot of squabbles, arguing over who got which view." Again, she saw he was teasing.

"You have a big family?"

"It's grown some since Vince and Jesse married. I mostly avoid them."

"Why?" She hadn't expected that answer.

"No reason. I'm just talking."

She knew he wasn't, but she didn't probe. She walked down the row of rooms, peeking in each one. One had a complete roof and at the back was what looked like a cave. She looked back at Cole who had followed her.

"Holly said they hid things in those rooms sometimes," he said. "They also buried their dead in the floors of the rooms when they were family or like children. Outsiders got buried farther away."

"It must have been exciting being on the dig with her, so much to learn. She was always so excited about prehistoric cultures."

"Yes, she has been that." When he didn't say more, something in the tone of his voice told her to let this also go. Perhaps someday he'd want to tell her his secrets. Then she remembered her own and it dampened her joy in the day.

"Seen enough?" he asked, as they walked back to his horse.

"Yes, thank you so much for bringing me. It's let me understand a little of what Holly feels for such places."

"My pleasure, ma'am." He helped her into the saddle and then leaped up behind her.

"I don't suppose it helped us find the key to the cipher though."

79

"I am going to concentrate of the receipts, billings, facts he had amassed. From the little I've seen, it looks as though someone was buying supplies but then overbilling their client. When I have a chance, I'll talk to my brother about suppliers in the Bay area. As a trader, he knew which businesses to avoid and which to trust. A couple of those names didn't look right."

"You'll have to go home to do that then?"

He turned his horse and started him back down the trail. "I could write him a letter or for a faster reply, wire him some of the names."

"We'd go back to Payson then, or would that be just you?"

"Your choice."

She thought about that. She wanted to keep riding with him forever, with those muscular arms brushing against hers. She wanted to lean back against his chest and give herself over to his strength. She had no rights and needed not to forget that. An hour and a half later, they rode into the cabin yard and he slid off his horse before helping her down. "I'll let Zinnia out and start dinner," she said as he nodded and headed to the corral.

By the time Cole came into the house, she had shredded potatoes and onions to make potato cakes. She sliced off some of the ham and fried it alongside the cakes. Nothing fancy but then she wasn't actually that great a cook even with her cookbook. She wondered if Cole liked gourmet foods. So many questions to which she imagined she'd never learn the answer.

After they'd eaten and he'd helped her clean up, they sat out on the bench to watch the lake. She sipped sherry while he whiskey. Zinnia sat at his feet. Willy didn't mind that the little dog had taken to Cole so quickly. She was unsure though whether either of them could keep her. She wanted to, but her life was unpredictable as it stood. If she couldn't get this new book started, her only income would be from the university, which would not begin again until the next term. She had a little savings. Maybe selling her home in San Francisco would be the prudent choice. But then, where would she go? Rent a room from someone was most likely and cheapest.

"You are thinking deep," he said, taking a sip of his whiskey.

"Just trying to plot out my next move when I go back to Frisco."

"You thinking of visiting Holly before you do that?"

"I'd like to see her, but would she want a visitor with a new baby to care for?"

"When do you leave here?"

"Originally it was to be middle of December, but now if someone really does buy the cabin, I might have to leave sooner. I've certainly been a failure on this idea of mine."

"Had you figured how much snow this cabin likely gets in winter?"

"Oh… I guess I had not. Would I have been snowed in?"

He smiled. "Not a bad fate if you had food anyway."

"I was too much the Californian, I guess. I forgot about winters and shouldn't since I went to school where there were very much winters." But someone took care of snow removal.

"Mid-November would probably get you out of here before it hit —most years."

"When do you have to leave?" she asked feeling a sense of loss that she hadn't expected to be so strong. She barely knew him. It had only been a few days since he'd arrived. How could he have come to mean so much to her life in such a short time?

"I had hoped to solve your mystery first. Let me see how I do on the evidence your father had gathered. It might tell us what was going on even without his journals."

"I am half scared of the possible answers in those."

He smiled and reached out with his finger to touch her cheek. She nearly sighed with pleasure at the soft stroke, the rough texture of his skin. She'd heard gunmen had smooth hands, easier to draw their guns. Obviously, Cole worked with his hands enough to keep that from being true of him. When he used his finger to move her face, she knew he meant to kiss her. She should have stopped him, but she wanted that kiss. She realized that she'd wanted it since the day he'd arrived. Even when she'd looked at him from the lake as he leaned over his pommel watching her in the water. She'd been more angry at that feeling, than at him coming on her that way.

When he bent, his lips lightly touched hers, a mere brush. She wanted more, and she leaned into him. Perhaps he had meant the kiss as a good-night kiss. Whatever he'd originally intended, his eyes showed his change of mood. He bent again and this time, he put his arms around her, pulling her against him. She moved her hand up his arm, that muscular arm she had wanted to touch for so long, and then to his shoulder, his neck as she embraced him too. The kiss went on deepening as their lips moved against each other. When she opened her mouth, he thrust his tongue within. She had a moment of shock before she felt the impact travel through her body.

Pulling back, his gaze met hers. "I am sorry."

"For what? For giving me what I have wanted since I first saw you." Maybe from long before.

"It can't be for us. We both know that."

"Just a kiss?"

He smiled then brushing his finger lightly over her cheek. "You know that kiss was heading somewhere, don't you, sweetheart."

She knew he didn't really mean she was his sweetheart. It was probably what he called all the women he kissed, but she liked the sound of it. She found herself wishing he had meant it. As to where the kiss was heading, her body was suggesting several possibilities. She supposed Cole was right. She didn't want him to be right. She cuddled against him. "Are you sure?" she asked when she felt his arms tighten around her.

"It'll only be harder later."

"You sound like you know."

"I'm not totally inexperienced if that was what you were asking, but there's been nobody serious for a reason."

"You don't want to be hurt?" She understood that. Love was painful but wasn't it possible that sometimes it was worth it?

"I don't have the kind of life that a woman would want to share." He didn't take his arm away and kissed the top of her hair.

"Were you thinking to tell me what kind of life that is?"

"Are you familiar with paladins?" He laughed then.

"Holy warriors, who promise to protect the weak, bring justice to those who are unjust, and fight to end evil. Originally Charlemagne's twelve foremost warriors, I believe."

"Other than the holy part..." He chuckled again. "It's what I've done since I finally was free to do it, and yes, it sometimes involves guns."

"You use them for good?"

"It's what I try to do. I take money for my services, so it's not charitable... usually. Sometimes it's been to help someone, like you with bringing out a truth. What I do though involves a lot of travel, some risk, and no way to be there for anyone."

"I should be paying you then," she said running her hand lightly down his shirt. She was distracted from his words by his body. She wondered if his chest had hair on it. When he'd washed and shaved at the lake, it'd been too far away for her to know.

"You don't fit a category."

"Do most?"

"Generally. Like a marshal who needs to bring in a wanted man and nobody nearby is capable of helping him."

She remembered then what Jim Wilson had told him. "Was that what happened with Johnson?"

He nodded. "With his brother. It was in Springerville, east of here by a few hundred miles. Johnson had rustled thirty head of cattle. It wasn't the first. I had been there with another issue. I knew the sheriff there. I liked him and he asked me to go along when he arrested Johnson. I didn't expect it to lead to shooting, but it did. I haven't killed a lot of men, sweetheart, but when you put yourself out there, it can happen. It did that time."

"As part of keeping the law."

"Brothers don't see it that way, of course."

"I suppose not. So, you lead a dangerous life."

"I grew up with that. It's ironic as there was a time I resisted wearing a gun. I knew I was good with it, but eventually I didn't find I had any other talents." He gave a little laugh. "I justified it by seeing myself on the side of the law, of good. My people weren't always."

"But your brothers, Holly's husband?"

"They are good men and no, they are not outlaws. Jesse trains horses, has a nice little ranch. Vince ranches some and is a trader, who avoids traveling as much as possible these days. He also helps Holly with her digs, when she's not pregnant." She could hear the smile in his voice. Now was the time she should tell him, but she couldn't bear to have his arms taken from her, and she knew they would be.

"You could choose a different life too then... if I mean, if you wanted to."

He took her hand from his chest and kissed her fingers. "Sometimes it's too late for a man."

"You mean karma will get you?" she teased. She freed her hand and ran it over his stubbly jaw.

"I mean somebody like Johnson will. It's just inevitable and more complicated now by those damned books."

She felt herself pale. "How?"

"It's a reputation that I don't have, but some think I do. Sure, I've been involved in some shootings, but nothing like that character in the fictional books. The trouble is the ones looking for a reputation of their own won't believe that."

She hadn't thought of that. "Can't you just explain it's not you?"

He snorted. "Like that kind care. They want the rep. In the case of Johnson, the rep stirred up an old grudge."

"He won't find you out here."

"He probably could if he hangs around long enough. I think I have to go in. If he's still there, I'll talk to him to prevent that."

"Please, don't do that."

He bent and claimed her lips again. Another kiss that she felt through her whole body. "I better head for bed," he said then as he rose, "before this goes further." She watched him walk to the corrals.

She didn't know how long she sat there feeling frustrated at herself for not having told him when he brought up the book. He was going to feel deceived whenever she did it now. The silvery sliver of moon was risen in the sky as she thought about her options. Zinnia had stayed at her side but now seemed anxious to go in. She could do that or…

She walked down toward the corral. If he was sound asleep, that would settle it. "Cole," she whispered to alert him, not wanting to get shot by startling him.

"Is something wrong?" he asked, his own voice didn't sound like he'd been sleeping.

"I need to tell you something."

"All right." When she got to him, he held up his blanket for her to slide in beside him. He was wearing jeans but no shirt. Even in the faint light, she could see he had only a smattering of hair on his chest. In moments, he had pulled her to him. "Nights getting colder," he said as he pulled the other blanket over her.

"You could sleep in the house."

"Not a good idea."

She sucked in a breath. "Well, wanted you to know my mother's maiden name."

"And this is important why? A key maybe?"

"Yes, but not to what you think. I… I hope you can forgive me but… when I wanted to go to college, to get more education, there was no money for it."

"You're a bank robber," he suggested with what sounded like a smile in his voice.

"Not quite. I always could write, and I got this idea when I was almost through with high school, that dime novels were selling quite well. I thought maybe I could do that."

She felt him stiffen. "What is your mother's maiden name?"

"Tremaine."

He was silent as he took that in. "So Will Tremaine is…"

"Me."

"Damn." He sat up and looked back down at her. She was glad in the dim moonlight that he couldn't see her tears. "You wrote those cursed books." It wasn't a question.

"Yes, but I had no idea that there was a real Taggert. I had no idea it could cause anyone problems. I had been writing other dime novels for several years, and they'd been selling enough to pay my tuition. Then I got the urge to create a new hero. The Taggert name was good because it was real and yet not real. From all I could find, there was no sign of where they'd gone after they left Kansas. That seemed perfect."

"Of course." She knew he was gritting his teeth. "Not real at all," he added with a low growl. "Why tell me now?"

"What you told me today about your background. I was holding out on you, and then you said that about Johnson and his looking for you because of the books."

He sucked in a breath. "But mostly for killing his brother."

"But he might have forgotten about you if not for the books."

He didn't look down at her. "Those things have a way of happening. I can't say he's your fault."

"I blame myself. I am so sorry. I never meant to cause anyone trouble. I didn't feel good about the books anyway as they felt deceptive. Then there was the other thing."

"That being?"

"The last Taggert began to feel too real to me. I... couldn't keep writing about him without... Well, I told my editor before I left San Francisco that there'd be no more."

"There are plenty already out there from what I've been told."

"I know. I am so sorry."

He shook his head and let out a breath. "Thank you for telling me," he said in a cold tone.

She understood his anger. She deserved it. She resisted wiping her eyes as she stood and walked back to the cabin. Once she got inside, she'd have a good cry. She'd endured a lot of losses, her mother, her father, the doubts over her father's honesty, but this one felt worse as she'd done this to herself. The books had only been words until she met Cole. How she had felt him, known what he looked like, so many things about him, and then the ones she hadn't known, she couldn't explain any of it. She wished she'd never written them but wishes didn't help anything.

For the first time Zinnia climbed up on the bed by her pillow as soon as she pulled up the covers. She guessed it was getting colder for the little dog, or was she trying to comfort her? She felt the tears leaking under her lashes. There was no making this right, and she understood. Probably Cole would ride out in the morning and never want to see her again. She wouldn't blame him.

After Willy had left him, Cole lay awake a long time trying to reason through what she'd told him. He lit a cigarette and stared up at the starry sky. With the moon a faint sliver, the stars were more intense than at any other time, especially at this elevation.

He didn't really blame her for what she'd done. She had needed the money. The books had been written as fiction; so it wasn't as though she claimed it was him doing all that she'd written about. What the hell had she written about? He knew Vince had liked them. Would he admire her skill as a writer if he read them? Nah, that wasn't happening. He just wanted to forget they existed. If she truly wrote no more, maybe people would forget about that last Taggert who was better at a gun than any man could be.

Not being angry at her didn't mean he'd let her know that. He'd come way too close to taking more than kisses from her. Maybe if she thought he was angry, she'd keep a distance, and he could keep his. He needed to find the evidence that she had to have regarding her father. If there had been cheating, it didn't mean the accountant had anything to do with it. The Hemstreets could have been playing fast and loose in their construction methods. If that was so, then when Butler found out, maybe they killed him. He had doubted the suicide all along. A man with a daughter like Willy would not take his own life.

His doubts about the suicide had nagged at him all along. Willy had left San Francisco to have time to put together what had happened. She hadn't realized or maybe she had by instinct, that she might be in danger there. He couldn't just get her the evidence. He'd have to be sure she was safe, and it would take that happening before he could leave her. If her father had been killed, whoever did it wouldn't have anything stopping them from killing her too if they felt it was necessary. He put the thoughts from him. He had to steady his thinking if he wanted to be effective, to find an answer for her.

The Milky Way was visible as a frothy swath across the blackness. He'd read that some of those stars might have planets like Earth. Maybe there were unknown worlds. He'd read many ideas about what life was about. It had all been abstract in the sense of wanting the information but not needing it for life. What if he did need it? What if there was a being out there who cared about man?

He snorted at the thought. His own life with Asa had been a constant cruel reminder that life was not fair. If he'd not known it before, the murder of their mother that had finally been revealed by Jesse told him how there was no ultimate being rewarding good and punishing evil. If there had been, his mother, as good and godly a woman as possible, would have been saved. Or if there was such a deity, that God only cared about other families, other people. He could not count on a God to protect Willy. He'd have to do it and stay with her until he did-- no matter how difficult it became.

His mind went in circles and finally he sat up and lit another cigarette. He leaned back against the corral post and stared toward the dark lake. He was being sucked into a vortex of a sort. He knew the word from one of the books he'd read. It suited how he felt. No way out and heading into darkness.

South of Apache Junction, September 21

The campfire was dwindling, and Nate fed it more twigs. He knew Jeremiah Taggert had been sleeping because of his snoring but now the snoring had stopped. "You got to get some sleep, kid." The voice surprised him.

"The name is Nate."

Jeremiah sat up with a grin. "Someday you'll like being called kid."

"The day's not here yet."

"So you love that gal." It wasn't really a question.

"I met her when we were both in grade school. She had long braids, cutest thing you ever saw and so gutsy and smart."

"Didn't answer my question."

"Is it your business either way?"

"Nah." Jeremiah lit a cigar. "Just nosey is all."

"I love her. Not sure though as you mean. She's always been mine in some strange way."

"She wouldn't marry you?"

"I never asked."

Jeremiah nodded. "Your family dislike her?"

He considered that. "My father liked her when he was alive. My mother not so much."

"Ah, she wasn't good enough for you then?"

"I don't know. It's hard to say with Mother. She's got her own way of thinking, a manipulative woman. I just don't know to what level."

"After you told us about Hamilton, I went out to the bar to get a gander at him. I wanted his measure. He might be working as a major-domo, or whatever the hell you called him, but I've seen his kind plenty in my days. He's a mean jasper, and the two with him would do whatever he asked and feel no guilt. Soulless, I call them. Your mama know what kind of man he is?"

Nate had been asking that question himself. "I don't know," he said finally.

"Want a cigar?"

"Does it help?" He'd never taken up smoking but was beginning to think he needed something.

"Makes it seem like it does." He handed Nate a cigar and lit it. "Man takes the smoke in, lets it out, and maybe problems go with it."

Nate smiled doubting that to be true. He took a light draw on the cigar finding the flavor to be to his taste "You sure they didn't follow us?" Nate asked finding his worries weren't leaving with the smoke.

"Positive."

"Did anybody else know Holly was friends with Willy?"

"You really do work up a passel of worries, son."

He didn't like son better than kid, but let it go. "You see me as quite the dude don't you?" he asked after smoking in silence another moment.

"You are, aren't you? Although I got to say you handled the bronc better than I expected."

"I haven't lived in your kind of world, but it's not to say I know nothing."

"You handle that gun good?"

"Or I wouldn't have it."

"Good answer. And as to your other question. Holly had no reason to tell anybody in Tucson about her friendships back East. She's not a woman to gossip if that worries you."

Nate considered that. "I wish I knew more what led Willy to leave Frisco. I don't know if she was running, on a vacation, or... She has always held back from me, I guess."

"Not a woman to spill her guts."

"Definitely not and very independent. I would have tried to help and yet..."

"Gotta respect that in a woman."

"Up to a point, but having a friend possibly in trouble and knowing they'd not tell me hasn't been a good feeling. For all I knew, she was off on a romantic rendezvous."

Jeremiah chuckled. "You think that likely?"

"I didn't before but now..."

"You'll see her soon enough and can ask. For now, get some sleep." He rolled back into his blanket and was soon sleeping and snoring. Nate lay down, but sleep was hard to come by as he considered the possibility that Willy did have a lover. He didn't much like that idea."

CHAPTER 8

Willy didn't blame Cole for talking little to her as they struggled again with the receipts, invoices, billings. He didn't mention her books and for that, she was grateful also. She kept an eye on Zinnia for any signs of labor as she continued to cook meals from the cookbook she'd brought. Cole was politely appreciative regarding the food, felt of the dog to make sure all was going well, but it was as if they were two strangers and their wonderful day at the ruins had never existed. She knew she should feel lucky he hadn't ridden out, but it wasn't easy having him there when he treated her as a stranger.

She had finally had a success with what became a delicious loaf of sourdough bread. She used the starter to make dinner rolls and again was pleased with the result. She'd read that you could keep the starter for months, but she had her doubts about that. She watched carefully for any sign of it turning bad. It wouldn't do to make themselves sick or worse Zinnia, who had quite the fondness for bread. She had very much come to love the little dog who followed Cole or her everywhere. If Cole wasn't interested in talking to her, she was happy to have someone who still was willing to listen.

Down at the lake, having left lunch for Cole while he continued to sort her father's piles of possible evidence, she tried skimming a rock. She'd seen it done but maybe the rocks weren't right. Zinnia watched with limited interest as each rock sank without a bounce.

She heard Cole's step but didn't turn. "It's in the flick of the wrist," he said. He picked up a rock, gave it a toss that sent it bouncing four times before it fell to the bottom.

"Beautiful," she said admiringly. She tried again but once more her rock sank.

He came up behind her and took hold of her wrist, turning it a bit and then pushing it forward with a quick movement. "Like that."

She nearly melted at the touch of his hand on her skin and was very aware he had quickly moved back. "Try it," he said.

She bent, picked up a likely rock and tried again. This time she got two bounces before it dropped. She laughed clapping her hands and immediately tried again, with the reward of three bounces. "Thank you," she said. "I've always admired those who could skim rocks. Back in Boston, there were ponds, and others did it so well. I just never had the knack."

"It's not a skill most care to develop."

She considered that. "I don't know why I saw it that way, but it seems beautiful to me. What is the most you've been able to keep one going?"

He picked up a rock, leaned a bit to the side and let fly. She counted seven bounces before it disappeared beneath the surface. "About that many," he said.

"Did someone teach you?" she asked hoping to rebuild the rapport they'd found so briefly.

"No. Like you, I just wanted to do it. Asa wouldn't teach anybody anything. Vince left when I was small. We had a little pond, when it wasn't dried up. It's where I taught Jesse, who quickly did it better than me." She glanced over and saw the faint smile.

"You haven't talked much about your brothers."

"Jesse was called slow-witted, but he was physically better at everything than I ever was. He can fork any bronc but even more teach it to behave and do what he wants. He stayed away from home though as much as he could. Pretty much, it was up to me to keep the ranch going. It wasn't good land, nothing like here. Hardscrabble ranching is what it was."

"You were glad to leave it then?"

He glanced over at her. "You want that for your next book?"

She managed a smile unsure if he was teasing or angry. "I don't plan to write more dime novels."

"You will write more when you need the money." Now, she knew he was irked, and any momentary camaraderie was gone.

"I have apologized. I don't know what you want from me. A pound of flesh? I can't undo those I already wrote."

He snorted and moved to sit on the large boulder she'd used so many times. "I came down to tell you that I may have found something for you." He lit a cigarette and drew in the smoke. "There are five names that show up repeatedly. I began sorting these billings by date and company. Several companies were only a small part of the Hemstreet constructing, but five were far more. I will wire Vince to see if any mean anything to him."

"Is that likely?"

He shrugged. "Maybe. Over the years, his dealings involved warehouses and stores. As a trader, he not only dealt with bringing in goods but looking for what was recently arrived. I don't know that he will be familiar with the names, but it's a start."

"You'd have to go into Payson though to send him a wire." She didn't like that idea. She remembered a man had been there who wanted to kill him.

"Unless I can get someone to send smoke signals," he said with a laugh.

"It might be dangerous for you to do that. Maybe I should go."

He snorted. "You who ride so well."

"It's my fault you'd be facing danger. I should go."

"And I can hide behind your skirts?"

"Well, I was thinking it just made sense, Mr. Taggert." She was beginning to feel a little irked with him too. It made sense for her to go, and she could ride well enough... she hoped. "Tell me the names and..."

He put up his hand. "Get this through that beautiful head of yours. I am the one going."

Disturbed as she was by images of him being shot, she hadn't missed that he had called her beautiful. She'd never thought of herself as beautiful, certainly nothing like Holly but maybe he did think so. She knew she shouldn't care, that it wasn't enough, but despite her fear for him, she felt an odd sort of pleasure that he might see her as attractive.

"You could wait a day or so. Mr. Johnson might get tired of waiting and leave."

"Or find out I'm out here. No, it's better that I go now for a lot of reasons. Besides, I'm not in the habit of running from things or people."

She didn't like the sounds of that. She knew she could not stop him, as she thought of all the gunfights she'd written with no clue as to what any of them had meant. Cole could be killed.

Maybe she could help. He needed to take her since this might be her fault for the books. Books that made Cole a possible target. "We should both go," she argued.

"What about Zinnia?" he asked.

She looked down at the little dog. "You think her puppies are going to come soon?"

"From the looks of her, I'd say yes."

"How can you tell?"

"It's like all animals. Swollen, redder than normal where they come out. Feel her teats. They're swollen. Top of that, she's sticking close to you, no running around. She trusts you."

"I wouldn't know how to help her if she had trouble."

"It won't take me long to go in and wire him."

"You can't call him?"

He smiled at that. "It'll take a while for Payson to get phone lines. No, we're lucky they have the telegraph."

"Why does it have to be right now? Why can't you wait and do it another day or even let Mr. Contrell take in a letter?"

"What would that change? Besides, I don't believe we should wait on this. This isn't just about money but maybe shoddy construction and could endanger the public."

"You think that's what it is?" She felt a cold chill.

"From what I can tell, yes, among other things. It's something that needs to go to the law if it's what I think."

"Will you wait then for a response?"

"I'll go back in a couple of days for the answer."

"It's too late today anyway. It took us two hours to get here," she said feeling stubbornly determined he should not go even if it he was convinced it was the right thing to do. She had a bad feeling about it.

He knelt down by Zinnia and felt of her again. The little dog rolled onto her back and let him have a good go at it. "I'll be back before she whelps," he said looking up at Willy.

"I guess I can't stop you."

"No, you can't." He rose and headed for the corral.

"You mean to go right now?" she asked following him. "You won't be back tonight then?"

He called for his horse, which came right to him. Cole threw the saddle blanket onto his back and then the saddle, expertly tightening the cinch and throwing down the stirrups. "The sooner I go, the sooner, I'll be back."

"You can't come after dark. The moon is still not giving much light. Your horse might fall and…"

"I'll be back long before dark." He put the hackamore over his horse's head and then took the reins as he mounted. "Don't worry about this. Chances are good that Johnson has gone elsewhere when he didn't find me right away."

"And if he didn't?"

His lips tightened. "Then he and I'll have a little talk. Should still not be a problem." He tipped his hat to her, the expression in his eyes impossible to read before he kicked his horse lightly in the side, and rode off at a quick canter. She watched until he was out of sight.

Reaching down, she patted Zinnia's head, hoping he was right, and she'd not be faced with birthing puppies without him. Zinnia was such a little dog. What size had the male been who was the father. Silly thinking, but she needed to think of anything but what was actually on her mind.

Back in the cabin, she heated water for tea and then went to the table and sat in front of her typewriter. She wanted to start on her next book except who was the hero? What about a villain? Everything she'd written had both.

She worried then about what Cole had said about possible fraud and her father either had discovered it or was he involved in it? Could Nathan have been involved? She could not imagine her tall, handsome friend being crooked. Money had never seemed to matter that much to him.

In the kitchen, she drained the red beans she'd been soaking, and started a big pot of chili. She added lots of chili powder convinced that Cole would want it that way. To go with it, she set out to make cornbread. Again, the Farmer cookbook gave her a recipe she could follow. She was using a bit much of her butter, but hopefully the cornbread would be worth lowering her supplies.

Two hours had passed and she felt a sense of panic. Cole had to be in Payson. How long would it take to send a wire? Although it was not yet three, she was convinced he'd not be able to get back before dark with the nights coming faster as the seasons changed.

She sat back on the sofa, and Zinnia jumped up beside her. She had not tried to stop her from sitting on furniture. It was comforting to run her hands over the little dog's coat, to feel her nestling against her hip. She probably should have tried to work on cracking the code again, but all she could think about was Cole and what he was doing.

When it was done, she pulled the cornbread from the oven, stirred the chili and went back to the great room and Zinnia, who had not followed her. She wondered then if she should prepare a kind of nest for the dog to whelp as Cole had called it. Although she knew the word, she hadn't ever used it or thought she'd have reason to.

There were some extra blankets in the bedroom. She took one of them and folding it, along with a towel, put them on the floor in the corner near her typewriter. If Zinnia wanted to be near her, that might work. She laid one of the chairs on its side to provide a kind of nest. Sitting on the floor beside it, she patted it to encourage Zinnia to give it a try.

The dog came over and sniffed before moving onto the padding and lying down. She seemed to be panting a little. Was that a good or bad sign? Willy went into the kitchen and pumped some water into a bowl to bring back and put by the new bed. Zinnia looked at her but didn't move toward it.

Leaning back against the wall, Willy wondered where Cole was. How long would it take him to return? She tried to imagine what he might be doing. Maybe riding back toward her or... She couldn't bear to think about the or.

She had been unwilling to write the next book of the last Taggert because she knew she'd have to kill him. It would go with the mythic traditions she had been following in her stories. She knew she'd never write that ending and that Cole was wrong. She would not write another of the dime novels even if she had to go without food. Silly thought, as her salary as a professor did cover the basics. When she sold the Butler home, she'd have an emergency reserve.

She loved her home, liked its cozy neighborhood. They weren't fancy homes like Nob Hill but the neighbors were nice people, helpful even. She remembered the meals they had brought after her father died. It was too big a home though for a woman by herself. She could rent a room easily in someone's home, as she wasn't there a great deal anyway with the responsibilities not only of teaching but other obligations toward her students and the faculty. She petted Zinnia absently, trying to comfort her as she felt the dog was acting uncomfortable.

It was almost dark when she heard a horse coming into the yard. She rose and went to the door, watching as he rode his horse to the corral, slowly dismounted and then unsaddled and released it before closing the gate. He walked up to the house without his usual quick stride. When he arrived at the porch, she said, "Are you all right?" Just as she heard a little yelp from Zinnia.

Cole didn't answer her question but went to the dog. "Good idea to give her a private place," he said as he felt of her side and then looked at where he had indicated the pups would appear. "Good girl," he said in a soothing voice as Zinnia strained and out popped a wet little body.

Willy had a towel ready to dry the pup, but he said, "No. Let her lick it off."

Soon another pup, a darker color than the first also appeared. Willy watched with amazement as Zinnia licked them both. When what she knew had to be the placenta had passed, Cole pushed the pups to Zinnia's nipples and in a moment, both were sucking noisily.

"I've never seen anything like this," Willy said feeling teary. "So beautiful. Should I clean up that?" She pointed to the placenta and fluids.

"Let her decide if she wants to eat it," Cole said. "Sometimes they do if they need it." He rose slowly and moved to take the chair by the table. She lit the lamp and saw why he seemed unnaturally stiff. There was blood on his left shoulder.

"What happened?" she asked as she moved to his side, trying to assess how much blood he'd lost. She felt a sense of irony or was that déjà vu for all the times she'd written a scene where a man was shot or knifed and blood flowed. She had sometimes wondered how she'd react if in that situation. Now she knew. Determined.

"It's not much. Keep an eye on Zinnia, make sure she gets up soon and drinks some water. I am going to lie down. Call me if there's is problem."

When he started to rise, she pushed him back. "You are going nowhere. What did the doctor say?"

"I didn't see a doctor. I told you, it's nothing."

"Then come into the kitchen and let me see it."

"Not necessary."

"I will follow you to the corral if you don't let me take care of this in the kitchen."

He shrugged, winced, but finally nodded. "You learn about wounds from your books?" he asked as he followed her and sat at the table. His lips were set, his eyes narrowed. She could see he was in pain whether he admitted it or not.

She turned up the lamp. "Take off your shirt," she said as she gathered her medical supplies.

When he fumbled with a button, she bent and did it for him, a little shocked at her own steadiness. She pulled the shirt from his shoulders and tossed it into the sink later to rinse the blood out. Using a clean, wet cloth, she carefully washed blood from the skin around the wound in front and then in back. She realized the hole was smaller in back.

"Someone shot you in the back?" she asked as she stood back to assess the damage. It was high on the shoulder, in the muscle, above the bone. Likely, if it didn't infect, it would be what he had said-- not of major significance other than the lost blood.

"You do know some about wounds." His voice sounded surprised.

"Research and a first aid class with Clara Barton."

He whistled. "Impressive."

"I have carbolic acid. Carbolic is more painful but also better at preventing infection." She studied the wounds again, casting glances at his muscular chest and arms as an unfortunate side effect. If she'd been attracted to him before, being so close to his bare torso wasn't making it easier. She'd never touched a man's unclothed chest. While she might be steady where it came to his wound, his body was a whole other thing.

"Do what you need to do," he said with a note of resignation.

"It does look like the bleeding has stopped, but you lost blood. I don't think we have to stitch the wound closed. I brought gauze and surgical tape in case of an accident, not that I imagined a bullet causing it." She talked as she worked to keep her mind off the fact that she had to be hurting him. He stiffened at what had to be excruciating pain with the carbolic but didn't let out a groan as she had expected, at least based on her father's propensity for moaning over even a sliver.

Finally, she was able to put gauze pads over each hole and secure them in place with the surgical tape. "I have aspirin. Would you like some?" She sat across from him studying his face for paleness or signs he might be about to faint.

"Nah, it's fine."

"What about this?" She reached into the kit and pulled out the whiskey flask.

"You were holding out on me," he said as he took a swig.

"I thought the occasion warranted something more than sherry." When he handed back the flask, she took a swallow, choking on it. "You going to tell me how it happened?" she asked when she could speak again.

He smiled faintly. "Stupidly as this kind of thing always does."

"You've been shot before?"

"This for your next book?"

"You are being mean. I told you I wouldn't write about you again."

"Cut me some slack. I am a wounded man." His smile seemed more genuine.

"You should lie down."

"I'll get myself down there in a minute."

"You are staying in the bedroom here. I won't listen to any excuses. If you do get an infection, you'll be where you can get water, stay warm at night, and I can check on you. If you don't, you can help me with making sure Zinnia is all right. By the way, what could still go wrong with her?"

"I don't look for anything. She popped those pups out without trouble. Sometimes though it weakens a dog; so we'll just watch her."

She heard the sound of paws on the kitchen floor and smiled. "I guess we don't have to worry about that." Zinnia checked for food, which Willy replenished, before the new mother returned to her pups.

"I want you to tell me what happened," she said, "but you need to lie down. If you won't take the bed, I'd have to bundle up Zinnia, her pups, and all of us sleep down by the corral."

His smile was crooked. "Okay, I give up." He rose, steadied himself with his hand on the back of the chair and headed for the bedroom. She followed him to the door where he turned. "Unless you planned on helping me undress, you better stop right here."

"I will just help you get your boots off. Is that all right?"

He stopped and gave a little laugh. "I could do it but... Yeah, it's all right." She knew he wasn't a man used to accepting help. A few moments later, she had pulled off both boots and set them by the foot of the bed.

"I'll be back with a glass of water." She gave him enough time to get out of those jeans and under covers before she returned with water, aspirin bottle, and the whiskey flask. While he drank the water, she sat on the wooden chair alongside the bed. "Zinnia is cuddled with her babies. It looks like she'll be a good mama."

"She's a good dog."

"Try to sleep. I'll check on you later to be sure you aren't running a fever."

She saw by the look in his eyes that he was surprised at that. "You aren't going to ask again about how this happened?"

"You'll tell me when you feel better."

He smiled. "I was being stupid and would just as soon get telling you over with."

"All right." She moved her chair closer to him and felt of his forehead. "No fever yet; so guess you aren't delirious."

He snorted. "I won't even know it happened in two days. I'll be mad at myself a lot longer."

"Then tell me."

"I sent the wire, headed for the general store, bought something that I left in my saddlebags down at the corral. When I came out, Johnson was waiting for me. I told him he and I had no grudge and explained how it had been with his brother. He didn't believe me. No surprise in that, I guess. I still figured I could avoid trouble with him. A lot of men are blowhards. He struck me as one." He sucked in a breath.

"You can tell me tomorrow," she said putting her hand on his forehead and brushing the hair back. "I can see this is difficult to remember."

"No, better now. I guess what happened came out of the fact I've always hated guns."

"But you wear one."

"Now, because I need to. It doesn't mean I don't hate using them. Despite how it sounds, I have not killed so many men that each doesn't bother me. I do what I can to avoid trouble. This time, I thought I could ride off, and he'd let it go. I turned my back on him and headed for my horse. A lot of men won't shoot another in the back." She saw the muscle jump in his cheek. He wasn't looking at her but instead out the window into the darkness. "I listened because I knew what his brother had been like. I should not have turned my back. It was a fool thing to do... I heard the sound of him pulling his hogleg out of its leather. I spun, knew I'd been hit as I dropped to one knee. I fired at the same time he fired again. His next shot missed. Mine didn't."

She wanted to comfort him, saw how pained he was, not so much at the wound, but at what he'd done to survive. "You had no choice," she said, moving her hand from his temple to his neck. "I am so sorry I wrote those books."

"Don't feel guilty for that," he said. "I won't say it hasn't been a burr under my saddle, but this thing with Johnson was going to happen whenever he and I crossed paths."

"You are trying to make me feel better." She managed a smile despite her worry about whether he really was going to be all right-- coupled by the knowledge of how easily it could have gone the other way. Again, she was struck by how little she'd understood the books she'd written. She'd followed stereotypes, used the classics, and been clueless about real life. She had blamed herself for writing what she regarded as trash. Now she felt the crime had been worse than she'd known as it had led to a distortion of reality. Being a writer shouldn't have been only about vision, and craft, but one also of conscience.

Seeing he looked exhausted, she rose. "Sleep now," she said. She wondered if he'd say more but his eyelids had already closed. In the main room, she knelt by Zinnia and her babies. She petted the dog, ran her fingers over the still damp little pups as they slept soundly at her side. She was unsure what she could do about them. Could she secure the three a good life? She had no idea how she'd get them back to San Francisco. Selling her home would leave her without a place to keep them. But her home was too large for her to afford. Her thoughts went in circles as she though then of the man asleep in the bedroom, wounded not just physically but emotionally. She'd not remotely captured the essence of the last Taggert.

With morning, Cole got dressed, stiff as he'd expected, his shoulder painful, but no more than was manageable. His spare shirt was outside in his saddlebags, so he had to walk into the main room with a bare chest. Since she'd seen it already, he didn't think it'd bother her. In the kitchen, he smelled coffee and saw Willy was mixing up some dough. "You are up," she said with surprise. "Sit at the table, and I'll get your coffee. Your shirt isn't quite dry."

"You washed it?" Another surprise. He wanted to be mad at her for something but anger was proving impossible to hold onto, as she really had done nothing wrong with writing those fiction books. In addition, she had tended his wounds more competently than he'd imagined possible.

"I think the bloodstains are all gone. How do you feel?" she asked as she sat across from him to sip her own coffee.

"I've felt better but not bad overall considering. Thank you for what you did last night."

She smiled at that. "I was glad to do it, be able to do it. I'm just sorry it had to be done."

"It's something we both have to let go. Some things are meant to be." He wasn't sure he believed that, but then he couldn't explain life all that well anyway. Sometimes it all seemed to be going into what appeared to be a pattern, and then it'd blow up and nothing would make sense. He'd long ago quit trying to figure it out.

"Zinnia is proving to be a good mama. Her babies are so cute. How long does it take for them to open their eyes?"

"It depends but ten days to two weeks."

"She licks them a lot, very loving mommy."

"That helps them… eliminate." He smiled as he realized much of what he knew about dogs didn't fit into polite conversation. "What are you making?"

"It is supposed to be noodles." She pointed to the cookbook she had open. "I had thought you'd be in bed a few days and chicken noodle soup is good for invalids. We had some chicken left, and I figured I could make the noodles. Except now it appears that I don't have an invalid." She made a pouting face.

He smiled at her sense of humor. "Still will taste good."

"What would you like for breakfast?"

"What do you have?"

"The usual, hotcakes, eggs, bacon, salt pork."

"I need to get my gear. Eggs would be good, if we have enough."

"Scrambled?"

"Great." He walked outside. The morning air was growing crisper, and he was glad to get his shirt from the saddlebags. Pulling it on, he drew out the small package he'd bought at the store and headed back to the cabin. Inside, he knelt gingerly to check Zinnia and her babies, who currently looked more like little rats than dogs, as they nuzzled at their mother's nipples, and quickly fell back asleep.

"Are they doing all right?" Willy asked from the kitchen door.

"So far so good." He straightened with a wince. "I bought you something."

"For me?"

"Well, they won't fit me." He held out the small package.

She opened it and smiled. "Knit gloves."

"You'll need them soon."

"I keep forgetting it will get cold here. I did bring a heavy coat."

"Good. I wasn't sure but thought if you hadn't, I could get you that when I go back to see what Vince knows about those names."

"But not for several days-- giving yourself time to heal, of course," she remonstrated.

"Sure." He knew his time of taking it easy would be less than she expected, but he had no reason to argue with the woman who had bandaged his wound. "How are the noodles coming?"

"They rolled out nicely, surprising me a little, I cut them in strips. I need to hang them to dry. Maybe the chair backs after breakfast. They at least look like noodles... I think. I love this cookbook."

He was surprised by that too. His stereotypes of educated women from big cities were going out the window. She still wasn't anyone for him, but she was quite a classy lady with more character than he'd expected. No wonder her books had sold well. For the first time, he was tempted to read them. Maybe he would after she'd gone back to her home.

They took their coffee into the main room, where Zinnia was torn between staying with her pups and coming out to be petted by them. The little dog went out to the kitchen and ate some of the scrambled eggs that Willy had left for her before returning to curl up with her offspring.

"I wish most that I could read Father's journals," she said sipping the coffee. "I keep thinking I will get some great inspiration and they'll open up to me. I mean, why leave them if he didn't believe I could read them?"

"Good question. Do you really believe he killed himself?" he asked because the thought had been on his mind.

"I did at the time but through the summer, I began to doubt it. That morning, he hadn't seemed he was depressed. Was I really so into my problems that I didn't see it? I've thought back that he had seemed concerned to get to work, but that wasn't unusual."

"If he didn't kill himself, then you're aware the papers might've been why someone faked his suicide."

"I hate thinking he was murdered but suicide was worse."

"There's more to it than that."

"What do you mean?"

"You could also be in danger. Did you leave Frisco with that thought in mind?"

"Not consciously. I just felt I couldn't do what I needed to do there. I also wanted to have a cleansing experience. The writing of the dime novels, yours not the only one, were making me feel as though I had no real purpose beyond making money. I was grieving Father's death. But even more, I needed a change."

"You did find it with the Mazatzals."

"I did. I had no clue how much I would love being here, love this air, the little cabin, the lake, the... dog." She stopped then and took another sip of her coffee. "I was wondering... will there be any legal repercussions from the shooting?"

"You mean the killing," he corrected. "It was seen by several including Contrell and Wilson. They don't have a full-time sheriff, but Wilson said he'd tell their deputy when he got back from Flagstaff. They were going to bury him in their cemetery."

"Did he have family to notify?"

He shrugged before he remembered that wasn't a good idea. "I don't know." He smiled then. "Maybe I'll find out someday."

"That is not funny!"

He laughed. "You're telling me."

"Where did he live?"

"I don't know. He wasn't with Al on the rustling anyway."

She hesitated. "Are there a lot of men out there who would like to get revenge on you?"

"You are way too much the writer."

"What does that mean?"

"Asking questions and looking for complications before they exist."

"You also did that with my father's death."

"I'll give you that. Yes, I am used to working out mysteries. I don't think Clement Johnson was much of a mystery. That was straight out revenge with maybe a goal of getting a rep for killing me."

"Have you killed other men?"

He rose and walked to the window staring out at the lake. "Two before him. Always in self-defense and when it involved the legal system. I might want to reconsider working for the law." He smiled wryly.

"Can't you find something safer to do?" she asked with a note of irritation in her voice.

"Like teach at a college?" he asked looking back at her.

"I suppose options are limited, but you know how to ranch."

"I also know how little money there is in it."

"Be a trader like you said your brother was."

"He knew the tribes, and things I do not know. Besides he doesn't need to do it anymore, not after marrying Holly."

She sighed. "Did he marry her for her money?"

"Almost didn't marry her for her money."

"He saw it as a barrier?"

"Very much. It can be when two people come from such different worlds." He saw she didn't like hearing that, but he needed to remind himself of it as much as her. She was all too tempting looking as she did, her thick, wavy brown hair hanging loose, the questioning look in those beautiful eyes. He needed them both never to forget some barriers could not be crossed.

CHAPTER 9

Two hours later, Cole had settled onto the bench on the front porch. The sun warmed his skin, helping to ease the ache of his torn flesh. Willy was in the kitchen working on that soup, he guessed. When he had disappointed her again, she'd smiled and turned to her work. He could have been looking through the billings again, but until he knew if the names meant anything, he was accomplishing nothing. It was proving as frustrating as trying to find a key to decipher the journals.

Hearing the sounds of riders approaching, he reached for his rifle and rose to lean against the porch post. Two riders appeared at the top of the ridge and headed straight for the cabin. Willy came to his side with her rifle. It reminded him of the first time he'd seen her, the day he'd had it pointed at him.

When he recognized the first rider, he swore under his breath. Willy had stacked her rifle against the wall. "Nate," she cried running down to greet the men as they dismounted. "What are you doing here?" The stranger swept her up in his arms. Cole stepped off the porch. "You two planning to stay awhile?"

"A night or two," Jeremiah said.

"Then put your horses in the corral. Tomorrow we can figure out a place to tie them with some grass."

"Sounds good to me," Willy's friend said. She walked with them to the corrals as they took care of their mounts. Cole watched, wondering what this man meant to her. He knew who the stranger had to be—Nathan Hemstreet.

When the three returned, Jeremiah plopped saddlebags onto the porch.

"So what are you doing here?" Cole asked his father.

The old man grinned at him but looked tired. "I can tell you one thing. I'm getting too old for this shit," he said as he sat down next to Cole. "How are you, boy?" He slapped Cole on the shoulder, causing him involuntarily to groan and jerk away.

"I feel a bandage there. She shoot you?" his father asked with a chuckle.

"Sure and with good reason."

Willy and the tall, blond stranger came up on the porch. "Cole," Willy said, "I want you to meet my best friend other than Holly."

The stranger put out his hand as Cole rose. "Nathan Hemstreet," he said as they shook hands.

Interesting. Cole managed a smile. Friends or more?

"And you must be the *other* I keep hearing about," Hemstreet said.

"Could be." He looked at Willy, trying to read her face. She was smiling broadly, obviously very glad to see this man. As a Hemstreet, she didn't regard him as the threat Cole was thinking, after going through the billings, that he might represent.

"You must be Cole's father? I see the resemblance." Willy smiled as she shook Jeremiah's hand. "Can I get you both something to eat? How far did you ride today?" she asked, her arm again linked to Hemstreet's.

"Not that far and what do you have?" Hemstreet asked.

"I figure you're the reason we rode up here. Yeah, I'm Cole's daddy. Call me Jeremiah. You wouldn't happen to have some whiskey, would you?"

"I can manage that. I also have bread and ham for a sandwich if you'd like that too."

"Let me help you," Hemstreet said as he followed her inside.

Cole stared at the lake, not wanting to think of the questions that were coming to him. "How bad you hurt?" his father asked.

"Not much."

"I know it wasn't the filly. Who was it?"

Cole told him the basics. "Does he have any relatives apt to continue the vendetta?" Cole asked his father when he'd finished.

"Let me think on that one. Springerville, huh? I only rode through there a few years back. Rough place?"

"About like a lot of towns on the Rim."

"If one was rustling, likely the other was too. Figures they could have some more varmints but would they brace you now, after killing those two? Not likely unless it was a shot in the back. No trouble with the law over the killing?"

"Shouldn't be unless the Taggert books stir up something." He still felt irked at their existence. He'd already said it when he realized Willy was at the door with a tray. He met her gaze, saw the troubled eyes, but was in no mood to comfort her over the guilt he knew she shouldn't feel. Guilt though was something with which he was quite familiar, and she'd have to work it out on her own.

She set the tray on the barrel alongside the bench along with the slices of bread and ham, which his father happily put together along with his shot of whiskey. Nate made himself a sandwich before settling on the step, leaning back against the post. "So you're another Taggert," he said with narrowed eyes.

"Vince and Jesse's brother," Cole said.

"And in case, you've read the Will Tremaine books," Willy said "He's not the last Taggert. I know because I wrote them."

Hemstreet looked at her blankly while Jeremiah grinned and gave a laugh. "Never would've guessed a female wrote them stories. Real good job, you did."

"You've read them?"

"Every damn one. You are a heap better than the average dime novelist, gal. You tell a rip-roaring good story."

"You didn't mind that I used your name?"

"Wal, it wasn't me." He took a bite of the sandwich. "Sourdough. I like the bread. You make it?"

She smiled with what Cole saw was pride. "Yes, I did."

"You've been writing books?" Hemstreet asked between bites. That actually helped Cole's mood some that she'd not confided her secret in her *best* friend.

"They and many other pulp novels are how I paid my way through college," she said.

"I had no idea," Hemstreet said with a smile. "Would the books be in the library?"

Willy laughed and shook her head. "No chance. They are not exactly a respected genre."

"Except by the folks," Jeremiah corrected.

"There is a lot of fighting in them," she said, "and the heroes are often western outlaws."

This time Hemstreet looked at Cole. "Him?"

"I had not met him when I wrote them."

Feeling a sudden need of a stiff drink, Cole took the whiskey bottle and poured himself a shot.

"I need some tea," Willy said. "Does anyone else want some?" When no one took her up on it, she picked up the now emptied tray and went back into the cabin.

"So what are you two doing here?" Cole asked sipping his whiskey.

"Had some concern about the gal," Jeremiah said.

"Also some information for her," Nate added.

A silence descended on them as Cole didn't ask the questions, to which he most wanted answers. When Willy returned, she had a teapot and cups with her. "In case anyone has changed their minds," she said as she set it down on the barrel. "Coffee is still hot on the stove."

Hemstreet joined her in the tea, but Cole and his father stuck to the whiskey. Cole was undecided as to what he thought of the city slicker, but his father had brought him, and Holly had to have helped him come. He'd reserve his own judgment as he was beginning to realize his problem was jealousy.

"I have some bad news for you," Hemstreet said after emptying his cup. His gaze was now sympathetically focused on Willy.

"All right."

"Your home was burned."

She whitened. "Destroyed?"

"I am afraid so."

"How did it happen?"

"Arson."

"The police know that?"

"I am not sure if they know it, but I do. I had been there that night. I overheard my mother and Thomas Hamilton talking." He looked toward Cole. "Hamilton is my mother's majordomo, the house steward, who runs things for her," he added. Cole smiled faintly. The man obviously didn't think he'd know what a majordomo was. He nodded but said nothing, as he waited for the rest.

Hemstreet looked back at Willy. "They had had a conversation, which I overheard, eavesdropped, you might say, concerning papers your father had amassed. Mr. Hamilton had apparently looked for them the day of the funeral and then they felt evidently they were hidden too well for anyone to find. When you left abruptly, it aroused their doubts. I decided that I should try to find what they wanted, which was why I was in the house. I left when I realized others had entered, but I watched from a distance with no idea what they were going to do. I know they started the fire but wasn't close enough to be sure of who they were. One, however, had the body type of Thomas Hamilton."

"Why now though? I mean Father killed himself in February. Why burn the house now?"

"I can only guess that they assumed no one would find them. Then when you left, they were afraid you had. If you hadn't, they would make sure they weren't still there for anyone to find."

"You took a risk going there," Willy said concern in her voice as she also obviously tried to take in her loss of all she had owned.

"The whole thing proved upsetting to me. I began to wonder about your father's suicide."

"You believed until then that he killed himself?" Cole asked. He knew his voice was cold and unfriendly. He was unsure how much to trust this man.

"Mr. Butler was a good man. Yes, I didn't doubt it at the time. I was busy with trying to take over some of the Hemstreet businesses, but now, I am not sure. It doesn't seem in character."

Zinnia came out the door and nuzzled Willy's skirt.

"You have a dog?" Hemstreet asked, "or is she yours?" he looked up at Cole.

"She's mine," Willy said. "She also has puppies. I guess she's hungry. I need to get her lunch." She managed a smile, which Cole felt was pretty gritty, considering the news she'd just been given. He wished he could comfort her for the loss, but Hemstreet would do that. And in moments the city slicker had followed her inside.

"She's a purty little thing." His father reached for the whiskey bottle and poured himself another drink.

Cole didn't have to ask which female he meant. He finished off his whiskey and reached into his pocket for a cigarette.

"Thought ya gave up the devil weed?" his father said watching him intently now.

"It comes and goes."

"Mostly comes when under pressure, huh? The shooting bother ya, or is it that little gal?"

Cole had gotten good at ignoring his father and put that to use by lighting his cigarette and taking a long draw on it.

"Nate thinks she's in danger."

"It seems likely."

"That Hamilton followed him to Tucson. I got a gander at him before we left. He's a hoodlum, call himself by fancy names or not."

"You tell that to Hemstreet?"

"I did. I guess he already knew it. What he doesn't know is about his mother."

"How deeply she's involved in this?"

"Yep."

Hemstreet and Willy came back outside. He sat on the step, while she moved to the other end of the porch and sat there. "The nights are getting colder," she said not looking at any of them.

"Does that in high country," Jeremiah said when no one else replied.

She looked back at Cole. "You never thought he killed himself, did you?"

"It didn't fit." No man would kill himself with a daughter like Willy. Given the things Cole had worked with, seen, murder had come to him sooner than it would with many who lived had lived less violent lives.

She looked back at Hemstreet. "Cole has found a pattern of names that Hemstreet Enterprises were doing jobs for. He sent a wire to his brother to see if any of the names meant something. You could look at them and see if you recognize them."

"I'd do that, but I have to admit I wasn't involved with the business much. Mother wanted me to but... It wasn't really in my area of expertise or of my interest. I, of course, blame myself for that now."

"What is your interest?" Cole asked letting smoke out as he studied the smooth talker.

"Willy—at the moment," Hemstreet said smiling at her.

"I very much appreciate your letting me know about the house," she said. "I am shocked, of course, especially that... well anyone would do such a thing. Now though I have time to think about what I want to do when I go back."

"Was it insured?"

She shook her head. "There'd never been enough money for that. They weren't able to recover anything?"

"It was on fire so quickly and done so well. An inferno. A total loss. I am sorry, Willy. I hope you will return with me now. I will help you, you know that."

"I am not leaving yet, Nate. My lease is not up until the middle of December, at least I hope. More than that though, I have been working on..." She glanced over at Cole. "Actually, Cole has and whether he wants to share it with you is up to him."

Hemstreet stood. "Wait, are you writing a book with him?" He jabbed his thumb at Cole.

"No." She looked at Cole. "Do you want to tell Nate what you've discovered?"

Cole saw it then, how she had come to trust him, and more than she did her best friend. He didn't know how that had come to be, but it was, and Hemstreet saw it too as he turned to look at him, the look as unfriendly as he knew his had earlier been.

"Well?" the man asked with his lips set in clear frustration.

Cole thought about that. Hemstreet had the name of the business in concern, but he had revealed the fire when he didn't have to. "How much involvement do you feel your mother had in the arson?"

Hemstreet clenched his jaw and took a long moment before answering. "I'm afraid if she didn't directly order it, she let Hamilton know she wanted it done. So, too much involvement. I would add the fear goes to Mr. Butler's death. I don't believe he killed himself. If your next question would be whether my mother ordered his death." He stopped and took a long breath. "I wish I knew."

"Let's go in the cabin," Cole said, crushing out his cigarette with his boot before he put it in his shirt pocket. "I want you to look at what Mr. Butler had put together as well as those names to see if any mean something to you."

Inside, Cole showed his father and Hemstreet the way he'd laid out the receipts, billings, invoices, and using dates and companies had found a pattern.

"So," Hemstreet said when he'd taken it all in, "our family company has been overcharging, creating false billings, and… do you think some of these companies don't exist?"

"From the looks of it, shoddy construction was in a lot of it. Using a reputable name, which apparently your father had built up, this all worked and maybe would have for a long time. The figures grew larger and what appear to be shell companies, with more money involved. It is possible that when Mr. Butler began keeping track, he wasn't sure himself what was going on but he had an instinct."

"Might it have gone back to when my father was alive?"

"These records start in '01. When did Hamilton come to work for your family?"

"Let me think." He stared out the window. "Is any of that whiskey left?" he asked.

Jeremiah poured him a shot, which Hemstreet took in a single swallow. "He came to work in 1899. The year my father died."

"And what happened to your father?"

"It was… a fall. He had been going down the stairs and tripped near the top. We found him at the bottom. He'd broken his neck."

"Anybody home when it happened?"

"No… You think?" He stopped and took a breath holding out the glass for another shot. "It is possible. My father hired him in… June. Father died in September."

"I suppose Hamilton had good references?"

"I don't know. I was back East when he was brought into the company. I dropped out of school, didn't actually have a major that I gave a damn about. I came home immediately but Mother was running the company.

She acted as though she wanted me in it but more on the level of looking good than truly involved."

"With Hamilton her right hand man."

"Pretty much." He sipped this whiskey more slowly. "You think Hamilton... got my father out of the way? I just... never imagined."

"Time to imagine. Now the question that is harder for you has to be about your mother. Was she happily married to your father?"

Hemstreet looked back from the window and glared at Cole. "You don't mean to suggest?"

"Look, I run into all sorts of people and the things they do in my line of work."

"And that is?"

"Straightening out businesses that are having problems, serving with a marshal or sheriff, a little of this and that but mostly my requests come from something going wrong and nobody able to figure out why. They want an outsider."

"Who uses his gun then?" Hemstreet asked, his tone not particularly friendly.

"Not usually."

"You are then a detective?"

Cole shrugged. "You want a definition. It works as well as any."

Hemstreet walked to the door. "I need to think about this."

"Did you recognize any of the names?"

Hemstreet swallowed hard. "Miller Dry Goods, Schaeffer's Emporium, Milford Shipping. Maybe one other but all businesses that I have been in. They are reputable as best I know."

They weren't the names that had triggered Cole's interest. "What about Collins, Smith, Polk, Jones?"

"Contractors, I think. The names though are less familiar to me."

Cole felt suddenly tired. He managed to take the chair by the typewriter.

"You need to lie down," he heard Willy saying, and he knew it was true. The constant pain and loss of blood had worn him out more than he had expected. Her hand was on his arm as she encouraged him to rise and then walked with him to the bedroom. He hadn't wanted either his father or Hemstreet to know where he had been sleeping. He was past arguing with her. He'd spent more energy than he had.

In the room, she pulled off his boots. "I'll call you for dinner," she said and closed the door. He was asleep as soon as he closed his eyes.

Walking into the kitchen, Willy tried to think what she could prepare for the evening meal. Jeremiah was sitting at the table. She was unsure where Nate had gone, but he hadn't been very happy. Maybe he had needed a walk.

"Need help fixing supper?" the old man asked. He was handsome, bigger boned than Cole, not quite as tall. He had a full head of silver hair and a big mustache. She could see his son in him.

"That's exactly it, Mr. Taggert. I was trying to think what I have. The Contrells bring out supplies twice a month, maybe on Tuesday. I am kind of getting down there a bit."

"You better call me Jeremiah."

"Then you call me Willy."

He grinned. "I still have some supplies in my saddlebags. I left them out on the porch. Beef jerky, a can of beans, a few potatoes, a few chili peppers, flask of whiskey, of course." He grinned. "Why don't you let an old outlaw do the cooking tonight? Nothing fancy, but it'll get us by."

She liked that idea a lot. "I have the half the loaf of sourdough bread, some butter left."

"Then trust me and I'll take care of the vittles. Got any eggs?"

"Half a dozen."

"I'll fix you a western meal you won't forget. You could go talk to Nate while I get to work here. He came a long way to help you."

"I know." She sighed.

"I'm still trying to get my head around you writing them books. You do know how to write a shootout, ma'am, if I do say so myself."

"I read a lot. I knew nothing about its reality."

"Cole's not been very happy about the books, but Vince likes 'em too."

"I suppose only Cole really fits them."

He sat across from her. "That is a little surprising."

"You should have seen me when I saw him the first time and realized... I hadn't any idea I was describing a real person."

"Drawn to him though, I reckon."

"I must have been. I just didn't think of the damage I was causing. All I could think was it paid my tuition and got me an education."

"You got one of them doctor's degrees?"

"I do. In English. It's what I teach at Golden Gate University."

"Too bad about you losing your home."

"I had counted on being able to sell it. Of course, there were the photographs, books, all the things my family had collected." Not to mention all of her clothing, her father's that she hadn't given away.

"Nice home?"

"Nothing special. Average, I guess. Not like where Nate lives on Nob Hill."

"You in a hurry to go back there?"

She'd been asking that question herself. "I like the ocean. There's the bay, shipping, always something going on. This has been just a little vacation. San Francisco is my home." That was until she'd seen this cabin, the lake, and Cole....

"You buying the cabin for a sort of summer home?"

"Even before I lost my home, I didn't have the money to buy this. I might've hoped to rent it again except Mr. Gibbons, the land agent, said someone was interested in it. I guess it's just a temporary stopover for me."

Jeremiah looked out the back toward the forest. "Right pretty place. Marry Nate, and he'd buy it for you."

She looked at him and saw the sly smile. Obviously, he had a way of getting information and not always by direct methods. "I hadn't planned to marry."

"Education seems to ruin gals." He grinned again.

"An education and a job gives a woman more options."

"And one option getting' thrown out is marriage."

"Not everyone has to be married, you know. Now, may I ask you something?"

He chuckled. "Might not get any more answers than I got."

"Well, you seem to drift between using cowboy vernacular and pretty good English. Is there a reason for that?"

At that, he guffawed loudly and slapped his knee. "Besides English," he asked with another chuckle, "you didn't study psychology did you?"

She smiled. "It's the writer in me. Language is my tool. I am guessing that you tend to use your speech to relate to people in a way that gets you what you want. Maybe put them off their guard to see you as a... uhmm good old boy perhaps." She could have said it was manipulative, but she wanted to be polite.

"Won't work with you though, I see. Might I be interesting enough to end up in one of your books?"

She smiled. "I can't say that's never happened, but I am planning to stay away from westerns now."

"That'd be a shame. You're damned good at them."

"Thank you, and I just didn't feel good about what I was writing even before..." She stopped at seeing Nate come in the door.

"Can I talk to you, Willy?" he asked.

"Of course, want some coffee or would you prefer tea?"

"I meant alone."

"I understand," Jeremiah said. "I'll just get started on the vittles." He grinned at her as he used the word.

"All right." With the air turning a little nippy toward late afternoon, Willy grabbed her jacket and then followed Nate down to the lake where they each sat on one of the boulders.

"I want you to come back to San Francisco with me," Nate said. "I want you where I can protect you."

"From your mother?"

"If required."

"I am not going back now. I want to get the details lined up; so I can go to the marshal or someone with legal authority, while still in Arizona."

"Why here?"

"Because I wouldn't know who to trust there."

She saw he was gritting his teeth. "And you do here?"

"I have Holly here and now the Taggert family."

"Outlaws."

"That's not true."

"We stopped in Payson for supplies. I heard in the store about Cole Taggert killing a man."

"In self-defense."

"Was it?"

"You know it was, with witnesses. Cole told me about it."

"And he wouldn't lie?"

"Nate, what are you trying to do here? Please don't ruin our friendship."

"Does it have to be just friendship?" He moved off his rock and pulled her into his arms. "Willy, please be my wife."

She shook her head. "You don't love me that way, Nate. And I don't love you that way. We are like brother and sister and that's a good thing. It's not a basis for a marriage, and you know it."

"Friendship can be a strong basis for a marriage."

"Not for mine."

He released her and stared out at the lake. "I am losing you and probably my mother."

"You won't lose me, Nate. We will always be friends."

He tried again to pull her into his arms. She knew he wanted to kiss her but wasn't going to let that happen. She pushed back. He let her go. "Don't ruin what we have," she said.

"You're in love with him." It wasn't a question.

"I don't need to be in love with him to say no to you. Nate, you are upset and with good reason, but don't take it out on Cole. It's not his fault."

"I think you fell in love with him while writing all those books."

"Which you haven't read."

"Jeremiah told me about them as we rode north. Of course, then he had no idea who wrote them, but he was telling me how the writer told stories of the values out here, values that weren't in cities like Frisco."

"If he said that, he was wrong. I learned those values from books and while in cities like San Francisco and Boston. Values are values wherever people are."

He let out a sigh and turned again to look at the water. "I'd like to make good what happened to your home," he said finally.

"It wasn't your fault. I don't want your money, Nate." She knew she was probably being foolish, but she also knew she'd not take a dime from the Hemstreets, not even the man she had considered a best friend.

"What can I do then?"

"You did what you could by warning me and letting me know about Hamilton and my home. You can't do more."

He turned back to her. "You want me to leave then?"

"There really isn't room here for the three of you."

"Then why not them? I'll stay and help you."

She smiled. He was more determined than she had remembered. "Maybe you can find out more about the names Cole was concerned about if you go back and see what you can learn." Then she realized that might not be safe. "Why don't you stay in Tucson until I get down there, and we can go back together."

"What about him?" He gestured with his thumb to the cabin, and she realized for the first time that Cole had come out onto the porch, was sitting on the bench, and smoking.

"He will do what seems best for him."

Nate let out a low growl. "You shouldn't trust him."

She laughed and shook her head. "And your reasoning is?"

He let out a reluctant laugh. "Do I need reasoning?"

She reached out and gave him a hug. "He's a good man. I know he is. He is a detective, who can help figure this all out." She had started to think of Cole that way after Nate had used the word. He was good at looking at piles of figures, at evidence, and he would figure it out.

"I see I can't convince you," he said as they slowly walked back to the cabin. She looked again for Cole, but he was gone. She hurried her step a little as she was concerned he had taken ill. Inside, in the kitchen she heard his voice and then his father's.

When she entered, Cole, sipping a cup of coffee, didn't look up. She tried to read his expression but it was impossible. If he was getting a fever, if his wound had infected, would he tell her? She had to know.

"Are you feeling all right?" she asked as she walked to him and felt of his forehead. It was cool. She brushed the dark hair back.

"I'm fine," he said in a brusque tone.

"Supper's about ready," Jeremiah said. "Don't mind Cole." He turned to Willy. "He's been in a rotten mood when he's sick since he was a tyke." He chuckled and then pointed to the pan of food. "This is called toad in a hole. Remember it, Cole?"

"Didn't think you knew how to make it."

"Why shore I do." He chuckled again as he winked at Willy.

"What is in it?" she asked looking at what appeared to be bread but with something poking up through it at regular intervals.

"I had to use the dried beef, soak it a little in whiskey, waste of good whiskey," he said with another laugh. "Mix up eggs, flour, little salt, your dried milk, water, and pour it over the meat. It can be done in an oven, but I used the cast iron pot and lid. Just cook it until the dough is done. In my case, I chopped up some of my chili peppers to add some spice to it. You need to get some black pepper." He smiled at Willy as they sat at the table, and he dished it out.

When she ate, she complimented the cook. Simple and good. She'd have to remember to request black pepper. It seemed men liked such, if Cole and Nate's reaction to the meal was any indication.

An hour later, she had helped Jeremiah clean up the kitchen and then joined the silent Cole and Nate who had gone out onto the porch. While Cole was smoking, Nate was staring at the lake. Their silence made no secret of the fact they didn't care much for each other. While it was because of her, in regards Nate, what was Cole's reason? Did he believe Nate had more to do with what went wrong with Hemstreets than he admitted? Having known Nate as many years as she had, she doubted that to be the case, but Cole didn't know him at all.

"Reckon we should leave tomorrow," Jeremiah said bringing a chair out and sitting on it, leaving the bench for Willy but she was reluctant to take it given how Cole was acting. He didn't appear to want her anywhere near him. He blew out the smoke but didn't react to his father's statement.

Nate looked back at Cole then, his expression no friendlier. "You going with us?"

"Us? You are leaving?" Cole asked and then looked back at Willy.

"I am not leaving," Willy said, feeling annoyed with Cole. "They are." She wanted to ask if he was going with them but was afraid of the answer. Instead of staying where the atmosphere was frigid, even though the temperature was not, she walked inside, checked on Zinnia, mixed her up some dried milk and water along with the leftovers from dinner, refilled her water bowl, and then headed up the stairs to her loft. She wondered where Cole would sleep. Would it be his last night at the lake cabin? She'd only know in the morning.

CHAPTER 10

Having opted to sleep down by the corrals, leaving his father and Hemstreet to have the floor of the main room, Cole woke at first light. He rotated his shoulder, pleased it moved with no limitations even if it still was painful. He lay in his bedroll as he watched the sunrise. His mood was dark after seeing Willy in Hemstreet's arms the day before. The man had made his move, and he hadn't seen any indication Willy had resisted him. He wondered if she wanted him to be the one leaving. Maybe it's what he should do.

Knowing her home had been burned, that Hamilton had followed Hemstreet to Tucson made him reluctant to leave her alone. She wasn't going to leave right now. Maybe Hemstreet was staying after all. He'd find out for sure. Then he needed to ride into Payson to see if his brother had answered his wire. Knowing more about Hamilton, he hoped the wire hadn't provided a trail that he'd never intended.

Before he could decide what was best, he heard the door to the house open and saw Willy heading toward him. Before she got there, he was out of his blankets and had pulled on his boots. "Why didn't you sleep in the cabin?" she asked in an irritated tone as she knelt beside him, again feeling of his forehead.

"No need," he said, knowing his voice sounded as annoyed as hers.

"Are you leaving today?"

"Do you want me to go?" he snapped back.

She glared at him. "You are a very intelligent man. How could you ask that question?" With that, she turned on her heel and left him.

He spent some time currying Boomer, in no hurry to go up to the house and face any of the three. Maybe he did know or had known, but then she'd let Hemstreet take her in his arms. He saw his father leave the cabin and waited.

"So," Jeremiah said lighting a cigar, "where are you going now?"

"Just to get a response to my wire hopefully. You don't have to leave today."

"Best if we do. You could come along. She was fine here before you, will be fine now. She's a tough little thing for all that learning." He grinned as he let the smoke out.

"Why'd you bother saying that? You know I won't do it."

His father snickered. "She's too classy for the likes of you."

"I am aware."

"It would be smart if you just let it go."

"There's nothing to let go." He walked off only to run into Hemstreet blocking his way. "Excuse me," he said attempting to go around.

"I'd like to talk to you."

He let out a breath hoping this wouldn't turn ugly. "All right."

"Down at the lake."

"Fine." He followed the man to the lake edge. It looked like he was never getting his coffee for breakfast or maybe no breakfast at all. He turned and lit a cigarette. "About what?"

"Your intentions toward Willy."

"And this is your business, why?"

"Because she is mine. Maybe not the way I want but my responsibility. If I am not going to be here to look after her, I want to be sure the man who is means well by her."

"You have got to be joking." This was getting weirder and weirder.

Hemstreet gave him a look. "Why would you think that?"

"You're the man who had her in his arms yesterday. Maybe you should stay here and look after her."

"You saw that, did you?"

"Of course."

"Well, I'd do that… if she wanted me to. She does not."

Cole was having a hard time understanding why they were having this conversation. "I am not sure I get your drift."

Hemstreet snorted. "If you don't, I'm not about to help you." He walked back to the cabin leaving Cole to ponder what the hell that meant.

An hour later, after eating breakfast, Cole went down to the corral to saddle Boomer. His horse was eager to get out of the corral. It reminded him he needed to find feed for him if he planned to stick around for long. The meager grass around the lake wouldn't last long. It was possible the stable would sell some small bales, enough to get him to when she was finally ready to leave. He could have them bring that out with her supplies next time.

Maybe he should have waited for his father and Hemstreet to leave, but he'd decided he didn't have the time. Besides, they seemed unsure of when they were going. If they decided to hang around, which seemed possible, he needed to know if Vince knew any of those names. He also wanted to talk to the land agent who handled Willy's lease.

He led Boomer to the cabin where his father and Hemstreet were sitting on the bench and watching. Willy came out. "You should not be riding," she protested with a shrewish tone.

"I need to know about the wire and a few other arrangements. When are you being resupplied?"

"Tuesday." Her tone was definitely displeased.

Cole looked over at the two men. "You two hanging around a few extra days?"

"We were discussing that."

"I'll get enough food in case you do." With that, he swung onto Boomer and rode out of the yard, in frankly a rotten mood. As he headed down the dirt road, he considered what he'd heard from both Hemstreet and his father. Both discouraged him from Willy. It wasn't that he had any intention of moving forward with her. Yes, she was out of his league. She'd never seriously consider him as a husband even if he was so inclined to want a wife. Ridiculous even to consider it.

It was just over an hour later when he rode into Payson in no better mood than he'd left the cabin. He stopped first at the telegraph office and picked up the wire from Vince. The names had meant nothing to him, which didn't tell him anything by itself except Vince was familiar with some of the businesses along the waterfront and these names should have meant something to him.

At the stable, he had Boomer put in a stall with oats and hay. He learned he could buy three or four twenty-two inch bales of pressed hay, as well as a sack of oats. He stopped next at Cantrell's to be sure he could get them out to the cabin.

"Shore, I can bring them out. You fellas planning to spend a while out there helping Miss Butler?"

"Not sure."

His next stop was the land agent, who was at his desk when Cole entered.

"May I help you?" Gibbons asked rising and taking Cole's hand.

Cole didn't smile. "You can since you are the land agent for Payson."

"As well as justice of the peace, attorney, and accountant."

"I am interested in the Smith lake cabin. You said it was for sale."

Gibbon's smile widened. "I did meet you out there, didn't I?"

"You did."

"What do you need to know?"

"How many acres come with the cabin?"

"One hundred and sixty, with more available."

"Do you have a plat map?"

Gibbons went to his file and laid the drawing on his desk. "This pretty well defines it. You interested in a cattle operation. As much as a thousand acres are available."

"Interesting. No other buyers to worry about, are there."

Gibbons narrowed his gaze. "The other people weren't serious apparently… I can get you a good price."

"I am sure you can." He had figured that the talk of another buyer had been to pressure Willy into buying it. "What is the asking price?"

"Cash only. Five hundred dollars."

Cole considered. "Three seventy-five, and I can wire to my bank to get it transferred."

Gibbons considered. "Four twenty-five."

"Four hundred."

"Cash?"

"Cash."

"I can draw you up a contract today, Mr. uh?

"Taggert."

Gibbons paled. "You are the man who killed a man."

He nodded. "I might be interested in options on the other thousand. Find a good price on that too so I can think about it."

Gibbons swallowed. "All right, I can get everything ready for you in say an hour, Mr. Taggert."

"I'll get to my bank and arrange the transfer."

Outside, Cole thought about where he could kill an hour. He had operated on an impulse to buy the cabin. It wasn't just knowing how much Willy loved it but also aware of what she must have felt at having lost her home. He wasn't sure how much she'd even want it, but it was what he could do for her. He was glad he still had his share from the sale of the family's Utah ranch. It had brought in more than he'd expected even with sharing it equally with his father and two brothers. He could buy more than the cabin if he decided he wanted that. Right now, he was operating on instinct, and none of it was aimed at being logical.

To add to his foolishness, he walked back to the stable. "I was interested in buying a horse. You have anything right now?"

The young hostler took him to the back corral where there were two swayback mares but also a nice gelding, not young but seemed in good shape. He lifted its hooves to assure himself of no foundering. Running his hand over the horse's neck to his rump, the animal felt solid. His teeth indicated about nine years old. "Let's saddle him. I want to see how he handles." In half an hour, he'd ridden the horse out of the stable, down the street, let him run, seen him respond quickly to a pull on the reins, even when heading back to the stable. "How much?" he asked and the dickering began. He paid for the horse, gear, and feed.

By the time Cole went back to the land agent, he had the money order to sign over. "All right, Mr. Taggert," Gibbons said as he put the papers out for him to sign. "I am pleased with this. I am sure you will enjoy the property."

"I will."

Cole strode back to the stable and saddled Boomer, taking the reins to the new gelding. "He have a name?" he asked the hostler.

"Boots for those front feet."

"Good enough. Contrells will be here Tuesday for the hay and oats." The man waved him off. As Cole headed out of town, he saw his father and Hemstreet riding in. He pulled his horse to a stop along with Boots.

"You bought a horse," his father said needlessly.

"You both decided to leave." It was equally evident.

"It was time to go. We'll stay in the hotel tonight though," his father said.

Nate looked at him with no more friendliness than before. "I guess you bought the horse for Willy."

"I like to ride Roman style sometimes," Cole said.

Nate smiled for the first time. "You will look after her."

"You know that, or you'd not have left."

"I did. I won't say I liked it."

"I understand."

Jeremiah looked at him then. "When you be back in Tucson?"

"Mid-December at the latest."

"Take care." He nudged his horse in the side and rode on into town.

"I might be there," Hemstreet said, "to be sure you do right by her."

"Not worried about her doing right by me?" Cole said with a half-smile.

"I know her."

"She is not my woman." He didn't know why he said as he wasn't sure himself. So much had happened so fast, and his feelings were undergoing changes like he'd never imagined.

"Maybe for now." With that, he gave what Cole considered a reluctant grin before nudging his horse and following Jeremiah.

Just over an hour later, and not much before dark, Cole rode into the cabin's clearing. Smoke was coming from the kitchen chimney, but she didn't come out to greet him. He took both horses down to the corrals, unsaddled and put them into the enclosure. Walking up to the house, he was unsure what response he'd be getting.

She was sitting on the floor by Zinnia, petting her. She looked up as he entered. "Until you got closer, I didn't know it was you. Why two horses?"

"You will need one."

"Why?"

"For now, to go to the natural bridge."

"Natural bridge?" She wasn't smiling.

"North of us by maybe twenty miles or so. A prospector, David Gowan hid there when Apaches chased him. He claimed it by squatter's rights. His nephew and the family built a home. It's a natural travertine bridge, over 180 feet high." He smiled. "Be good in a book."

She just looked at him, ignoring his small joke. He wondered what she was thinking. Finally she rose. "Are you hungry?"

"I could eat."

In the kitchen, she ladled out soup into a bowl and then a slice of bread. "You already ate?" he asked as he sat down.

She nodded.

He tried to work through what was going on with her as he ate the delicious soup, a kind of beef vegetable with maybe what was left of his father's chilies. "Are you depressed that Hemstreet left?"

"Why don't you ever call him by his name?"

"Nate. Are you missing him?"

She rose and walked to the stove before turning. "Do you honestly think that?"

"I don't know what to think." He remembered how she had trusted him to make the decision on whether to draw Hemstreet into the mystery they were trying to unravel. He had appreciated that but hadn't said so at the time. Some of that was because he had felt almost sick, thinking what he was coming to feel for her. Everything was deepening his ties to her and yet he hadn't pulled away. He was contributing to his own downfall. What made him buy the horse for her? Even worse, the property?

He knew why he'd bought the land. It wasn't just feeling sorry for her in losing her home. It came down to his own belief he'd not live a long time. He'd had the money from the ranch, invested it, but done nothing with it. Finally, he had something he could do, someone he could make happy with it. He hadn't asked for the title to be in her name mostly because it would have required her signing it and he hadn't trusted

Gibbons. He would though take care of that in Tucson with a lawyer he did trust. He wasn't sure when he'd tell her about it. Not soon, as he didn't want her feeling obligated to him.

"Cole, why do you dislike Nate? Do you honestly believe he's in on whatever his family has been doing?"

"I don't know him well enough to rule that in or out, but no, I don't think he's in on it."

"Then why?"

He felt suddenly tired beyond thinking. It was the way it had always been with him. He could push it to the limit and then be ready to collapse a moment later. He kept underestimating his need to build back up strength. The ride into town had maybe been a mistake so soon after being shot. He had needed to do it though. Now he was too exhausted to deal with her questions. He looked up at her trying to think of a way to tell her that.

"Let's talk in the morning," she said as she took his emptied bowl. "Pour yourself a little whiskey, I'll have a sherry and then let's go to bed."

He looked at her but nodded. He wanted them to talk, but he had no idea what he would say or what he wanted to hear from her.

They went into the main room and sat on the chairs by the fireplace as they sipped their drinks. Zinnia quickly came over. "She looks good," he said reaching down and petting her.

"She seems to love having the babies. They are making more sounds, but still no eyes open. When they begin to move more, the chair won't be enough to keep them in the nest."

"I can make something that will do that," he said watching the little bodies as they nuzzled around the nest trying to find their mama. Instinctual love was one of those things no one could explain and yet it was heartwarming to see. It didn't always work out that way. He knew a lot about that.

"Go to bed and damn it all," Willy said, "in here. It's not like I'll attack you."

He smiled. "Maybe I'm worried I'll attack you."

"I'll fight you off. You're safe." She went up the stairs, leaving him to put out the kerosene lamp. He went into the bedroom and thought about his bizarre day, as he got undressed. His wound was doing well, no infection. Tomorrow he'd pull off the dressing. He wasn't sure what he'd tell Willy. The things he was thinking were out of the question.

When Willy walked down the stairs at first light, she checked on Zinnia and then went into the kitchen to light the stove and make coffee. With the bedroom door closed, she had assumed Cole had spent the night in the bedroom, but with him, who knew.

She was sipping her first cup of coffee when he came in looking tousled and very desirable. She'd never imagined a woman could feel that way about a man. Writing about those feelings and experiencing them herself turned out to be very different. She needed to get control of her wayward emotions. "How are you feeling?" she asked as she poured him his coffee.

"Good. I ought to be able to chop you some wood today." He smiled at her grimace. "I was thinking the wound's dressing should come off if you don't mind."

She looked at him to be sure he meant it. Not mind? Not mind touching him? She nodded though. "It will also let us be sure there is no infection. After breakfast?"

"Good."

She fixed hotcakes and bacon. "Did you see Mr. Contrell in town?" she asked as she poured more coffee before putting the pot back on the stove.

"Yes, among other things. Vince didn't recognize the names I sent him. That alone kind of makes me wonder but maybe your friend will have better luck figuring this out as to which companies were fronts."

"I hope it doesn't endanger him. I still can't get past them burning my home. All probably to get rid of the papers we have here."

He nodded. "Which tells you how dangerous this is."

"It does. I think though if we can put together the evidence, maybe the sheriff in Tucson will see to an arrest and that could change it all."

"If it turns out that clear."

"You know a lot about that, don't you?"

"Some."

"How did you… end up being a detective?"

He considered that. "It was what I could do, I guess. I was good at figures, thinking, and putting one fact with another. Most of the time it doesn't involve people like Hamilton. It's most often those who twisted their lives up trying to make money, while cheating someone else."

"Money can be important."

"Having enough is but when it goes beyond that." He shrugged.

"I wonder if it's just about money. I only met Nate's mother a few times, but she didn't strike me as someone who would order a home burned or someone killed."

"You'd be surprised how seldom those who do something violent look like they would."

"I suppose."

"I was thinking we'd stay around here today while we wait for the

Contrells. I can fix the fence to give our horses a little more room. I ordered hay and oats, and Amos said he'd bring them out with your order."

"You really bought me a horse?" She still felt surprised. She'd never owned any animals and now she had a dog, two puppies, and it appeared a horse.

He nodded. "He's responsive, steady, and should get you not only to the natural bridge, but also we can use them both to head south when the time comes."

"Not take the stage?"

"You can if you want. I just think keeping a low profile might be smarter until we are with friends. The dogs wouldn't likely work on the stage either."

"I hadn't thought of that. I guess you are right. You really think I can learn to ride well enough to do that?"

"If you want."

"How will I get the typewriter south with me?"

"Leave it here or box and ship it."

She considered that. She hadn't much liked the stage ride on the rough road. Riding a stage with strangers would mean she'd not be alone with Cole or with Cole at all. She smiled then. "So riding to the natural bridge is a test of me being able to do a longer ride south."

"I know you can do it," he said with the most gentle smile she'd yet seen on his face. "It's all about whether you want to do it."

"Will Zinnia have to walk south with us?"

"Even without the pups, that's not feasible. I've thought on it. I'll make packs that will let her and the pups ride safely behind us. Dogs on one side of the horse and their food on the other."

She knew it then. If she'd had any doubts, his tender thoughtfulness on the dogs put them away. She was in love with this man. It might be impossible for them to have a life together, as he had said, but she loved him with every fiber of her being. Maybe Nate had been right, and the love had begun even before she met him. It didn't matter. The real man was so much more than the one she'd created.

"So when do we ride to the natural bridge?" she asked confident he'd not have her do it if it wasn't safe.

"I want you to have a day or two riding around here first. You need to get used to Boots and him to you."

"Boots?"

"Boomer and Boots. Good mix, huh?" He smiled again.

"It works for me. Now do you want me to take the gauze off your wound?"

He unbuttoned his shirt and shoved it off his shoulders. She moved behind his chair and took the shirt further down. "I should soak it first." She smiled as she went to the sink and found a cloth, which she moistened and then returned to stand behind him. She braced her hand on one shoulder as she put the cloth over the pad. She moved her hand along his shoulder to his neck, feeling his muscles tense. She dropped the cloth to the table and slowly began edging away the surgical tape on the back bandage.

"Do it fast," he said finally.

She didn't want to do anything fast, but she worked a little faster, had the tape gone and then slowly pried off the gauze. "It looks good," she said. "Now turn around so I can get the front one."

He looked up, met her gaze but then did it. She pushed herself between his legs, and using the damp cloth, against wetted the gauze before removing the tape. This time it caught a few of his chest hairs causing him to grimace. "Remember, fast."

"Is fast good?" she asked with as teasing a tone as she could put to her voice.

"For some things." She knew he had clenched his jaw. She had made up her mind how this morning was going to go, but she hoped he would be of a similar mind. She worked on the gauze. This wound had been larger as she knew from her reading that the exit tore more skin. Slowly she peeled off dressing without starting bleeding. She applied new dressings to both wounds Mostly to protect them from being torn open.

When she was finished, instead of moving away, she sat on one of his legs. "I was thinking..."

"I doubt that." His breathing had quickened.

She ran her fingers over his uninjured shoulder, running it down his bicep. Her own breathing wasn't coming easily. She had never imagined a man's body could be like Cole's. Although the shirt was not all the way down, she could see his chest, nipples, the light hair covering it, the ridges of muscle. She wanted to see more and set herself to unbuttoning it to his belt. She pushed it down his arms, before sitting back a little to look at what she had uncovered. His belly was flat, more of the ridged muscles. The hair traveled from his chest in a narrow line that went below the buckle. She wondered what that would look like when it got to...

"Willy, you can't play with this."

She laughed a little. "I wasn't thinking of playing but... now that you mention it." She ran her fingers down his belly to the buckle.

His hand came up, and he put it to the back of her neck. "Is this what you want?" he asked as he brought her lips almost to his.

"It seems a good start." She pressed her lips against his, opening her mouth and felt his tongue delve within. She moved her hands now down his back. The muscles flexed. She felt her body heating up and wondered if he was feeling any of the same things. Before she could decide on another move, she felt the brush of fur against her leg. A little whine came next. She opened her eyes and looked down.

"Forget to feed her?" he asked with humor in his voice.

"Apparently." Reluctantly she got off his lap and went to the stove for the food she'd had cooling for Zinnia, who ate with gusto. Willy looked back at Cole wondering what he was thinking. Was it an escape he had wanted? His eyes looked warm, inviting, and the slight quirk of his lips gave her encouragement.

"You know," she said, when Zinnia had gone outside, taken care of her needs, and returned to her babies. "I am not very experienced at this."

"This?"

She knew he was teasing now. "Seduction," she said with an answering smile.

"Then you have a natural talent for it, or did you learn that from writing your books?"

"He and she never got that far. He was always riding off on some dangerous quest."

"Did he have a woman in every town or make that book?" he asked rising to retrieve the coffee pot and pour himself another cup.

"Of course not," she snapped. "He was in love."

"But it didn't work out or did it?"

She smiled. "You should read the books."

"I might, but for now, tell me about the woman." He leaned back against the counter, one boot over the other.

"What do you want to know?"

"The man was fantasy. Was the woman also?"

She knew then what he wondered. Had Lucy been her? She had to think about that. Parts of her certainly. "Well, Lucy did teach school. A lot of women could if they could read and do sums."

"Was she beautiful?"

"He thought so."

He smiled at that. "What color was her hair?"

"Plain brown."

"Like yours?"

"I suppose so." She hadn't thought of that. Maybe she had been Lucy.

"Do you know your hair isn't plain anything?"

"Of course it is. It's not blonde like Holly's."

"No, it's a rich brown, like the woods, the deepest riches soil, but with red highlights especially when the sun hits it. Glossy and makes a man want to run his fingers through it as it's so thick. Did the last Taggert ever get to touch Lucy's hair?"

She shook her head. "They never even kissed. He kept her away from him for her safety."

"Noble fellow for an outlaw."

"He wasn't so much outlaw anymore. His family had been, but he was just trying to stay alive in a world where many saw him as the enemy."

"Kind of weak?"

She glared at him and saw the humorous glint in his eyes. "Well, I guess," she said with her own smile, "where it came to Lucy, he was. He should have claimed her for both their sakes."

"Ah, was there some dastardly villain after her?"

"Of course. And wanting to kill him."

"From where did you get your plots?"

"Imagination, of course," she said and then shook her head. "No, I stole them from classics. Ivanhoe, Sir Lancelot, Achilles." She threw in Redmond Barry wondering how well read he really was.

He grinned. "Seriously, not him. How do you make him into a hero?"

"You read *The Luck of Barry Lyndon*?"

"I like Thackeray for his satire."

"Of course, you would." Cole was such a mix of her dreams and his reality. She imagined if she spent years with him, she'd still never truly know him.

"How about Ahab?" he asked. "Did he find his way into becoming one of your heroes or is that antiheroes?"

"A man on a quest that would destroy him?" she asked. Ahab had been at the base of them all and his earlier mention of it being a favorite of his had shocked her at the time. Even more than he had understood the deeper meaning. Her last Taggert wasn't nearly as deep as the real Taggert.

"He sounds like the perfect inspiration," he said as though reading her minds, "for a man without a strong life force."

"How can you say that? He fought the elements."

"And for what? An obsession that had no meaning."

She had to think about that. She was at the same time a little frustrated. She had not wanted an esoteric discussion. She knew now what she did want. She looked at him as he sipped his coffee and knew he'd deliberately sidetracked all of that. Perhaps he didn't really desire her.

"You are like an open book yourself," he said with another of those smiles that melted her to her toes.

"So you know what I'm thinking," she said rising and taking the dishes to the sink.

"Right now, and I am thinking it too. I want you. Don't think I don't, but we need to both be sure before we take a step we might regret."

She nodded, pumping some water to fill a pan to put on the stove and wash the dishes. "You know so much about regrets," she said unable to hide her irritation.

His smile this time was sardonic. "What do you think?" With that, he walked from the room.

CHAPTER 11

Cole spent the morning splitting kindling, while Willy washed clothing, studied her cookbook, and came up with a recipe that didn't seem beyond her for dinner. She had come to love *The Boston Cooking-School Cook Book*. It made anything seem possible, even a soufflé, though she wasn't about to try that.

The biggest temptation was to find wild mushrooms to add to the next meal. She had learned something about them from her mother and then when in Boston. The question is which ones might be in the Mazatzals if any. She went out to where Cole had been carrying in the last load of kindling. "What do you know about wild mushrooms?"

"They can kill you," he said piling the kindling at the top of the wood-pile on the porch.

"I mean the safe, delicious kind."

He leaned the axe against the wall. "What do you know?"

"I went with my mother in San Francisco and we found morels, chanterelles, porcini. I was curious which might be in this area."

"Ever know anybody who died from them?" he asked with a grin.

"No, but I do think it's safer to stay with the ones that don't have a poisonous relative that looks a bit like them."

"Which means?"

"Probably morels or chanterelles. If they are here."

"Where is most likely?"

"Along the lake maybe. How far around do you think the lake is? Does it have an inlet and outlet?"

He tried to remember the plat map. "Just guessing, a mile around. You'll find out about inlets and outlets when you start out."

"I guess I will. Does this lake have a name?"

"Hey, you're the one who rented a house here." He smiled to soften the words.

"I don't recall it being mentioned. Maybe it's too small for a name. Should I call it Taggert Lake?" She looked up at him to see if he'd laugh.

"How about Willy's Lake?"

"Zinnia's?" She went back into the kitchen for a basket she remembered seeing. Zinnia showed no interest in following her but she closed the door anyway. Starting out, she hadn't expected Cole to come with her, but he was there with his rifle.

"You expect somebody bad to attack us?" she asked, happy at his company.

He shook his head. "It's off the beaten path, but this area has bear and cougar. I don't expect them either but better safe than sorry. Isn't there a saying about that?"

"It comes from Irish novelist Samuel Lover's *Rory O'More*, which began as a song."

"Well, it's my philosophy."

She looked over to see if he was teasing her. "And you have so lived your life that way, haven't you? Choosing safety at any price."

He laughed. "Well, maybe not so much."

"I live my life that way or have. Too much so."

"And it's why you chose the wilderness cabin as a retreat?"

"I hadn't thought of that. Maybe. I needed to do something I hadn't done, something that was far from what I knew. I had been drawn to the Rim by the descriptions Holly had told me about in her dreams and her research. I liked the idea that prehistoric people had made homes in these mountains. I didn't though have a real plan for where I'd go. Just get to Payson and the rest would take care of itself. And as it turned out, it did."

As they walked, in some areas, the boulders were large enough to skirt around. There were grassy beaches as well as those of mud. Around the cabin had been mostly tall pines, but the vegetation changed as they got farther around the lake. The pines were mixed with groves of white-barked sycamores and ash trees. In a clearing, she saw the ridge above the lake had junipers, pinyon pines, and sagebrush.

Several times Cole looked at the tracks in the mud and told her the animals that had likely made them. Deer, antelope, wolves, coyotes, beaver. Rabbits appeared most common. He pointed to one set of tracks. "Weasel and you don't see them often here."

"No cougar?" she asked as she kept her own eyes peeled for the right habitat for the mushrooms she sought.

"Not yet."

When she found the first chanterelle, she had a eureka moment and gave a little yip.

"You sure these are safe to eat?" he asked as he helped her gather them.

"Positive. Morels are the same. They don't have a deadly brother. She pointed to another mushroom further back in the woods. "That one I'd hesitate about. I think there is one like it that is a hallucinogenic but also potentially deadly. I just want the ones that taste good."

He took the basket as they found more of the chanterelles in the marshy areas at the edge of the pines. Then she found a few morels. "They say they will return to the same area if you are careful how you gather them. Of course, I won't be back here likely but for the next renter."

He nodded and smiled. With enough mushrooms for several meals, she stopped looking and instead enjoyed the lingering wildflowers. The most common were the yellow poppies and a few sunflowers but then she saw a purple nightshade and a penstemon putting forth its last spikes. Walking with him around the lake was a pleasure she hadn't expected. When he pointed to rounded prints and said, "Cougar," they weren't that far from the cabin.

"Might it attack the horses?"

"It'd be unusual or desperate if it did. A horse would kick and break its jaw, crippling or killing it. Zinnia was more in danger."

"What about humans?"

"It happens but rarely. Children would be at more risk. If you ever see a cougar, meet its gaze firmly, give it a glare, get as big as you can, and yell at it."

"Same with a bear?"

"Opposite with a bear, especially if it was a big one like a grizzly. Not likely you'll see one of those though. They are being killed off. Still, with any bear, don't dare it. Don't run. Wait it out and sometimes they run at someone as a sort of challenge, but they back off. That's most of the time."

"Is your rifle big enough to kill a grizzly? Seems I heard they are hard to kill."

"Hit it in the right spot and yes."

"You know the right spot?"

He smiled. "I haven't had to put that to the test."

"I don't like a cougar being around the cabin." She looked toward the woods. "Zinnia does go outside when needed."

"She'll be fine when we're around. When we go up to the natural

bridge, we should close her in—like you did today. Better safe than sorry."
He smiled when she looked at him. "Hey, I can worry about her too."

She liked that. She had liked everything about this day with him. Back at the cabin, she put together Zinnia's meal, then set about cooking their dinner which involved frying the remains of their beef with the mushrooms. She boiled five of their potatoes, assuming Zinnia would eat them with some meat and then mashed the ones for their supper. She longed for fresh vegetables but that would have to wait for being in a town. For the first time she thought about what Tucson might be like and where she could stay while there. She didn't think she'd want to live with Holly and her family. She supposed the only alternative would be a hotel room. Where would Cole live, or would he leave her as soon as he got her somewhere he regarded as safe?

She had no eagerness to get to the future. She wanted these days in the forest with him. She loved the cabin, living by the lake. She supposed with winter, it'd not seem so idyllic, although she could imagine being snowed in with white beauty all around her. Fall was wonderful as the few deciduous trees and bushes were beginning to change color.

As they ate, Cole was complementary on the mushroom and beef and helped her clean up before pouring himself a whiskey and her a sherry. Out on the porch, the moonrise was just beginning.

"The circular sliver is so beautiful," she said. "I wish I was a painter."

"Writers paint with words."

"The kind of writing I wish I did."

"It sounded like, from what my brother and father said, that you write an exciting story. Don't put that down."

"Thank you." She was glad he had been kind enough to say it. Especially given how much he had disliked being the main character in her books. She reached up and kissed his cheek in appreciation. He had shaved sometime when she hadn't seen it. She liked the feel of his skin with the bristle gone, the smell of soap.

"You don't wear a mustache or beard," she observed as she stroked his cheek with her fingers.

"Hair on my face has always been irritating." He bent toward her and lightly brushed her lips with his.

"I like your jaw. I like it even better clean shaven." She moved her fingers to his neck. "I like it when you kiss me too."

"You know where this is heading," he said. Again, it wasn't a question.

"I know where I want it to head."

"And you know a lot about that."

"You know I don't."

She saw him consider that. "Why me? Why now?" he asked.

"Why not you, and why not now?"

He smiled at that. "Kiss me." He pulled her over onto his lap and waited. She pressed her lips against his, saw that he wasn't going to do anything to help her and then liked the idea of being the aggressor. She used her tongue to open his mouth and delve within. She explored him and then felt his tongue move into her mouth, teasing and causing her body to grow warm and then hot.

"Should we stay out here?" she asked.

"Who would watch?" he asked unbuttoning the top of her shirt. She had worn a chemise, and in moments, it was all she was wearing above her skirt. He brushed the straps off her shoulders and kissed the tops of her breasts. She'd never felt anything like the sensations that were aroused. It was as though not just her breast was being touched but her whole body. She wanted to touch him the same way and took some time unbuttoning his shirt, pushing it down his shoulders to bare his torso. She loved his chest and to explore it with her fingers was exciting her as much as his fingers on her own flesh.

The night air was soft, almost no breeze, but she felt it on her skin in a way she never had. When he bared her breasts, he sucked on first one nipple and then the other. They grew tight. Her whole body was filled with yearning for him, for his touch, for them to be together more completely.

He picked her up and carried her into the cabin, kicking the door shut with his boot. He set her on her feet and kissed her again, pressing her against him as they clung together. Then he stepped back.

"You don't mean to stop now," she protested.

He laughed. "Not unless you say no. I have something to get, and we should make sure Zinnia is set for the night—if we don't want more interruptions."

She had forgotten about the dog. "All right," she said feeling a little sheepish, and then wondered if he had changed his mind.

"Your bed or mine tonight?" he asked. That answered that question.

"What would you prefer?"

"Whatever you want. And if you change your mind about this, that's all right too, sweetheart. We'll take it slow, and you let me know at any time if…"

She reached up and put her fingers over his lips. "I won't change my mind. And let's use your room, and then if there's a problem with Zinnia tonight, it's easier to get to her." She wanted to belong to him in ways she'd never imagined a woman wanting.

She went out to the outhouse and then he did. They both washed up in the kitchen. She realized her anticipation had only grown with the brief intermission in their lovemaking. She had not put back on her blouse, nor had he his shirt. Being half naked added to her sense of anticipation. He was right. No one would see them. The thought was liberating.

With the dog settled, she started for the stairs. "What do you want from up there?" he asked from the doorway to the bedroom. He had lit a kerosene lamp and put it on the dresser.

"My nightgown."

He smiled. "You won't need that tonight."

She swallowed, feeling suddenly nervous as she walked into the bedroom. "What... what do I do?"

"Whatever you want." She realized his smile had changed to one she'd never seen. It was seductive and soft, as though he felt all she did and maybe more. His eyes held a quiet confidence that excited her even more.

"Could we just sit on the bed for a bit?"

He guided her there and sat beside her. "We don't have to do this."

"Cole, do you love me?"

His smile was crooked. "Why don't we put this off for another time or maybe not if you would rather?"

She put her fingers over his lips again. "You don't have to love me for us to do this. I just wondered is all."

"Would you like to be married first?"

"You would marry me? You didn't want to get married."

"I hadn't met you when I believed that. I know we can't really be together all the time or work out what some might regard as a real life, but I'd like it if you were my wife."

"I don't need to be your wife to do this."

He smiled then. "Modern woman, eh?"

She gave a nervous laugh. "No, not that so much but... I am your woman, Cole. Did you know that?"

He took her in his arms. "From the day I saw you swimming in the lake. I just fought it because I knew how complicated it would be."

"I am a city woman who lives in San Francisco."

"And I'm her outlaw lover in her fiction and a range detective in reality." He brushed her forehead with his lips.

"It can't possibly work, can it?" She drew his head down for another kiss, and this time pressed her breasts against his bare chest.

"Probably not." He laid her back on the bed. "Want me to take your clothes off or would you rather do it?"

She laughed. "Are you trying to talk me out of this?"

"Could I?"

"Not a chance but uh, don't you think we should turn out the light first?"

"Uh uh. I want to see every beautiful inch of you."

"Well…. I'd like to see you too."

"First?"

"Would you mind?"

He stood and unfastened his belt buckle. She stopped him and undid the buttons on his jeans. Slowly, brushing his skin with her fingers, she pushed the pants down, seeing that arrow of hair and then more hair. She had read enough biology books to know what to expect when she finally had him nude. She had though never imagined how large a man, who was in a state of arousal, would be. He was impressive and a little frightening. Goodness. "You are rather big, aren't you?" she asked as she wondered how that could ever fit inside a woman.

"Average I'd say." He sat back on the bed and reached for her buttons. When he had them unfastened, he laid her back, and pulled first off her boots, socks, then undid the buttons on her skirt and removed it with her undergarments until she was as naked as he. He lay beside her then, using his fingers and lips to touch her places she never imagined a man might want to touch a woman or that she would ever permit, let alone ache to have him do. As she writhed, she realized she wanted to have him feeling all she was.

"Can I touch you too?" she asked.

He lay back and let her experiment, touching his skin, his nipples, then down his belly and to his thighs. She avoided the body part that most fascinated and yet frightened her at the same time. She pushed his thighs apart and soon had him in the same condition she was.

"Are you ready for me?" he asked.

She nodded, as she felt his fingers probe to assure that she was indeed. He stretched her a little and then stopped and reached for something.

"You aren't stopping," she said thinking she might hit him if he was.

He laughed. "Protecting you from getting pregnant." He had a little packet in his fingers. Breaking it open, he pulled out a sheath. She did know what it was. How did he happen to have it? Had he known this would happen between them? Then he was back, and she lost all thought as he pushed her legs apart and moved between them. She felt him push against her most intimate place. In another moment, he had pushed inside, slowed, and then when he felt her acceptance of him, thrust hard to enter her fully.

The next moments were lost to her as they became one in the fullest sense of the word. When she exploded with the kinds of sensations, she'd never imagined, she felt him groan and join her. He lowered himself to the bed, pulling her to her side. They stayed joined as they both fell asleep. An hour or was it more, she knew he had moved to blow out the light and then pull the covers over her. She slept again, not waking until morning, when they made love again.

In the kitchen, sipping coffee, Cole thought about the night they'd spent, how certain he'd been that he'd never fall in love with a woman, and how quickly the world had changed. Nothing fit together for the two of them, except the feelings.

"Are you sorry?" she asked as she sat across from him. She was wearing the plain cotton skirt and white shirt, very plain garb and yet, on Willy, anything she wore only made her more beautiful. He smiled. Better yet when wearing nothing.

He laughed as he made himself get back to her question. "Isn't that supposed to be my question?"

"I suppose but… well, maybe you feel I took advantage of you."

He shook his head. "How the hell did I get involved with an educated woman who writes books?"

"I lured you to me, possibly," she suggested.

"You might have." He put his hand across the table and took hers. "You are my fate. I won't say if that's good or bad, but it's a fact."

She smiled at that. "I think it's the other way around."

"You do huh?"

"I do. I started writing about you before I met you. Long before. What were you doing when I wrote the first Taggert book?"

"What was its date?"

"1899. I wrote my first dime novel when in high school and it was published right after I graduated and before I started at Wellesley. There were different heroes, stories, all with elements of the classics or mythology. I got tired of that and decided to write about just one hero. I was in Yale at the time. I spent time at the library, read through their archives of old newspapers from particularly Kansas. That's when I came across the Taggert outlaws."

"My grandfather and great uncles."

"I suppose. They had seemed to disappear. I liked the name. I wanted one hero and to carry him through adventures. Moby Dick was the inspiration in many ways, which led to my nearly choking when you said you had a copy with you."

"A man on a quest to die or conquer a dangerous enemy," he suggested with a chuckle.

"I suppose. So what were you doing that year? Out robbing trains?"

"You wish," he said with another laugh. "After finishing school in '81, that is eighth grade in case you wondered, I was determined to make our ranch pay enough to keep us eating, worked to avoid being killed by Asa, or going out to rob a bank and ending up in prison." His smile was sardonic. "The year of your book, we were in the midst of the worst drought to hit Utah. It lasted until we sold the ranch in '01 when Pa decided to settle in Tucson."

"Did you want to keep it with all that work in it?"

He shook his head. "It had more bad memories than good ones. Since I'd been the main one working it, he asked me to sell it. We got more than I expected with the drought still on. I had done a little research and found out those hills had minerals, the kind they were starting to need for some industries. Sold it at a good price to a conglomerate from the East."

"You sound more like a financial manager than an outlaw." She smiled

"Sorry to disappoint."

"Back to the first Taggert book. What about your father. Perhaps he was robbing trains in '99." She gave a little laugh that had him thinking more of kissing her, than her question.

"He likely wished he was. No, those would be the years he was mourning the loss of the outlaw way of life. Nothing was working well for him. His first wife had died having Vince. His second, my mother died in '96. We had thought she was sick but found out later Asa poisoned her."

"His own mother?"

"You had to know Asa to understand how that could be. She was a Bible fearing, good woman, and I guess Asa got tired of her trying to turn him around. Vince came back when he heard she was sick."

"Back?"

"He had gone when he was maybe fourteen. I was seven and mad at him for leaving us. That lasted awhile."

"You did though forgive him."

"He did what he had to do to survive. It's what we all do."

"It's hard for me to grasp all of this. And I write books." She shook her head.

"Nobody should understand someone like Asa. Look, I don't really want to talk about this and doubt you do either."

She got up and headed to the stove. "I'll fix us breakfast, but if you do want to talk about it someday, well, I will listen. I may not understand, but I will try."

He resisted the temptation to ask if it would be research. He had to quit digging at her. It was unfair. He'd said the truth. Everyone does what they must to survive.

As they were finishing breakfast, he heard the sound of a wagon in the yard and went out. In moments, James Wilson had pulled the wagon to a halt. "How you folks be?" he asked as he jumped down before reaching back for a sack of supplies.

"Good. I'll take the wagon to the shed and unload the hay and oats," Cole said as he and Willy helped Wilson unload everything else. At the shed, he broke open one bale and gave two flakes to the horses, who quickly showed their approval by chomping down. They were getting along well, which was good since geldings didn't always. By the time, Cole had brought the wagon back to the cabin, Wilson and Willy were sitting on the porch drinking coffee.

"Real pretty place here," Wilson said. "I'd be buying it myself if it wasn't so far out from town."

"It is a few miles," Cole agreed. He still hadn't determined when he would tell Willy that she was going to own the cabin and the 160 acres that went with it. His reluctance came down to his uncertainty of how she'd feel about it. Maybe she'd think he was trying to buy her affection. He knew that was foolish since she and he had already come together in the most intimate way a man and woman could. He would tell her. Just not until he had the deal finalized in Tucson. As it stood, it might look to her as though he had tried to buy it out from under her.

"The hay look fine to you?" Wilson asked as Cole lowered himself to the front step.

"Smelled sweet, and the horses went for it."

"Horses?" Wilson looked toward the corral. "I hadn't realized you'd had two," he said rather redundantly in Cole's mind.

"I will be riding him," Willy said.

"Oh, then you bought him."

"Cole bought him but for me." She smiled. At that point, Cole realized by the disappointment on Wilson's face, that he had also had hopes where it came to Willy. Something about her seemed to draw men to her like bees to honey. He resisted the smile as he did know just how sweet she was and could well understand the appeal. Not that long ago, he'd have felt jealous. He recognized the feeling now but since she had given herself to him, he found that feeling gone. All he wanted now was to keep her safe, to see her happy. Maybe he wasn't the man to do that but for as long as he could, he'd sure as hell try.

When Wilson had gone, Willy suggested they go for a swim.

"It'd be nice but how about a little ride first."

"Horseback?" She sounded edgy.

"It'll get easier every time you do it. Then we can wash off in the lake, get rid of the horse smell."

"I guess that sounds logical… All right. What do I wear?"

"For riding, those boy pants you've got. I'll saddle the horses. And close the cabin door when you come out. We don't want Zinnia trying to follow us and getting herself lost again."

She smiled and disappeared inside. By the time she had changed, he had both horses by the front of the porch. "You know the basics, right?" he asked as she mounted Boots, and he handed her the reins.

"Barely."

"Take your foot from the stirrup." He adjusted its length and did the same on the other side. Then stepped into his own saddle. "It's not that complicated. Use one hand to hold the reins, balance yourself with your knees, relax."

"That last part is impossible." She smiled though. She looked at him again with a frown. "You're wearing the gun again."

"Did you notice your saddle has a scabbard? I will want you carrying your Winchester when we head south."

"Not today though?"

"We aren't going far. It wouldn't hurt though when we head to the natural bridge. It's not a long ride, but more chance of the unpredictable."

"I suppose you live that way, expecting the unpredictable?"

He laughed. He supposed the questions would never stop with her. "Take the reins and give a gentle pull to the right, let's save arguing for when we get back."

"Are we going to argue?" This time her smile had turned soft.

"It's possible with a feisty woman like you."

"Ah, so it'd never be your doing." She pulled on the reins, and Boots responded by turning and heading at a walk toward the dirt road.

"He wants to please you," he said as he brought Boomer alongside her. The two animals were taking to the trail well, with neither desiring to prove who was alpha. He wouldn't take that for granted, not with her on the new horse.

"I guess this is fun," she said without much enthusiasm after about fifteen minutes.

He grinned. "Turn him here and let's head the other way." That went smoothly. He let Boots take the lead this time and watched the gait, her seat in the saddle. "Want to try a trot?" he asked as he moved alongside her.

"How would I tell him to do that and not end up having him run? We are heading back to the cabin. Might he start to run?"

"I'll stay a little ahead of you. Just nudge him in the side. Pretty soon, you will find you quit thinking what you're doing. You will look around you at the pines and those aspens turning gold down by the lake. You'll even be looking for mushrooms."

"I doubt that." She gently nudged Boots with her heels, and he picked up his gait. "Good," Cole said as the cabin came back into view. "Want to do some more?"

"Only if you insist." She smiled at him, and they rode the horses to the corral.

"Good for a first day. I'll unsaddle them. How about you find some towels, soap, and we'll clean up down at the lake when you get back." He saw she liked that idea as she ran back to the cabin. Not doing too much, too fast was good for not getting sore. She had a pretty good seat on the horse, and this would work for them to ride back to Tucson, taking it slow, camping more than he would've by himself, but it'd be good. The only real glitch would be how well Zinnia would take to being in a sort of pouch with her pups. He'd see what he could do about making it such that she could look out as well as lots of stewzaops to let her exercise and lose her anxiety.

When Willy returned with the towels and soap, he met her at the lake's edge. "What about your wound?" she asked.

"It's closed up enough now not to worry. These lakes at this elevation are pretty clean. When we get out, I'll have you take the pads off."

"One other thing… are we going to swim without clothing?"

"My dear English professor, you aren't sure about bathing together after all we did this morning and last night?"

"When you put it that way but just I worry about someone coming along."

"How many folks have come this way while you've lived here, that is who weren't coming here?"

"Nobody."

He unbuttoned his shirt and threw it onto the boulder, his holster and belt followed. He sat on the rock and pulled off his boots and socks and then turned back to see she was also starting to strip. In a few moments, they were both naked and wading into the lake. The water was not particularly warm but not so cold that a good swim wasn't possible. He stroked out into the lake. His style was nowhere as perfect as hers, but he had more muscle, which made them well matched for how far they went before turning back. At the shore, he went for the soap.

"How about you pulling off the back pad?" he asked as he yanked off the front one.

She went at it slower but soon they'd both been removed. "It does look good," she said studying it and then back to looking him over. "May I wash you?" She reached for the bar.

He remembered the first time he had seen her swimming in the lake. He supposed he'd been a lost cause from that moment. He handed her the bar.

She sudsed it up and then using her right hand, she began soaping his body, moving down his biceps, his torso to his thighs and then to his buttocks and back to the front where he was now fully erect. She cupped water and used it to sluice off the suds.

"I've never washed a man before," she said as she stood back to admire her handiwork.

"I'd have never guessed," he teased, as he returned the favor of washing her from her neck down and then rinsing off the suds.

He supposed he'd have done something else if he hadn't heard the sound of a horse's hooves. Maybe this hadn't been such a good idea. He strode quickly to the rock, drew his revolver from its holster, handed her a towel to wrap around herself, and then faced the approaching rider. The man had long white hair, a beard of the same color, half of an old United States uniform, and hadn't drawn the gun on his belt.

"You got reason to be here?" Cole asked, with his Colt pointed at the now smiling man.

"Sorry to catch you folks unawares," the stranger said. His smirk did not look sorry but mostly amused.

"Turn that horse around until the lady has a chance to get dressed," Cole said not lowering his gun.

"Shore. Be glad to." He did it while Willy quickly pulled on clothing. She took the gun then long enough for Cole to pull on his jeans.

"All right, you can turn around. What's your business?" Cole asked in no friendlier a tone.

"I own the land a mile to the southeast. Just wanted to see who was livin' here."

"You came from town though, didn't you?"

The man grinned more widely. "You are a slick one, son. I know you?"

"I don't know you, so it's unlikely."

"Wal, I was in town and heard I had a neighbor, that's all. You ain't real friendly."

"I've been caught in better times," Cole said with his first smile.

"Sorry about that. I wish my property was on the lake, be swimming myself if I knew how anyways. I do have a small creek."

"Do you have a wife at your home?" Willy asked with some interest obviously at the idea of a woman nearby.

"Sorry to say, I do not. You folks mind if I dismount? I been on Hank here too many hours."

Cole noted the filled flour sack on the back of his horse. Maybe his story was true. "All right, go ahead and dismount, just don't pull that hogleg."

"Wouldn't think of it, son."

Willy pulled on her boots. "I am Willy Butler," she said as she stuck out her hand. Cole supposed that if he wasn't going to be friendly, she would try to make up for it. It made some degree of sense if the man was actually trustworthy. After all, she'd be the man's neighbor someday—if she decided to stay up in this country.

"I'm Lars Ericson." He looked then back at Cole.

Always reluctant to share his name, Cole gave it anyway. When Ericson showed no reaction, he hoped that meant he didn't know his name or his family's.

"Would you take supper with us, Mr. Ericson," Willy asked with that smile that melted most men.

"Shore would appreciate that, ma'am."

Cole realized he was still holding his gun and slid it back in his holster before he finished getting dressed but belted it back on before heading to the house. "I'll put your horse in the corral while you eat, if you want," Cole said.

"That's be right kind of you. It so happens I have bottle of brandy in the sack. You want a nip?" When Cole nodded, Ericson got the bottle out of the sack. He followed Cole to the corral where Cole helped him with the saddle. The old man looked like he'd seen a tough time or two.

"You smoke, son?" Ericson asked when they reached the porch.

"I do but not inside."

"Got a spare cigarette? I ain't got the money to buy them but sure would appreciate one."

Cole shook his head but sat on the porch bench. He pulled out cigarettes and also lit the old man's, taking a long draw as he studied the stranger. Before he could make up his mind what he thought about him, Zinnia came out.

"I wondered where she got to. Glad she didn't get ate by a bear," Ericson said as he reached down and petted the dog, who had come over to him.

"She's your dog?" Cole asked thinking this was not going to make Willy very happy.

"Nah, but she was with me a week and then went on. I figured her for a drifter but guess she settled here."

Willy came out and saw the brandy bottle. She returned with a tray and three glasses. "I wouldn't mind a little brandy too, if you have enough, Mr. Ericson."

"Make that Lars." He handed her the bottle.

"Then you must call me Willy." She poured a little in each glass.

He gave her a questioning smile but nodded. He lifted his glass. "To good neighbors." They each took a sip. "I live out a long way mostly not to see folks but then got curious about who bought this place."

"I am just leasing it, Lars," she said sipping again of the rich burgundy liquor.

"Wal, whatever the case. Glad the dog found a home here that she likes."

"Zinnia's roaming days are probably done," Cole said. "She's got pups."

"You don't say." The old man slapped his knee with the hand that held his cigarette. "Ain't that the thing? What'd she have?"

"Two, both females," Cole said.

"You never told me that," Willy said.

"Didn't figure you cared."

"Wal, good for her."

"Their eyes aren't open yet," Willy offered. "I am looking forward to when they get more mobile, although that will present its own problems, I guess."

"It shore will. They'll end up bear bait for sure."

"I think we can prevent that for a while anyway," Cole said when he saw the distress on Willy's face. His time of being able to protect her would be limited. This was one small thing he could do by creating a pen to keep playful puppies from getting in trouble. The rest would be harder.

CHAPTER 12

Half an hour later, the three had consumed the black bean soup and cornbread that Willy had prepared for dinner. "Sorry it's not fancier," she said as she cleared the dishes.

"Best cooking, I ate in weeks. Most likely months. Thank you."

When the men retreated to the porch, Cole brought out his whiskey bottle. He and Ericson had a snort and then the man mooched another cigarette off him. He'd have to remember to buy more his next trip to Payson, or he'd have to break the habit the hard way.

Smoking, he thought of the worn uniform. "You were in the army then?"

Ericson nodded. "Right up until the Washita. Damn never seen anything like that. That bastard Custer."

"Black Kettle and his people?" Cole did remember the story.

"I was with the 7th when we hit that Cheyenne camp. Battle, hah!" He snorted. "It was a massacre and worse than that were all the horses got killed to keep the Cheyenne from being able to fight back or follow other than on foot. I felt ashamed of being in the cavalry, the first time ever."

"That was 1868, wasn't it?"

"Surprised you knew that. Yep, November 27, 1868, snow on the ground, cold and them Injuns peaceful, no clue what was comin' down on them, women, children, running, and no escape. I figured if a man can't find a better way to earn a living, he might as well die."

"I was born in '67, but my family talked about what happened there on the Washita. No two people told the same story though. Guess now I know why."

Ericson nodded. "That's why. Plumb ashamed. After my enlistment was up, I drifted, did some mining, worked in saloons, ranches, whatever brought in a little change."

Cole realized that Willy had come out and sat on the porch step. "Fortunate you didn't stay with Custer," she said, "given what happened on the Little Big Horn."

Ericson snorted. "He got what he deserved, that's all I got to say on it."

"You want to sleep here tonight?" she asked. The sun was starting to go down, and it would make sense, but it also would mean he'd not be able to sleep with Willy. He wondered if she was changing her mind about them. Or was she just polite."

"I'd like that," Ericson said. "Be better than breaking his and my leg heading out with dark. I can sleep down by the corral by Hank."

"No need for that," Willy said. "The sofa is comfortable or on the rug by the fireplace."

"I'd worry about Hank but appreciate the offer. Been a cougar nosing around my place. You seen him here?"

"Just tracks," Cole said finishing the last of his cigarette.

"They're pretty smart, ya know."

"I do." Cole considered lighting another cigarette, but if he did, he'd have Ericson bumming another. He smiled at his own parsimony but did without to save what he had for another day. He looked up at Willy, who he imagined was wrestling with her need for being proper in the eyes of others. "We'll see you in the morning," he said, with a smile, as though this was routine for him also to go down to the corrals at night. His bedroll was still down there.

She nodded and went into the house closing the door to keep Zinnia with her.

"She's a right nice lady," Ericson said as they walked down to the corrals. "Unlikely sort to be out in a place like this."

"Not the trapper kind, huh?" Cole asked with a grin as he spread out his blanket and pulled off his boots.

"She running from something? I'd help a lady like her if I knew she needed it."

Cole gave up on cigarette saving and offered another to Ericson. They lay in their blankets staring up at the starry sky. "Nice of you to want to help her," Cole said letting the smoke out.

"Don't see many ladies in my life."

"Where do you come from?"

"Wisconsin first and drifted a lot like your little dog."

"Were you in the Civil War?"

"In the cavalry then, but on the Plains trying to hold the ground we were losing to the Injuns. Them was the years they figured they'd won. Then Custer and his ilk come back and showed 'em otherwise."

"You really didn't like him." It wasn't a question.

"Not much. Cocky son of a bitch. I don't like men put themselves above others."

"Some thought highly of him."

"I reckon. Likely didn't serve under him." He snorted.

"He had a hard road too after the war, trying to find a place where he mattered. Civil War was that way for a lot of career soldiers."

"I suppose..." Ericson hesitated and levered himself on one elbow. "I keep thinking I know you except I can't figure out from where."

"Maybe you knew my father." Frankly, he hoped not, but it was possible. "Jeremiah Taggert."

Ericson shook his head. "Nah. I'll figure it out. I always do. You look like a tough bastard" He grinned and lay back down.

"Not a bastard and not that tough." Cole wasn't about to help him.

The old man chortled. "See if I'd said that to Custer, not that he'd have talked to a lowly enlisted man, but if I had, he'd have said he was."

"He was in a job where he had to convince people of that. Sometimes convincing someone you are tough can make the difference between a fight or not."

"You know something about fights?" It was another probing question.

"Something."

"I noticed you had a fresh scar on your chest."

"True."

"A Taggert killed a man in Payson. Would that be you?"

"It was."

"They said self-defense. Was it?"

"Would I tell you if it wasn't?" He was beginning to feel annoyed and more wondered why the old man kept asking questions.

"Testy too.'

"At times."

The old man laughed then. "I'll figure it out, why I know you from before."

"You do that."

In a few minutes, Cole heard him snoring. It took Cole longer. He thought about Ericson's disdain for Custer. Most likely, he didn't understand why some men need a reputation. Reps could be bad and good. Custer's might've cost him his life-- his need to hold onto it. He'd seen that happen to men who had a name with a gun and were forgetting that world was over. He looked up at what he figured was the constellation

Orion, the warrior in the sky. Maybe that world for him would never be over. Live a warrior and die one.

In the morning, Willy fixed a big breakfast and waved Lars off with half a loaf of her sourdough bread. "He seemed nice, didn't he?" she said to Cole who, with his usual enigmatic expression, was sipping his third cup of coffee.

"Okay, I guess."

"You don't take much to people, do you?"

He smiled at that. "Not right away."

"When are we going to see the natural bridge?"

"You want to do it today?"

"I was thinking today maybe would be another practice ride… maybe even of you on me." She smiled broadly, as he swept her off her feet and into the bedroom.

Hours later, she began to think that maybe they should get something to eat. She heard Zinnia come in and out enough times to indicate she needed to go out. "I should get up," she said finally moving to the edge of the bed and looking around for where her clothing had been strewn. In the beginning, she had felt uneasy being seen naked by Cole but that was gone. Now she liked knowing his gaze was on her body, and the glow in his eyes showed he appreciated what he saw.

"You know my condoms will be gone soon," he observed with his hands under his head watching her as she pulled on clothing.

"Did you buy them in Payson?"

He shook his head. "My brother gave them to me. Said I might need them." He laughed. "I told him not a chance."

"Well, would Payson have them?"

"Maybe. What kind of cycle do you have?"

"You mean, am I regular? Unfortunately, not so much. I've only had one period since I left San Francisco, but that was not long before we… er you know."

He smiled. "You aren't still shy about saying we are making love, are you?"

"Maybe a little."

He sat up and reached for his jeans. "A lady of words, and she can't use them for herself?"

"It does tend to be that way sometimes, you know."

"I never thought to ask… are you shy?"

"You're the detective," she said working to get her hair back up in a tidy bun. "You tell me."

"The evidence would be you are. Only a reserved person would want to live this far from other people. There are reasons people though can be reserved, for instance fear. But you don't strike me as fearful, not with going East to school, putting out those books."

"The books don't require much from me beyond writing them. Because my editor agreed that it was best Will stayed a man, there could be no book signings or lectures."

"Would there have been otherwise?"

"You mean do dime novels have enough prestige to be considered important?"

"Possibly." He grinned and began buttoning his shirt.

"They make money and whatever makes money has importance of a sort anyway. I didn't want to do that though; so woman or man, it wasn't happening."

"Yet you can get up and lecture in front of a class. That makes you a bit of a paradox."

"No more than you to be a man who speaks of an eighth grade education and knows a word like paradox."

He smirked. "Dictionaries can be used by anyone."

She sighed. "I think that was a putdown."

He held his index and thumb a small distance apart. "A tiny one."

"So, we aren't either all it might seem," she said as he also dressed and they went into the main room. When he opened the door for Zinnia, he grabbed his rifle and went out with her.

"You didn't do that before."

"I hadn't worried about a cougar coming up and grabbing her before," he said with a smile as he stepped off the porch to stay with the little dog as she explored different scents.

"Lars did say that."

"He did. I suspect Zinnia is woods smart but still we don't want to figure out how to raise two puppies without her, do we?"

She giggled. "So it's all practical concerns."

"Could be."

After taking care of her needs, Zinnia was willing to be ushered back inside.

"We spent too much of our day... er riding," she said as she tried to figure out what they would have for supper.

"I am sure I can think of something." His smile was sensual and made her forget they'd spent the morning doing just that. But then, this was so new to her. "And then, tomorrow, we go north."

"I worry about that."

"Don't. You will be fine and Boots is fine. Wait until you see the bridge."

"All right." She smiled. "How long will it take us to get there and back?" She was hoping it would not mean a night out as how would that work for Zinnia?

"We'll take gear to spend a night if required, but I don't look for that." He smiled at her worried expression. "Listen here, writer lady, you are one to anticipate all that could go wrong. Why don't you leave that up to me this time?"

She smiled then. He was right. He was as used to thinking up problems as she was. This time, she'd just go along for the ride.

Cole prepared a small set of temporary saddlebags from the feed sacks. In addition, they would carry extra water and a blanket roll each, along with biscuits and dried meat for breaks. He had some concern about 20 miles on the horse when she had only been out an hour or two, but the trip to the ruins had gone well. She was tougher than she looked.

Early, right after first light, they left the house and headed due north downstream to the East Fork of the Verde River, crossing at the old Indian ford. The water was low, but gurgled around the boulders in the streambed. Debris from a recent flashflood was caught in the willow brush along the bank. It would not do to cross with storms in the area, but today the sky was clear.

Moving diagonally east up the slope away from the mine road, a short cut took them to General Crooks trail. Near the top of the ridge there was an overhang with a small rock and mud dwelling built into the cliff, partially hidden behind a sycamore, close to water and yet defensible. He pointed it out to her and they stopped to study it.

"I wonder what they had been protecting," she said.

"No idea. Maybe, a mineral outcropping of magical powers, or the burials of venerable leaders—which sometimes ended up having the same meaning." He nudged Boomer forward and Boots followed at a steady gait, not trying to pass the other horse. These two were operating like old buddies.

At the top the old wagon trail made it easy to travel northwest across the high plateau at a fast pace. Although he had assured her that there'd be no problems, he'd had his own concerns. These roads changed with every season. She was doing well in handling her horse and found all the plants fascinating as the vegetation gave way to mostly taller pines, cypress and madrone.

At the narrowing of the plateau, Cole stopped and encouraged a break for water and a biscuit. When they left the road, he headed west down a fainter wagon road which led to the rim of a vast expanse. From there, the trail dropped precipitously diagonally toward an apparent wall. They dismounted and started walking their horse down the slope with Cole in front encouraging her to focus on him and not scream if a few rocks slid on the trail. He knew Boomer was stable, but he had less familiarity with how calm Boots would be. By leading and talking as they went, he figured it would work fine.

He saw the sign of others having passed, horse tracks as well as deer and what looked like a bear track. From the first time he'd come this way, someone had dug into the cliff to make it safe enough for even the narrow wagon tracks he saw. Ahead lay a lush green valley. He stopped their horses and again let them drink from a small stream, while they sipped from canteens.

"Last time I was this way, I came in from the north and didn't see that someone has been rebuilding the cabins."

"Did you come to view the bridge?"

He shook his head, in no mood to relive the hunt that had brought him to this place. He'd been in Phoenix on another job and called up to help track two men who had killed five people in Pine during a botched bank robbery. He hoped she'd let it go as he pointed to the orchards. "This is a real homestead now."

"Do you know the people who live here?"

He shook his head. "No smoke from the chimney. Maybe if we are lucky, they are gone."

"That's an unfriendly thing to say."

"Not everybody likes strangers passing by." He smiled at her disbelief. For an educated woman, who had written all those westerns, sometimes she seemed unbelievably naive.

He pointed to the narrow canals. "Look how they diverted the water from Pine Creek. It's why they can get their garden and those fruit trees to survive the occasional dry seasons." In this country, water was the difference between survival and death.

He helped her onto her horse and swung up onto his own. They rode past horses grazing in a log-fenced pasture. A few hundred feet beyond, the trail took a drop where the canyon walls narrowed and the creek disappeared from view. The view was striking with the dry hills of scrub pine and cypress beyond, lush green to pale greenish yellow and occasional bright red of the sumac in fall. It was a world removed from the desert below and the rim above-- a mini-paradise. It though took a unique brand of human to want to put up with the difficulties in living so far from others with a land that could make any mistake a final one.

At the base of the trail, Cole saw man and a half-grown youth approaching, both wearing holsters and carrying shovels. "How do you do," the man said as they stopped. "My name is David Goodfellow, owner of this property, well along with my uncle." He spoke with a heavy Scottish brogue.

"Glad to meet you," Willy said with an answering smile. "I am Wilhelmina Butler." Cole didn't volunteer his own.

"It's bit late in the year for visitors," Goodfellow said not seeming to mind the omission. "The cabins are not ready. If you wanted to stay the night, it will take some doing, but we will welcome you."

Cole glanced at Willy, who gave him a smile, which he understood meant—see, people can be friendly.

"We just wanted to see the bridge. We have to be home before dark," Cole said, still not offering his name.

"Well, enjoy yourselves and don't break a leg by going into the tunnel under the arch. That is really slick under there, and I had to pull the guide rope so that I wouldn't lose it in the freshen. The main pool is 20 feet deep, and you have swim to get past it. If you slide off the ledge below, the buzzards will pick you up a mile downstream." He looked at Willy and then back at Cole with a questioning look. "You look familiar. Do I know you?"

"Don't think so." God, Cole hoped not. He waved and led the way for Willy to follow him. The trail along the creek had little side loops to the water under the overhanging rock shelves with water dripping from the moss. Wild grapes and vines made a strong contrast to the dry red and brown a few hundred feet away. The bridge itself was not visible until they came to the edge of a wide spot in the lower canyon. The creek disappeared into what appeared to be a cave, except the water flowed through. At times it had room for a river to rage past with the freshen.

"This is beautiful, almost mystical feeling," she said as he helped her from her horse. "The top looks like marble. You said travertine, didn't you?"

"It's what I was told. It does dwarf a man. The travertine is interspersed with Coconino sandstone. My guess is that big marble slab resisted the water and freezing better than the sandstone, which led to what you see today, a nature made masterpiece.

"It is amazing. I've heard of natural bridges, but this is the first I've seen."

"The Indians in this region called it the garden spot of the gods. They considered it sacred. Warm in the canyon, sheltered from the winds and cold of the high rim."

They took a break along the banks, near the waterfall and ate the bread and meat that she had packed. Sitting in the sun, it would have been tempting to tease her into making love again except Cole wasn't that certain the man or his son would not be back. He settled for long kisses and a promise of more when they got back to the cabin.

Reluctantly, they mounted and rode up the trail past the cabin again. Cole saw there were several smaller cabins set back in the pines. The man stopped them, handing Cole a small sack of apples.

"Be sure you tell people that we'll be taking visitors soon enough," he said again looking at Willy. "Reasonable charge with a hearty breakfast and supper."

"Is this going to be a hotel?" Willy asked.

"It will if we can make enough money starting small. Wish you could have met my wife. She went into Pine with my uncle, picking up more supplies.

"Pine growing?" Cole asked.

"You been there?"

"A while back."

"It 'tis up and down. You know how it is with villages. It doesn't take much to crush them. Pine has those though who will stick with it. Nice little general store there now."

"Good."

He turned his gaze back on Willy. "Whether we make it out here though, that will depend on word of mouth. Hope you folks will tell others about our cabins. One of these days, we'll build a hotel here. The bridge should be seen by lots of people."

"We will certainly spread the word where we can," she said.

"I appreciate that. We want to stay here, make it available to all, but it will take visitors." The man grinned and waved them on their way.

Five hours later, beginning to feel the soreness that she knew the following day would make more apparent, Willy was happy to see their cabin. She headed inside to let Zinnia out while Cole took care of the horses. She realized she had thought of it as theirs, and yet it never would be. Someone else would buy it before she ever earned enough money to own her own paradise.

When Cole came in, she had used the leftovers to make something the cookbook called Cottage Pie. In a baking dish, she had layered mashed potatoes, roast beef cut in small pieces followed by a final layer of mashed potatoes.

"Tomorrow, I'll go to town," Cole said as they ate.

"I could go with you."

"You could but are you up to it?"

She smiled. "Probably not. If you go, will you get in a fight?"

He chuckled. "More likely if you were with me than without you."

"Why is that?"

"Beautiful women often lead to fights."

He had said that before and she liked hearing it even though she didn't think of herself as that attractive. Still, she'd take the compliment and smile. "Why do you need to go?" she asked as they finished eating, and she cleared the table.

"I want to get us a tarp, some oilcloth for when we head south. Also nails, leather, and cord to make a kind of crib for the pups. I'll use that to make a traveling basket for the dogs when we travel south. From the looks of it, tomorrow you may see their eyes open and from then on, they'll be a handful for their mama and then you. Make me a grocery list of what you need. As things are going, we'll need more condoms. Hopefully Payson will have them."

"It is a pretty small town." She sat back across from him. She loved watching his face when he talked. He was expressive, that slightly sardonic smile appeared less and less. His eyes were thoughtful and always attentive to her when she talked. She liked feeling important, the way he made her feel.

"In which case, I'll have Vince mail me more. That will take a while though which means we'll have to show some restraint." He smiled as he reached across and stroked her hand.

"At one time, I'd never believed that could be difficult." She took his hand in hers and turned it over to look at the palm. The lines were long and strongly defined. She tried to remember what each one meant, from the time she and her friends at college had visited the fortuneteller. None of them had believed a word the woman had said, but she had explained the lines. "You have a long life line," she said running her finger along it where it curved around his thumb.

"You believe in that stuff?" he asked.

"You don't?"

"No. I admit though some do see more than we do."

"You've known some like that?"

"There is a woman in Tucson, Connie Sicilla. I think she does. My brother Jesse, he does too, but he never says much."

"You don't?"

He shook his head. "I am satisfied with the here and now." He stood and pulled her to him. "Especially the now." He sat back with her on his lap. She ran her fingers through his hair.

"We have one left, right?"

"We do. I want you to think seriously though about the question I asked you earlier. Marry me."

"You didn't want to be married. You'd be sorry that you got yourself carried away with it on a whim."

He chuckled. "You are no whim, Willy. You are the real deal, and I know we can't work out a life together for a dozen reasons, but marriage, doesn't require that."

"So why do it?"

"Protection for you."

She smiled at that and began unbuttoning his shirt. "I don't need protecting. Just a mystery solved, and you have put enough together that I think we can get the law at least interested in looking for more."

"You forgot about your home being burned?"

"I wasn't in it." She moved her fingers down his bare chest.

"You think it would have stopped that sort if you had been?" He took a breath as she pushed his shirt off his shoulders.

"It wouldn't?" Her own breath was coming more unevenly. She did love his body, never imagined a man's body could seem so beautiful. It was certainly not all she loved about him. The word love came so easily to her now but only in her thoughts. She did love him but love never was enough—not in the end. Then he began to touch her and she forgot the rest of what she was thinking.

When Cole rode off to town the next morning, Willy decided to take advantage of time alone, well alone except for a dog and two puppies, who had begun making whimpering sounds whenever their mother left. Zinnia was taking breaks to check out the food supply, drink water, and maybe just get a rest from puppy needs.

At the typewriter, Willy wrote the description of their ride to the natural bridge. It had been a magical day-- possibly another piece of a puzzle where nothing went together for the book she hoped to write. Still, she kept with it describing her increasing ease of being on horseback. Even going down a few steep slopes, well, steep by her definition, she had leaned back in the saddle, had her legs out in front, and she hadn't worried she'd slide off.

It had been interesting meeting the family, who lived above the natural bridge. They had seemed friendly. She hoped their business would flourish. It was a long ways for people to come, but the bridge was unique and the scenery around it relaxing, a place to recreate one's self.

Like anything though, it needed to have people know about it. She recalled the magazine *Cosmopolitan* had been purchased by William Randolph Hearst. His reputation was one of creating new things, increasing their value. Maybe writing pieces for magazines could be a new direction for her as well. Her position as a professor might give her enough credibility to get her work at least looked at. She considered more carefully words that might get her a sale as well as help the Goodfellows find more visitors.

When she heard the sound of a horse coming down the road, she knew it was too soon to be Cole unless he had forgotten for something. She pulled her paper from the typewriter, picked up her rifle, and went to the door, Zinnia right at her heels.

When she saw it was Lars Ericson, she put her rifle down. He dismounted by the porch. "Is your man around?" he asked.

"He went to town. May I help you?"

He looked concerned. "Missy, do you know who that man is who you're here with?"

"Cole?"

"Yep, him."

"I think so."

"You know he killed a man in Payson."

"I do and was shot in the back before he did."

"Didn't know that part. Wal, there's somethin' more. There's been books been writ about that one. He's a gunman, an outlaw. Killed a lot of men."

"Mr. Ericson. Those books were not about Cole."

"They shore were. The last Taggert. I ain't read them all, but *Taggert's War*, that one had him killing fifteen men."

"In fair fights."

He looked at her with a monetary look of surprise that she knew the story. He quickly recovered. "Ain't no fight fair with a man like that one. He just makes it look like it is. The last one I read, can't remember the name, 'cause I borrowed it from the store, had to return it, but he was sent to Yuma. He must've busted out being here now."

"I know you mean well but… Cole isn't that man." She hated having to tell another person of her own infamy, but it appeared she had no choice if she didn't want Lars waiting to bushwhack Cole. "I know because I wrote the books."

He snorted his disbelief. "You love that man, missy. That much is plain as the nose on my face. I see you wantin' to protect him, but you didn't write them books. Will Tremaine wrote 'em."

"My full name is Wilhelmina Agatha Tremaine Butler. I did write the books and many others. The seventeenth Taggert was my last."

He sunk onto the porch step. "You don't..." It was a few moments before he said, "How'd you know all that stuff you wrote? He tell you?"

"Mr. Taggert came here at the request of a good friend of mine. She was concerned for me being up here alone." She saw no reason to fill him in on the other reasons for Holly's concerns. "Mr. Taggert hasn't even been here a month. He has only been a help to me since he arrived."

"I'll be jiggered... You really mean you wrote 'em all?"

"I do. I swear it" She crossed her heart with her index finger.

He looked away then back at her. "You got any extra copies around here. I liked the ones I read. Danged good stories is what they were."

She managed a smile. "I only brought one book with me."

When he looked encouraged, she laughed. "The 1896 Boston Cooking-School Cook Book."

He looked surprised for a moment and then grinned. "Wal, can't say I'd complain about that."

"Would you like to stay for a meal?"

"Your man be bothered if I show up here again, him not here?"

"He's not the jealous sort." She hoped. "And he's not really my man. He's my friend." She didn't know why she'd said that. She wasn't as modern a woman as she wanted to think if she had to hide what she felt for Cole. She'd think about that someday as to why she would be reluctant to admit who she really was.

"Good man then... even if he's got an outlaw name."

After he put his horse in the corral, Lars sat to play with the puppies, who now had their eyes open and were crawling with mixed success. The larger of the two was catching on faster but that seemed to spur the smaller to try harder. The whole operation was fretting Zinnia, who relaxed considerably when Lars kept them corralled.

Willy got the oven stoked to the right temperature, as she mixed up a batch of biscuits. While they were cooking, she decided it would be a shame to waste the heat and began sorting through the cookbook until she found a recipe that would use the apples they'd been given. She didn't feel up to making a pie but the recipe for apple fritters looked simple enough. When the biscuits came out, the fritters went in. Twenty minutes later, she felt proud of the results. She had cooked very little in her life, as someone else was always around, who enjoyed it. She hadn't realized until she got to the cabin that she also enjoyed it—once she had some simple instructions.

"That sure does smell good, missy," Lars said at the door.

"Well, wash your hands and I'll heat up some coffee. We can see how they are."

As they sat at the table eating, with Lars complimenting her lavishly,

Zinnia came to the door. This time, two puppies trailed her. While they were still unsteady on their feet, they managed enough mobility to keep their mother in sight.

"They'll be a handful soon," Lars said as he sipped his coffee.

"It was one reason Cole went into town. He planned to create a kind of pen for when we weren't watching them."

"Good idea. He handy with his hands with other than a gun that is?" he cackled. Willy blushed thinking of how many ways he was good with his hands. When she looked up and met Lars' eyes, he laughed harder. "Don't bother telling me," he said, "I got it."

"Have you ever been married, Lars?" she asked refilling their coffee cups.

"Nope. I left for the cavalry when I was a sprout. That's not much of a life for a woman, not when he's an enlisted man. Most places I was stationed, the only women around were… well, not the sort a man would marry."

"What about after you left the military?"

"No money. I didn't live much of any place long. When I found out my ma died, I went back there and was surprised the folks had left a small inheritance for my sister and me. I used mine to buy a piece of land and build my cabin up here. I like being alone now, not like I'd want a woman around telling me what to do."

"Maybe she'd be a friend." She wasn't sure why she was asking him about marriage. Maybe it came down to her own reluctance to say yes to Cole's proposal. At twenty-nine, she had not expected ever to marry and then along came a man out of her fantasy world. She should have jumped at the chance, especially since he was more than she'd ever imagined of her fictional hero. Maybe she was afraid that tying him down would change everything in a negative way. He said he'd understand them not living together but would he over the years? She certainly could not imagine him living in a big city.

"You arguing me into it or yourself?" Lars asked with another chuckle.

She laughed with him. "I guess both."

Lars took a deck of cards out of his pocket. "There is one thing I miss about living alone. Only can play solitaire."

"I never learned it."

"You know any card games, the kind two can play?"

"Well, I did play some poker in college."

"How about a game?" He looked more excited than he ever had.

"Sure, I could do that. Play for matches?" She had a box of them on shelf by the stove.

"Works for me or a penny a hand?" He gave her a sly look.

157

"Let's make the matchsticks worth say five to a penny, keeping this friendly but also worth playing."

"Want me to deal first?" Lars asked as he began shuffling what looked like a well-used deck. She realized he could easily have marked the deck, but if he had, it wouldn't take her long to figure the marks.

"I'll cut," she said with a smile that mimicked his own.

CHAPTER 13

W hen Cole rode into the cabin yard, he felt some concern to see Ericson's horse back in the corral. He didn't particularly see the man as dangerous. The question was what had brought him back. Willy came to the corrals to watch while he unsaddled and put Boomer in the corral. The other two horses greeted him like an old friend. He untied the food sack from the saddle, as well as the length of cord, and then turned to her. Lars was right behind her.

"I'll tell ya, son. I come here to warn her about you." He chuckled. "Should've been warning you about her. You know she's a card shark?"

Cole looked back at her. "You are?"

"He exaggerates," she said with a little grin.

"My foot," Ericson said. "We played for matchsticks. Five to a penny. I am down two bits." He gave her an accusing look.

"Stud or five card draw?" Cole found it amusing, and at least now, he'd be forewarned, that she not only could play, but play well.

"Five card," Lars said shaking his head. "Never seen a woman so good at counting cards. Must be all that college."

"Of course, I had one other advantage," she admitted with a sly smile.

Lars gave her a look. "You figured that out did you?"

"I did which is why I won't take your twenty-five cents."

"What exactly did you figure out?" Cole asked as they walked up to the cabin. He would unload the sack himself since it had a few personal items he preferred Ericson not see.

"He marked his deck."

More than her even winning the games, Cole found that amazing. "You knew about marked decks."

"I did. College students do it too, you know."

Ericson shook his head. "Danged, educated women. Hope you know what you're in for, boy."

"I doubt it."

In the cabin, he saw the pups following their mother around and Zinnia with a more bedraggled look as she had to deal with their mobility. "I see they are on the move," he said.

"What are you going to call 'em?" Ericson asked.

"We hadn't gotten that far," Willy said. "I made an apple fritter, Cole. Would you like a piece with some coffee?"

He nodded. "Let me unload the sack. You had the clerk running around trying to find ginger but she finally did."

"Wonderful as I have plans for gingerbread cookies next."

After complimenting Willy on the dessert, Cole turned back to Ericson. "What had you come up here to warn her about me?"

"About you being that man in the books, an outlaw and supposed to be in prison." He cackled. "Back then, seems like a long time ago, I was plumb surprised she wrote 'em, and that they ain't you. Now though, after the way she snookered me at cards, I ain't so surprised." He laughed more loudly.

"She can surprise a man. I'll agree with you on that." She'd done it to him more than once.

"I should get back to my cabin," Ericson said clearly reluctantly.

"Stay for dinner," Willy said.

"Nah, but I'll be back in a few days just to check how the gingerbread cookies come out."

When he went outside, Cole followed him down to the corral, and helped him saddle his horse. "You're welcome to stay if you want."

"Nah, young folks need to be together. You two planning to winter up here?"

"No. Willy has to teach spring term at her college. We'll spend Christmas though with my family in Tucson. At least that's my hope. Since her best friend, Holly, is my brother's wife, I think she'll want to spend the holidays there before she takes the train back to Frisco."

"You leaving the dog here?" His expression was inquisitive.

"You are joking. I'd be leaving her here if I did." He shook his head with a laugh.

"How you taking them three?"

"I've got a plan."

Ericson considered that a moment. "Tucson, eh. My sister lives there. I ain't seen her in too many years. She wrote me two years ago. I should've wrote back, but I didn't."

"She have a family?" Cole asked knowing this conversation was definitely not going where he'd want.

"Two boys, reckon they aren't boys anymore. Laura married young but lost him five years back. She works in a café or that's what she said. I am a poor excuse for a brother." Personal experience told Cole there was poorer possible, but he said nothing. When Ericson didn't mount, Cole wasn't surprised at what came next. "When you folks head south, any chance I could ride along? I admit I am not eager at my age to go by myself and can't afford the stage fare."

There was no way to say no. "It won't be for a month if the lady sticks with her original plan."

"Before first snow?"

"Or right at it?"

"I'd appreciate it if you'd consider it."

"The road's free. If you want to come when we go, no problem. Willy has figured the first full moon in December but I got a feeling, if the weather turns cold, the first snowfall will change her mind."

"Mind if I come by now and again? I'll make plenty of noise," Ericson said with another of those smiles.

"That's fine. Why don't you draw me a map to your cabin? If plans change, I'll ride over and let you know."

Ericson's face changed from one of surprise to warmth. "I appreciate that, son. Reckon you are a good man, like she said." With that, he mounted and rode off.

Tucson Arizona—September 29

"You figuring on heading back to Frisco soon," Jeremiah asked Nate.

It was the question Nate had asked himself as soon as they'd ridden into Tucson. "Not right away," he said but wasn't sure why.

"You're welcome to bunk with me while you're here. It's not that fancy for a jasper like you, used to mansions, but it's clean. I got a spare room since a friend moved out."

"That is generous of you." He considered that. He'd actually gotten to liking the old outlaw in the process of the many miles they'd ridden together. "I would like that for a time at least."

"You got any gear stowed other than what was in your saddlebags?"

"It's at the hotel. I can get it and meet you... Where is your home?"

"Walking distance from the hotel, but I'll tag along with you. It won't hurt to look around town some."

"To be sure Hamilton is gone?"

"Would you recognize his crew?"

"Some of them, not by name but if I had seen them with Hamilton, I'd know their faces. Say, before I head to the hotel for my things, where can I get some of those cigars you've been sharing with me?"

Jeremiah chuckled. "Got you hooked have I?"

"I never really took to cigarettes, but a cigar is different somehow."

Jeremiah's grin widened. "'You got that right. Let's head over to Sicillas. Del knows his tobacco and stocks the best. Reckon you can afford the best."

"And repay you all the ones I smoked around a campfire."

"You don't have to do that. Of course, if you want to." He chuckled. "I'm not a man to turn down a cigar."

"Especially the finest. Tell you what, I'll treat you to lunch first. Anywhere good to eat here?"

"Wal, not like eating at the Palace Hotel." Nate glanced over at him and again saw the sly smile.

"You eat there often?" he asked as they stepped up onto the boardwalk in front of the small café.

"Once. Not really my place, but it suited my sense of humor. There I was at a table, with all that fine china and crystal, flowers on every table, eating with opera stars and city big wigs. Them not knowing that the man who was wearing a good suit robbed a bank earlier that month."

"I don't suppose you brag about that often," Nate said as a waitress seated them. She managed a smile, which appeared practiced more than sincere. Salt and pepper hair was pulled into a tight bun. She looked thin, a bit past her middle years, and he felt a strange sort of sympathy for her. A woman her age wouldn't choose to be a waitress, unless she needed the money.

"My name is Laura, and I will be your waitress today," she said as she handed them single sheet menus. "Our special is chicken fried steak with mashed potatoes and gravy."

Nate glanced down the items listed. "I don't see any salads."

She gave him a look. "We don't get much call for salads. What kind would you want?"

"By that expression on your face, I am guessing my options are limited. Think you can rustle me up something?" He grinned not only as a way to be friendly but amused at the western lingo he'd picked up after less than two weeks with Jeremiah. He'd be barely understood when he returned to Frisco.

"I guess I can make one. Lettuce, tomato, whatever fresh vegetables are back there," she suggested, writing a note on her pad. "What dressing?"

"Are there options?" He smiled again but wasn't getting one in return. He regretted making more work for her, but it was too late to back out now.

"Not many. Oil, vinegar come to mind."

"Perfect, just bring them to the table, and I'll mix my own. Oh and half a ham sandwich, just butter on it besides the ham, of course." Again, she didn't smile.

"I'll take your special," Jeremiah said. "Go light on the gravy though." When he grinned, she responded with brightening eyes. Maybe they knew each other apart from the café. Jeremiah was still a vital, handsome man. He supposed a woman Laura's age would be aware of that. But would he see past the worn down visage to the younger woman she had been? Jeremiah was his usual charmer but not in a way that indicated interest in Laura beyond their food.

When Nate realized what he'd been doing, he shook his head. Maybe he should have been the writer—but a romance writer. "Coffee, black," he said. Jeremiah held up two fingers. She nodded, went off with their order, quickly returning with the coffee pot to fill both their cups.

The café held five booths, three tables, and had a counter for some to eat. It was half-filled, even though it was past the usual lunch hour.

"Keep your eyes out for anyone you'd recognize," Jeremiah said. "We need to know if he cleared out his bunch or left some behind as lookouts."

"You think the latter, don't you?"

"I'd put chips on it. They know you stopped here. They likely believe she sent for you or you were following her. Hamilton most likely went home to keep things the way he wants there. He wouldn't go though, without leaving someone here for when she shows up. By now, he knows she had a friend in Holly."

"How would he know that?"

"It's not hard to find someone's trail when they ain't looking to hide it. Holly and Lily went to school together, talked of their friendship. Then you came to Tucson where she lives."

"Holly wouldn't be in danger?"

"Not unless the man's a fool." He chuckled. "No, he'll just have them here to wait for Willy to show up, and men like that don't mind being paid to do nothing and get drunk."

"What can we do about it?"

"If you recognize any of them, we'll warn Cole by wire, so he doesn't walk into this blind—not that he likely would anyway." He smirked. "Actually, I'll do it in case they are tracing you."

"You think Hamilton has that kind of power?"

"I don't know enough about him right now to be sure either way." Jeremiah smiled at the waitress, as she came with a loaded tray. Deftly sliding the correct plates before each of them, she returned with more coffee and disappeared again.

The sandwich looked fine. The lettuce was a little brown around the edges but was edible, and he ate hungrily, as did Jeremiah. He wished he understood more of the sort of man he was dealing with in Hamilton. He thought of his impressions in San Francisco. Until the fire, he hadn't seen him as physically dangerous. Could he be dangerous to his mother? He'd been suspicious of her involvement with Hamilton, and then the possible fraudulent activities, but now his concern shifted to one for her physical safety. Still, the one at most risk would be Willy. He needed to learn more about Hamilton and how much power he really had.

Half an hour later, they entered Sicillas and were greeted by Del. "You look a little more worn in than the last time I saw you," Del said to Nate as the three men shook hands.

"I can believe that." He'd had a big disappointment with learning Willy would never really be his more than as a friend. Going north, he supposed that he'd hoped to be a Galahad. Turned out someone had beat him to it.

Del chuckled, maybe at the expression on his face. "Once upon a time I had a wandering itch. Too old for it now." He turned to Jeremiah. "You seem still up to it though."

"Only when there's a reason. Otherwise, I'd just as soon set in my big old stuffed chair and read a good book. Got anything new?"

"None by Tremaine that you hadn't already read, but there is this new author you might like." Del held up a dime novel with a flashy looking gambler on the cover. The man held a revolver pointed right at the reader, behind him was a roulette wheel and a table with several poker hands spread on it. Nate had never seen a book like it and realized there was a whole world out there that he knew little about. Would such books fill him in? How the hell did Willy learn about that world if she hadn't gotten her information from Cole?

"Looks like a tinhorn, but might do," Jeremiah mused looking through it. "My friend here needs a few cigars. What have you got?"

Del smiled and led them to a glass display case. "Just got in a new shipment. I'm not a smoker of cigars, but the rich fragrance from some of these could even tempt me to give them a try. What's your preference?"

"Give him a sampler with some of them really good ones." Jeremiah suggested.

Del looked at Nate, "How much you up to?"

"No limit." Nate smiled broadly.

"Well, from Old Havana, we got Fuentas, Larangas, La Coronas and a special Henry Clay-- Sobrano Gold. Then the lower level Swishers. Now, what style and how dark or mellow a flavor? I suggest that they store better if they are tapper rolled each end, that allows an even better, secondary fermentation for next year, if they last that long."

"Whoa… too much information. There were men in Father's club that paraded their big fat, dark Havanas like they were jewels. I know nothing about what is best. Tell you what." he looked at Jeremiah. "Pick out what you'd like best. I'll trust your judgment."

"Gonna cost you," Jeremiah said with a sly smile. "Sobrano Golds run five bucks each."

"You want a box of those?" Nate asked.

"Not me. I lean more toward La Coronas. Figure you're up to fifty dollars plus two of those Sobrano Golds, so make that sixty?"

"I can handle it. While you pick out the right ones, I'll head for the grocery store and stock up on food."

"You need a humidor if you want to put that kind of money into cigars," Del said.

"Sure." He looked back at Jeremiah. "You visit awhile. I'll make a stop at a bank and be back to pay you."

"Jeremiah can take them, and you pay me tomorrow." Del grinned.

Nate chose the Consolidated National Bank of Tucson, which appeared to be the biggest in town. After he confirmed they had direct telegraph access, he presented his business card and asked for the manager. He wanted to create an account in Tucson with money from his San Francisco bank. He decided transferring $5000 was sufficient, with $300 cash for whatever he needed immediately. By the time the transfer was complete, he'd become the manager's new best friend. He hoped the transfer of funds wouldn't be something Hamilton could trace; since this account had come from an inheritance from his grandparents.

At the grocers, he ordered fresh vegetables, surprised to find such a tasty variety after the café's disinterest in them. From then it was steaks, potatoes, eggs, bacon, two bottles of whiskey. He chose their best brandy, and all the staples and spices he could imagine two bachelors might need. As the order stacked up, he realized he'd have to figure out a way to get them to the house where he had no idea of its address. He paid, requested the items be boxed, and he'd return for them.

Walking from the store, he ducked back into a doorway as he watched two men stride down the boardwalk to the bar. He was sure he'd seen them before. Jeremiah had been right. Hamilton had left these, maybe more, to report on his return or Willy's arrival.

When he got to Sicillas, Connie, Del and Jeremiah were drinking tea. Connie poured a fourth cup. "Very good tea," he said.

"I get it from the East. My mother used to send it to me before she died. Now I have to work some but I like the blend of fruity and exotic."

"I suppose you read tea leaves too." Nate said.

"I can but not often. Palms are better. Have you had yours read?"

"No."

"Want me to tell you what I see?"

He considered that. "Sure, but I won't believe it."

"Ah a man of practical nature. Well, palms, despite what you might've been told, are not about fortunetelling. They are about our natural abilities and yearnings, our life energy… and our loves."

She reached across the small table and took his right hand. Someone entering the store took Del away, but Jeremiah watched as Connie studied Nate's lines. She ran her finger along the one that circled his thumb. "This is called the lifeline and some believe it determines how long someone will live. I don't believe that. It shows instead the strength of that person's life energy. Look at how strong your line is, no deviation except toward the top of it. It begins high on your hand, which means you are a man of ambition."

"Funny, I haven't seen myself as that."

"Perhaps you have not yet found your purpose. That's what you are doing now, finding that purpose. When you do, the ambition will be clear." She pointed to various lines with what they meant. Then she ran her finger along a strong but short one alongside his hand. "The marriage or love line. You have one, very defined. You will have one strong relationship, which may be a marriage but may not. It could be a strong love."

He smiled at that. It could be Willy, but then she was not feeling the same thing toward him. Had he really felt all he should have for her? He knew he would die for her, but did he feel the sort of things a man should for the woman he would live for? For that, he didn't have answers.

"How about Jeremiah?" he asked when she released his hand. "He got a lot of love lines there?"

Connie smiled. "He and I have discussed it before." Jeremiah put out his hand where Nate could see for himself. Three lines and very well defined.

"It ain't true though," Jeremiah said with the twang he sometimes used when he was playing the bumpkin, which by now, Nate knew him to be anything but. "Not gonna marry again, not for love nor money."

"Marriages can be good for a person," Connie said with a knowing smile. "Think of Ollie and Rose. It enriched both their lives to find love again when they were old."

Jeremiah snorted. "That does remind me though." He looked back at Nate. "We need to get up there and talk to Ollie."

"Should I know him?"

"You should and you will." Jeremiah rose.

"Thank you for the tea, ma'am," Nate said as he paid for the cigars and humidor.

"Remember. It's Connie, and you're welcome."

Outside Nate stopped Jeremiah. "You were right. I saw two of his henchmen. I recognized them from being in my mother's home with Hamilton."

"Did they see you?"

"Unlikely. They were headed for the bar."

"All right." Jeremiah considered. "How does it sound that we hire a wagon to get your gear, the food, and us to my place. We'll take it slow tonight, and tomorrow head up to talk to Ollie Oliver."

"You haven't yet said who he is."

"Ollie goes beyond explaining. You have to meet him."

"Sounds fine."

Jeremiah's home was a tidy looking cottage with surprisingly nice furnishings and a good feel to the interior. The wagon driver helped them carry the goods into the house, and Jeremiah took to stowing away the groceries in the appropriate cupboards. Nate found it surprising that the old outlaw kept his home clean and in order. It was not what he had expected. The bedroom he had been assigned had clean bedding and included a wardrobe and dresser. He walked back out to the kitchen and saw Jeremiah was starting their supper.

"I figured those steaks and frying up some potatoes. That sound like enough for you?"

Nate would have liked some of the vegetables, but his energy for fixing them was less than the old man's. When Jeremiah handed him a whiskey, he sipped it cautiously-- afraid he'd go straight out if he drank much. "You are a tough old bird," he said watching as Jeremiah expertly turned the steak and then the potatoes.

"Comes from a hardscrabble life, son. You got toughness. I see it in you, and yet, you came up the easy way, didn't you?"

"I never thought of myself as tough or even that I needed to be."

"Watch the steaks, don't let them get tough. Need them still red inside."

"All right. Where are you going?"

"I'm going to call Vince. I want him to wire Cole but coded enough that he'll know what it means without saying it. I don't know who to trust in Payson or even here in the telegraph office."

"Surely you can't think Hamilton would have cohorts there."

"Live as long as I do in my world, you don't go by thinking but what you know. Watch the steaks."

He picked up the receiver, tapped the phone a few times before giving Vince's number. More moments went by. "And when he answers, get off the line, Tildy," he said laughing and then nodding with satisfaction as he said, "Hello son." There was a moment and then Jeremiah said, "Send Cole a wire in Payson. Say Asa is back. He wants to meet your sister. More when we know more." There was silence on Jeremiah's end and then he chuckled. "You don't need to know what it means. Send it in the morning, early. I'll explain tomorrow. We have to go up to Ollie's. Want to meet us there? Yeah, say about ten. Take care, boy." More chuckles. "You know what I mean."

"You really think someone would listen in on the phone?" Nate asked, taking the steaks from the pan and stirring the potatoes again.

"Tildy does if she isn't caught at it. Nosy is what she is. You let the steaks cook too long."

Nate snorted. "You want them blood red?"

"Or straight off the steer." Jeremiah poured himself another whiskey.

After dinner, they sat in the small parlor, Nate trying to avoid falling asleep. "How about a cigar?" Jeremiah asked.

"Will it keep me awake?"

"Maybe. Let's save the Golds for another day." Jeremiah reverently opened the box and then put the cigars into the humidor, which he set on the small table by the lamp. "You can bite off both ends or much better trim the outer end with a blunt cut about three quarters inches wide. On the draw end, make it one half."

"That's important?" He knew he was too tired to make sense of this, but he was trying to follow the fine points of smoking a cigar.

"You do it to get a nice even burn, assuming you roll it between draws."

"Is this a smoke or a dance?"

"Have some class, boy!" Jeremiah chuckled. "Now, let the match burn a couple seconds to get past the sulfur and lightly, touch the end, gently draw. No inhaling yet, just get it started."

Nate followed his instructions.

"Smooth, eh?"

"It is. Smells good too."

"Now, inhale... not too deep. Sort of like how it is with a good woman."

Nate gave him a look.

"Wal, it's not like I'm so old I don't remember." Nate looked at him for a long moment as he drew in the smoke from the cigar. They laughed together.

~

Mazatzals September 29

Lying in bed as comfortably as though they had slept together for years, Willy remembered the passion of the hours before they fell asleep. She had never dreamed a man could be such an ardent lover, could so touch her all the places that brought her the greatest pleasure. He must have had many lovers to be so skillful. She felt jealous of them. She wished she had been his first as he had been hers.

His arm tightened around her. "What are you thinking?" he asked kissing the top of her head.

"You ask that at the worst times," she said stroking her hand down his side. She loved the muscles in his body, the ridges and bumps, the hard places and then the silky skin that covered it all.

"Ah, then it's something bad."

"No, just jealous. I wish you'd never had another love before me. Like I hadn't before you."

"I hadn't."

"Not possible. You couldn't be such a gifted lover if you hadn't been with hundreds of women."

She felt the breath of his laughter against her hair. "It doesn't take hundreds. To be honest, I've had no lovers like you. But I have been with women."

She sat up and looked back down at him. He turned onto his back, his hand now under his head. "What kind?"

His smile was crooked. "The kind who teach a boy how to do it right."

"Prostitutes?"

"More or less."

"You paid them?"

"My father did."

She felt horrified. What kind of father would do that? "What did your mother think of that idea?"

"Probably much like you do. She wasn't asked. I wasn't really either."

"Oh." She tried to take that in. "They forced you?"

169

"It doesn't take forcing when you are sixteen. It takes a kind of seduction, I guess. I didn't understand much about it, but I did learn what women wanted. Then... yes, through the years, I've paid women. I wasn't about to seduce a woman when I knew I'd not be there for her."

She guessed that was honest in a sort of a way. Still, it bothered her.

"There weren't that many, and I always used something to avoid disease or getting a woman pregnant."

She lay back beside him, running her hands down his chest, to his belly. Her mind more on his body that what he'd said. "I suppose that was fairest... in a way."

He took her hand into his and brought it to his lips. "Fair or not, it was what it was, and as I said, there weren't a lot of them."

"Were you ever in love?"

She felt his smile against her palm as he kissed it and then blew lightly on it. "You are in a questioning mood tonight. Another book germinating in that beautiful head of yours?"

"You think I am beautiful?" She had heard him say it many times, but she liked hearing it again.

He turned until he was leaning over her, his finger lightly streaking her cheek. "Ravishing, gorgeous, the most beautiful woman I have ever seen."

"You aren't telling the truth. Holly is the most beautiful woman you will have ever seen."

"I'm not that attracted to blondes. No, you are the most beautiful. And before you ask, my brother Jesse is married to Holly's sister, who has black hair. She's lovely, but you are more lovely than her too."

His lips were so close to hers. She wanted him to kiss her, but he was staring into her eyes as he ran his other fingers through her hair. "It's more than beauty though, with you," he said, now kissing her cheek and then her nose. "It's the whole package. You are smart, kind, sweet, innocent-- for all your knowledge. It's all of you."

"You've never said you loved me though."

"No, I haven't but not because I don't feel it. I do love you, Wilhelmina Butler."

She swallowed feeling happiness flowing through her, her body warm and almost on fire with it. "I love you too, Cole Taggert."

"So, let's go into Payson Monday and get married."

"It's not the right time for that."

"You think there will be a right time?" He lay back on the bed staring up at the ceiling. The room was dark with little moonlight seeping in through the windows. She wished she could see his face. Had she hurt his feelings? She didn't know why she hadn't said yes. It was true that she loved him, but still, was that all marriage required. Did they have the rest of what it took? Would they end up like so many couples, old bitter and hating each other.

She wanted to make it up to him, to say something that expressed some little part of what she felt for him. For a writer, she was surprisingly without words. "I hope so," she whispered feeling a tear at the edge of her eye. She felt whatever was missing was in her, not in him. What would it take to...?

"And now, it's a right time for?" he asked.

"This." She supported herself on one elbow and bent over him to kiss his lips, running her tongue along the edge before she thrust within.

In the morning, after she'd fixed the two of them breakfast, he set about creating two play areas for the pups. He made them high enough to keep the babies in but let Zinnia jump out for her breaks. The first one was in the kitchen. "This is so they can be with us when we are here and easier to clean this floor. They are getting big enough for that to be a factor."

"I like that thinking."

The other he made outside for fresh air and to learn what the world was like-- but in a safe way. She saw that it was protected by the outhouse beyond, the woodpile and hopefully would keep them out of the eye of predators. They had yet to see a cougar, but one was likely to live in the vicinity. While a puppy would be a small treat, it could be tempting.

After that, he began the dog pack that would let them be on the back of the horses. Even Zinnia wasn't up to keeping up with them with all the miles they'd have ahead.

"What will we feed her when traveling?" she asked. At the cabin, she'd used leftovers, but she doubted that would work with the kinds of food they were likely to be heating up over a campfire.

"Make up some hard tack biscuits. Wheat flour, grind up some of the vegetables, and juice from the meat, bake them hard. I'll see if I can find some of those Spratt's Cakes when I go to town next."

"What is that?"

"Dry dog food. That with dried milk for her, should get her to Tucson."

"All right."

"I don't think I mentioned Ericson wants to go with us when we leave." He punched holes in leather and then using twine, secured two pieces together with a small piece of wood at the bottom.

"He does? Why?" She was surprised at that.

"I guess the winters get tough up here. He's not a young man. He said he didn't have the money to take the stage. I suppose he worried about doing it by himself."

"But why Tucson?"

"He has a sister there and two nephews. I'll be honest, I don't know. Maybe being with us like he's been, he's feeling the isolation up here."

"You'd think he'd adore it."

"You do like it, don't you."

"I've never felt anyplace that felt so much like home. Certainly not the house in San Francisco. I feel bad at losing all my things, the books, letters, but I planned to sell it when I got back. Once Father was dead, it wasn't the same."

He stopped his work and looked up at her. "You came up here to write. Why don't you do that now?"

She smiled. "I guess I wanted to be with you more. And then what would I write? I thought I'd write a novel but nothing has come to me."

"Another Taggert book? This time Taggert gets what's coming to him maybe?" He gave her a teasing smile.

She didn't find it humorous, not since she had already known if she wrote the eighteenth Taggert western, she had felt she had to do just that —albeit with a fancier title. "You have come close to death more than once, haven't you?" she asked unsure why she wanted to talk about something that was a part of her doubts involving any future between them.

"Why do you ask?"

"I've seen other scars."

"Then you know."

"Not what it's like to face down death. I wrote from a safe distance. Do you ever think-- this time it could be me?"

He went back to using the awl on the leather. "I always know it could be me, but that is true of most of life. A horse can fall and pin a man, crush him to death. A tree can fall in the woods, one you never saw coming. Lightning out of a clear blue sky, and it hits you. A bear comes down the path and is in the wrong mood when you surprise him. You must have thought of some of that when you came up here to be what you thought would be by yourself."

"I honestly hadn't. I was coming up here only seeing it as an adventure. I was naïve, I suppose."

"You were but not a bad way to live. Living in fear is no way to live at all. I like what Mark Twain said about it, "The fear of death follows from the fear of life. A man who lives fully is prepared to die at any time."

"So you have thought of dying?"

"Of course. It just comes a little quicker in my line of work but think how my mother died, poisoned by her own son."

"She didn't know though."

"She said she did."

"Before she died?"

"No, after. Connie Sicilla does readings. Mother told Jeremiah that she'd been murdered. Jesse already knew, but I didn't. Vince didn't. Pa didn't."

"And you believed that kind of thing? I admit that I don't have much faith in séances."

"Well, in this case, later Asa told Vince to goad him into drawing recklessly. So, it was true."

She knew what drawing meant but Cole had said it so casually. It disturbed her. She shook her head, trying to clear it. "Horrible to imagine a son would do that to his own mother, kill her."

"We shouldn't talk about this."

"I think about such things."

"Morbid?"

"Maybe all writers are some. I mean we write about life and death. We have to go there, mentally at least, to write about it. And then, it was even more after my father chose to end his life without a word, with no clue it was coming. I wondered if he'd thought of it ahead of time."

"I doubt it."

"You don't believe he did, do you?"

"I think it's unlikely. The house burning further convinced me. He was murdered. And hearing how Mr. Hemstreet died, broken neck, falling down stairs, convenient for someone, wasn't it?"

"Thomas Hamilton."

"He did profit from it by then getting control of the business."

"Are you distracting me from thinking about your own dangers?" she asked with a knowing smile.

"You're onto me huh?" His smile was amused, but he quickly went back to work without giving her the answer she had wanted. Was his life dangerous? If she risked it all by marrying him, would he leave her a widow, and the worry and sacrifices she knew would be involved in loving a man would all be for nothing? She managed a self-deprecating smile. It was too late to avoid loving him.

CHAPTER 14

Tucson, October 1

Nate was surprised at the adobe home nestled in the foothills of the Catalina Mountains. He had expected something plain, severe even. Instead, it sprawled out several directions and even had a gazebo that overlooked what appeared to be a small stream.

A balding man walked out of the house and waved as they stopped their mounts at the corral below the house. "So how the hell you been?" he asked as he slapped Jeremiah on the back.

"Raising hell, of course," Jeremiah said with a chuckle as the two hugged.

"So who's this dude?" the man he knew had to be Ollie asked. So much for clothes make the man.

"Nate Hemstreet, meet Ollie Oliver, and if I tell you his real first name, he'd have to kill you, so best you stick to calling him Ollie."

A beautiful older woman came out onto the covered veranda. "I'm Rose. You all come on up here. There's lemonade for those who like it," she said as she waved at Jeremiah. In a few moments, the three men were sitting under the cover of what was some sort of lanai, only he doubted that was what it was called. The lemonade was not too sweet or sour. He smiled his thanks to Rose, as he took a sugar cookie from the offered plate.

"I'll leave you to your secret dealings," she said with a little laugh and went back into the house. The view from the veranda was beautiful as it looked across the valley. In the distance, Nate saw the dust from a fast moving horse. He had no doubts who that would be. Ten minutes later,

Vince had taken a glass of lemonade and Rose had once again left them with a refilled pitcher.

"So what was that all about?" Vince asked his father munching on a cookie.

"You send the wire?"

"I did."

Jeremiah told him what they'd uncovered at the cabin in terms of probable fraud as well as the coded notebooks, which had yet to be deciphered. "The real problem though was that Hamilton left behind two, maybe more men."

"We could take care of them," Vince said with a cold smile. Good Lord, Nate thought, not for the first time-- Who are these men?

Ollie chuckled. "Them is the old days, boy. Now we got to do things legal."

"That's where you come in," Jeremiah said looking at Ollie. "Here's what I believe. Thomas Hamilton has another name or a couple. Once we find his names, we can find out if he has a record."

"You figure to consult both sides of the law-- Cord and Sam," Ollie said as his face turned contemplative. "You write them a good description?"

"I already did that." Jeremiah handed him a piece of paper.

Ollie studied it. "Could fit more than one. Ya know it'll take a spell to get word to either of them. You got that time?"

"The last I heard, Willy won't be back until the middle of December. That means a month unless things change up north. When Cole gets word of what's waiting here, he isn't likely to be in a hurry to leave the cabin."

Vince chuckled. "Maybe he'll have other reasons to stay there as long as he can."

"Might be." Jeremiah laughed with Ollie joining in. Nate didn't find that humorous. He did, however, like these men, liked how quickly this became a mutual problem for them to solve. He had never had a deep, male friendship. There'd always been Willy, but it wasn't the same. He wanted to earn the friendship of such men, where money didn't decree importance, but something deeper and more inherent. He wasn't even sure what that was.

An hour later, Rose came out to tell them she'd prepared enough for supper, if they were so inclined. "Royce will be out of school early today," she reminded Ollie.

"My grandson," Ollie said to Nate. "He twelve and gets fine marks, smarter than me by far. The teacher brings him to the end of the road down there a piece, but I usually meet him with a horse, just so he gets the practice on horseback." The pride was evident in his voice.

Ollie walked off, using just a hackamore, leaped on his horse bareback, with all the agility of a younger man. Nate sucked in a breath thinking how his life had been hollow in ways he'd never imagined until he got to Arizona. He didn't have a family, not like these people did. If he didn't get himself together, he never would. Should he try harder to get Willy to marry him, or was his real problem his own uncertainty as to what he wanted to be when he grew up? Hell, he was grown up. It was time to stop playing at life, at least after the Hamilton problem had been resolved.

"You add to that description as to what you know about how the man operates. That might tell Cord and Sam more," Vince said. "We can take it to Trask too."

"I was thinking perhaps we should hire a detective."

"Sam once rode on the other side of the law," Jeremiah said. "He knows men from those days. Cord was a US Marshal. They are brothers."

"Interesting. You really think either can help?"

"With as much description as we can give them, it's possible," Vince said.

"Another question. Should I stay away from the places Hamilton's hoodlums will frequent?"

"That would be smart," Vince said.

"He's staying with me but that's too close to town," Jeremiah said.

"How about helping us build the barns out at the adobe ranch," Vince suggested. Nate liked that idea. He liked it a lot.

Mazatzals October 9 Monday

With a week of solid work behind him, Cole came into the cabin from out where he'd been improved the shed by strengthening its walls, patching the roof, and building a feed bin and box for salt. In the cabin, he saw Willy hadn't left the typewriter, and if the piles of crumpled papers were any clue, she was continuing to have more frustration than success. He bent and kissed her neck.

"Is it time for lunch already?" she asked looking at the clock on the wall. "I am sorry. I got wrapped up and then… lost track of time."

"Not a problem. How's it going?"

She rose with a sigh. "It's not as you can probably tell."

"What are you trying to write or is that a secret?"

"No secret. I wanted to write about out here, about just ordinary people living in a place like this."

"Doesn't a story need a problem?"

"Well, that's the problem." She smiled.

"You know, you can write about that crooked Taggert if you want. I am used to the idea of it now, and if it's the story that comes to you, well, go for it."

"That's sweet of you but... No, I want to write something different. I just haven't figured out what that would be. I have been trying to write something for a magazine, using that trip to the natural bridge for one."

"So what's the problem? It seems like a good idea."

She shook her head. "I can't seem to get a good start with any real energy anyway." She went out into the kitchen, reached down to pet the puppies and Zinnia before she looked at their options for lunch. "Sandwich maybe?" she asked.

"How would you like to ride into Payson for lunch?"

"Isn't it too late for that today?"

"Not really. You've gotten better on horseback. I could use more nails. That saw I'm using is worse than useless. I thought I'd buy a new one."

"You are putting a lot of work into property that isn't yours."

"Get changed, and let's head out," he said ignoring the opportunity to tell her the property was his and soon to be hers. "There is a little café across from the general store. Let's try it out."

She smiled and headed up the stairs. He gave Zinnia a chance to take care of her needs, refilled her water bowl and set her back in with her puppies in the kitchen pen. When Willy came downstairs, she was wearing jeans with a skirt bunched to her waist. He got the idea. In town, she could lower it and look proper. He smiled.

Ten minutes later, they were riding up the trail toward town. "Why don't you practice letting Boots gallop," he suggested when they came to where the road stayed level for half a mile or so.

She looked at him with some doubt but then leaned forward and gave Boots a harder nudge with her heel. Cole liked her seat, how well she was handling the horse. He hung just behind her until she slowed Boots to a walk. "That was more fun than I thought," she said.

"When you get confidence you can handle a horse at a dead run, then it won't scare you. Just be sure you pick your spots to do it until you are more confident."

She smiled at him. "Like you?"

"I grew up in the saddle. It does change how you see a horse."

"How old when you first rode by yourself?"

He had to think about that. "I was walking," he said finally with a little laugh. "I honestly don't know how old. I just always did."

"Didn't your mother worry about you on such a big animal?"

"Maybe but she had so much else to worry about that not sure it ranked high." He saw the first buildings of Payson as they reached the edge of the town. "Do you want to get yourself anything at the general store?"

"I haven't been in a store in such a long time. I may have forgotten how to shop."

"Do you need money?"

She laughed. "I am not so poor I can't buy a few things myself."

Remembering his purchases of the condoms and that pickle faced female clerk, he knew it would be best he not go with her to give the woman more reasons to wonder about what was going on out at the lake cabin. He put their horses in stalls at the stable, with a portion of oats as a reward, while Willy brushed her skirt down and pushed her hair into a semblance of order. Personally, he liked her tousled, but he supposed it wasn't how she wanted to be seen by others.

"I need to check the telegraph office and will meet you at the café." He pointed to a small building, with checkered red and white curtains and a sign above-- Adele's.

"Why the telegraph?"

"Just to be sure all is well in Tucson. Remember Holly is having a baby. I don't expect trouble but want to make sure they aren't needing to reach us."

"I had forgotten about that." Her brow furrowed. "You don't think she..."

He smiled at his worrier. "No, I don't. Now get on over to the general store and meet me at Adele's. I'll be the one sipping coffee and looking up at the clock."

At the telegraph office, the clerk was in the backroom but came out. As soon as Cole told him his name, he handed him a wire. "Been here almost a week."

"I don't get in all the time. Thanks." On the street, he opened the wire, read it, read it again, and then folded it and put it in his pocket. Vince had sent him a warning but without much information to go on. He'd have to wait. Maybe more would come. He only hoped he could decode it when it did. Damn, what was it with codes? It was obvious Vince didn't trust the delivery system, maybe worried even about the telegraph operator at this end. How much trouble did he feel Hamilton could be? Enough to warn him. He'd wait to tell Willy when they got back to the cabin.

Before he could enter the café, he heard her call his name. He turned and watched her stride across the dusty street. She looked furious.

"What's wrong?" he asked as she grabbed his arm and pulled him away from the café.

"That woman in the store." She made a low growl. "She treated me like a trollop. She said." She stopped and growled again.

And then, he put it together. The condoms, the woman's disapproving expression when he'd purchased them, small town, and maybe even the freighters, who regularly went out to the cabin with supplies. Likely, half the community knew who was staying there. He looked down at Willy wanting to find words to make her feel better. He'd already said the only ones he knew, which could fix the problem in the eyes of the religious. She'd turned him down.

"There is an easy solution to this," he said giving it a fourth try.

"Go back and poke her in the eye?" she suggested.

"We get married. Then nobody questions the use of a condom."

"That's no reason to marry, and you know it."

"Fine. Let's get lunch."

"I don't like being treated like a whore."

"Sweetheart, do you want to live by someone else's standards or your own?"

She pouted out her lip. "You are making this sound logical. I don't want to be logical right now. I am mad."

"And I'm hungry. You aren't going to tell me you're afraid of a little diner."

She stiffened her spine, took his arm, and together they turned and walked into the diner. It had five tables, only one of which was occupied. For a moment, Cole hoped this wasn't going to prove a mistake and then a heavyset, smiling woman, with the reddest hair he'd ever seen, came out of the back. "I am Adele, owner, proprietor and sometimes head chef, when my husband is gone. You can tell we have many tables reserved," she added with a giggle. "Did you want a window table? Might have to wait an hour for that."

The couple at the other table chuckled. "Watch what you eat here," the woman said as she smiled at Willy. "It makes you fat because you can't stop."

Willy smiled reluctantly and then looked back at Adele. "How about your best table?"

"Well, they have that."

In moments, Cole and Willy were seated and had a menu. It was a single sheet but with quite a few choices, all of which looked good to him.

"Want some coffee?" Adele asked.

They both nodded. "What do you recommend?" Willy asked as she looked up from the listed items and met the friendly older woman's gaze.

"For lunch, I see you as the sort to enjoy the cream of tomato soup with a lettuce and cucumber salad."

"That sounds wonderful. I haven't had fresh greens in too long."

"We have a cold frame and hot bed. We are building a greenhouse.

Anything that lets us keep the greens going before the winter sets in with a passion. This has been a warmer than usual year; so no hard freezes, but that seems due in a week or so. The cucumbers we are getting right now from Flagstaff."

"I'd love it."

"How about you, mister?" Adele asked holding a pad expectantly.

"Sliced roast beef sandwich. You wouldn't have horseradish, would you?"

"Shore do." She grinned, filled their coffee cups, and disappeared into what was apparently the kitchen.

"I didn't know you liked horseradish," Willy said sipping her coffee. "We could order some, that is if I didn't have to go back to the store to do it." She made a face.

The husband at the other table said, "You talking about Ruth?"

"Is that the name of the clerk there? If so, yes."

"It's her name. Ruth and Dennis Vashons own it. If it wasn't so far to the next store, they'd be out of business. I've never known more of a busybody."

"I thought it was just me, and I hit her wrong," Willy said. Cole understood for the first time how much of the teacher was in her personality as she was seeking to be kind and not add to the problems of the community.

"No, it's her."

"It's a nice town here," Cole said sipping his coffee.

"Everything is changing," the older man said. "There is a lot of uncertainty as to how it'll be with the forest service regulating the lands."

"Change in what way?" Cole asked suddenly interested in land where he hadn't cared much a month before. He knew the reason.

"The talk is their regulations and limitations on who can graze where will ruin what has been a good thing. From the talk I hear, there will be trouble over it. People up here do not like outsiders coming in and changing things."

"Maybe it'll be good for the forests though," Willy suggested. Adele came out with a tray and set their lunches before them. Willy sighed with pleasure, as she took her first spoonful of the soup.

"That's not what I hear. The forests have been kept, as they are by those who know the land-- know its needs.

"First the Apache and then the early ranchers knew to start small fires to prevent big ones. It brought the grass and feed for the animals to flourish. The rangers they will put in charge will be appointees, political, with few knowing this land or these people. Change is coming."

"That's not always bad," Cole said taking a bite of his sandwich. When his eyes watered, he looked up to see Adele smiling.

"Want some water, sir?" she asked bringing two glasses.

Cole resisted the swear words that came to him. "You make that horse-radish yourselves?" he gasped when he finally could.

"We shore do. My husband, he loves it hot, which is why I added a little extra cayenne."

"Well… now that I can breathe again," Cole said with another big gulp of the water, "I agree with him." Adele giggled.

"Do you sell any of it? I mean bottled?" Willy asked.

"Sure do. How much you want?"

"Maybe half a cup."

Adele nodded and headed back to her kitchen. She returned with a small bottle, which Cole was pretty sure contained more than half a cup. "When I make it, I add a little vinegar, so it'll keep pretty well, but store it away from the stove."

Willy took it with a big smile. "I'll be paying the bill, so just add the cost to it."

"Since when?" Cole asked not liking the idea of a woman paying for his meal.

"Since I said so." She tilted her chin up and gave him a saucy smile.

"Give it up, son," the man at the other table said. "Woman says it that way, and you can never win fighting her."

Cole knew his smile was sheepish, but he nodded. "All right," he said finally.

Willy looked at Adele. "He's been my hired man, helping with the horse and well, he deserves a treat." She glanced back at Cole probably to see how he took that. He understood her desire to protect whatever was left of her reputation in this small town, but he didn't like it. She was quick to deny him any personal connection to her.

"I keep thinking I should know you," the older man said to Cole, sipping the last of his coffee before Adele came around to refill all their cups.

"I doubt it. I have been through here a few years back but not to stop."

"Wait, you worked with the sheriff of Springerville to break up the rustler gang, wasn't that you?"

"You were in Springerville back then?"

"I'm a lawyer, son. I work most of these small towns to keep enough business going. My name is Milton Freedman. This is my wife, Sadie. We make our home here as it's central enough to let me travel around or get down to the capitol when required, which fortunately is not often."

"Do you have an office here in town then?" Cole asked as he began to think this might solve a problem that had grown of more concern after his brother's wire.

"In Payson I work out of my home." Freedman reached into his jacket pocket for his card. "If I'm there, the office is open," he said with a smile. "Otherwise, Sadie takes messages, and I get back to clients when I return."

"You heard of the shooting here?"

"I heard there was one but hadn't drawn the connection. Sadie didn't mention it, and the boys at the bar didn't have names other than it was over quick and a stranger in town got what he was looking for in terms of trouble."

"My name is Cole Taggert." He didn't like giving it out, hadn't even before the books, but he was thinking he needed this man and better make sure this could work.

"I think I know your brother, Vince. He was working as a trader on the reservations."

"You get around," Cole said with some amusement at his own reticence to give his name, and then that it'd be Vince Freedman knew.

"I was born up here on the Rim. When I wanted to live here, it was obvious I'd have to travel some to keep enough business going. I share an office in Heber, Show Low, and Springerville."

"How long will you be here?"

"This week and leave next Monday." He smiled at his wife. "Needed some home time with my lady."

Cole nodded, not wanting to say more in front of Willy. "Important to know the name of a trustworthy lawyer when I am in an area. I travel a fair amount too."

"You figure you could trust me?" The man chuckled.

"I go by the look in a man's eyes." Cole smiled. "I'd trust you more than some." He was not surprised Freedman didn't work out of Gibbons' office.

When he and Willy walked out of the café, she immediately said, "I am sorry I called you a hired man. I just... Well, after that other woman, I was feeling guilty, I guess."

"I understand." He didn't really. He'd never had a reputation he had to worry about or maybe he had, but it had always been one to live down, not to protect. "It's all right."

"It's not. I let that woman impact who I was and that was wrong of me."

"You mean like hiding that you are the writer of the Tremaine books?" He looked at her to see how she took that. She looked a little shaken, but she didn't deny it.

Riding out of town, she said, "I do that, don't I? Try to be what others expect? Like using a skirt to hide the pants that made riding practical."

He saw she'd been chewing on it the whole time he'd been saddling and getting the horses loaded with the new supplies. "Well, you did with the books. Whenever I hear anybody talk about them, they praise them. You don't have anything to be ashamed of with them."

"They've caused you troubles."

"Hell, maybe they gave me business." He looked over at her and smiled. "I think though you should be proud of them, even do book signings like other authors do."

"Who would want that?"

"People who like the books."

"You can't mean I should be proud of them."

He shook his head. "You mean like you wouldn't be proud of being with me unless I was a hired man, like I am beneath you, and so is writing the books that come to you because your intellectual friends would not like it, they'd consider you inferior for writing them. You mean like that?"

"You make me sound like a snob."

"Are you?"

She stared straight ahead. "I don't know, I guess. I didn't think I was but…"

"Look, maybe we all are in some ways. Let's forget it."

She sighed. "I am not sure I can. You opened a door and…"

Two men rode toward them. They stared with curiosity at Cole and then Willy but passed without a word.

"Did you know them?" she asked when she came up alongside him again.

He shook his head. "Just their type."

"And that would be?"

"Opportunist," he said for wont of a better word.

"Is that bad?"

He laughed. "Only if they don't have ethics to go along with it."

"Ethics is a big word… I thought I had ethics."

"And now you aren't sure?" He had never met anyone who probed as deeply into feelings. He guessed it should not have surprised him but…

She interrupted his thinking. "Are you angry with me?"

"No."

"Disappointed?"

"No. I told you. I understand—well, except about the books. I still think you should be proud of them." He glanced over and saw she was smiling.

"You didn't mind my saying you are my hired man?"

"It was a good idea but may not save your reputation anyway. They might not believe you."

She smiled then. "You could be my hired man if I had enough money anyway."

"I could… and what would you hire me to do?"

"I'd think of something."

An hour later after a fast ride that encompassed some galloping, which helped Willy to feel more and more at ease on Boots, they arrived at the cabin. "I'll take care of the horses," he said as she dismounted at the porch. "You take care of Zinnia and the kids."

"Would a sandwich be enough tonight?"

"Sure. I'll bring the horseradish back with me."

Inside, Zinnia was eager to go out back. Willy put the pups in their outside corral. They were moving around and sniffing of the air. Zinnia came back to her and pushed her head under Willy's hand. She petted her, pleased with how the little dog's coat had improved even with feeding her babies. She praised her as she stroked her under her chin. Zinnia seemed to purr with the strokes or would have had she been a cat.

"She's looking good," Cole said as he strode up from the barn. "Did you notice we are going to get a storm?"

She looked toward the south and saw dark thunderclouds building. "A bad one?"

"Hard to say. It's late for the monsoons, but you never can tell. The wind has picked up. Let's get the dogs in." He picked up the pups. Once inside, he took the horseradish from his pocket and set it on the counter. "If you eat any of it, just go slow," he said with a smile.

Instead of putting the pups into their pen, Cole brought them into the main room. "Let's let them get used to being in a house with some rules." He went to the wastebasket alongside her table and unfolded some of the papers without looking at them. "Puppies can learn to use paper. We'll see if we can housebreak them. They'll find better homes if they learn they can't pee just anywhere."

She didn't like thinking she couldn't keep them all with Zinnia but practically speaking, she didn't even have a home in San Francisco. She went back into the kitchen to slice bread and ham. "Do I butter the bread if we're using the horseradish?" she asked.

"You're going to try it?"

"I never have and not sure why, but yes, I am. How about some brandy?"

When he nodded, she poured them each a small glass, put the sandwich makings on a tray and carried it to the main room where he had settled onto the floor with the puppies and Zinnia. She handed him a glass of brandy. "Want me to make your sandwich?" When he nodded, she dipped into the jar of horseradish. Remembering how he'd reacted in Adele's, she went light on it and used butter on the other side. She handed him the sandwich, which he shared the places with the butter, meat, and no horseradish with Zinnia. She almost appeared to smile. The puppies played with a small piece, but they still were mother's milk oriented.

Willy made herself half a sandwich and put the horseradish on half of it. She was surprised to find she liked it. Next time she'd be a little more generous.

"I needed to tell you about the wire I got in town," he said.

"Holly is all right?"

"It wasn't about her. My brother sent me a warning that trouble is waiting in Tucson."

"What kind?"

"Most likely Hamilton."

"He didn't give you a name?"

"I am guessing on this but most likely Pa asked him to send it, and he didn't want to give anybody information that he didn't have to. So he used a code."

"I am confused."

"It seems codes are catching," he said with a smile that was a mix of humorous and cynical.

"Is this funny?" It didn't feel funny to her.

"Kind of. The wire said Asa is back and he wants to meet my sister. More info would come when he had it."

"And that means?"

"Asa is my dead brother. I don't have a sister."

"Why would he send such a confusing message?"

"I am guessing again but likely Pa is not sure how widespread Hamilton can reach so didn't want to send anything that would link me to you. The name Taggert is not connected to Wilhelmina Butler."

"Unless Hamilton knew about the books." She grimaced.

"The likelihood of him reading them seems slim. I think what Pa is telling us is either Hamilton didn't leave Tucson or he left someone there to report when you arrive."

"He would chase me?"

"That's what my family is hoping to figure out with more information to follow."

"Oh." She sucked in a breath. "What should we do?"

"Nothing for now." His smile changed to something softer. "Don't worry. I won't let Hamilton hurt you."

"What about you? Will you not let him hurt you either?"

He shook his head again with that faint smile that she'd seen whenever the subject of danger came up. "You think too much."

"It's not like I can change that at this late point."

"Try not worrying until you know there is something to be concerned about. Something solid."

"You don't seem worried."

"Nothing to do about it right now. No point in getting worrying when we don't have all the facts."

She smiled. "You find that easy to do?"

"It gets easier the more times you face it." He reached down and petted one of the pups who was nosing his jeans. She lit two of the lamps, sat on the sofa and watched him in the glow of their light. He looked up and met her gaze.

"I was thinking," she said, her breath coming a little faster.

"Uh oh. Not worrying, I hope."

"No."

"So?" he asked.

"Well, if you were my hired man, you'd have to do what I said, wouldn't you?"

"Depends on what it was, I suppose. I could always quit."

"But while you were."

He smiled. "All right, yes, while I was."

"You'd have to stand up when I said stand up."

Outside she heard the crack of thunder. Seconds later, the flash of lightning seemed to fill the sky. She felt as though the storm was filling her with an energy she'd previously never known. Or was it Cole who was doing that? "Stand up," she ordered and watched a slow smile spread across his face. He rose with that leonine grace she'd observed before. "Now... take off your shirt."

She heard the rain starting, hitting the roof, darkening the sky. The excitement of the storm was nothing to what she felt as she watched him slowly unbutton his shirt and then put it over the chair beside the table. The light of the lamps highlighted his muscles. Her breath came faster. "Now your boots and socks."

"Is this heading somewhere?" he asked as he sat on a chair and obeyed her. Half nude, he leaned forward his elbows resting on his knees.

"I want more. I want you naked." She tried to steady her breathing.

He smiled. "Should I put the pups away first, ma'am?"

She considered that. What she had in mind would take time, possibly a lot of time. She nodded, trying to put a highfaluting tone to her voice, "Yes, you should do that and then come back... and I want to see you. All of you."

When he returned, He undid his belt buckle, then the buttons on his jeans, but he didn't drop them. He looked at her with an expression in his eyes that was as hot as the lightning she saw strike the other side of the lake with an instantaneous boom of thunder that seemed to rock the cabin. The rain thundered against the shake roof. She tried to steady her breathing as she picked up one of the lamps. She led the way to the bedroom stopping at the door to look back at him. He had not moved. His smile was crooked.

"You have to do what I say," she reminded him, "as my hired man that is."

"You think so?" He bent and blew out the other lamp and then came to her in the doorway. "You better be sure the pay is worth what you are asking of me."

She went into the bedroom and put the lamp on the dresser before she turned to watch him in the doorway. "What do you think your pay should be?" she asked as she slowly unbuttoned her shirt.

He moved across the room, his pants unbuttoned but held on now by a stiff erection. Before she could think of something to say, he had pulled her into his arms. Her ability, to think what she wanted next, disappeared as he lifted her into his arms and carried her to the bed where he made fast work of her clothing. Nude, she watched him as he reached for the condom. "Wait," she said. "Let me do it this time."

He pushed his pants down and lay beside her on the bed. She'd never opened the package before and she was shaking, but she got it done and then bent over him, unrolling the sheath over his hard length. From then on, she lost track of anything, but their bodies coming together.

CHAPTER 15

Three days later, the last of the storms had passed. The land felt fresh and clean after the rains, and Cole knew he'd put off going back to Payson as long as he could. He didn't want to go. His life with Willy had fallen into a comfortable routine where he worked on improving the buildings, doing the repairs, even cutting down a few trees to dry for more firewood, while she wrote, of what he had no idea and tried out new recipes—to his benefit. At night, he would build a fire in the fireplace and they'd play with the puppies, when they weren't playing with each other. They'd even played poker which he found she was good at but not better than he was—especially when he had a motive to try harder for something like strip poker. It felt like what a normal couple would experience, what he'd seen of his brothers' lives. The fact that he knew it was temporary for the two of them didn't change the way it felt.

Walking into the kitchen, he said, "I need to go to town. Do you want anything?"

She looked up from the dough she was kneading. "Why? I mean why go?"

"I need to wire Vince about the baby and see if they have learned more about Asa's return." He smiled. "I will hang around long enough to get a reply; so that means I am going to be riding hard. You're not up to that yet." He also had a personal purpose that he was unwilling to tell her about yet.

She looked unconvinced, but she wrote five pounds of flour, baking powder, butter, rolled oats before she looked up. "Could you also get a leg of lamb if they have one?"

"I'll ask."

"Are you really willing to dare that harridan?" she asked as she handed her list to him.

"If that means shrew, yes I am." He bent to kiss her forehead. When she reached up to pull his lips down to hers, the kiss deepened. "I definitely will hurry back," he said with a grin as he went out the door before he could change his mind.

As he rode hard, as he'd told her he would, he thought about his hope to find Freedman and have him draw him up a will as well as start the transfer of the cabin to Willy's name. He hoped that could be finalized before they had to head south. It wasn't that he had a premonition of his death. He wouldn't have paid it any mind if he had. His life though had been such that any day could see its end. He'd lived with that knowledge, but not until her had it mattered that he assure himself someone else would be all right when he was gone.

Riding into Payson, Cole stopped by the telegraph office and sent a wire to Vince inquiring about the baby's arrival. Then he rode to Freedman's home, hoping the lawyer wouldn't be busy.

"Good to see you again so soon," Freedman said as he ushered him into the front parlor which served as his office.

"I have a need of legal assistance, Mr. Freedman," Cole said.

Mrs. Freedman came to the door. "Can I bring you gentlemen some tea?"

"That would be nice, Mother," Freedman said then looked at Cole. "That is, do you like tea?"

"I do."

A few moments later, the tea had been poured, and the door closed. "So how may I help you?" Freedman asked after taking a sip.

"This first." He got the deed from his pocket and handed it to Freedman.

The lawyer studied the paper and then looked back at Cole. "It looks as though it was properly done."

"I want to transfer the ownership. Do I need the other party to sign to do that?"

"Not really, although if the party later refused, they would have that right. Is there a reason for secrecy?"

"For now."

"I can take care of getting it legally filed. Is there a reason you didn't go back to Chester Gibbons?"

"Is there a reason you don't share an office with him?" Cole smiled.

Freedman chuckled. "Good point. All right, I can do it. Who will be the other party?"

"Wilhelmina Agatha Tremaine Butler." He handed Freedman a second piece of paper. I also want this will legally filed. It has her name on it."

"I see." He studied Cole. "You are her hired man and yet you wish to transfer your holdings to her. I won't say it doesn't happen, but I haven't had it since my time in the law."

"She's a good woman, and she recently had a loss of all she owned. She loves that cabin. I want her to have it. As for the will, I don't plan on kicking the bucket anytime soon. I just want to be sure she gets my possessions if that happens when I didn't plan it."

"In your line of work, I expect that does happen."

"It does in life period, Mr. Freedman."

"Make it Milt, please."

"How long will all this take, to get it filed and official?"

Freedman looked back at the papers. "A few days. I will have to go around Gibbons just to be sure. I actually was heading to Phoenix this coming week with some court business. How would that be?"

"Fine." Cole reached into his pocket. "What do I owe you?"

"Ten dollars should do it including the registration fees."

"You are joking."

"This isn't much work, and I'll be there anyway."

Cole rose and paid him. "I'll check back next week."

"I should have it all ready for you."

After stabling Boomer for some oats, Cole checked again on the telegraph but wasn't surprised no message waited. Reluctantly, he headed for the general store not eager to deal with the unfriendly woman. It was the only place he had much hope of getting the needed supplies.

Once he was in the store, the woman gave him the same evil eye he'd seen before. "My boss asked me to pick up these items," he said handing her the list.

"Your boss is she?" The woman smirked as she scanned down the list. "We don't have the leg of lamb."

"A nice rib roast?"

"We can find that." She hollered at her husband, in a back room, to wrap a roast. She began gathering the supplies in a flour sack. A brow-beaten looking man came out with the roast, glanced at Cole but said nothing as he put it on the counter and disappeared again.

"Better add a pack of cigarettes and five more condoms."

The woman snorted, but she kept filling out the list. She looked up when she had it all tallied. "Anything else?" she asked again with that smirk.

"Any chance you carry Spratt's Dog Cakes?" he asked hoping he had the name right from what he'd seen his brother sometimes feed his dog Bear.

"Why you needing that? You in the dog house?" she chuckled at her joke.

"Do you have them?"

She pointed to a barrel. "How many you fixing to need?"

He had to think. It would be six or seven days and a lactating dog. Dried milk would supply some of her needs. "Twenty, if you have them. And how about rawhide chews?"

"You mean to say you got a dog?"

He nodded. "One with puppies. Her two babies will need something to teethe on soon."

She walked to the back of the store and reached into another bin. "I can let you have these." She handed him some pieces of rawhide. "No charge." Her expression had softened. "Just a minute." She returned with some bones with a little meat still on them. "For your dog." This time she managed a genuine smile.

Walking out of the store, Cole thought about the softening of the tough, older woman, all because of a dog. He stashed his goods with his saddle and then gave the telegraph one last try. This time a wire waited for him. He smiled as he read it. Finally, good news. Holly had her baby, and her name was Lucinda. As he rode back to the cabin, he thought it was time they named the puppies.

Tucson, Arizona October 17

Riding up to the Oliver home, Nate was feeling particularly good about the full day's work he'd done out at the adobe ranch. With Vince caught up with his blonde, baby daughter, who had he made no secret of adoring from the moment she'd been born, it had been good Nate was there for getting more work done on the barn. He was glad he felt good about something, as swinging by the Taggert ranch, Vince had told him his father had called, and he was to head to the Olivers. He wasn't much for expecting bad things before they came, but in this case, it seemed unlikely he'd be hearing anything he liked.

Dismounting at the corrals, Nate put his horse in with the others and walked up the hill to see Jeremiah and Ollie sitting under the veranda and sipping whiskeys.

"Want one?" Ollie asked.

Nate shook his head. "Water would be good though."

A few moments later, Rose came out with a glass. Royce followed her and would have sat with the men except Ollie said, "Didn't you say you had homework?"

His grandson groaned but went back inside.

"I heard from Cord O'Brian, used to be marshal here," Ollie said. "From the physical description of Hamilton, and the possible way he's operating in Frisco, Cord said it sounded like Harold Thomas. He swung a wide loop in first West Texas, then New Mexico, and Southern Arizona."

"Wide loop?"

"Involving a lot of shady dealings, fraud, crooked land deals. One of the men he cheated turned up dead, but no proof it was Thomas. He got caught up in a bank fraud and spent time in Yuma."

"And from there?"

"With that, I visited Trask this afternoon to see what he could find," Jeremiah said. "Harold Thomas did five years in Yuma. He got out in 1897. Trask requested the mugshots, but when I called before I came here, he hadn't gotten them. If the pictures match, then he's the guy."

"It would fit with when he showed up in Frisco," Nate said.

"Yeah and maybe not a different way of operating."

"It won't prove he was connected to the shading dealings with my family operation, unless we can find he's been pocketing the money," Nate said.

"No, but it would make a person wonder why change his name."

"Some do that to get jobs, rebuild a reputation," Ollie said. "That is if he wanted to change his ways."

"It also won't prove he burned the Butler home," Nate said feeling disillusioned. It appeared the man was good at hiding his tracks. "Without proof, that he's behind the fraud, I won't be able to get my mother to fire him."

"Have you considered that she already knows who he is and uses it?" Jeremiah asked.

Nate sighed. "It is possible. I hate to... I could do with that whiskey."

After supper, the three men again sat on the veranda watching as the sun slowly sunk in the west. A pretty sunset if a man was in the mood for beauty. Nate wasn't. He wrestled with his conflicting emotions. Thieves, arsonists, and murderers did not people his world. Or so he had believed.

"What about the two men, who we believe work for Hamilton or Thomas?" he finally asked. "Find out anything about them?"

"They're not on any wanted posters. Ridge did get their names—at least the ones they admit to. Blackie Jones and Ike Smith. The third with them now is a local, who maybe has been hanging around them for future jobs. He's Alvin Smith. A lot of men are named Smith in Tucson." Jeremiah snickered.

"Possibly I should hire a detective," Nate said as he tried to think what other way they could get the information they needed.

"I was thinking if I can get their names to Cole, he can do some looking. The thing that bothers me though is the damned telegraph office. Who's been paid off? We can't take the risk that Hamilton connects Cole to Willy. If he's going to run into trouble, I want him to be here where he's got backup."

"How about sending him a letter?" Nate suggested. When telephones didn't work, how did someone communicate important information? Another aspect of life for which he had had little familiarity.

"I could try that. Not sure he'd go looking for a letter though. Maybe a wire but with enough codes to give him the info he needs."

"How is that possible?" Nate asked.

"We should wait until we see if the photo is Hamilton. That can't take much longer to get back to Trask," Ollie said.

"When is Cole coming to Tucson?" Nate asked.

"He's not going to leave her alone up there," Jeremiah said, and then added, "The original plan was she'd leave the middle of December and come down here for Christmas."

Something about the way he said that made it sound to Nate as though he wasn't convinced it would turn out that way.

"Would she contact her friends in Frisco?" Ollie asked

"I don't know who her friends were at the university; so can't say how close she was to anyone. I know she left Frisco without a word to me," Nate said.

"Would she write them?"

"You worried she'd write and Hamilton would intercept?" Nate asked.

"It would be a concern. Is there anyone else she might contact?" Jeremiah asked. "Like maybe the publisher of her books?"

"Since I didn't even know she wrote them, I'd have no idea who that would be."

Ollie put up his hand. "We're wasting our time jawing over this. We will have to wait this out. When we know for sure who Hamilton is, we can decide what to do next."

"Time is running out," Jeremiah said, concern in his voice.

"We still have a month," Nate reminded him.

"Unless something brings them to Tucson sooner."

"You have reason to think that could happen?"

Jeremiah stared into the distance. "The problem is I don't have a reason to think it couldn't. I don't want my son walking into this blind."

Riding back to Jeremiah's home, Nate thought of what had been said. He understood the love the old man had for his sons. He didn't want to ride under false colors. He waited though until they had unsaddled their horses and gone into the cottage.

"How about a cigar?" Jeremiah asked.

"Sounds good." They sat on the chairs smoking. "I need to tell you something," Nate said unable to find an easy way to work into this.

"Shoot."

"I did ask Willy to marry me before I left the cabin. She turned me down, but I am not going to give up. I believe she should marry me. I think I can make a good husband for her. When she is here again, and I will wait until she is, then I will again make my case."

Jeremiah smiled, letting out the smoke. "Did you figure that would bother me?"

"I know how loyal you are to your sons. I just wanted you to know that I will try to cut Cole out of her life."

"I told him, when we were up there, that you'd be the right man for her."

"You did?"

"I know you better now and see you to be a good man. You have the money to give her a good life. More important, you grew up like she did. She has no idea what it was like for Cole as a child, the life he has led. Frankly, I think the two of you would be a good match."

"I am surprised."

"Cole's a good man. He has a lot going for him to turn a woman's head, but she's out of his league. I think he will see it or maybe always has. If they tried it, it'd never work. I know what it's like when two mules are unevenly hitched. I had that kind of marriage. As much as I loved my wife, there was a lot of pain to it. I'd rather Cole found a woman from his background."

Nate smiled and took a long draw on the cigar. "I wouldn't ask you to help my case."

"I wouldn't do it either. In the end, a woman decides, but if she realizes a man from her background is better for her, I think it'll be best for Cole too."

"Good."

Willy woke in Cole's arms. He was still asleep. She lay watching him. He had thick eyelashes for a man. She liked watching him when he didn't know, when his overpowering intensity didn't suck her in and take away her ability to think.

When his eyes blinked open, she brushed her fingers over his bristly cheek. He looked at her and then out the window. "Did you see it's snowing?" he asked.

She turned then to see big flakes falling, almost like white feathers. She had seen snow when she lived in Boston, but the thrill of it never got old after growing up in California. "It's so beautiful," she said before she turned back to him. "I suppose snow is old hat to you growing up in Utah."

"We had a lot of it, and it can get in the way for feeding cattle, keeping water open."

"Will it be a problem for us here?"

"Not likely to last long at this time of year."

"Did you ever make a snowman?" She ran her fingers over his lips, felt the smile.

"I am guessing you have," he said without answering.

"I have… How about a snow angel?"

"What's that?"

"When the snow is deep enough, you fall back in it and move your arms up and down to create wings, then you stand up without ruining the image you created."

"I assume there is no rock sticking out where you fall back?"

"Naturally." She moved her fingers to his neck, running them lightly down to his chest. "I was thinking, after breakfast, of course, that we could make a snowman."

"If the snow lasts." He sat up and looked out the window. "I think maybe four inches now."

"Well, after breakfast maybe there'll be more."

He bent back over her. "I know what I want for breakfast."

"Fortunately, I want the same."

An hour later, Willy had dressed in her pants with a heavy sweater. In the kitchen, she began mixing up pancake batter. Through the window, she watched Cole let the puppies have their first experience with snow. At first, they didn't know what they thought of it, but they soon got the idea it could be fun. Zinnia was less impressed and at the door scratching. She let her in and watched as Cole picked up the pups and returned them to the kitchen. "I'll feed the horses. Be back in ten minutes," he said and strode off across a vision of white. She had thought the lake was beautiful when she had arrived, but seeing the trees iced with white, the snow falling and almost blocking out the opposite shore, this was like a Currier and Ives lithograph. Just watching it was enough, but she would want to go out into it, catch the flakes on her tongue, feel it all around her.

Considering what she'd need to go out, Willy remembered the gloves that Cole had bought her. She had a good scarf. With the cook stove heating the kitchen, they could dry their clothing when they got back. She smiled as she imagined stripping by the heat of the stove and making love in the kitchen. She couldn't imagine anywhere she wouldn't want to feel him with her and in her. Well, maybe not in the snow.

When he came in, stomping the snow from his boots, she handed him a cup of coffee. "How long do you think it'll keep snowing?"

"A few days maybe. The sky is dark to the south; so I think more is coming." He sat at the table and smiled up at her. "Enough for you to make your snow angel."

"I wonder what it would be like to live here through a winter."

"You aren't thinking of doing that this year are you?"

She shook her head. "I wish I could, but I signed a contract to teach which means by late January I have to be back in San Francisco."

"You don't sound like you are looking forward to that."

"No, I never thought I'd not want to go back but... I like Arizona. I haven't seen Tucson, of course, but I love it up here. The air is so fresh, so quiet and then the wind in the pines. I like the lonesome quality that somehow doesn't feel lonely."

"It is pretty country."

"Have you ever thought of settling one place?"

"Maybe someday. I'd have to figure out something to do though. My line of work requires travel."

She considered that. She knew he'd never want to live in a city like San Francisco. She could not imagine him keeping a store. Maybe he'd go back to ranching. It wasn't her problem-- even if she wished it was.

"You are thinking too much," he said rising and taking her in his arms. "Let the day take care of itself. And today is about snow, isn't it?"

She smiled as he kissed her lips. She had been wrestling with so many problems, doubts, fears, and maybe she did have to learn to let a day be what it was without looking ahead.

When they finished eating, she cleaned up and then joined him in the main room. "It's still coming down hard," he said as they looked out the window and he put his arm around her.

"It's so beautiful. I've seen snow when I lived back East, but this is different in the wilderness or it feels different.

"Get your coat and gloves," he said.

Half an hour later, she followed him down to the lake with the snow falling hard around them. They had left the dogs inside, even though Zinnia, and even the puppies protested being left behind. "So," he said, "what will it be? Snowman or snow angel first?"

"Snow angel. Yours and mine, side by side."

"I think it's deep enough here, no rocks that I remember," he said with a teasing smile. He let go and fell flat on the ground and then moved his arms as she had instructed. A moment later, he had risen up with the smooth grace she had seen so often from him. She looked back at his creation. It was a very tall angel but did look like one. So it was her turn. She faced the lake, let herself go and landed hard in the soft snow. She lay there a moment smiling before she reached out her arms to create her wings. Before she could rise, he had reached down and drawn her to her feet. Looking back, she saw the two angels, the one taller, and somehow surprisingly stronger looking, but the other clearly its mate or would be until it melted.

"So," he said, "still up to a snowman or are you getting cold?"

"I was thinking maybe a walk in the snow instead?"

He smiled, put his arm around her waist, and they headed up the road. She stopped where she had first seen the lake and cabin. "When I first got here, I was amazed how beautiful it all was," she said as he looked with her at the tableau below. "Now, it's like a painting." Even though they were always far from people, the snow gave it an even cozier feeling, like it was just them in the world.

"I suppose you paint too," he said teasingly as he bent and kissed her forehead.

"Not very well. Have you tried painting or drawing?"

He shook his head. "There wasn't a lot of time for play in my world and art would have been play." Slowly with his arm around her, they walked back to the cabin. Inside, they stripped off their clothing to hang on chairs by the cook stove and it was as she had imagined.

She ran her fingers over his body. She so loved his lean muscles, the way they moved or tightened under her touch. He left her only long enough to get the condom, and then they made love in the kitchen, by the stove, lying together when they had both found their fulfillment.

When he rose and went into the bedroom to get his clothing, he brought back hers and they dressed by the heat of the fire. She warmed up the coffee, and they took it into the main room to watch the snow as it fell. "Tomorrow we can make a snowman," she said.

"If this doesn't turn to rain first."

"You think it will?"

"With the mountains, you never know. I was up on the Sierras two years ago when we got caught in a storm."

"We?"

"I was with a rancher who was looking to prove his neighbor had been rustling his stock. It was not supposed to snow that early. He knew of a cave, and we took refuge there. Big enough to bring the horses in too. We built a fire but firewood was limited. The storm lasted just under a week, and by the time it finally broke, we were considering eating one of the horses."

She looked at him with shock. "You can't mean you'd eat a horse."

"Better than starving." He smiled at her, and once again, she was unsure if he was teasing or serious. The one thing she knew for sure is he'd lived a life she'd imagined.

"You know what you said that day when we left Payson, about my trying too hard to be what others want."

"Yes."

She pulled him to the sofa. "I have thought about it. I know from where it came."

"And?"

"My mother. I don't remember if I told you, but she had been born to money, more than my father ever could have made. She's the one who tried to get me to dress better, act more the lady, do what was important in society. I think she's the one who wanted Father to work for the Hemstreets. Money was always what she valued."

"And she's the reason you hid your books?" he asked when she stopped.

"Part of it. A start. Then I went to Wellesley and Yale. The women there were intellectuals. By then I was paying for my education with writing the western stories, and I knew they would find it beneath them. I let them believe I'd gotten a scholarship rather than let them know the truth."

"Holly too?"

"I told no one. I know Holly would have understood but hiding it by then was second nature to me. I was hiding men like you, the ones who others craved to read about and I was ashamed of writing." When he looked away from her, she turned his head so their gazes met. "I didn't really understand what I was writing about or the kind of people. I'd read a lot, of course, but I'd never met anyone like you."

"That's understandable."

She wondered if he meant that. "Is it? Then when I lied to that couple in Payson, trying to hide who I was, who you were to me. It was more of the same, and I didn't see it until you called me out for it."

"I told you it was all right."

"But it wasn't. Cole, it's not about you. It's about me. I should have been proud of my books. I am embarrassed now that I wasn't. I should have been proud of the people I wrote about. They call them salt of the earth, and I was worrying about what some elites thought more than the ethics of my stories. I wanted to look good to others and was less worried about being good."

He smiled and took her hand, kissing her fingers. "You are a very special lady. Do you know that?"

"You keep saying I think too much."

He gave a little laugh. "Funny if I've made you think I don't respect all you've done, I've grown to think how much you accomplished and how much I admire you for it."

"Really?"

He laughed and shook his head before he bent to claim her lips.

CHAPTER 16

Three days later, the snow mostly gone, Cole rode into Payson to see if there had been any wires. More importantly, he hoped Freedman would be back with the deed and will. He had also decided to stop by the land agent. He wanted the other thousand acres. If the government was going to regulate land usage, the value of private land would go up. He wasn't sure he wanted to go back to cattle ranching, but if he bought the land, the option would be there. He wasn't willing to admit that the real hope was for some kind of future with Willy. Maybe she could teach most of the year and come back to him for the summers. Was he ready to commit to a place as well as a woman?

He had been surprised that Willy hadn't argued with him about coming along, but she had been busy typing. Maybe she had gotten past the barrier blocking her writing. Frustrated in his own work, he was no closer to deciphering her father's journals. While there was sufficient evidence to show fraud and deceptions in the Hemstreet business, that would not link it to Butler's death nor prove Hamilton had any part of it. Clearly, someone was convinced the papers could prove a crime or there'd have been no arson. That wasn't enough to lead to charges.

After settling Boomer in the stable, Cole stopped by the telegraph office. He wasn't surprised but was still disappointed when nothing was waiting for him. He stopped next at Gibbons and told him the land he wanted.

"You can afford that?" the agent asked with some surprise.

"Would I come here if I could not?" His impression of the man's dishonesty hadn't changed.

"I suppose not." He rifled through his files and came up with a plat map. "Which portion do you want?"

"What's available?"

They worked out the details, signed a quitclaim, and a contract agreement to a warranty deed transfer. Cole went back to the telegraph office to have the funds transferred.

"Hey, son," the familiar voice called.

Cole turned to watch Lars Ericson walk up to him. "How things going?" the old man asked

"Pretty well. You think we're due for more snow?"

"The old timers say we might be."

Cole smiled as he wondered how old someone would have to be to qualify for being an old timer in Ericson's book.

"When you thinking of heading south?" Ericson asked.

"It will depend on the lady, but if hard weather is coming, she may want to go sooner than she originally planned."

"Tell her the Injuns say it's how it'll be."

"Which ones?"

"Jim Little Eagle for one. He's Tonto 'pache. He come by last week, right before the snow, and said it was coming, and be ready."

Cole considered that. Those who had lived in a region often knew.

"How about having a drink with me," Ericson suggested, pointing toward the closest bar.

Cole smiled as he recognized what that would mean, but he went anyway. The bar was small and smoky. It had three men drinking in a corner table.

"What can I get you two?" the barkeep asked.

"Beer," Cole said and Ericson nodded.

A moment later, he was sipping the first beer he'd had in months. He reached into his pocket for a cigarette and lit it, not surprised when Ericson bummed one. He'd have to buy several packs before he headed south with the moocher.

"What's the prediction for the winter?" he asked the bartender with a smile as he took a long draw on the cigarette.

"Gonna be a hard one. That's what the Tontos say. Early snow always means hard winter."

Ericson chortled. "Told ya so. Jim come in here?"

"Not to drink beer," the bartender said looking affronted. "You know the law."

"And I know you."

"Well, it was him—and that's all I'm sayin'." The barkeep smirked.

After finishing off his beer, Cole headed outside. Ericson followed him.

"Why don't you come by Saturday," Cole suggested. "By then I should know what she wants to do." Ericson grinned and nodded, before leaving him.

Cole walked up to the Freedman home and was glad to see the lawyer in and the paperwork ready. "I appreciate your work. I am buying land around the lake cabin, but that will stay in my name for now."

"Leaving it to her though, I suppose."

"The will stipulates all my worldly goods; so yes."

"I hope your boss..." Milt hesitated and smiled. "Doesn't have to find this out the hard way."

Cole smiled crookedly. "You and me both."

Stopping by the telegraph office, the funds had been transferred, but there was also a wire from Vince. He took it outside to read. "Asa is a Thomas. Yuma. Dangerous. Watch to the south. Support here." He didn't like the sound of that but needed to take care of his Payson business before he considered it further.

He took the money order to Gibbons, bought extra oats, got Boomer saddled and loaded. Before he had done more than mount him, he realized he needed one more thing. He rode to the general store and bought a padlock that looked exactly like the one on the cabin. He put the keys with the papers in his saddlebag. With his lack of trust regarding Gibbons, he didn't want him to have access to the cabin when they were gone.

Riding out of town, he was not surprised that Hamilton would have been an alias. The name Thomas meant nothing to him but Yuma did. The man had a record. Whatever was intended by Hamilton, Vince said it was waiting for Willy. He considered as he rode out of town if she'd be better off not coming to Tucson. He was certain of one thing. This needed to be settled. If she went to San Francisco without that happening, it would be more dangerous. Support was in Tucson. Eventually, word would get to Hamilton or rather Thomas as to where she was. Better to confront it.

He heard the horse behind him and slowed, his hand loose above his revolver as he waited until he saw it was Ericson. "Thought I'd ride with ya," the oldster said as he brought his horse alongside Boomer.

Considering the man's request to also ride south with them, Cole decided he needed to be fair. "I need to warn you that the ride south might not be the safest thing for you to do. If you want to stay up here for the winter and need help with firewood, I'll do that."

"Danger? What exactly you mean?"

"I might have an enemy. I don't have a reason to expect that person to reach me before I get to Tucson but... just saying."

Ericson chuckled. "I might like going with you more than I expected.

I'll get my rifle sighted up. I have plenty of ammo. What are you expecting?"

"That's the problem. I don't know. It involves a man called Thomas Hamilton from San Francisco, except, his last name was Thomas when he did time in Yuma."

"Strange." Ericson was silent as they rode up a ridge. Cole waited. "Could it be Harry Thomas?" Ericson finally asked.

"I didn't get both names."

"When I got out of the army, after Washita, I was riding for different outfits. On one of the ranches, the foreman was Harry Thomas. Maybe not the same man, but he was the meanest son of a bitch I ever met. A man like that sticks in a body's mind. He was cheating the brand he was riding for. Branding calves for another outfit and being paid for it. Changing the numbers when he took stock to the auction. When it was discovered, he was fired. Someone took a shot at the boss, missed, but some thought they saw Thomas."

"Where was this?"

"Let me think. Socorro, New Mexico. I would say it was '79 but just guessing. Working on a ranch, time gets away from a man. Anyway, I never saw him again, but if he's who you're talking about, he was a cruel bastard to animals and men."

"It might fit from what I've been told about him." He did some calculating. "Mid-forties now would fit for Hamilton's age. He works for a company in Frisco where fraud has been part of their game and maybe murder."

"And he's after you?"

"Willy."

Ericson choked. "That purty little thing?"

"It's about evidence she has. Maybe something more. At any rate, that's all I know."

"Well, I'll tell you this for sure. I'm with you and will do what I can to keep that sweet gal safe. Damn that bastard to hell."

Cole's smile was grim. That was his job.

Willy watched as Cole rode to the corrals and unsaddled his horse. She had prepared a special dinner and had hoped he'd be home before dark to eat it. She went back into the kitchen and put the last touches on the chicken cutlets, which used up the last of their chicken and the mushrooms she had gathered. The recipe had called for truffles, but she was pretty sure morels would be a suitable substitute.

When he came in, he set a bag on the counter as she handed him the whiskey he generally favored after a ride. "How were things in town?" she asked.

He took a sip and sat down. "How was your day?" he asked.

"Good except for missing you." She smiled. "Are you hungry?"

"As a bear—and not just for food." He smiled, and she turned back to the stove looking forward to the evening ahead.

She put the food on the table. They ate with little conversation. A few scraps found their way to Zinnia, who had gotten rather good at the art of begging. When they finished, he helped with the dishes before they went into the main room and sat on the sofa.

"Tell me about town," she said.

"I got a wire from Vince." He handed it to her.

'Asa is a Thomas. Yuma. Dangerous. Watch out to the south. Support here.'

"What does this mean?" she asked.

"It means Hamilton has an alias. I rode out of town with Lars Ericson, and he gave me what is probably the rest of his name. Harry Thomas. The reference to Yuma means he did time there. Vince didn't know for how long or there'd have been a number. The rest means that Vince is concerned and wants us where he can be backup. Sounds as if he's concerned Thomas can find out where you are."

"Could he?"

"You haven't told anyone where you went, have you?"

She shook her head. "I don't have many friends in San Francisco. My two best friends from high school have moved on with babies and married life. The university didn't have women I worked closely with. My best friend today is Holly. Woman friend that is."

"How about that publisher of your books?"

"I never told him where I was going or even that I was."

"How does he get your royalties to you?"

She smiled. "You know a bit about putting out books."

"I know a bit about a lot of things." He gave her that crooked smile that as always had her heart melting.

"Yes, I chose to take royalties rather than a lump sum. They are deposited in a San Francisco bank along with my college salary. When I left on the train, I took the money I thought I might need. At the time I left, I didn't have a lot to worry about. Can he find me?"

"If he wants to. You've been into Payson, and you stand out as someone different. Contrell and Wilson know your name. Nobody can really hide from a determined detective unless they stay completely away from other people."

"I hadn't thought of that." She felt a surge of fear.

"You know I'll protect you."

She did know that, and it was what scared her the most. "What should we do?"

"You came here to write and figure out what your father left for you. Your main purposes can be accomplished wherever you are. I know you love it here, but maybe it would be better if we got somewhere I wasn't your only protection."

She knew what that meant-- where he could be killed. "I suppose so." She didn't like the idea, but it was sensible.

"There is another consideration," he said as he went into the kitchen and came back with two brandies. "The talk is this may be an exceptionally hard winter up here. Even with heavy snow, we can still get out but it'd be harder on the horses and won't be much fun for you either."

"When do you believe we should leave?"

She saw him consider that. "I will need to let Ericson know. He wants to come. This looks like a break in the weather that can get us south. We can leave with the supplies we have and get more in Jacobs Corner. It had a nice little store last time I was through there."

"Not in Payson?"

"It's best if we don't. The less people who know where you are, the better."

"So we go to Tucson. Do we take the stage route?"

He shook his head. "There is a shorter route but it will take five nights from here. Head south from Payson to Jacob's Corner. From there to the Salt River crossing. Next town is Globe which has a hotel if you want a room and if not, we'll camp south of it in one of the little side canyons with a spring. The next day we cross the Gila and head up the San Pedro, camping along the river. We'll probably stop at Mammoth or Oracle, take a hotel room, get cleaned up, and from there it's about thirty miles to Vince's ranch. I am not sure though if they will still be there, or if they will have moved out to the adobes."

"This sounds like a long journey."

"Almost 190 miles. You'll be a real horseman by the time you get there."

"If I don't fall off due to total exhaustion."

He chuckled. "You are a strong gal. You won't do that, but if I think you're getting too tired, we'll hole up somewhere a day or two."

"Will any of this be dangerous?"

"Traveling the backcountry always has risks. Even trains and stagecoaches get held up. Haven't you written about a few of those?" he asked with that bantering smile.

She put her fingers up and stroked his cheek. "Have I ever told you how cute you are?" she asked.

He snorted. "Nobody has ever told me how cute I am, which is because I am not cute."

"You can be when you get that look in your eyes, when you show how amused you are, when you smile with just one corner of your mouth tilted up. You are very cute."

"Must be one of those in the eye of the beholder," he said as he bent and kissed her lightly.

"You really believe we should leave soon?"

"We don't have to. It's up to you. I am laying out the facts for you, sweetheart. You decide."

"And I can't take my typewriter?" She hated leaving it for the owner or next renter, but it was bulky for packing on a horse and likely would destroy it anyway.

"Get a new one in Tucson," he said with that smile that had her thinking about anything but her typewriter. Well, maybe it did a bit regarding writing, as she wondered why she'd never thought to give the last Taggert such a playful smile. She guessed she'd thought if a man lived with danger, he'd have no sense of humor. Knowing Cole had changed all that. She understood such a man might find more reasons to laugh knowing his life could be cut short.

"I am only delaying the inevitable, I guess," she said with a sigh. "I am scared though. I admit it."

"Look into my eyes." He tilted her chin up so she gazed straight into his. She saw truth and determination. "I will do anything for you," he said. "I will keep you safe. I won't promise there may not be trouble ahead, but you will get back to San Francisco, and when you do, it'll be safe for you. I promise you that too."

"Will you promise you'll be safe too?" she asked knowing he wouldn't but wanting to ask it anyway.

"I will do my best," he said with that grin and rose. "So when do we go?"

"How soon can we be ready?"

"Start packing your clothes, the papers of your father's. I'll ride over to Ericson's in the morning, and I think we could leave in two days. It'll be a new moon. Good time for traveling."

"Why?"

"Dark at night and others can't move around so easily, not so easy to find our camps, or at least, it's more unlikely. Besides, isn't there something about planting by the new moon?" Again, the teasing smile.

"I've never planted a garden and know next to nothing about them. I want to someday. Talking to Adele gave me ideas. At least, whenever I have a home again."

"I hear the Bay Area is good for growing. Milder climate."

"I guess." She wondered if he hoped she'd stay there. Maybe he'd had enough of her problems, the ones that didn't give him any profit. Then she felt annoyed with herself even to think that. He had come to help her, never asked anything. "Are you tired?" she asked.

Again, that smile. "Not too tired. Let me take the dogs out for one last romp."

She headed for the bedroom, stripped and put on her nightgown, blew out all but the one lamp on the dresser. When he came in, she watched in its glow.

"We should name them," he said when he sat on the edge of the bed.

She reached up to rub his back as he unbuttoned his shirt. "How about Petunia and Poppy?" she suggested as she ran her ringers along the large muscle ridge that ran down his back to his belt.

"Good enough."

When he turned, he kissed and then touched her. Lost again in the magic that had consumed her since the moment she had seen him, she loved the feel of his skin under her fingers, how the muscles moved and then...

October 26

In the morning, right after breakfast, Cole rode to Lars Ericson's cabin. It was well set beneath a colorful cliff, with a little stream winding below the house. Ericson stood on the porch. "Come on in for coffee," the older man said.

Cole dismounted and entered the tidy cabin. He sat at the table and took the coffee cup. "Don't have no sugar or cream," Ericson said.

"I take it black. Day after tomorrow. Can you be ready?"

"Shore can, but I do have a problem."

"And?" Cole studied him over the rim of his cup.

"I got a mule. Horace. I can't leave him here."

Cole considered that. "Actually that could be good. I made a pack that will hold the dogs with oats balancing it out on the other side. I had figured to put it onto my horse, but a mule would be better."

"Works for me if it's not too heavy. Horace ain't young."

"We'll divide the gear between our horses. The way I figure this is we will leave at first light."

"Want me to come back with you now? We could figure out the pack better that way."

"Can you be ready to leave?"

"Been ready."

"Good. One other thing, when we get to Payson, I want you to take Willy around town. Make sure she's not seen."

"You want me to know this now and not her until we get there."

"You're a smart old-timer. Yes, I don't want to scare her."

"You're in love with her, ain't you?"

There was no point in lying. "Yes."

"When you marrying her?"

"She turned me down and she's right. She's... Well, it wouldn't work. I'd die for her but I can't live the life she'd want her husband to live."

"You know that for a fact?"

"It's obvious."

"Son, a lot that seems obvious, ain't so much when it gets right down to it."

"Well, this is. There is another man. He'd suit her better. Better when she's not tied to the wrong man."

Ericson chuckled. "She agree with that?"

"She will."

"Back to when we get to Payson, since I can see you're stubborn as my mule. Why are we separating?" He poured them each more coffee.

"I have to go into town long enough to tell Contrell that there won't be more supplies going out to the lake house."

"Makes sense. All right."

"I'll meet you two a mile beyond town. I remember a copse of trees. Hang back and wait for me there."

"You expecting trouble?"

"Not so much but you never know. I told you about the situation with Thomas. He's had time to start looking around Arizona for her."

"Makes sense. You are good at strategy. Would've made a good soldier."

Cole snorted. "Other than the taking orders part, you mean."

"Other than that."

Tucson, Arizona October 27

Nate sat on the bench in front of the new adobe he'd just helped Vince, Holly and their two children move into. Alongside him was Jesse, Vince's youngest brother. The man talked little but what he said always made sense. Nate felt jealous of Cole for having two such brothers, for having this wonderful family. His own had been cold, never much support. Well, his father had tried. Thinking of his father brought him to his mother and full circle to the man who was a threat to Willy if not to his mother also.

"You're doing some deep thinking," Jesse said sipping his beer.

Vince joined them sitting on one of the garden chairs. "He's worried about what I'm worried about," he said opening his beer and taking a slug from the bottle.

"That jasper who wants to kill Holly's friend?" Jesse asked

"That's the one. Cole will stand between her and a bullet," Vince said with a glum expression. Obviously, the downside to having brothers was having to worry about them. "Of course, I don't want anything to happen to Willy but..."

"We might have a little something to say about that," Jesse said his jaw set.

"If we get to be part of the play," Vince argued.

"They may not be here until the middle of December," Nate said.

"The wire I sent Cole likely will change that," Vince said.

"Is that good or bad?" Nate asked.

"Some of both. I worried that Thomas would be sending out feelers, and he'd find them up there with only Cole to protect her and keep himself alive. Still, if I was wrong, then it brings them here with those yahoos in town, ready to let Thomas know when she gets here."

"I don't want to sound ignorant," Nate said, "but what's a yahoo?"

Despite his grim demeanor, Vince chuckled. "Didn't you ever read *Gulliver's Travels?*"

"Maybe I did a long time ago. By Jonathan Swift, right?"

"That's the ones. Yahoos resemble humans but are filthy, with disgusting habits."

"Sounds about right then. I didn't pay enough attention to literature I guess."

"Or to the underbelly of life."

"Maybe I was more connected to that then I knew. If the man we now know as Thomas came to work for my father shortly before his death, it seems likely Mr. Thomas was behind it. But was my mother also? Is that how she kept her Nob Hill home?"

"And paid for your keep," Jesse added.

"True. I'd have profited from the thefts, I guess." His horse, his education, his spending money. No, he had that from an earlier inheritance, his mother's mother.

"Learning that can be upsetting," Vince said with a wry smile. Nate recognized that from what Jeremiah had told him of the Taggert family, these two understood more about his concerns than most ever would.

"And then... burning the house and... did it involve two murders? My father and Mr. Butler? Maybe others, if someone found out what he was doing." He set down his empty bottle and set his head onto his hands. "Life is sure not much like I thought it was."

"Those things happen. So what do you do about it now?" Vince asked.

Nate looked up from one strong face to the other. "I could whine for a few hours... or days. Then, maybe I should ride back to the lake house and see what they have decided."

"Give it a week," Vince said as he lit a cigarette. "I suspect Cole will be here within that."

"Why?"

"Because he will have thought it through and know he's got to get her out of there and here where we can keep her safe when he..."

Nate stared at him. "When he goes after Thomas?" He got it now.

"He won't leave him out there."

"Would he... murder him in cold blood?" For all he knew, it's exactly what he'd do.

"No, he'd never do that," Jesse said. "But he'll make Thomas go after him, and then he'll kill him." The words were said with no emotion. Nate looked back at Vince, who nodded.

"Maybe we need to draw Thomas out," Vince suggested as he stared into the desert beyond his new home. "Save Cole the trouble."

"How would we do it?" Jesse asked but was smiling with approval. What the hell kind of men were these to discuss something like this with so little emotion. It could all end in their deaths. Didn't that worry them?

"Let me think on it." Vince said. "Maybe we won't have to. If he's sent out runners, then he'll eventually find where Willy went. She'd stand out in Payson. It'd take them awhile to get there, but they will. When he finds out she's not there, he'll be on the train to Tucson or Phoenix first. We need to start looking for names arriving either place. He won't know we're onto him or that we know both his names.

Jesse nodded. "Sounds like it should work.

"You both have young families. You can't be putting yourselves at risk," Nate said.

They looked at him with that hard smile he'd seen on Cole's face. "We're brothers. It's what you do."

As Nate rode back to Jeremiah's house for the night, he thought about it. Brothers did that for each other. Friends did too. He didn't have many friends, but Willy was one of them. He couldn't let her be killed. He guessed he better put in some hours practicing with his gun. It might be needed.

Putting the pack on Horace was the last step before bringing down the dogs. Cole had suggested Willy play with them, get them exercising, so that they'd hopefully sleep as they rode in the pack. The first day or two would be the roughest in getting them used to travel. Fortunately, Horace had a calm, even disposition, a sweet temperament, especially for a jack.

He walked up to the porch where she was closing the padlock on the hasp. He hadn't expected she would notice he'd changed it, and she didn't. She held the key up. "Remind me to get this to the land agent when we go through town," she said.

"Give it to me. I can get it to the owner," he said. For a moment, he wasn't sure she would, but then she handed it to him and he put it in his vest pocket.

"I will miss this place the rest of my life," she said putting her arms around him and staring toward the lake.

"It is beautiful here."

"I suppose by the time I could consider renting it again, someone will have bought it."

"You never know." He had put the papers with the keys to the new lock in his saddlebag. He still wasn't sure when he'd tell her that the home was now in her name. Maybe before she headed to California for her job. "I don't want you going into Payson. Ericson will take you around it, and I'll meet you a mile south of town."

"Why?" She dropped her arms and looked up into his eyes.

"I don't want anyone knowing you left here. I will tell Contrell and that's it."

"You think…"

"I don't know, and it's why this is best. I will ask him to tell no one you're gone. I trust he won't."

"What about Mr. Gibbons?"

"You still have it leased for a month. You can write him when that's up."

"You really think that Hamilton or rather Thomas would be trying to find me?"

"He burned your home down. Yes, I think he will try." He smiled at her brushing the hair loose hair behind her ear. "Wear your hat low in case we run into anybody on our way to town. Let's not help them."

"All right."

Putting Zinnia and then the pups into the pack took a little time to reassure the anxious mother. He'd placed a blanket into the bottom to make a cozy nest, and they finally settled into the compartment. He tied shut the rawhide thongs to keep them there. Horace had behaved admirably through the process. "He is a good mule," he said to Ericson.

In moments, they had mounted and turned their horses to the road. Willy looked sad, but she didn't look back as they cleared the ridge, and the lake and cabin disappeared from view. They talked little on their way to Payson. Half a mile from town, Ericson called a halt. "This is the way we have to go."

Cole smiled at him. "Take care of her, Lars."

The older man grinned at him. "Took you awhile to call me by my first name."

"Takes me awhile to trust someone."

"Good wisdom."

"This isn't dangerous for you, is it?" Willy asked as he bent from his horse to give her a light kiss on the forehead.

"No reason for it to be." He smiled, tipped his hat, and rode off.

CHAPTER 17

Cole loosened his revolver in its holster as he rode into town. He had no reason to believe he'd run into trouble, but then trouble had rarely found him when he was expecting it. He pulled up in front of the freight office, stepping from his horse as Amos Contrell came to the door. "Was kind of expectin' ya."

"There a reason for that?" he asked as he walked up to him, pulled out a cigarette, and lit it.

"A body been here yesterday askin' about Miss Butler. Two it was."

Cole took a long draw on the cigarette as he considered that. "Give their names?"

"Nah, but they were toughs, not from 'round here."

"They still here?"

"Not sure. Said I never heard the name. They headed to Adele's and the general store. We all talked later, and told 'em the same thing. Don't know nobody by that name."

"That was good of you folks." He was thinking especially of the lady at the general store.

"No business of strangers. But they headed for Gibbons. He's not likely to do likewise, now is he?"

No, Cole thought, he likely would not. He seriously thought about looking for the two men, but the truth was he couldn't afford a fight, not when the real danger to Willy was not here. "I appreciate that." Then he thought of something else and reached into his back pocket, unfolded a ten-dollar bill, and handed it to Contrell.

Contrell frowned. "Ya don't need to pay us for being decent folks."

"I didn't intend to. What I want is a favor. If a stranger comes in, with maybe five or six hard cases, he's likely to go out to the lake cabin, come back spitting mad, and head south. After he's left, would you wire Sheriff Jace Trask in Tucson. Just say. "It's gone.""

"You expectin' trouble, young'un?"

"Maybe."

"I will do that." He smiled then, with the solid look Cole had seen on many older men who were tough as rawhide.

After shaking hands, Cole stepped up on his horse. "Thanks again. Be seeing you."

"I shore hope so."

South of town, Cole saw that Willy and Lars had dismounted and were waiting for him in the grove he'd suggested. Zinnia was feeding her pups. "Might be we should make a leash for them all," he said as he rode up. "Those pups will be getting adventuresome soon."

"We could cut up one of my skirts," Willy suggested.

"I have some leather strips that should do the trick. When we camp tonight, I'll see what I can do."

"See anything interesting in Payson?" Lars asked.

"Nope but got out of town as quick as I could to avoid that possibility." The more he thought about it, the more he decided the two looking for Willy would wire their boss for instructions. Would that bring Thomas back to Arizona? It was likely. If so, he'd take the train as far as Phoenix, rent a rig or horses to ride to Payson. He'd come with men. He wouldn't be coming the way that Cole had planned to go south. He smiled grimly. He was buying time.

"What are you thinking about?" Willy asked as she handed him one of the biscuits.

"How do you know it's anything?" he asked a mix of dismay and amusement at her knack of reading him.

"You have creases between your brows, your eyes are narrowed, and your lips tightened."

He laughed. "All right, it was something but now I forgot when you did that."

"Did what?"

"Looked at me that way." He bent and kissed her hard ignoring the fact that Lars was watching.

"Want me to take the dogs for a walk?" Lars asked with a chuckle.

"No need right now. Ask me again later." Cole winked at Willy.

"All right, you distracted me, but now I want to know what you found in Payson that upset you."

"I'm not upset. I'll tell you while we're riding." He scooped up the dogs, settled them into their pack and swung up on his horse.

She came alongside him. "We're riding," she reminded him.

"You come up too, Lars," he said and told them what he'd learned in town. "My thinking is Thomas will come up here. He will find the house deserted, and then he'll head south, most likely for Tucson. That means we have a week and a half from now until he gets back to Tucson."

"I suppose Mr. Gibbons will tell him of my leasing the cabin."

"If it can profit him." What Cole didn't add is the probability that Gibbons would also tell him about Cole's involvement. Willy had no reason to know about it yet. He still wasn't ready to tell her why he had gone to Gibbons. It was possible the land agent wouldn't tell the jasper, but more likely, that he would, especially after Thomas went out to the cabin to find nobody there. It'd be the first time Thomas would know that he was facing Taggerts. With his background, he was likely to know the name. It wouldn't take long to find Taggerts now lived in Tucson, where Nate had first gone. When he got back to Phoenix, he'd hire more men before he came. When Cole got to Globe, he'd call his father to tell him what he knew. His brothers and father would need some time to prepare their end. He wished he could think of a way to keep them out of what was likely to come. He couldn't think of one.

When they rode through Jacob's Corner, Cole asked Willy if she wanted to spend the night. "We can go farther, can't we?" she asked feeling actually good about how the ride was going, and the dogs were not minding the pack. They stopped only long enough to purchase more eggs, flour, powdered milk, and a new bottle of whiskey. Willy had brought her half bottle of sherry.

Five miles farther on, Cole pointed to a small canyon a bit off the trail, and there they made their first night camp. While she and Lars built the fire, Cole secured the horses and mule with a rope corral where there was some grass. The canyon itself helped to corral the pups who were beginning to explore as Cole had predicted.

Willy fed Zinnia the first of the Spratt's cakes and was pleased she gulped it down and even drank the milk she'd made up for her. She showed less enthusiasm for the hard tack Willy had made, but she nibbled at it. The little dog then lay on her side and drew the puppies to feed.

Lars helped Willy heat up the can of beans, and they ate more of the biscuits. After they ate, she enjoyed watching the flames, leaning back against Cole's muscular chest and feeling the warmth of his body warming hers. The pups had nestled down with their mother and were sleeping. "It's pretty like this," she said. "With the moon barely a sickle, the stars show up so much more."

"Do you know their names?"

"The constellations?"

"Yes."

"The Big and Little Dipper. That's it. I am not much of an astronomer."

He pointed to the southern horizon. "I don't know a lot but over there, that's Orion, the warrior. See the sword."

She brushed her fingers over his bristly jaw. "You would know that one."

"It's easy to see and use to travel at night by."

"You need a shave."

"You're telling me. I hate the feel too but not going to be doing much about it while we're traveling."

Lars poured Cole and himself a whiskey. Willy made a face when he suggested she might like one. She would save her sherry for a night she needed it more. She'd have no problem falling asleep after the day they'd had.

"Do you want a tent?" Cole asked. "With the tarp, I can easily rig you up one."

She shook her head. "I like it under the stars. I've never slept out like this."

When he got up, he made up her bedroll and his beside her. He stripped off his shirt and boots, helped her pull of her boots, before he rolled up in his blanket. Lars put his bedding closer to the horses and mule. The puppies and Zinnia curled up next to Willy. She knew when Cole fell asleep, but she lay awake longer than she had expected. She watched the coals slowly darkening as she thought about what he'd said regarding the men in Payson. She suspected he'd left something out. He wanted not to worry her, but he didn't understand she did better when she understood it all.

She thought then of her father's desire to protect her. He had left all the evidence for her to deal for what was clearly a crime, and yet he'd never told her when he knew it. Was it to protect her or because he thought she had stronger feelings for Nate than she did? She didn't know when she fell asleep, only when she woke to the first light with Cole's arm tightening around her.

"How did you sleep?" she asked kissing his chest.

"Good. And you?"

"Well, other than Lars snoring," she said teasingly, "I did fine."

"Today you'll see the Salt River. I hope it'll be low enough for an easy crossing."

"If it's not?"

"We'll deal with it when we get to it." He rose, and with a few twigs, he stirred the fire to life. As the coffee began perking, Lars joined them.

"You feel it?"

"Maybe storm coming?" Cole asked.

"Feels like it."

"We better make good time then today. We have to cross the Salt and don't want to do it when it's in flood."

"Will my father's papers be safe if it rains?" she asked as she saddled her horse while Cole set the packs back on Horace.

"I wrapped them in oil cloth. You need to find your coat." She dug it out of her saddlebag. He handed her a cloth that felt slick. "Oil cloth for you too. If it starts to rain, put it over your shoulders, keep as dry as you can. The air is getting colder. Don't want to take a chill."

"What about you?" she asked as she stepped up on Boots.

"I'm used to being rained on." He grinned at her as he nudged Boomer into a fast walk. They stopped only once in the afternoon to eat and give the dogs a short break. When they got to the Salt, the gravel bars extended most the across to the rocky bluff. If the storm had hit earlier they would have had to wait because the narrow channel would deepen fast. As it was, Cole stayed at Willy's side as her horse crossed, but she had no problems. She waited while he rode back across to make sure Horace crossed safely with the packs and dogs.

"He pointed to high bluffs. "None of this will look the same in a year. They are building a dam here. We crossed the last time we likely will of a free flowing Salt. They say that dam will be one of the highest in the world."

"It's a changing country," Lars agreed. "Nothing gonna be the same."

Cole let out a breath. "It was a good way." He gave a little laugh. "But can't stop progress… or that's what they call it."

They climbed the opposite ridge and rode another mile or two before Cole signaled them to the side and a grove of trees. "It'll give us some shelter," he said as they went through the familiar routine of unsaddling and unpacking the animals. This time she was able to find small branches and get the fire started before Lars and Cole were finished. The wind was getting stronger, and she could smell moisture in the air. After they ate a simple meal, Lars sipped whiskey and Cole lit a cigarette, leaning back against a tree.

"This time, I will make you a tent," Cole said as he studied the blackening sky. This time, she didn't argue and watched as, using a knife she saw for the first time he had on his belt, he cut off straight branches from the junipers, peeling off the smaller branches and needles. He, studied the sky a moment, then laid out the tarp, and lifted it with what had become poles. Using pegs that he pulled from a pack, he secured the tarp to the ground. Unless the wind blew fiercely, she saw she'd stay dry and protected.

"You will sleep with me in it, won't you?" she asked as she saw him only lay her bedroll within the tent.

"Best I don't tonight. Storms make the animals edgy. Keep the dogs with you. I'll stay by the horses. We don't want them running off."

No, she didn't want that, but she would miss the feeling of his long, lean body next to hers. She realized how much she'd grown accustomed to that. How many more days would they have together? She didn't have to go back to San Francisco until mid-January. However, would she be welcome in Tucson where she was clearly a threat with someone coming after her? Foolish thought which she quickly discarded. Holly was a courageous woman who would never turn out a friend. It didn't change Willy's concern, as she also didn't want to endanger a friend, her husband, and even more Cole. The thing was-- where could she go? She fell asleep without an answer.

When the rains came, they were heavy and beat against her tent. She worried about how Cole and Lars would fare, but she was grateful she was staying dry with the dogs. She remembered the oilcloth. Maybe Cole and Lars were using that to protect themselves. She fell asleep again, with that thought the last she remembered.

The next morning the air felt clear and fresh. The storm had passed and left behind only puddles as they rode south. By late afternoon, they were entering Globe. "Do you want a hotel room tonight?" Cole asked.

"Would it be safe?"

"We have the time. You won't be able to take the dogs or me though." He smiled. "Reputable hotels rent to married couples, not those fornicating."

She slapped his chest. "I don't feel like that's what we're doing."

"It's how they'd see it."

"How do you even know that word?" She glared at him.

"Don't forget, I was raised by a Bible reading, God fearing mother. She drilled it into my brothers and me. Not sure that it took on anybody but Jesse-- maybe. Not that he'd talk about it if it had."

"Hmph." She didn't like the word or what he'd said one bit, but she knew he was probably right as to how their relationship, such as it was, would be seen by others. It was so much more than that on her end, and he had asked her to marry him. She was having a harder time under-standing why she'd said no. "All right then."

"We'll meet you…"

"You didn't let me finish. No man, no dog, no hotel." She smiled.

"You'd be able to have a bath," he added to the tempting side of the ledger.

"I can do that when we get to another river too. No, I want us to be together as much as we can."

Lars had been listening but not getting into the debate. "If you two have worked that out, I can stop at the grocery store to get more supplies if… well, I'd need some cash."

That didn't surprise Cole. He delved into his back pocket, came up with a twenty and gave it to the older man. "Be sure you get food too."

Lars made a pouting face, which on a man of his age, with his white mustache, had Willy giggling. She had some money too and handed him a five.

"Meet us on the other side of town," Cole said as he rode toward the stable to get more oats. Willy stayed with Horace talking to Zinnia who wanted out of the pack, once they'd stopped. Where Willy didn't expect they'd be there long, she reassured her that her time was coming. When Cole came out with the bag and put it on the opposite side of the pack, he said, "I need to call Pa."

"Where will you find a phone?"

"I know the sheriff. He has one."

He would know sheriffs, probably everywhere, she thought with some irritation as they rode to the office. "I'll wait for you here," she said keeping the brim on her hat down as he'd requested. With her hair mostly covered, she didn't think she'd look much like a woman. She hoped.

When he came out, he looked irritated. "What was wrong?" she asked as he mounted his horse.

"Pa wasn't there."

"Isn't there anyone else you can call?"

He shook his head. "The adobes don't have phones yet, if ever that far out. Vince and Holly are moved out there. Nobody at their ranch either."

"And a wire?"

"Not this time." She looked into his eyes and saw once again some-thing he wasn't telling her.

"All right, then I guess we find Lars and go?" she said forcing a smile.

"No argument?"

"You'll tell me when you want me to know."

"Low blow."

"Women don't fight fair. Didn't you know that?"

He laughed. "I guess not, but I am learning. We'll talk about it when we camp for the night."

Joining up with Lars, they rode south, crossing the Gila a few miles south of Globe. It was not as big a river as the Salt. Several miles south of it, Cole led them to a campsite half a mile off the road. As they put together their camp, Cole handed her the straps he'd cut for the pups and Zinnia. "Tonight keep them on the leash." She didn't ask why but did it. Then she heard a wolf, soon answered by another. They tethered the horses and mule together and kept them near to the camp.

"No point in taking chances," he said as another wolf howled. She liked the sound, almost beautiful, at least when she wasn't worried about a pack attacking her pets or the horses. After they'd eaten, she sipped a little of her sherry while Lars and Cole shared the whiskey.

She had the pups on her lap. Petunia and Poppy. She had to start using their names. Zinnia was lying with her head on her leg.

She wanted to be held by Cole, but he was in a thoughtful mood, maybe enhanced by their getting closer to Tucson. Was he worried about a confrontation there with Thomas? She still hoped that if they got the proof of theft to the sheriff, the law would arrest the man, or maybe he'd run for it if he decided he'd been found out. Maybe he'd change his name again.

Cole lit a cigarette and then looked at her. "You wanted to know why no wire."

She was glad he hadn't forgotten and nodded.

"I have every reason to believe Thomas will know I am with you. He will know my name because of the shooting, maybe other reasons."

"The books? Or because we were seen together in Payson?"

"Some of that. The result is, I can't wire my father or brothers and take the chance Thomas has a source working in the telegraph office either place. I don't want him to be totally sure where we are right now or where we are heading."

"Maybe we shouldn't go to Tucson," Willy suggested. "We could just sort of disappear."

He smiled at that. "I guarantee you-- unless someone hides in a wilderness and never comes out, it's impossible to hide forever."

"So what are you expecting?" Lars asked. Surprisingly, to Willy, he seemed more interested than afraid of what he was hearing.

"I expect him to go to Payson with the belief Willy is still there. Asking questions in town, he'll head for Tucson as it's common knowledge Taggerts live there. With the men he left in town, he will know Hemstreet is still there. He's going to expect that's where Willy headed. I believe he will come with more men than he might've if he'd thought she was alone." He turned back to her. "If you thought he'd forget about you after you put the evidence of theft into the sheriff's hands, he won't. It's not how men like him operate."

"So what's the plan?" Lars asked.

Cole's smile was crooked. "We will be in Tucson hopefully at least four days, maybe five ahead of him. That gives us time to talk to my family, get Willy somewhere safe, and make sure we meet Thomas where we choose."

"If he's after me, why don't I go back to San Francisco and trust the law there to keep me safe?" she asked. "I don't want anyone else being hurt because of me."

He took long draw on his cigarette, long enough that she thought he wasn't going to answer. "If you thought I'd let you do that or my brothers would, or my father, you don't know the Taggerts-- writing about them or not."

"Hell," Lars said with a laugh, "I only read the books and met this man a short time ago, and even I know he'd not let you do it."

"Well, it's not like I knew them then," she said defensively.

"You do now. So put that thought out of your head. We will work this out, and in the end, Thomas will be leaving you alone, one way or the other, and you can go back to that university of yours and teach those classes."

"You a professor?" Lars asked.

"English."

"Wal, I'll be danged, and write all them rootin' tootin' fightin' books." He shook his head. "You just never know with women these days."

Riding south and heading up into the Mescal Mountains, Cole saw the glint of steel on the right side of the trail. Looking left, he saw movement. The birds had gone quiet. He put out his hand.

"Lars, get out your rifle, keep a tight hold on Horace in case this goes bad." He glanced back at Willy as he pulled out his Winchester. "Drop a little behind us. Hold tight to your reins. Don't let Boots go."

"What's wrong?"

"Just do it and make sure you can grab your rifle if need be." He was relieved when she did it without argument.

He laid his rifle across the pommel of his saddle. There were two, one on each side of the road. Whether they were road agents or worse, they would see that there was no taking them by surprise.

He kept his horse at a slow steady pace, as they rode past, where he knew two waited.

He smiled as he looked into one of the men's eyes. The man had backed off, didn't have his rifle pointed, and tipped his hat as they rode by.

"You think they'll be trouble?" Lars asked when they all were well past them.

"Not now."

Their next camp was past the community of Winkelman, this time along the San Pedro River. "How far ya figure to Tucson?" Lars asked him, as they got the horses settled.

"Two days maybe." The air, even in the lower desert, was getting a nip to it in the evening. It had to be November. In the distance, he saw clouds building. As they ate their simple supper, the thunderheads passed to the south and traveled up the Winchester range. Cole was not surprised that there was little talk as each of them were into their own thoughts as to what lay ahead.

In the morning, they left at first light. "How many miles to go?" Willy asked as she rode alongside him, using her hand to ease her back.

"Maybe forty. One more night on the trail. You up to it?"

She nodded but he saw she was tired. "Where will we go when we get there?"

"Vince and Holly's ranch. It's north of Tucson, has open ground around it. If they have moved out, like I figure, they'll be fine with us staying there while we work out what happens next."

"Lars too?"

"If he wants. It's a big house. Remember though that he has a sister in Tucson." The older man had dropped back a bit with Horace. The ride had been hard on them too. Soon, they'd have time to recuperate.

"Then do I take what we'd gathered to the sheriff?"

"Remember when I earlier asked you if your father had a pet name for you? Something he would call you other than Wilhelmina or Willy. Have you come up with anything?"

About the time, he had decided she wouldn't answer, she said, "I've tried, but nothing's coming to me."

"We need a key. Maybe in your childhood? I keep thinking the journals could be what tie Thomas to the evidence you have."

"You really think so?"

"I'd put chips on it. He stacked them with it. They extend over a period of years. He was worried they would fall into the wrong hands and that's why he not only hid them away but counted on you being able to decipher them as you'd be the only one who could find them. It's possible what's in them will lead us to his killer."

"You really don't think he killed himself?"

When he nodded, she was silent. He looked over and saw tears on her lashes. He knew some was she was tired, but she needed to know what had happened, that her father hadn't chosen to leave her. Cole instinctually believed that to be the case. He had to prove it for her as much as to finally have something solid that would draw the law into this.

When they rode past Steam Pump Ranch, Cole turned them west. An hour later, they were at his brother's ranch. Whenever he rode into its yard, he admired the setting. High enough above the Santa Cruz to avoid the potential flashfloods, that were part of desert living, the two-story farmhouse was shaded with tall cottonwood and sycamore trees. Painted white with green shutters, Cole knew the shutters weren't just decorative but could be used to batten down the home against storms or other dangers. Vince had lived long enough with danger to know the need for a defensible home, and he had made sure it was where he situated his family.

"Nice spread he has here," Lars said as they all dismounted.

"He's moved, built a house out near Jesse's, farther from towns."

"Now why'd he wanta do that?"

"Family. Jesse and Vince married sisters, now they each have two children. Out there, they can grow up together, support each other."

"It would be nice to be with family," Willy said stretching her back. She smiled then. "It'd be nice to even have a family."

"Yeah," Lars said, looking out across the pasture to the river, "but look at that grass. I see he's still got a few cattle here. He going to lease it?"

"I haven't heard his plans." Cole lifted the pups and Zinnia out of their pack. Willy went ahead of him and opened the gate to a picket fence that surrounded the front porch. He set the dogs down, and they rolled in the dirt and ran toward the porch to explore. They would be safe in the yard, as any rattlers could be seen and removed. Willy stepped up on the porch. "Nobody is home," she said. "What do we do now?"

He went to the left side of the house, lifted a piece of siding, and came up with the key. He put it into the deadbolt, heard it click and opened the door. He hadn't been sure if there'd be furniture left, but although he could see familiar items were gone, it still had a sofa, chairs, end tables in the parlor, a table in the dining room with chairs. He led their way back to the kitchen and saw pans and dishes had been left. When he opened the pantry, it was fully stocked.

"There's a note on the table," Willy handed it to him.

"It says, '*Figure you'll be here by Saturday. Make yourselves at home. We'll be back early Saturday morning to figure out what we do next. Vince.*' Wonder what the hell day this is."

Lars pulled out a pocket watch. "It's Friday, November 3. Need the year too?" He chuckled at his little joke.

"I can manage that one."

"So we can use the bedrooms?" Willy asked moving back to the hall and looking up the stairs.

"Take your pick.

He heard whimpering at the front door.

"Can the dogs come in?" she asked.

"They did good on being housebroke at the cabin, I think it'll be fine." He opened the door and in the three hurried, looking around, and then quickly returning to Willy.

"I need to unpack the mule, get the horses into the corral, why don't you check which bedroom you want, and maybe take a little nap," he said as he headed out the door. He hadn't expected Lars to follow him, but the older man helped him unload Horace, put their packs and bags on the porch and went with him to settle the animals in the corral.

"You are pretty spry for an old guy," Cole said as they walked back up to the house.

"How old you figure I am?" Lars grinned.

"You were in the military a long while, before the Civil War, you said."

"I joined up when I was fourteen. I am sixty-two."

"Younger than Pa. Your white hair had me fooled."

"Thought it might. I got some good years left in me."

Cole smiled as they walked back into the house to be greeted by the dogs. He heard rustling from the kitchen and went out to see Willy had started cooking something that smelled good. She looked up and met his gaze.

"I picked out *our* bedroom and put your saddlebags and my bags in it." She emphasized the *our* and gave him a look that dared him to deny them sleeping together no matter what anyone else thought about it. He was in no mood to deny anything. It'd been too long since they'd made love. He wanted what time he could have with her before all hell broke loose.

"What are you cooking, gal?" Lars asked.

"With a refrigerator full of food, including vegetables, and cut up chicken, I am making chicken gumbo. One of the few dishes I know how to make without a recipe. Holly knows how much I love it and even left okra for it."

"Okra?" Lars asked with doubt oozing from his words.

"Wait 'til you try it," she said grinning as she measured out water and put it on the stove to boil.

"Lots of peppers, I hope," Cole said as he opened the sideboard, found the scotch and poured himself and Lars each two fingers. Seeing a nice bottle of red wine, he opened it and poured her a glass. "They have a bathroom with a tub if you didn't already see that," he told her. "Vince brought an electric line out here and got a hot water heater as soon as he could. Nothing but the best for Holly."

"I will very much appreciate his magnanimous nature."

"Well, it was her money," he reminded her.

"I suspect it took more than money to make this home as comfortable as it is."

"That's true. Vince is handy with his hands." He gave her one of those smiles. She answered it with a teasing one of her own. Because Lars was there, he resisted the impulse to tell her all the ways they could enjoy that hot water."

"I love this house," Willy said. "I can feel the love that has been here. And it's wonderful how the dogs have a yard where they can be out without us having to worry about them being out in a pasture trying to chase cows." She giggled and took another sip of her wine.

"The benefits of small children. Vince takes no chances where it comes to his family."

"Good. I also found that Holly left some dresses in the armoire. We are the same size. Her note said I would probably like to wear them. I suppose Nate told her I had lost my clothing in the fire. I have just what I brought to Arizona. Not much money to buy more right now, although when I can access my bank account in San Francisco, I will be all right."

He hadn't thought of the needed clothing once they'd left the mountains. He was grateful for Holly's thoughtfulness, as he wasn't anxious to have Willy going to town, shopping, and being seen—not yet. He wanted Thomas to be guessing as to where she was. He watched as she dumped the rice she'd measure into the boiling water and put a lid on it. She stirred the gumbo and then sat across from him sipping her wine with that contemplative look on her face.

"When were you thinking we'd try the code?" he asked

"I suppose after supper."

"You need a bath and some time to relax. Maybe tomorrow morning. Vince and Jesse will be here in the morning. We can put all our brains to it."

"What are you two talking about?" Lars asked.

"We've been trying to break my father's code," Willy said. "He left behind journals that might tell provide proof connecting Thomas

Hamilton or rather Harold Thomas to the graft in the Hemstreet business."

Cole rose and looked out the window with a smile. "I hope you made a lot of gumbo." He walked out onto the porch. "It didn't take you two long to get here," he said as his father and Nate Hemstreet swung down from their horses.

"Been checking every night this week. Took you long enough," his father said. "Hey, Zinnia is becoming a beauty and these are her babies. Little cuties."

Cole accepted the hug from his father and a handshake from Hemstreet; then stood back as the dude nearly swallowed Willy in a huge hug.

"God, it's good to see you and looking so well," Hemstreet said as he stepped back to look at her and then draw her back in his arms.

Jeremiah looked over at Lars. "Do I know you?"

"Don't think so. I reckon you're Cole's papa."

"I am."

"I can see it in those eagle eyes and the strong jaw. Now, this blond who's been hanging onto Willy as if he owns her, who's he?" Lars asked. His look was less than friendly toward the city man.

"He's my best friend from years and years back, well, other than Holly." Willy smiled. Cole figured he was about to be relegated to hired man again. While he understood, he didn't much like it.

"Any chance we can bunk here tonight?" Jeremiah asked as they walked into the house.

"Sure, you know there are plenty of bedrooms. Jesse and Vince will come in the morning, and we can figure out the plan for how we proceed," Cole said. He didn't look at Willy, who still had Nate holding onto her. He understood how long her friendship went back with Hemstreet and how much she cared for him. Maybe he was the real reason she had turned down his marriage proposal. In the mountains, it'd been one thing, but now they were back on more familiar ground and Hemstreet was familiar.

When Willy said she had to stir the gumbo and check the rice, Hemstreet followed her inside. Cole lit a cigarette and leaned against the porch post trying not to think about what might be happening in that kitchen.

"Want a cigar, Lars?" Jeremiah asked as he pulled one from his pocket.

"Ain't had a good cigar in years. You bet," Lars answered and soon the two older men were sitting on the porch swing and smoking.

Taking another long draw on his cigarette, Cole turned back to see their satisfied smiles. "They must be good ones, I am guessing," Cole said.

"Want to try one, son?" Jeremiah asked.

"No thanks, one bad habit is enough." He managed a smile he wasn't feeling as he heard the laughter from the kitchen. That was better than the low voices and silence.

"You should go join the young folks," Lars said. Cole shook his head.

"So what's your plan for when Thomas gets here?" Jeremiah asked watching him through the smoke.

"The usual," Cole said with an ironic smile. "You know, bang bang, shoot 'em up and avoid getting killed."

Lars chuckled. "That the usual?"

"In the books," Cole said with a snort.

He looked at the door and saw Hemstreet. "She said the gumbo is ready." He turned and went right back into the house without waiting for them to respond.

"He didn't look in a good mood," Lars said.

"I suppose he's worried about her. I am trying to decide if he could get her out of here before Thomas shows up and…"

"No, he couldn't," he was interrupted by Willy. She walked up to Cole, pulled his head down for a long kiss where she delved within his mouth with her tongue, shocking him enough, that he had nothing to say when she let him go.

"Reckon that says a lot. Does it explain why your friend is not so happy?" Lars asked.

"It might," Willy said. She took Cole's hand and pulled him off the porch to the edge of the yard. "I explained things to Nate."

He felt stunned enough that he couldn't immediately think what to say. "Want to explain it to me?" he said finally.

She growled at him. "You know what it is. We are fornicating and plan to continue."

He saw she was annoyed. He was having a hard time keeping up with her. Added to that was the tension he felt, based on the near future that promised to be violent. It all added up to his being angry too. "I asked you to marry me."

"Tomorrow?" she asked.

"Now it would be after things are straightened out with Thomas."

She whitened. "You are afraid you will be killed." It wasn't a question.

"It's possible. You don't think he'll go down easy, do you? He's put too much into what he has with Hemstreets. He has to believe you could have evidence to end all that."

"So we take it to the sheriff, and you let him do what must be done. It's what he's trained for."

He lifted her chin to look into his eyes. "You know that it's what I am trained for also."

"You asked me to marry you, but where would we live? How would it work where we come from such different worlds? I also cannot imagine what it's like for a woman when her husband goes off over and over again facing danger where he might be killed. This has been my first real experience with that, and I don't know how I'd manage to live with it." She turned from him and stared down at the river.

"So then marry Hemstreet."

She turned on him so fast that it was a blur. He thought for a moment she would slap him, but she just glared before running into the house.

The next step he heard at his back he recognized. "Looks like you handled that well," his father said, still smoking his cigar.

"You said it could never work out," Cole said lighting another cigarette. He knew none of this drama was good for his need to keep a level head. How did it all come to need resolution at the same time?

"And you were going to take my advice for the first time in your life."

"It's not a choice I get to make. I asked her to marry me, but she asked questions I couldn't answer."

"You love her."

"Enough to die for her."

"But not enough to live for her, I reckon."

Cole smoked not wanting to think about that. "She'll be happier with Hemstreet."

"He's a good man. I agree with that, but who she'd be happier with is up to Willy. I'd say she made up her mind."

"Women often unmake it up just as fast."

"That's your real fear, isn't it? Not that you can't work out a compromise, but that she will leave you anyway or it'll end up like me and your ma."

"Look, I can't do this now with you. In a few days, things will be better and then, I can think clearly." He hoped.

"You mean after Thomas."

"He kills anyone who gets in his way. We need to decode the damned journals, get the evidence to Trask, and maybe he can arrest him, and it won't go like I am expecting."

"You believe any of that?" Lars asked who had come up and been listening to the last of their conversation.

"Not so much."

"Here's the thing with him when I knew him," Lars said. "He's a cruel bastard, and he holds a grudge. He's been put out by this. He's been pushed where he didn't want to go. I suppose it's possible he's changed, but if he ain't, then he's going to come here wanting revenge and frankly you'll be as high on his list as Willy."

Cole had already assumed that. In fact, he wanted it to be that way. If he could get the man to be distracted from her, then he'd finish it before she was in danger.

CHAPTER 18

Willy pinned her hair on top of her head as the bathtub filled. She'd been surprised to find a tub in the bathroom off the bedroom she had chosen. Hot water would feel good, even if it wouldn't solve all her aches, the ones of the heart. She fought back tears.

The tap at the door interrupted her feeling sorry for herself. "What?" she asked thinking too bad the door hadn't had a lock. When it opened and Cole stepped in, she dropped the bar of soap. He had taken off his shirt and boots, wore only jeans and the top button was undone.

"Need someone to wash your back?" he asked as he leaned against the door, a soft smile on his face.

"Only if I get to wash yours too." She watched then, her breath coming faster as he undid the buttons and dropped his jeans to reveal he was wearing nothing under them. She loved his naked body, the muscles, the way they moved as he walked to her.

"I shaved and washed up down at the river," he said, "or I'd not think of doing this."

She smiled as she realized what he intended when he pushed her forward in the tub and settled himself behind her with her between his legs. "I won't be able to wash your back," she said in a mock protest as she turned in his arms until she was kneeling and facing him. She delved for the bar of soap. Creating some suds, she ran her hands over his shoulders, down his chest as he returned the favor. His hands moved slowly, stroking down her breasts and belly to her most sensitive areas.

When she washed him, she delved beneath the water down the line of hair to his hardness. He was so ready for her, and she wanted him so much. He rose and took her with him. Pulling the plug, he ran water into the tub to rinse them both off, and then towel dry before he carried her to the bed where they were lost in each other. The past, the future, nothing existed except the moment. When she woke later, he made love to her again.

"I'm sorry," he whispered against her earlobe.

"Not for making love? Surely not for that." She thought she'd cry if he meant that.

"I didn't use anything to protect you. I lost my head."

"I wouldn't mind having your baby, Cole, but I finished my time just before we got here. You are safe."

"You mean you are."

"I guess we both are for now but someday... someday I want your babies. As many as we can have."

"It's a nice dream." She heard in his voice that he didn't believe it would happen. She did. She now knew it would. It would take time, but they could get there. She would make it happen and whatever she'd been determined to make happen always came to pass. They could work this out. She fell asleep with a smile.

At first light, she opened her eyes, still nestled in his arms. She loved the feeling of his skin against hers. She wanted it to be that way all the time. She realized he was awake and watching her as he brushed his fingers over her lips.

"How long do we have?" she asked. She was shocked she could keep her voice so level and not show any of the emotion that surged through her at the thought of what lay ahead.

"Three days, I think. We'll know more after I talk to the sheriff. After Vince and Jesse get here, I'll ride into Tucson and ask Trask to come out to see what your father amassed."

"Why shouldn't I go with you?"

"Mostly it's trying to keep the advantage on our side. I'd as soon Thomas' men didn't see you. I want him to come with some uncertainty."

She ran her finger around one of his flat nipples. Then she remembered her dream. "When I was a little girl, my hair was considerably redder than it is now. My father called me Red. Mama hated it as she was determined I'd be a lady. Eventually, he stopped and of course, my hair darkened."

"Bet you were a cute little girl."

"I didn't think so. I had long braids and got teased a lot. Could red be the key?"

"We'll find out after breakfast."

As Willy dressed in a burgundy gown of Holly's, the scent of bacon wafted up the stairs. She worked on her hair to get it into some sort of tidy bun for meeting his brothers. She hoped they would approve of her. The reason she hoped clearly related to her thinking more and more about being his wife. They would then all be family.

Cole dressed in a white shirt, black vest, dark pants, and wasn't wearing his holster for once when they went downstairs. Seeing him without it, looking so at ease, had been rare since she'd known him, and she reveled in it. It would be what it'd be like if they could manage a real life someday.

She sipped coffee as Jeremiah and Lars took over fixing eggs, bacon, hotcakes, and frying some bread. Nate didn't say much, but he didn't seem angry, maybe more resigned. She was sure the day would come when he'd know he had never loved her and would be glad for the decision she had made.

It was as the food was being put on the table that she heard horses. Cole strode out, grabbing his gun as he went through the hall but stuffing it in his belt when he saw it was his brothers. The three men laughed and hugged each other. She was amazed how much the three resembled each other and yet each with distinctive qualities.

Cole came up the steps with them and stopped to introduce them to Willy.

"I am so glad to meet you. I've heard so much about you," she said as each gave her a gentle hug.

"Don't believe what he said," Vince said with that teasing smile that reminded her of Cole's.

"It was all good."

Cole laughed. "Of course, it was."

"Hey, you have dogs?" Jesse asked pointing to Zinnia with her pups who were keeping a low profile in the corner of the kitchen.

"Hope that's all right with you," Cole said looking at Vince.

"No problem. Cute pups. They have names?"

"Tentatively Poppy and Petunia. Zinnia came to the lake cabin as a stray."

"She's a pretty dog," Jesse said as he went over, hunkered down, and let her sniff his hand before he petted her and the pups. "The kids will go crazy for the puppies. They keep wanting Bear to have one," Jesse said as he rose with a grin.

"Sit down boys, while the old man cooks up some hotcakes," Jeremiah said, and soon they were at the table.

"Already ate before we left, but those are good," Jesse said as he dug into his third.

"So what do you know that I don't?" Cole asked Vince.

"I talked to Trask, he got the mug shots. Pa identified him as the man he saw in town, who Nate said was Hamilton. There are no further records of arrests, and Trask says he has no record after the time in Yuma."

"What was he in for?" Cole asked sipping his coffee.

"Manslaughter. He killed a man who had been a partner, but he claimed the man had tried to kill him first. There were no witnesses, but his story didn't hold water. It also didn't allow them to hang him."

"Lars, tell them when you knew a man called Harold Thomas."

The old man repeated the stories of the man's abusive behavior on the ranch, his theft, and his final taking a shot at the owner. "Happened in New Mexico," he concluded.

"He good with a gun?" Jesse asked pushing his emptied plate away.

"He acted like he was, but he did miss the owner that day. I never saw him in a gun fight."

"So what's the plan?" Vince asked lighting a cigarette and leaning back to study Cole.

"You figure there is one?" Cole asked sardonically.

"Knowing you. Yeah."

"How about sort of a plan. By my calculations, the soonest he could have gotten to Payson was Friday even if all his travel goes smoothly. He had two men waiting but they won't know Willy left. Let's say Saturday morning he heads for the cabin. Nobody is there. He turns around mad as a hornet. The town folk have been stonewalling him with one exception-- the land agent, Gibbons. That man will tell him about the shooting and anything else to take the pressure off him. Thomas will put it together with Hemstreet being in Tucson and head south Sunday. That puts him here the soonest Monday and if he decides to get more men in Phoenix, maybe Tuesday."

"More men?" Willy asked.

"He will know there is more than one Taggert here. I don't know how many men he took up to Payson but he won't brace us without..." He considered a moment. "There are two here, two up there, what he brought with him... Let's say ten men."

"Can't we see him arrested in Phoenix?" she asked. She wondered if Cole's brothers would have resented her interrupting their debate. Some men thought women should remain silent when men talked. Then she remember how outspoken Holly had always been and likely her sister was too. The Taggert men were probably used to women speaking up.

"That is unlikely but would take very solid evidence if we can put it together fast enough," Cole said.

"So what have you got so far?" Vince asked and they went into the dining room where the billings, receipts, lists had been piled at one end, the journals at the other, with the tablets and pencils in between.

"I doubt Mr. Butler collected all the work that was being done by Hemstreet," Cole said as he organized the billings into the stacks he had put together at the lake. "What he was doing was compiling where the problems lay and had been going on for four years."

"You don't believe Mr. Butler was involved in anything crooked, do you?" Nate asked.

"It doesn't fit what I have been told of him, but someone was cheating people, using billings that didn't match with supplies purchased, and sometimes with companies that look to be shells, nothing inside."

"So that person was cheating other businesses and probably my family operation."

"From the best I could tell, Hamilton was in a good position to do that. But believing something and proving it are two different things. I think that's why Butler collected so much evidence. He was looking for the who behind it and something definitive that he could take to the law or maybe to the head of the company." Cole looked at Nate. "Your mother." He opened one of the journals and showed it to his brothers and Nate. "Willy and I recognized this is a code, a cipher. Without a key, we got nowhere. It had to be something she'd recognize enabling her to read journals that may tie Thomas to the rest of what Butler had gathered."

"And your idea is?" Nate asked.

"We try red."

Cole wrote down the gibberish of the first line. "Here's what I know about codes. Below each letter, I put its numerical order in the alphabet; then because of R's order, add eighteen. So that makes the first letter a B. The second letter is offset by five since that was an E. The third letter by four."

She watched, but the letters still didn't form words. Cole drew in a breath. "That didn't work."

"So no key," Willy said showing disappointment on her face.

"I remembered something you said. Your father spoke some German. What is red in German?"

"Rot," Nate said.

Cole took another piece of paper and this time, when applied, words emerged.

'Because of my suspicions regarding suspect dealings at Hemstreet Enterprises, I have...'

'Looks like we have it," Cole said with a satisfied laugh. "But with four journals, it's going to take more time than we have."

"It'll go faster if we make a translation table," Nate said. "Do you have a ruler?"

Vince dug into a drawer and put the items on the table. Taking a pencil, Nate made five columns each about half an inch wide, running the length of the paper, then turned the paper sideways and drew twenty-seven evenly spaced lines across the five rows. "That will be twenty-six boxes," he said as he worked. "Fill the top row with numbers one to twenty-six. The next row is the alphabet. A under 1, B under 2, C under 3, and so forth. The next row begins with R where A is R; B is S; then the row below A is O."

"And the next with T?" Cole asked.

"The pattern repeats every three letters. He could have done this other ways, made it harder, but I knew Samuel pretty well, like a second father to me. He loved word games and especially ciphers that weren't that complex for those who understood the basics." His smile was grim. "He would have known that even if he got hold of the journals Thomas Hamilton could never figure them out. What I am guessing now is that Hamilton or rather Thomas didn't want to destroy them unless he had to. He believed that Samuel had put in names and addresses, things he could use. Burning the house was a last resort."

"So with this table, we each take a journal and get to work," Vince said.

"That's pretty much it."

"How long will it take?" Jeremiah asked doubtfully.

"Probably too long," Cole said. "We want Trask on our side before Thomas arrives."

"You hope for an arrest, not a shoot-out?" Lars asked as he took one of the books and looked at the letters.

"I don't hope where it comes to something like this. I just know it is the first choice."

"Not with Thomas. He won't give up."

"Then it'll be what it'll be."

"Best we start with the last book then," Nate suggested. "If Samuel was worried about what was going on, maybe it had something to do with his death."

"Sounds fine with me," Jeremiah said. "How we going to do this?"

"One read the letters for the other to write down. Work in teams of two. I guess the best idea is one team take the first journal and the other the last," Nate said.

Willy was a little surprised that Cole had stepped back and was letting Nate lead the work. She was actually impressed that he didn't need to do it when Nate was the one who understood the most about the process.

Then she saw by the expression on his face that he was thinking beyond this to what would come next.

"Why don't Jeremiah and I take the last one," Nate suggested and when Cole only nodded approval, he assigned Lars and Willy the first.

"Will reading his thoughts upset you?" Cole asked her.

"No, I needed to understand what led to his death. I feel relieved that's maybe possible."

"Good enough. I need to ride into talk to Jace in an hour or two."

"Why don't you call him?" she asked.

"Because I don't want anyone listening in. Until I need to go though, I can work with Vince on the third. Jesse, you take care of the horses and keep the coffee coming."

Jesse smiled with obvious relief and went out to unsaddle and put his and Vince's horses into the corral.

"I would really like to see Holly," Willy said as she sat at the table next to Lars. She needed counsel, loving support, and a woman's voice.

"She's anxious to see you too," Vince said, "but she's not up to riding yet and sure not leaving Lucinda with anybody."

"I can ride out there maybe tomorrow." She looked at Cole to see his opinion, but his expression was still distant. He sat at the table and began to work with Vince on the third journal. Whatever he was thinking, he wasn't ready to tell her.

After an hour, finally able to read her father's words which she carefully transcribed onto one of the notepads, Willy felt a mix of sadness and relief. She could hear the strength in his purpose and his decision that it would take a lot to bring down a man who had covered his tracks as well as Hamilton as even in the beginning he saw the likely one behind this to be the majordomo of more than a household.

Two hours later, Nate looked up from what had been the last page. "We skipped ahead and glad we did," he said. "It's clear that Samuel believed TH had betrayed the family and others. He makes a reference to one of the clients having met with a suspicious end and… Well, I'll read it to you if you want."

Cole rose and went to stand behind Willy's chair. She appreciated his hand on her shoulder. "Please do read it," she said.

"March 17. This should be a good day to speak with Mrs. Hemstreet regarding my suspicions, which now have gone beyond that to certainty. I am not sure how she will take it since she is so dependent on TH. I won't tell her everything I have come to believe. It might frighten her to realize he is capable of murder. There is no other logical explanation where it came to Jackson Turnbull's supposed accidental death. Once I saw the way he'd been cheated, I knew TH had made sure he wasn't able to bring charges. No, I need to be cautious what I tell

her. For one thing, I do not know how much she already knows. My appointment at ten am should tell me that. I will go through my accusations but will not bring the evidence. Fortunately, Willy will be out until early evening, with meetings after classes. I can take as long as required. Hopefully, the dear lady will not find it too much to absorb."

Nate took a deep breath. "I wasn't there that day. Mother had asked me to go down to the docks and wait for the shipment she was expecting. The irony was she had the date wrong—or so I thought at the time. By the time I got home, she was primping for a luncheon engagement. I saw nothing of Samuel. Only the next day did I learn he had hung himself."

"Which is pretty obvious now he had not killed himself," Willy said, feeling again the comfort of Cole's hand on her shoulder, lightly pressing and soothing her. She fought back the tears. "I came home, and he wasn't there, then I saw the basement door was open. I… didn't dream. Sometimes he worked down there. When I saw his body swinging, the rope around his neck, my first thought was to get him loose." She couldn't stop the sob. "I ran upstairs for the butcher knife, came back down… righted the chair that had fallen over and got onto it, cutting the rope. I tried to hold him but he fell to the floor. I knew he was dead. I…" She could stop the tears no longer and rose from the table hurrying into the kitchen.

She knew Cole had come with her when he put his arms around her. "He was a brave man and when the whole of the journals have been deciphered, we should have more than theft to hang Thomas with. I know it doesn't bring your father back, but at least what he was trying to do, we can finish for him."

Smiling through her tears, she sniffled and nodded. "It's just hard, and it makes me angry."

"Good. Get mad. That monster deserves it."

"Do you think, based on what he wrote, that Nate's mother is involved in what happened?"

"I don't know. It wouldn't be provable unless Thomas confesses."

"You expect that?"

"He will have a chance to surrender, that's all I can tell you. After that, I don't know but based on what Lars said, on what would happen to him if he did give himself up, I think he won't."

"I wish you'd let the sheriff take care of this and stay away until it's been settled."

He tilted her chin up until their gazes met. "You don't expect that, do you?" He grinned then. "Surely not the bloodthirsty author of all those western shoot 'em ups."

She slapped his chest. "It's not funny."

He gave a little laugh. "Come on. Not just a little?"

"All right... just a little."

"I need to ride into town but will be back by supper. You should try and take it easy today. Play with the pups."

"Will you sleep with me tonight?" she asked.

He smiled. "Sweetheart, I'd like to sleep with you every night."

As she watched him saddle his horse and ride off, she waved as he disappeared from view. She also wanted to sleep with him every night. How was it possible though? Even if they did get Thomas arrested, and it all went well, she had obligations, a contract, a...

And then, she stopped. Things had changed. Her life had changed so much since her father's death in March, then the loss of her home, finally meeting the man she'd been fantasizing about for years in her books. She had a lot to think about. She needed a friend, a woman to get advice.

In Tucson, Cole stopped by the sheriff's office first, only to find he was out. His young deputy, Clarence something or other, said he'd be back in an hour. He rode then to Sicillas.

"How you doing?" Del asked as soon as he had taken off his hat in the store.

"Fine. I need five condoms." He wasn't sure he'd be alive long enough to use them all, but his brothers could take the leftovers if he ended up underground sooner than he hoped. "And something pretty in a nightgown."

Del grinned. "Didn't know you got married, or are you buying this for your brothers?"

"That was a snoopy question," Connie said coming from her side of the store. "Del, you package the condoms, and I'll show Cole the latest we have in nightgowns. Any special color?"

"What goes good with brown hair with red highlights?" He knew nothing about women's clothing, let alone what Willy would like.

"I can see this with that color." She held up a peach colored nightgown with lace around the neck and at the cuffs. It was so thin that he worried he'd put his fingers through it. Next, she held up a black one with a sort of satin looking fabric. Finally came one in a soft cream with thin straps. "This one comes with a peignoir," she said, holding up a garment that looked like a robe. The fabric was a bit thicker but still soft and comfortable.

"That one," he said. It was the first time he'd bought a woman any garments. Maybe it'd be the last time, but he was enjoying himself and ended up also finding a burgundy dress that he thought Willy would like. She should have more than Holly's castoffs. Before he could get out of the store, he saw little white gloves. He'd bought her gloves for the outdoors, but these were different. They were what a lady would wear. "I'll be broke if I don't make it out of here soon," he said with a laugh as she tallied up the garments and condoms.

When he paid her, she took his hand. "You look stressed. Is everything all right?"

"Sure." He knew about Connie's readings but had no interest in one for himself. He pretty well knew his future, and nobody was going to change it by any hocus-pocus. He needed to concentrate only on what lay ahead and make sure he did that right whether he came out of it or not. The more he'd gotten to knowing Nate Hemstreet, the better he felt Willy's future would be assured, if he was killed. The thing with the decoding had made him appreciate the man's intelligence. Nate would take care of her. It was Cole's job to make sure he had that chance.

Because an hour hadn't gone past, Cole went into the café. "My name's Laura. What can I get you?" the waitress asked as she came up with a pad and pencil. He had seen the older woman before but hadn't paid her any mind. Now he realized she looked familiar and knew why.

"Coffee," he said. When she came back with it, he asked, "You wouldn't have a brother named Lars by any chance?"

"How'd you know that?" She said. "I haven't seen that reprobate in years, but yes, I do."

"He came south with me. He said he had a sister here, but I didn't connect it to you until now."

She sat across from him. "He came here?"

"He's been helping me with a project, but he'll be around in a day or two."

"He wanted to see me?" She looked surprised.

"He said he did."

"Where's he been all these years?"

He considered that as he took his first sip of the coffee. "You know he was a soldier."

"I do, but I thought he got out." She had to get up and deliver food to another customer but then returned.

"I think it took a lot out of him. You know wars do that."

"He wasn't in the Civil War though."

"Harder. The Indian wars."

She swallowed hard, and he saw tears at the edge of her eyes. "I will be glad to see him. He has my address."

"I think he did."

She took her pad and wrote it down. "Give him this if he doesn't. I have two sons, but they both left Tucson; so I live alone. I would be glad to see him," she repeated.

"Good." He finished the coffee, left her a generous tip, and headed for the sheriff's office. This time, Jace was in.

"Good to see you didn't get yourself killed yet," Jace said with a chuckle as he poured Cole coffee he didn't want.

"Well, the day's not over," Cole said with a grin.

"True. Are you here for a reason or just to chew the fat?"

"Both." Cole took out a cigarette and lit it. "When I was in Payson, I asked the freighter to send a wire to Tucson and you. It'll just say, It's come." When that wire gets here, I'd like you to call me out at Vince's ranch with just that message, nothing more."

"I thought he moved farther out near to Jesse."

"He did. I am staying at his ranch."

"You going to explain this to me?"

Cole gave him the gist of what he knew and what he expected. When he finished, Jace blew out a whistle. "You weren't kidding about the day's not over."

"I don't expect him here until Monday at the soonest, maybe even Tuesday. But that wire will let me know more."

Jace gave a yell for Clarence. "Head on over to the telegraph office and bring back any wires for me. If there's not, tell Jack to bring one to me as soon as it arrives."

The young man hurried off.

"Seems like a nice kid," Cole said taking another long draw on his cigarette.

"He's learning. Tucson has been pretty quiet... until this anyway. You really expect Thomas to show up here?"

"I do. He wants what Samuel Butler compiled and now he wants Wilhelmina, Samuel's daughter. From what you found on his record, he is the kind of man who doesn't much care about rules or life."

"I was hoping for a quiet week."

Cole smiled. "Go fishing."

Jace laughed and pulled a cigar from the desk drawer. Lighting it, he said, "I was a kid when Cord O'Brian was marshal here. I still remember how I admired him. He's a man who never ran from anything. I won't either."

"Come out to the ranch tomorrow, whether the wire comes or not. I'd like to show you what we've found, what Harold Thomas has been up to, and what you'll be up against."

When Cole got back to the ranch, Willy was in the kitchen, his brothers, Nate and Jeremiah had gone back to their homes leaving her chatting with Lars. "I fixed a beef roast. How does that sound?"

"Like we're living high on the hog." He handed her the package. "I got you something," he said, "but open it upstairs. Want me to do anything about the dinner?"

"Cut up some vegetables maybe for a salad. I thought I'd mash potatoes and make gravy if that sounds okay." She smiled and ran upstairs with her package.

"How did the deciphering go?" he asked Lars as he washed his hands and set about doing what she had asked.

"Got over half the last journal and looks like Thomas killed that other jasper. But he got away with it by it looking like an accident. Butler didn't buy it. I'm guessing there'll be more than a few of those in the journals, again with no proof."

"Hope it's enough to get a warrant," Cole said.

"Want a whiskey?"

Cole smiled. He knew who did, but he nodded. "I saw your sister today."

"Laura?" Lars handed him the whiskey. Cole nodded. "She is looking forward to seeing you and said if you don't have her address, this is where you can find her."

"I suppose I should go see her."

"Anytime you want."

"First I help you settle things with Thomas."

He leaned back against the counter to sip his whiskey. "Lars, I don't want you going with me when this goes down."

"I'm too old?" The old man looked hurt.

"No, I know you're not. It's two reasons. One your sister. I looked into her eyes, and I can't be the one who takes the chance you get hurt or worse. She needs you. The other is in case this doesn't go well, I want you at the adobes with Willy and my family. Charlie will be there. You haven't met him but he'd go down before he let anything happen to them. I want you there because if it goes against us, they will find the Taggert homes. I know my sisters-in-law can shoot as can Willy. I don't anticipate that happening, but nobody can guarantee anything when something like this goes down."

"Your brothers will go with you then?"

"I couldn't stop them if I wanted. I trust you, Lars. Will you do it?"

"What do you trust him about?" Willy asked from the door. "You didn't get far on the vegetables."

He smiled at her. "I got distracted by whiskey." He heard Zinnia scratching to get out and let them into the back fenced yard. Turning back, he saw Willy wasn't very happy with him.

"Did you like the dress?" he asked to distract her.

He saw her make the effort to smile. "I loved it and the other. Just..."

"I'll do it," Lars said, "but I don't like it any more than she does." He gave Cole a look that had him laughing.

Hours later, after he'd made love to her until they were both satiated, Cole held her in his arms enjoying the beauty of the candlelight as it accented her high cheekbones and followed the hollows in her throat. "Now tell me what's going on," she said.

"After making love, you want to talk about business," he teased. "Is this how it's always going to be?"

"Probably. Now tell me."

He told her about the sheriff, the wire he'd requested Contrell send. "It'll give us the edge when Thomas gets to Tucson," he said finally. "I've seen more than a few of these things, Willy. Trust me about it."

"I do trust you but..."

"Think positive, sweetheart. Imagine when this is past, and we can enjoy Thanksgiving with my family, Christmas. Someday, I hope they will be yours too."

She let out a sigh. "I'd like to think that way, but the things we found, as we finally were able to read my father's journals, it's very upsetting to know what kind of man Mr. Hamilton or rather Thomas is."

"That's our advantage. He doesn't know we're onto him. He wanted those journals or to have them destroyed. Now the evidence is going to be on record. I think Jace can get a warrant. It is possible he'll just give up in the end."

"How many men will he have with him?"

"I don't know. I'll have a better idea if he takes the train down from Phoenix. What I do know is he will know he faces Taggerts. He won't come alone."

"And you want me to hide out at the ranches while you face that?"

"How do you think you'd help if you came with me?"

She considered that. "I suppose I couldn't, could I?"

"No, you couldn't. Besides, if this goes wrong, which I don't believe it will, you will need to be ready there with my sisters-in-law. From all I know, Thomas won't be the type to let this go even with all the proof against him. He'll go after revenge. If he gets by us, I want to know you are ready for him."

"You are scaring me."

"Be a little bit scared but remember this. My brothers and I are also good at what we do."

"What about Nate?"

"I'd like him to stay with you, but I'll talk to him after I know more."

"Make love to me, Cole."

He laughed. "You think after all we did, I have the energy for that?"

"I know you do."

Sunday morning, Cole's brothers, father and Nate had returned to the ranch in time for a big breakfast and then to begin work on the deciphering. When Willy saw a handsome man with a badge come riding up, Cole went out to greet him. When he came in and was introduced, he accepted a cup of coffee with a big smile. He then turned to Cole. "Your wire came this morning at eight. It said, 'Just gone by wagon. 7. Phoenix road."

Cole smiled. "He's in a hurry. So, Monday, not Tuesday—if he comes straight here."

"If he takes the train, I'll find out and when he's likely to arrive."

"That means nine unless he picks up more in Phoenix or the hanger-on joins in," Vince said from the doorway where he'd been listening. He didn't sound any more worried than Cole.

Cole refilled his coffee cup. "How about looking at what Samuel Butler put together, Jace. Let us know if we have enough for an arrest."

For all the times Willy had written such scenes, she felt shocked that these men didn't seen nervous, shaky, or even concerned. They might as well have been planning a party. Didn't they feel any of the fear that she did?

After the sheriff studied the billings and read the interpreted journals, he smiled and looked from one to the other. "Looks good. We have a smart, strong judge in James Hutchinson. He's a fair man. I will ask for a warrant. That may even get Marshal Merritt interested."

"Is it possible that it won't come down to shooting?" Nate asked.

"Can't say but less chance if we come at it with enough force," Jace said. "The truth is you never know. Anticipate trouble and it doesn't happen. Not look for it, and it does."

Willy gave a huff. "That sounds like something Cole would say."

Jace chuckled. "Birds of a feather or something like that."

"Something like that," Cole agreed.

Vince turned to Willy. "What do you say to coming out to see Holly today?"

As much as she wanted to see her, she more wanted to be with Cole. She looked at him to see what he wanted.

"You could go out with Nate and Lars," Cole suggested looking at Nate as he said it. "Spend the night."

She felt angry with him even as she understood.

"I will be with you when you confront Thomas," Nate said meeting Cole's gaze.

"You ever been involved in a shooting?" Cole asked.

"No."

"You know it's not about target practice. It's about knowing you might have to kill a man to stay alive yourself."

"You think I can't do that?"

"I don't know. Can you? It's not easy. To hesitate gets you killed."

"You've done it." Nate looked around the room. "All of you have except Willy and me."

"The thing is this will go down fast when it does," Cole said. "If you aren't a help, you will be in the way and might even get killed."

"As could you."

Cole shrugged. "If he killed your father, and it looks like he did, I guess it's your choice. But just be sure. You don't have to be there."

"I know that. I will be there, and I will not be afraid."

Vince chuckled. "Then you'll be the only one."

CHAPTER 19

C ole walked upstairs to where Willy was packing her bag. She didn't look up when he entered. "You mad at me?" he asked. He did it only to get her talking as he saw from the way she was throwing her clothing into the bag that she was angry.

"Now why would I be mad?" she asked in a snide tone. "Maybe because you want to give away what might be our last night together by sending me off to the adobes to be *safe*."

He considered that. "You taking that nightgown?"

"Why would I?" She glared at him.

He turned, walked downstairs, went to the dining room where they were working on the deciphering. "It turns out Willy will go out tomorrow morning." He heard a snort from Vince but didn't look back as he walked up the stairs.

In their room, he shut the door. "You can go tomorrow."

She turned, tears streaming down her eyes. "You mean that? You can change your mind?"

He smiled. "You can change my mind." He reached out for her and took her into his arms. "I told you I want us to sleep together every night. I just also want you safe."

"But tonight he can't get here, can he?"

"Not even if he rode down."

"Then…"

After making love, dressing, and going back downstairs, ignoring the jibes from his brothers, Cole took Willy outside with him. They sat on the porch and threw sticks for the dogs. Zinnia immediately got the idea of what was happening, but the pups took a little educating. Vince and Jesse came out and walked down the steps. "We're heading home," Vince said.

"Good."

"We'll be back early," Jesse added.

Cole nodded. He understood. He wished his brothers would not go with him to face Thomas when he arrived. He knew it'd be pointless to tell them that. He watched as they rode off.

"It's my fault," Willy said reaching out to stroke his cheek.

"It's only one man's fault and those who ride with him," Cole said. "It's not like we could let him go on murdering and stealing, could we?"

"I guess not but..."

"There is no *but* for this. You didn't ask for this and neither did your father. You were brave enough to go looking for answers. You know as well as I do, that when something rotten is uncovered, it has to be dealt with or we can't as a people go forward can we?"

She smiled through tears. "Can I use that line in my next book?"

He reached over and kissed her lightly. "So what will the last Taggert be doing this time?"

"Getting married, I think, to Lucy." She cuddled against him.

"Lucy teach at a university?"

"I was thinking she might... I mean Arizona is developing a pretty good one here. That is if she isn't too busy having babies."

"You want children?" he asked as he took her hand and kissed it.

"I never used to think so but yes... yours."

"It's a good dream."

"Make sure it happens."

"I'll do my damnedest."

The door opened again with Nate and Jeremiah the next to leave. "We got as far as we can go today," Jeremiah said. "See you in the morning."

The evening meal was all the leftovers Willy could put together. They went upstairs early while Lars stayed below with the dogs and to read. Vince had brought him a stack of the Will Tremaine books.

With first light, Cole woke to feeling Willy running her finger around his nipple. "You never told me the whole truth about why Thomas knows about you." It wasn't really a question.

"I didn't?"

"You know you didn't."

"All right. I guess this is the right time for it." He met her questioning gaze. "He will know about me because of Gibbons."

"If I recall, when he came out to the cabin, you didn't tell him your name."

He had hoped to wait for this until she was ready to leave Tucson, but maybe there wouldn't be another time. "I visited him in Payson."

"To see who else wanted the land?"

"To buy the land."

She drew her hand away and sat up. "What?"

"I wanted you to have it. I bought it but had it transferred to your name before we left Payson."

"Why didn't you tell me?" In the early morning light, he saw tears glistening on her eyelashes.

"I didn't want you to feel obligated to me for it."

"You are insane. I can't believe you did this."

"You lost your home. I wanted you to have one. I also bought the thousand acres that surround it. I didn't transfer that to your name, but I did have Milt Freedman draw up a will. It's in my saddlebag along with the deed."

He could see her struggling to process what he was telling her. He had known it would be a shock. "Who is Milt Freedman?"

He wasn't sure what she was feeling as her face was giving him no clue other than the tears running down her cheeks. "He's the lawyer we met that day at Adele's."

"You really are a detective aren't you?"

Her tone hadn't made the statement a compliment. "I know how to put things together if that's what you mean."

She lay back down in his arms. "Cole, I want to be your wife."

He smiled. "You should have made up your mind earlier." He ran a teasing finger over her lips. "Now you have to wait until I finish with Thomas."

"You better live through it," she growled as she nipped his finger.

"And what will you do if I don't?" he asked with a laugh.

"Write you a despicable and even cowardly ending in the last book."

He laughed louder. "That does it. I have to make it to prevent you ruining my reputation." With that, he bent and claimed her mouth. He'd make love to her again and then he'd have to put her and all of that from him. In a few hours, he'd have to focus only on one thing—getting the job done.

While Willy was cooking breakfast, the phone rang. Cole got it. "He'll be in on the eleven am."

"Any idea how many?"

"Seven and him. I got the warrant. We'll try to arrest them all and sort out if they have any posters on the others afterward."

"The two in Tucson though didn't, did they?"

"Not that I ever found."

"Okay."

"Marshal Merritt is with us on it. I won't though bring my deputy. He's a kid and not that experienced."

"Sounds good. We'll be in town by ten." When he hung up, he saw Willy watching him with her jaw clenched.

"Don't burn the bacon," he said teasingly. She growled but turned back to the stove. He was drinking his second cup of coffee when Jesse and Vince rode in. They strode into the kitchen, took coffee, but turned down food.

"I told Jace we'd meet him at ten. Train comes in at eleven"

"Sounds good," Jesse said.

Vince turned to Willy. "Are you ready? Holly is excited about you coming."

"I am not ready, but I guess I have to go. What about the dogs?"

"Leave them here for now in the yard with water. It won't be that long, and we'll be back," Cole said, "then out to get you." He smiled. He wanted to reassure her, but she wasn't a fool. He couldn't give her guarantees.

Nate and Jeremiah rode in about the time that Willy and Lars were ready to ride out. "It's easy to find," Vince repeated with again giving instructions. "Charlie is waiting for you along with the gals at Jesse's place. The kids are playing together. Have a good lunch and all."

Cole saw Willy wasn't pleased, but she didn't argue. Ten minutes later, he'd kissed her again, lifted her onto her saddle and watched the two ride off. Zinnia whimpered from the yard, but she was placated some by Cole sitting on the porch and reaching down to pet her.

"How do you figure this?" Vince asked as he sat beside him.

"First-- none of us get killed."

The Taggerts laughed and Nate just looked at him with disbelief. "Is this how it usually goes down? Making jokes?" he asked.

"And the alternative would be?" Vince asked with a chuckle.

As Nate rode into town with the four Taggerts, he realized once again that he'd never known anyone like these men. Their play was rough, their humor amazing, considering what lay ahead, but the love was so great that he could feel it all around them and their father. They may have had tough times when younger, but somehow that had healed. It made him miss his father. Maybe soon, he'd be seeing him, as he faced realistically that he would be the most likely target for Thomas as soon as he saw him.

Staying with Jeremiah, he had been given some of Willy's books to read, and they had him just as amazed about his best friend, who he had thought he knew. How had she written such hard-hitting western tales? She'd never known any of what she wrote, at least not first hand. Well, he was about to, and that shocked him as much as the rest.

At the sheriff's office, they stabled their horses rather than tying them to rails, after Cole suggested it would be smart. "We don't know how long this will take," he said leading his into a stall and giving him oats and a brushing. Again, his calm demeanor had Nate curious about how he managed it. Surely, he was afraid of what was to come. Finally, he could resist the question no longer. As Cole stepped from the stall, Nate asked him, "Vince said you'd all be afraid. Are you?"

Cole stopped and looked at him. "I honestly don't think about it ahead of time or during. Afterward, yeah, if I survive, then I'll be afraid." He smiled and walked back onto the street. Nate noticed he had the usual revolver in his holster but had shoved a second one into the belt at his back.

A moment later, all of the Taggerts were at the depot. Cole had lit a cigarette and was leaning with his elbows against a hitching rail as he smoked, watching up the tracks. The sheriff and marshal stood a little apart, both of them had a shotgun as well as a holstered weapon.

Nate recognized his own shakiness, but felt he was steady enough to use his gun when the time came. He wondered what the protocol was for such events. Did they just start shooting? Would Thomas shoot first? Or might the majordomo actually surrender? The few books he'd read of Will Tremaine's didn't prepare him for standing with these six men and waiting for what he had no idea.

Two men walked past them, paying little attention—at least not seemingly.

"Those are Thomas' men," he heard Trask move over to tell Cole, who nodded.

"Good. Better in front than behind."

Cole's brothers had moved apart from him but stood together. Jeremiah had taken a position near one of the buildings, leaning his shoulder against it. For all intents, none of them looked as though they were part of any concerted effort soon to arrest ten men.

Nate smiled then as he realized how he'd been dissecting the whole event, trying to take it apart, and make sense of it in some logical way. There likely was no logical way. He wished he had one of the cigars he'd bought.

When he heard the train whistle, he expected the others with him to do something. They didn't. Cole's cigarette was dangling from his lips. His gaze was intent on the stopping train, but he hadn't moved.

The men who got off the train were walking rapidly toward them. He didn't try to count them but the two who had come from town joined them, standing talking a moment.

"Harold Thomas, throw your gun down and put your hands up. You're under arrest," the sheriff yelled.

The marshal added, "Anyone not connected with Thomas, throw your gun down and lie flat."

Thomas stared at the sheriff, shock on his face. He did have a gun, but it wasn't in his hand yet. Nate realized that Cole had shifted away from the railing. He had thrown down his cigarette but hadn't grabbed his revolver.

"What's this about?" Thomas asked as he scanned the men, clearly looking for what he was facing. He stopped when he saw Nate. Then he smiled and drew his gun.

Cole moved faster than Nate had realized a man could as he shoved Nate aside and drew his own gun, firing at the same time that Thomas got off his first shot. Nate, lying on the ground, grabbed his revolver from its shoulder holster and pointed it at the man next to Thomas. Guns blasting and sounds of men grunting or screaming filled the air. The blast of a shotgun threw one of the men off his feet and to the ground. It was then that Nate saw Cole hit by one of the shots. He twisted with the bullet hitting his right shoulder, dropped that gun while he yanked the one from his belt with his left and kept firing.

In the confusion, the noise and the energy of men falling and killing others, more blasts from the shotguns, Nate realized Cole had been hit again and had gone to one knee. He didn't stop firing. Then the air was silent except for groaning.

"You're hit," Vince said limping to Cole.

Jeremiah, having shoved his gun into its holster came to his other side. "He's hard hit. I am getting a wagon." The tough old bird stalked off.

"No," Cole said putting his left hand to his bloody shoulder. "Not much or…" Then his eyes closed, and he fell to the dust.

"Where's Doc Hadley?" Jesse asked standing beside Vince.

Sheriff Trask came over while the marshal was handcuffing and examining the survivors among the Thomas gang. "He works out of St. Mary's now. Cole is losing blood. We need to get him there fast. He shoved his scarf against the shoulder wound.

"It looks bad," Vince said with a groan.

"You need him too," Jesse said.

"Just a flesh wound in my leg." He had tied his bandana around it.

When Jeremiah returned, they lifted Cole into the wagon along with two badly wounded from the other side. Thomas and five of the men had been killed. Nate was uncertain what to do, but then knew he'd need to let Willy know. She would be worried, and she'd want to be with Cole.

"Where's St. Mary's?" he asked as he turned to head toward the stable. Jeremiah yelled instructions, as Jesse shoved his father aside to drive the wagon, with Vince holding Cole's limp form.

As Nate rode toward the adobes, he understood what Cole had meant about feeling afraid afterward. He had no idea how he'd done when the shooting had been happening. He had shot at men but had he hit one? The chaos was like a smokescreen to keep him from facing what he might've done. He felt no guilt either way. He'd done his best. Maybe that's all Cole had meant. His thoughts turned to him, and the fear now that Cole had been hard hit, that he might die.

On the turnoff beyond the ranch, he saw riders coming toward him. He stopped and waited. He knew by her hair flying that one was Willy, and the other had to be Lars.

"Where's Cole?" she asked as she pulled her mount to a halt.

He nodded. "He's at the hospital."

"He was hurt?"

"Yes. Come on."

He turned his mount. They rode at a gallop back into town and then up to where he'd been told St. Mary's was. Willy jumped from her horse and ran in the front doors. Nate and Lars followed as she was pointed toward a room where Jeremiah and Jesse sat.

"Where is he?" she asked.

"They have a room here just for surgery. They took him there. Vince is being patched up behind that curtain."

"Is he... Is he going to die?" she asked her voice quivering. Nate understood then that it wouldn't matter if the man died or lived. He was going to hold her heart for the rest of her life.

"Of course, he's not," Jeremiah said with a tired grin, as he rose and pulled her into a hug. "He's too tough to die from a measly bullet."

"Or two," Jesse added with a smile.

"He was hit twice. Where?"

"Shoulder and side. Maybe hit a rib with that one. He was conscious afterward."

"For a while," Jesse added.

"You are not helping, son," Jeremiah admonished.

"Just calling it like it is." Jesse turned to her. "You know I sometimes hear things others don't."

"Please don't tell me he's going to die," she begged.

"No, he's going to be fine. Just hurting for a time. Be patient with him. I just wanted to warn you. He doesn't take well to being hurt." Jesse smiled at her.

Vince, limping, emerged from behind the curtain. "Yeah, listen to him. Cole is a bear when he feels weak."

She'd already seen that when he got shot in his left shoulder. She forced a smile. "I'll try to remember that."

"You got here awful fast," Jesse said.

"She was already halfway here when I caught up with her and Lars," Nate said.

"Weren't you supposed to wait with Holly and Lily?" Vince asked.

"I had a bad feeling and turned around as soon as we got out there."

"Not very obedient."

She gave him a look and then realized he was teasing. "Guess not," she said finally.

"Make a good Taggert wife that way." He and Jesse both chuckled.

Willy had no idea how long it had been, but seemed hours before the doctor came out and looked around the waiting room. She felt a wave of fear over what he had come to tell them.

"How is he?" Jeremiah asked rising.

"He'll be down for a week maybe with blood loss, bullet broke a rib but no splinters nor hit anything vital. I got the bullet and bone pieces out of his shoulder which will need some therapy but, barring infection, he'll be back to normal in a month or two."

Jesse chuckled. "A month huh? How about two days if she holds him down."

"Well, he'll be out for a bit from the chloroform. Is there a Willy here?"

She rose and walked to him. Her knees felt shaky with lingering fear or maybe relief.

"You're Willy?"

She nodded.

The doctor gave a little laugh. "I did wonder about that. He asked for you before I put him under. You can sit with him if you want. We put him in a room." He looked then at Vince. "You need to get home and to bed. The leg wound was not nothing. Use a wagon for a few days."

"I will stay with him," Jesse said. "Just to be sure none of the jaspers got away and come looking."

Willy paled. "You expect that?"

"No, but…"

Jeremiah shook his head. "I'll stay. You both go home and reassure your wives."

The doctor led Willy down a hall to a room where she saw Cole's long length under a sheet. His face was pale, his eyes closed. "He should be coming around soon," the doctor said. "He might not make much sense to begin. Chloroform does odd things to people."

She sat on the chair, glad she'd worn her own gun. If anyone dared to threaten his life, she knew she'd use it. She watched him as he slept and then as he began to move, groan a little before his eyes opened. He looked around the room before his gaze settled on her. She put her hand out and pushed the hair back from his forehead.

"Where am I?" he asked. His pupils were wide, made his eyes look almost black.

"St. Mary's. It's a hospital."

"I want to get out of here."

She smiled and moved to his bed. "In a few days."

"Now."

"What are you wearing?"

He reached his hand down his side and came to the obvious conclusion as he winced. "Where are my clothes?"

"I have no idea as I didn't get to take them off you." She bent and kissed his forehead. "Didn't you promise not to get hurt?" she teased.

"I think I said I'd try to stay alive. Looks like I did."

"You better."

"Who came out to the adobe to tell you?" She saw the confusion in his eyes with no idea how much time had passed.

"I was on my way in, and it was Nate."

"You were supposed to stay where it was safe."

"I did until I knew you were hurt. I could feel it, Cole. I had to get to you. Lars came with me. I have my gun. We met Nate probably halfway."

"I remember my brothers are okay and father." She saw him grit his teeth against the pain.

"Vince had a wound treated in his leg."

He licked his lips and let out a breath.

"I can get you a glass of water and see what they have for the pain," she said.

"Water is good. No painkillers."

"Why not?"

"Addictive." She saw him stiffen in pain.

"I'll be right back."

In the hall, she saw two nuns. "He needs a glass of water, please, and is there anything he can have for the pain?" she asked.

One nun handed her a glass of water, the other nodded. "I will get the doctor."

Willy went back into Cole's room. His eyes were closed again, but she knew he wasn't asleep. A few minutes later, the doctor entered. "How are you doing?" he asked as he took Cole's pulse.

"When can I get out of here?" His tone was testy and not at all as appreciative as Willy would have expected. He should have been grateful for the care he'd been given. It might've saved his life.

"Three days maybe. You lost blood. Your rib was broken by a bullet, which glanced through your flesh out your back, but fortunately didn't nick an artery or vein. I dug a bullet out of your shoulder. Overall, with therapy, you will be good as new in a month or so."

"I want to leave now."

"You think you could walk out of here?"

"If you get me my clothes."

The doctor stood watching him with his hands folded over his chest. "You need to at least stay the night."

Cole groaned but sighed. "Where are my clothes?"

The doctor chuckled. "Let me see how you are in the morning." He tipped his hat to Willy and left the room.

"You are one very stubborn man," she said. She lifted his head and held the glass to his lips.

"I am not an invalid," he said testily when he'd taken several sips.

"Sleep now. I'll be here when you wake."

"You should go back to the ranch house, eat, and get a good night's sleep."

"You have to be joking. I am not leaving you. And Lars went back to take care of the dogs."

"You're as stubborn as I am."

"It might just be possible." She smiled and brushed her hand over his eyes closing them. "Sleep, get strong."

He woke again when it was just turning dark outside. He swallowed hard. She lifted his head and again put the water to his lips. He drank more then said, "Could you get a nurse?"

"Are you in pain?"

He smiled. "In need of a bedpan or helping me up."

"Oh, well… actually, I can handle that." And she did.

The nun entered, checked his pulse, temperature, and then left.

He smiled then. "Actually, you know despite the pain, I feel pretty good. I ended up alive."

"You didn't expect to?" She curled up on the bed alongside him, careful not to touch any wounds.

"I don't go into something like that with expectations."

"Will there be more such episodes in your future?" She knew her tone had turned cool, but she couldn't help it.

"I didn't plan this one." He moved a little to get more comfortable.

"What can I get you?" She sat up.

"Nothing."

"Thomas was killed," she said watching his face for reaction.

"I know. I killed him."

"I didn't know that."

"I took him out first. He fired at Nate. I pushed him aside and made sure my shot was a good one. From then on, I can't say what happened. I was hit, then hit again. The firing stopped. It was over about as fast as it started. A lot of loss of life and for nothing."

"Your father said he'd wait. Want me to see if he's still here?"

"He should go home."

"Maybe he did. I'll be right back."

She saw Jeremiah sleeping in a chair in the waiting room. He woke when she entered. "How is he?" he asked. He looked older. She guessed she did too.

"Come see for yourself." She led the way back to Cole's room and sat on the bottom of the bed, for Jeremiah to have the chair.

"I will be out of here tomorrow," Cole said when his father asked how he was.

"Want me to bring a wagon for you?" he asked not arguing. "You shouldn't ride yet."

"I guess. Tie on Boomer behind. Did they arrest the others?"

"All but those killed with Thomas. Two ended up here. I didn't hear what their condition was."

"I doubt Jace can hold them."

"Other than trying to kill a US marshal and Tucson sheriff, you mean," Jeremiah said with a tired smile.

"Yeah, other than. Guess that would do it for long enough for them to forget us."

"We can hope." Jeremiah grinned again, then said he'd see him in the morning if the doc really let him out.

"He will," Cole said with flint in his voice.

When they were alone, she said, "How about something to eat."

"Maybe in the morning. That chloroform made me sick."

"Oh, it wasn't the bullets or shock, huh?"

He patted the bed. "Come here. Sleep with me tonight."

"You think it's not against the rules?"

"Do we care?"

She lay alongside him, feeling his warmth, the strength of his body, relieved he was alive, hurt or not. No enemies lay ahead—at least none immediately. Of course, there were always those of their own making. His past. Hers.

"You are thinking again," he protested, his voice sounding tired.

"I am, but all of it can wait. We have forever now."

"We do, huh?" And then, she knew he had fallen asleep. She lay there wondering how they could work it all out. First was to get him strong again. The rest...they had time to figure out.

In the morning, Cole sat up with a groan. "Where'd you go?" he asked as he realized Willy wasn't still beside him.

She came in from the hall. "Your father is here," she said. "He's talking to the doctor."

"Where are my clothes?"

"You have to have permission to leave."

"Like hell. I'll walk out of here naked if I have to. I am not staying."

"You were shot."

His laugh was cut short by a groan. "I do know that. I'll heal better away from here."

Jeremiah walked into his room followed by the doctor. "I brought a wagon. Fixed up a bed in back."

"Good God, I am not on my death's bed here. I've been shot before." He glanced over at Willy, saw her pale and added, "but won't be again, of course." He smiled.

"All right," the doctor said. "I can't keep you. Just take lots of naps, drink lots of water, soft foods for a few days at least. Come back in a week to have the stitches removed that is if you don't tear them out with your teeth." He chuckled. "And it won't hurt you to lie in the back of a wagon."

Cole shook his head. "With my father driving it? You don't know my father."

The doctor laughed again and left.

"Now the clothes."

"The nun told me that they were bloodied and your shirt was cut up to treat your wounds," Willy said. She went to the cupboard and opened it to bring out jeans, boots, his hat, belt and gun. Taking them to him, she stood back while he pulled on the pants. "You need help with your boots," she said as he couldn't suppress the groan at straightening. "A broken rib will make that difficult or impossible if you don't want to poke the pieces into your lungs. Or is that something tough men ignore too."

He gave her as much of a glare as he could manage, as she helped him into the boots. He stood, felt a moment of dizziness as the pain surged through his body, but then he had it under control. He settled for carrying his holster, belt and gun. Walking to the door, Willy stayed at his side he supposed in case he fell. He wasn't about to fall.

At the wagon, much as he disliked the idea of lying in the back, Willy would need to sit next to his father. He gave up to their determination and let himself be helped to the bed. It felt surprisingly good to lie there. "How about Boomer?" he asked as his father stepped back down.

"Nate got the horses. He'll meet us out at the ranch—if that meets with your majesty's approval," his father said with a laugh before he helped Willy to the seat and flicked the reins to move the team forward.

"Taggert men don't take well to being sick," Jeremiah told her, irritating Cole further.

"I did note that," she said looking back at him, meeting his narrowed gaze and smiling. "I think I can handle it though." She winked at Cole, and he lay back resigned to being managed for a day or two... but not longer.

CHAPTER 20

A fter five days of being coddled, Cole had all he could take-- and the nights were in some ways more frustrating as Willy slept with him but insisted he wasn't up to more than sleeping. Worse, she had taken to wearing one of her old nightgowns, not the one he'd bought her. He was about to change things.

With the full moon, he didn't mind that she turned out the lights. "Take off that nightgown," he said before she could get under the covers.

"You are not strong enough for this yet."

"If you don't take it off, I'll tear it off you."

"You wouldn't." She didn't sound sure.

"I would." He reached out for her. She stepped back, but she did unbutton it and let the gown fall. When she pulled back the covers, she was nude. He ran his fingers down her side.

"I just don't want to hurt you," she whispered.

"You won't. Exercise is good for me. Besides, you can be on top this time." He didn't stop his touches, all designed to make her forget her doubts.

"I can?" She turned a little, to where she could touch him, running her hands down his chest to his belly and below.

"Get the condom. It's in the drawer alongside the bed." He was already swollen enough for her to easily slide it on. He pushed down their covers and lifted her to settle over his thighs.

"I know you shouldn't do that," she protested.

"Let me decide what I can do," he said with a smile as he brought her forward to where she now hovered over him. "But you can be in charge. What do you want, sweetheart?"

In moments, she had settled onto him. She began rocking forward and back, then in a little circle as she found what felt good for her. It all felt good for him. He lost track of what happened and how but he knew they were together. He wanted it to go on forever, but the feelings were building. She exploded with her release and he followed right after her. She rolled off him and to his side, her arm still across his now sweaty body.

"You sure that didn't hurt you?" she asked when she could breathe again.

He laughed. "You know the answer to that." In moments, they fell asleep.

When he woke in the morning, she was curled against him. "It's time," he said when her eyes opened, "for us to make plans."

"What kind?"

"A wedding and then what we do next."

"You are getting pretty bossy again."

He took her hand and kissed her fingers. "Before you go back to Frisco, I want to see a ring on this finger."

"About that..."

"I know we can work this out. I can spend time in Frisco, work from there as well as anywhere."

"Can we both compromise?" she asked.

"In what way?"

She sat up and looked back down at him. "I'd like you to stop being a detective or gun for hire, not even when it's the law. Can you give that up for me? I would feel so much fear every time you went out on a job. I don't know how I'd live with it, never knowing."

"Your teaching make enough to support me as a kept man?"

"Well, I had already been considering that. With my father dead and the house gone, I had nothing there. This week, I wrote a letter to the university resigning. It gives them time to find another professor for my classes. I couldn't see you living in the Bay area, and I like Arizona."

"You sure you want to do that?"

"Yes."

"So we're both without a job."

"There is my writing."

"Where would we live then? Wait, will you marry me? Let's get that out of the way first."

"Yes, I will."

He smiled and pulled her close to him. "I am not broke, and we can figure out work as we go. Maybe live part of the year in Payson and part in Tucson."

"I had thought about teaching at the university here, maybe one semester a year. That would let us be up there and here. I will have to apply though as I have no idea how well staffed they are. I wonder if we could lease this house from your brother."

"He mentioned he'd like us to live here; so yes."

"I'd like our real home though to be the lake house, us and our dogs."

"All three?"

"Yep, and whatever else we decide to add along the way."

"When you write though, I want you to be proud of what you write, do book signings, all the things writers do."

"Uhmmm, I guess I could. So, are you finally going to read them?"

"I hear Pa has them all, so yes, I will read them."

"And now I can improve them with a technical expert—someone very knowledge about the Taggerts." With that, she leaned over him and kissed his lips.

"So you figure out the wedding, and then we'll deal with the rest," he said as he kissed her hair. "You plan whatever you want, and I'll go along with it."

"I never imagined having a wedding; so I'll have to give it some thought." She would discuss it with Holly and Lily, as she had no idea what would be possible. On her own end, an elopement would be fine but maybe the family would want something bigger. She wasn't thrilled at that, but she had a family now and being part of that mattered more than her insecurities where it came to social events.

Sitting in Holly's new kitchen with Charlie Prevo and her future sisters-in-law, Willy sighed. "I still can't decide on what kind of wedding I should have. Cole wants to make plans. We had thought before Thanksgiving and that's only two weeks away."

"Rose will make your dress. She is a whiz with her needle and that little machine. Sicillas has some lovely satin and lace to die for," Lily said.

"Who do we have to invite and where would I have it?" Willy totally felt a dunce, but she had no clue nor even what Cole would want although she supposed eloping would be fine with him. But was it best for the family.

"We'll make a list," Holly said.

"And it should include everyone we can think of," Lily added. "I cheated our friends when Jesse and I got married."

"I suppose Vince and I did the same thing," Holly agreed. "I didn't even have you there."

"Did you both want a big wedding?" Willy asked.

Lily poured tea for them and Charlie, who was sitting at the other end of the table and listening with a grin. "It wasn't even a possibility. Jesse and I married with no idea it would be permanent. Well, he didn't." she grinned.

"I was feeling I shouldn't elope but..." She sipped the tea and felt a surge of renewed frustration. She was no good at social events, and she knew it.

Charlie, sometimes known as Jesse's handyman, but more now as a second grandfather, cackled. "There's an easy solution to the wedding?"

"What makes you an expert at them?" Lily asked with a giggle. "Not like you ever did it."

"Yes, I did. It just didn't stick."

"Where is Cole anyway?" Willy asked, more concerned about him than wedding plans. He had headed out to help finish Vince's barn, and she worried. He still did too much and ignored that he'd been hurt. That morning, when she had tried to explain he should take it easy, he had laughed and kissed her. The word relapse was not in his otherwise rather extensive vocabulary.

"You tryin' to avoid hearin' the best wedding plan you will ever hear?" Charlie asked.

"All right, let's hear it," Lily said, "since I know you're going to tell us anyway."

"Make it a triple wedding."

"But we're already married," Holly protested.

"No reason you can't do it again and do it right this time."

"Charlie, you are a devil," Lily said with a giggle. "This should be Willy's special day, not have us taking up the spotlight."

Willy smiled broadly and for the first time felt good about this idea of having a wedding. "I love the idea. Would you two do me the honor and get married again; so I am not the only one in the spotlight." She laughed at their expression. She also felt considerably happier as she heard all three Taggert brothers come riding in and head for the corrals.

"Actually," Holly said as Willy saw her considering it, "the idea is appealing to me too. I didn't even wear a white dress when Vince and I married."

"Neither did I," Lily agreed. "But could we now that we have two children and are old married women?"

"Of course, you could," Willy argued. "We should go to Sicillas and buy up all her satin and lace. I don't think Rose can make all the dresses though in this short of a time. Do you suppose she has friends to help?"

"We can find out."

Charlie chortled as he poured himself a cup of coffee.

"And what are you laughing at?" Lily asked as she went to him.

"Just seeing Jesse's face is all." He laughed again.

"Charlie, someone has to give me away."

He stopped laughing. "You don't mean... I mean wouldn't Jeremiah do it."

"He'll have to give away Holly. No, I'm afraid it has to be you."

He gave a half laugh. "Guess the joke's on me. Does that mean I have to wear a suit?"

"Of course."

"What about you, Willy?" Holly asked. "Would you want Jeremiah to do that too?"

"No, I'll ask Lars. Cole and I've become very fond of him."

"Then we're set," Holly said. "We are having a triple wedding. What date?" She took the calendar off the wall. "What do I circle?"

Willy looked at it thoughtfully. "Can we get it all ready by the thirtieth?"

"Thanksgiving?"

"Absolutely. I am so thankful to have Cole healthy and alive, to have enemies gone." She gave an unladylike snort. "At least as much as they can be for Taggerts. And now, to have two sisters. I am incredibly thankful."

"I think we can pull it off," Lily said. "You know, a better idea might be that the new dress shop in town has one section just for bridal gowns. Maybe we should see if Alberta has anything that would fit us."

"You mean buy a readymade gown?" Willy asked. "I don't have a lot of money." Actually, she had no idea how much money she did have since it was in a San Francisco bank. She'd have to get that changed and arrange book royalties to go to a Tucson bank.

"Money is not an issue," Holly said. The Jacobs money will stand this wedding." She laughed then. "I am getting excited. This will be such fun and then a huge Thanksgiving spread after it. Can we have it at our Taggert ranch?"

"I think we have to," Willy said, "if we want town people to come."

"Oh and we do," Holly said giggling. "This is going to be a real show for Tucson. Everyone will want to come."

"What are you gals plotting?" Vince asked as the brothers came through the door.

"Nothing much," Holly said with a huge grin.

"Just what then?" Jesse asked as he poured himself a cup of coffee, holding up the pot and having his brothers shake their heads.

"We're planning the wedding," Lily said as she went to her husband and put her arms around him.

"Uh oh, what's this about then?" Jesse asked with suspicion in his voice.

"Good on the wedding whatever it takes," Cole said. "I've been afraid she'll get cold feet." He sat at the table, and Willy quickly moved to sit on his lap and put her arms around him.

"No chance of that," she said. "You didn't overdo, did you?"

He shook his head and gave a snort. "What will it take to get you to quit mothering me?" She blushed, and the others laughed.

"All right, let's have it?" Vince asked as he sat at the other end of the table opposite Charlie. "What's the plotting about?"

"Gonna be a triple wedding," Charlie said snickering.

"How can that be?" Jesse asked and then his eyes widened. "You don't mean?"

"Yep. You're gettin' married again, son. And I get to give away the bride this time."

Jesse sunk down on one of the chairs and looked up at Lily. "You want this?"

"I do."

He smiled then. "If it gets Charlie in a suit, might be worth it." He laughed.

Cole looked at Willy. "This is what you want?"

"As soon as Charlie suggested it, I knew it was the perfect thing. I get three sisters. We have a big, fancy party."

"We even might buy dresses," Lily said. "That new dress shop has a bridal section."

"And we have to wear suits?" Jesse asked. "I don't have one and not sure any store can get one in my size."

"You three need to ride to town with us. We'll go to the dress shop while you order suits."

"Who watches the kids?"

"We'll take Lucinda and Ruth with us as they still nurse. I'll ask if Rose minds watching the boys for a few hours."

"Who will perform this?" Jesse asked.

"I'll ask Judge Hutchinson," Holly said. "I've always liked any dealings I have had with him."

"What date?" Cole asked.

"Thanksgiving," Willy answered. "It's the perfect time, and then we'll have a huge dinner afterward to celebrate with all the guests."

"Lot of work fixing that much food," Jesse said. Willy was unsure how the two brothers felt about it, but Cole seemed fine with sharing the day, or maybe he even was amused by it from the glint in his eyes.

"We'll bring in caterers," Holly said. "We're going to have it at the ranch. Put up a big tent outside, which will take care of the wedding and the reception."

"Looks like it's all figured out," Vince said shaking his head. "And to think we were ribbing Cole all morning. Looks like the joke's on us."

Charlie chortled. "And me. I never figured on wearing a suit ever, not even to be buried."

"Wait a minute, who give away the other brides?" Jesse asked.

"Pa could do them both," Vince said.

"Lars will give me away and, of course, then Jeremiah Holly. We worked it out. Well, other than asking them." Willy laughed too. She had dreaded the idea of a real wedding, and now suddenly she was incredibly excited at the possibilities, even the fun of going dress shopping with her sisters to be.

Other than Holly, Willy hadn't had many female friends. Mostly, she'd been too busy working. With her mother dying young and an elderly grandmother who hadn't encouraged noise or friends visiting, Holly had taken to herself when home-- writing and dreaming. When she'd gone away to college, she was working long hours to get her homework and her books finished. She hadn't realized what a hole had been left in her life that was now being filled.

After stopping to talk with Judge Hutchinson, who chuckling, heartily agreed to perform the weddings, Cole met his brothers, father, and the rest of the wedding party at Sicillas for finding suits. "You are a big one," Del said as he wrote down Jesse's measurements.

"Probably can't find one for me by the thirtieth," Jesse said, a hopeful tone to his voice.

"Ironically, you'll be easiest," Del said disappearing in the back and returning with a black suit on a hanger. "Lloyd Jessup ordered a suit and then... Well, might as well tell you, he died sudden like and never picked it up."

"Jessup?" Vince asked. "Died? I thought he got shot in a home invasion... or a sort." He chuckled.

"That's funny?" Cole asked examining the fabric on a suit on the rack.

"He had been courting Bennie Otten's wife, but Bennie found out and... He caught them."

"And the wife?" Cole asked, not finding it humorous.

"He forgave her."

"He doing time in Yuma then?"

Vince shook his head. "The jury found him innocent. Folks find a man courting another man's wife to be serious business, and that he got what was coming to him."

Cole still didn't find it funny. Then Nate Hemstreet walked in. He looked at Cole. "Can I talk to you a minute?"

"Sure." Cole followed him out to the porch.

"Willy told me about the wedding. She asked me to be there. I was thinking I should get on the train for home as you'd not want me there."

"Why would you think that? You are very welcome. I know how close you two have been, and she will not want to lose that."

"You sure?"

"I am."

"One more thing."

"All right?"

"I haven't thanked you for saving my life when you saw Thomas was pointing his gun at me. I saw the gun, but didn't react quickly enough. He'd have killed me if you hadn't pushed me down."

Cole smiled. "It was a first time for you, and it takes some getting used to. Hopefully, you won't have a second time."

Nate put out his hand. "You suppose you can call me Nate now?"

Cole took his hand. "If you get yourself a suit along with us."

When they walked back in, Vince was proving to be the hardest to fit with his broad shoulder but with adjustments, Connie assured them, they could would have it in time.

"We have the perfect one for you," Connie said holding a suit up to Cole. "Being tall and lean, you are easy to fit. I might have to have the waist on the pants taken in a bit but no problem."

"You are sure making us a good profit today," Del said. "Never sold this many suits in a day."

An hour later, they arranged for the alterations, and Vince had covered the cost. "Holly said it's on us," he said when Cole protested, "and that woman doesn't give up easily."

Cole smiled. He did know that about his sister-in-law.

"Are we invited?" Connie asked as she tallied the final cost, took the cash, and handed Vince the receipt.

"Anybody who wants to come is invited," Cole said.

"You sure about that," Del asked with a laugh. "Whole town might turn out."

"We don't have time to put out invites; so it'll be word of mouth. A Thanksgiving spread after the wedding."

"A lot of work."

"Holly is arranging with Elysian Grove and two restaurants for catering."

"I'd be glad to help," Connie said.

"We're covered but thanks."

"It should be beautiful. I am excited for you all," Connie said.

Cole knew she might wish to tell them something about it. He could almost see it in her eyes but no way. He didn't want any fortunetelling ruining things just in case it was not going to go smoothly.

The waning moon rose above the window as Cole and Willy lay in bed. "Did you find a nice dress?" he asked thinking about making love to her again... as soon as his energy returned.

"Beautiful. We all did. How did the suits go?"

"Even Jesse has one. It looks like this will come off. I have no idea how big a crowd though."

"I don't care now. Sharing it with Lily and Holly helped a lot for me."

"I told my brothers about the land we own in Payson."

"Oooh, I like that. Are they interested in it?"

"Mostly trying to figure out how it all fits together for us as a family. Tucson and Payson are a fair distance apart. We want to be close to them but do want to be up there a lot of the year, maybe all of it someday."

"I like that idea. Maybe they'd build homes there."

"I suggested they come up with us when the snow is off. Would you really like it if they decided to come up, maybe more of the year?"

"More like love it. I haven't had much family, Cole. Holly was my only real girlfriend. I am crazy about the idea of our children having family, grandparents, cousins, uncles and aunts. I also love the lake, but if it comes down to family or it, I'd choose family."

He smiled. "I don't think it will. Jesse said he feels like Tucson is getting too settled, spreading out too much. Payson has longer before that happens. Holly likes the potential for archaeological explorations up there."

She smiled and raised herself on one elbow. "As long as we are together, the rest, I don't care."

For the next week and a half, Willy dedicated herself to helping with whatever Holly told her to do. Frankly, her friend was amazing for her organizational skills. Sometimes Willy just babysat the boys while Holly and Lily visited businesses to arrange for the necessary items to be at the ranch on Thanksgiving. She knew they'd have done all this even if they had not been in the wedding, but that they were made it all so much more special.

Cole had gone out with his brothers to round up the cattle for branding the calves-- and whatever else they did to young animals. She knew so little about that. She guessed she'd be finding out. Another new thing for her life.

The invoices and transcribed journals had been turned over to the sheriff for them to be copied and sent to the authorities in San Francisco. Willy had no idea if it would lead to more arrests, but it seemed it had done what her father had hoped with making Thomas pay for what he had done. There would never be proof he'd murdered her father or Nate's, but at least he'd do no more damage.

"What are you up to?" Nate asked coming through the door she had left open for the dogs to come in and out.

"I was actually starting a new book. I do need to get a typewriter for here though as handwriting seems slow for me, especially when I have to get someone to type it up to send off."

"Another Taggert western?"

She smiled. "I am not sure but a western."

"Still as Will Tremaine?"

"Yes, he has fans." She grinned. "But now I'll acknowledge they are mine. I wrote my editor and he said it sounded fine to him. I also trans-ferred my bank account to the National here in town. There was more there than I had expected." She had been pleased with that.

"I read your books. They were at Jeremiah's. You are very good. Lots of action, some sentiment, and a classic sort of plot."

"I stole those from the classics," she said with a sheepish smile.

"There are no new plots by now. Yours aren't copied but inspired by."

"You always were my biggest fan."

"Still am. I just wish you had told me about them."

"I was having a hard time dealing with what I wrote. Would you like some tea?"

They went into the kitchen. As they sipped the tea, he said, "My big question now is what involvement my mother had in all of this. The jour-nals didn't answer that."

"It seemed my father didn't believe she did, or he would not have gone to her that morning."

"Yes, but was it what sealed his death? We know he didn't kill himself unless, of course, she threatened him with something that sent him into a depression. I don't believe that, do you?"

"No, I don't."

"After your wedding, I am going back. I hope to get some answers."

That worried her. "Be careful when you do. Don't let her know your doubts?"

"You think she'd be dangerous to me?"

"Do you?"

He smiled. "You're right. I don't know. I hope though to find the rest of the story when I go."

"I am glad you are staying for the wedding. I wanted you to be there."

"It appears it will be quite the event. I wouldn't miss it."

She looked up when she heard horses riding into the area of the barn and soon they had the corral filled with the bawling of cattle and dust riling the air. She and Nate walked to the porch. The dogs were excited at all the activity. Surprisingly, the three of them had proven not to be barkers, so they just watched.

Cole rode by the fence. He looked dusty and tired. "How was your day?" he asked.

"Are you sure you should be doing this?" she retorted.

He only laughed at her, gave a tip of his hat to Nate, and rode back to the corrals.

"He's quite a man," Nate said. "You are a fortunate woman."

"I am surprised you'd say that."

"Did he tell you that he saved my life that day?"

"No." She turned to him in shock. "What happened?"

He described the moment. "I've never seen anything like the Taggert men. You haven't written half enough about them," he said with a laugh. "I never knew men like them. Now... I have to admit, I'd like to be that kind of man but maybe it's too late. Born a city man and doomed to stay one," he said with a light-hearted sound, but she realized he wasn't joking.

"You are your own kind of strong man, Nate," she said trying to find words that would make him feel better but also show him that there is more than one way to be strong.

He laughed. "And that's why you chose Cole, huh?"

She shook her head. "Love isn't about that, Nate. The kind of love I had for you just wasn't the same as for Cole. It isn't his strength, although I do see that. It's who he is inside. He just pushed all the buttons I hadn't even realized I had."

"I can see that." He laughed, but this time he sounded in a better mood about it. "Maybe someday I'll find that also."

"I am sure you will."

~

The night before their wedding, the tent was up, chairs, tables, a trellis with roses for where the weddings would take place. Vince, Cole and Jesse were told they would not be sleeping in the ranch house that night. Cole's smile was crooked. "You aren't worried about bad luck at this point are you?" he asked Willy.

"Holly says it's an important tradition. We'll have the children, but you all must find elsewhere. The next time you will see me, I'll be walking down that aisle."

He laughed but didn't argue. Jesse and Vince were less convinced, considering they considered their case different, but in the end, they rode to Jeremiah's house to spend the night and return in the morning all suited up for the ceremony.

With the house to themselves, Holly, Willy, and Lily unwrapped the dresses and hung them in wardrobes upstairs. The boys were playing with the puppies, Zinnia was hanging around Willy as much as possible, and the infants seemed the least disturbed by the change in their environment. Maybe because for the last two weeks, they'd been moved around quite a lot.

With morning, Willy fixed them scrambled eggs, toasted some bread, and coffee with all their minds on getting ready. Rose arrived when they had barely finished. "I will be taking care of the babes," she said, "and Royce will watch boys and dogs." Her grandson was already eagerly at work with throwing sticks for Poppy and Petunia. Zinnia mostly wanted to be near to Willy. She supposed that was due to Cole being gone. The little dog was sensitive to change.

Upstairs, they began slipping into their gowns, which were all white but with varying trims of lace and ruffles. Willy had chosen a gown with a softly scooped neck, tiny pearl beads sewn around it, a skirt that skimmed over her hips with a bit of a bustle to emphasize her curves, the ones she had and didn't have. All three had been fortunate their figures were such that there hadn't been a need for alterations, especially given that Holly and Lily had given birth only months before.

Putting on her headpiece, a beaded cap with lace for a veil, Willy looked in the mirror and felt a bit of shock. She had kept her hair simple with pinning it back and then letting it hang down her back. She actually did look like a bride.

She helped Lily button up the back of her dress with a full skirt and then they both did the hooks on Holly's which was a straight skirt with long sleeves that ended over her fingers. "We look like brides," Lily said as the three looked in the mirror.

"I have a surprise for you," Holly said as she led them downstairs. A young man stood in the hall. He held a camera. "This is David Ryker. He's a professional photographer, who will be taking photos of the wedding. Us first."

"You stand over by the wall," David said for each one, before he shot the three together, arms around each other.

"You're using film, David," Holly said as she looked at his camera.

"Best for a wedding where we want lots of photos. Want a picture of the dogs and the boys?"

After he'd taken them, with more guests arriving, along with the caterers, Willy saw that their grooms were putting their horses in a temporary, rope corral. Buggies had their own place below the barns.

When he turned to look toward the house, Willy saw Cole for the first time in a fine black suit, white shirt, and a string tie. If he'd been handsome to her before, now he was everything she imagined a man could be, tall, slim, those eagle eyes that he shared with his brothers.

She didn't think he could see her as she was watching him through sheer cotton curtains. She wanted to suck him into her very being, to have their souls wedded together for this life and beyond. Then she wondered if they already had been. How else could she explain the stories she'd written about him before she so much as dreamed he actually existed? Except her stories had been faint impressions of what the flesh and blood man was actually like.

Cole then turned with his brothers, and they headed for the canopy where guests were seated in rows that would form an aisle. Holly had found a long carpet to form an aisle for the brides to walk to their grooms. She had even arranged for a harpist to play for them. The music and soft voices of the guests drifted to the house. Judge Hutchinson stood in front of a flower-covered trellis created by the magic of Rose Oliver and from her gardens. The flowers were a riot of colors. She had also made bouquets for each bride from lilies, bought from the gardens along the river.

"Hey gal," Lars said as he came alongside her. "You ready for this?" She turned and smiled. He was wearing a fine-looking, dark suit, as were Jeremiah and Charlie. They all looked so handsome and happy. She hugged each man and then took Lars' arm. "I am beyond ready." And it was so. With a signal from Holly, the harp music changed, the guests quieted, and looked toward the door.

Holly and Jeremiah were to be first as they entered the aisle to the powerful strains of *Mendelssohn's Wedding March*. Most details of the wedding, Willy had yielded to Holly's planning, as the one who knew more about how it should be. The music though was where she drew the line. Once she had explained the story of the opera from where the more usual bridal choice, *Wagner's Bridal March*, had come, her soon to be sisters made faces and totally agreed. They would all take fairies and elves any day over tragedy and betrayal for setting the tone of marriages to be.

The music began again for Charlie and Lily to make their way to the front where Charlie moved to sit beside Jeremiah, and Lily took Jesse's arm. Turning then with the audience to watch the door.

When it was her turn, she stood a moment at the back of the aisle, to take in the full view of what lay ahead. The aisle that led to the flower strewn trellis, the judge, so many smiling faces as they watched her start to walk. It was beautiful, but then all she could see was Cole waiting for her. On each side of Cole his brothers with her future sisters on their arms.

She walked slowly up the aisle, smiling and resisting tears as she thought of how happy her father would have been to have seen this day, to have met her wonderful, soon-to-be husband. She hoped, as some believed, that he was watching and could see her joy. Then all she could see was Cole standing with his own eyes showing a sheen of unshed tears.

Lars released her and then she was on Cole's arm, and they were facing the judge, the three couples, each repeating their vows. She had heard the words at other weddings, but when it was her turn to repeat them, they had new meaning. 'to have and to hold from this day forward.' She wanted nothing more than to go through life holding this man.

The brothers had decided they would be each other's best man. When it was Cole's turn to place a ring on Willy's finger, Jesse handed it to him. Then it was time for the grooms to kiss their brides.

She felt Cole's lips against hers, firm and tender, and she sank into his embrace. "You are the most beautiful bride I've ever seen," he whispered in her ear before they turned and faced their friends.

The judge smiled broadly as he said, "Now, may I present Holly, Wilhelmina, and Lily—the beautiful brides of the brothers Taggert." The cheers and clapping filled Willy's ears and heart as Cole again turned her to him and bent to kiss her.

Thank you for reading Bound For The Hills.

Keep alert for señor romance opportunity. The Ol' man isn't done yet.